DATE DUE

JIGSAW

JERRY KENNEALY

THOMAS DUNNE BOOKS
ST. MARTIN'S MINOTAUR ♏ NEW YORK

THOMAS DUNNE BOOKS.
An imprint of St. Martin's Press.

www.thomasdunnebooks.com
www.minotaurbooks.com

Design by Gregory Collins

ISBN-13: 978-0-312-35475-6
IBSN-10: 0-312-35475-4

First Edition: April 2007

10 9 8 7 6 5 4 3 2 1

FOR MY GRANDSON, JAKE

*Something to read while waiting
for the fish to bite*

ACKNOWLEDGMENT

Sincere thanks to Tony Hall for showing me
the hidden treasures of Treasure Island

ONE

The frescoed ceilings were ten feet high and the room was only slightly smaller than a football field, yet the din of the crowd made intimate conversation difficult. Jonathan Ashley, an elderly, woolly-haired actor, was nearly shouting into my ear. "It's a shame about what happened to Montgomery Hines, isn't it, Quint?"

"What happened to Monty?" I said. I'd been in New York for several days, reviewing off-Broadway shows. Hines was an actor who had never quite made it in Hollywood, and had come to San Francisco to work in local plays and commute down to Southern California for the occasional commercial or bit part.

"He was murdered," Ashley said. "In his shower. Early this morning. Stabbed to death." He grimaced. "The papers said it was very bloody."

"I'm sorry to hear that," I said sincerely. Hines hadn't been much of an actor, but I had respect for anyone who had the guts to get up on stage and perform in front of a camera or live audience.

"I hope the way you roasted his performance in the last play he was in had nothing to do with it," Ashley said with a lopsided grin.

"Me too," I responded and moved off, weaving my way past tuxedos and silk gowns until I came to the buffet table. I filled my plate with tiger shrimp, fried ginger pork, and miniature meatballs stuffed with garlic and cheddar cheese, then added some crab-filled cherry tomatoes.

By now my plate was stuffed and I had to get another one to hold the oysters and cold tagliarini salad. I did a balancing act with the plates and managed to wedge the stem of a champagne glass between my thumb and forefinger while looking for a space large enough to give me some elbow room.

Truth be told, the food was the main reason for my being at the party. The fact that I love to eat and hate to cook induces me to attend so many "show parties." When you consider the meager salary that the *San Francisco Bulletin* pays me as an entertainment critic, I'm more or less forced to go to the damn parties or risk starvation.

Tonight's affair was less of a bore than most because of the hostess, Gineen Rosenberry, the person most responsible for bringing the current revival of *Camelot* to San Francisco. Gineen is one of those all too uncommon individuals who combine enormous wealth with a strong sense of social responsibility. The fact that she is beautiful, charming, intelligent, and forgiving of small misfortunes made her unique indeed.

Of course, if I had known that the price for this meal would be accusations of theft and murder, and having the hell kicked out of me, I'd have hastened to the nearest Taco Bell.

I found a reasonably sized clearing alongside one of Gineen's latest acquisitions, a French art deco three-seat shoeshine stand that had begun its life in a Paris train station. It had been refurbished, with new black leather seats, handrails of gleaming steel, and intricate burnished bronze steps.

Two eager-looking men in matching double-breasted tuxedos occupied the outer seats, their attention riveted on the blonde in a chili-pepper-red dress with peekaboo shoulder holes wedged in the middle seat. The blonde appeared to have done everything possible to be a Britney Spears look-alike. She had succeeded amazingly well.

I slipped one of my plates onto the floor and went to work on the other one.

Gineen Rosenberry spotted me and glided over. Glided being the proper description—Gineen did not walk, shuffle, or stride; she definitely glided. She was wearing an emerald green silk dress that perfectly matched the thumb-sized single stone dangling from a platinum chain around her neck. Her honey-colored hair was styled in a fashionable upsweep. Copper-colored eyes under broad-arched brows sparkled at me. Someone had dubbed her the Satin Widow, due to the fact that she fancied satin sheets and her last two enormously wealthy husbands had died in bed, reportedly with smiles on their lips.

"Carroll, darling," she said, the trace of a South Carolinian accent still present in her seductively husky voice, "are you getting enough to eat?"

"Barely," I replied, wiping the remains of some of the shrimp barbecue sauce from my fingers before extending a hand. "You look gorgeous, Gineen."

"Thank you, dear." She glanced briefly at the two penguins and the Britney impersonator. "Ah, youth," she sighed. "How is that man?"

"That man" was my father, John Quint, who was what one of an unending line of female companions called "cat nip to us girls." He played piano at some of the posher restaurants around town, and at social gatherings such as this one. Somehow he'd been beaten out of this gig by a longhaired young man with a mournful face, who had been playing Gershwin since I'd arrived. Gershwin was losing.

"He's fine, Gineen, just fine."

"Is he," she paused and fluttered the fingers of one hand, "with anyone now?"

"Not that I know of." Though they'd been divorced some fifteen years, Dad still lived in the flat directly above my mother's. They often shared bread and breakfast—but nothing else, at least as far as I knew.

Her cheeks dimpled. "Good. Very good. I was so sorry to read about Montgomery Hines's death. The poor man. And the way that he died." Gineen placed a hand gently on my arm. "Carroll, have you thought that perhaps—"

It wasn't a sound of any kind that caused Gineen to stop in mid-sentence, it was the lack of same. The volume suddenly dropped to whisper decibels, a sure sign that "someone" had entered the room.

That someone turned out to be Peter Liddell, once an undeniable "movie star," whose track record of three Academy Award nominations was being lapped by disastrous outings in his last nine or ten films. Bombs would be a kind description. He had sunk to appearing in a TV miniseries and was now attempting to get back the adulation he thought he richly deserved by slipping into the slippers of King Arthur in the umpteenth revival of *Camelot*. Even if you didn't know he was a star, you'd know he was "someone" because he was *smoking* a cigarette. Indoors! Which was about as politically incorrect in San Francisco as being a Republican. There are more female priests in the Vatican than there are Republicans in the city. A hulking man in a shiny black suit and sunglasses was at Liddell's side, trying to look like a secret service agent.

Jules Moneta, Gineen's business partner—a self-described entertainment attorney—hurried over and gave me a lewd wink. Moneta was a slim, perfectly tailored man with dark wavy hair who made no attempt to disprove rumors that he was gay. "Darling, time to go meet the star," he said with an exaggerated lisp. His voice pattern changed to suit the occasion; he could sound something like George C. Scott doing General Patton during negotiations with actors, union agents, and bankers. Moneta was attempting to transform the Bay Area into Hollywood North, by using the abandoned U.S. Navy hangars on Treasure Island as movie and TV studios.

They rushed to meet Liddell and I went back to some serious eating. The sound level gradually built back up again and I watched the pseudo–Ms. Spears's head swivel back and forth between the tuxedo twins. She paused in midswivel once, gave me an appraising look, then went back to her adoring companions.

I was about to exchange the empty plate in my hand for the full one near the tip of my shoe when I saw Gineen Rosenberry leading Peter Liddell in my direction. The crowd parted like the Red Sea had for Moses as Gineen guided Liddell by his elbow. Maybe the hulking bodyguard alongside Liddell had something to do with that.

On screen Liddell still cut a dashing figure: well over six feet in height, his suntanned features included a chiseled chin, aristocratic nose, yellow-blond hair, broad shoulders, and flat stomach.

On stage, at least from a few rows back, the image remained pretty much the same. Up close and personal there were some visible flaws. The shoulders slumped, the stomach protruded, that glowing tan was more a nicotine-stain color, and a network of veins clouded the nose.

He was wearing a houndstooth sport coat and yellow turtleneck sweater, and had a chocolate brown scarf draped around his shoulders like a cloak.

Liddell kept his face frozen in a smirk as the ever-pleasant Gineen introduced him to the assemblage, an eclectic group of high society regulars, members of the *Camelot* cast and crew, local actors, and a few low class media types, such as myself. A vintage ebony cigarette holder was positioned in the corner of Liddell's mouth, jutting upward à la the way Ralph Bellamy portrayed Franklin D. Roosevelt in *Sunrise at Campobello*.

Actually the cigarette holder was in the position that Mr. Roosevelt himself was famous for; however, when your job is that of a reviewer, you always go with the actor.

"And this," Gineen said with an ingratiating smile, "is Carroll Quint, of the *San Francisco Bulletin*."

Liddell's cigarette holder dropped to half-mast. He blew a wobbly smoke ring in my direction. "The critic?" he said, pronouncing the word as if it were a highly contagious disease.

"That's right," I answered, trying to sound as if I was proud of my line of work.

Liddell leaned forward. The smell of gin came with him. "You reviewed *Four on an Island*, didn't you?"

"Yes," I said, not at all surprised that Liddell, who, to the best of my knowledge, had never made a movie or acted in a play in San Francisco before, was aware of the review. Some actors may have trouble remembering the name of their latest wife or coke dealer, their own phone number, or current address, but reviews, especially if they're not favorable, they can quote in their entirety.

"You didn't like the picture, did you, Carroll?" Liddell said, drawing out my first name as if it had four syllables instead of two.

The movie had been a financial and artistic flop, a heist adventure shot in Italy, with the entire crew performing as if they'd made a heavy dent in the local Chianti supplies prior to going before the cameras. "Not one of my favorites, Mr. Liddell."

"Carroll," he said loudly, in his best Shakespearean tones. "I always thought that was a pussy's name."

Liddell's sexual preferences were well known: "Boy, girl, man, woman, bicycle. He doesn't care as long as there are moving parts" was the way one Hollywood know-it-all had described his libido. "Since when could you tell the difference?" I said.

It seemed to take Liddell a second or two to get my meaning, then his watery blue eyes turned cold. He squared his shoulders, drew his scarf around his neck, then slapped me across the face, causing my glasses to fly off.

If a mother, with all good intentions, saddles her only male offspring with a name like Carroll, because it means Champion in Gaelic, and said offspring starts wearing glasses at an early age, and lives in the Mission District, the oldest and toughest neighborhood in San Francisco, he learns very early in life that other people are going to make fun of him, so he is left with two choices: run away, or fight like hell. I wasn't very fast on my feet. My father had taught me the basics of fisticuffs, the rest I'd learned on the streets.

I put my arms out in front of me to block Liddell's next punch. Without my glasses the world takes on a fuzzy appearance, like a French impressionist painting shown on an out-of-focus TV set. I easily slipped his punch, then sent an open palm into his chest with enough authority to knock him to the ground.

Liddell's bodyguard stepped in and landed a real blow along the side of my head. I swung blindly and made contact with something.

There were shouts and screams. Someone grabbed my arm and before I could pull away, Gineen Rosenberry said, "My God, Carroll, you're bleeding. And look at poor Peter. I hope you didn't hurt him."

TWO

"Poor Peter" was out of my vision, which was directed up at the ceiling, which depicted flights of chubby, pink-faced, winged angels circling around a God-like figure holding massive outstretched hands toward distant clouds.

I remembered that from previous visits. Now it looked like mashed potatoes with little pink spots. I also knew from all too many past occasions that the best way of stopping my honker from bleeding was to tilt my noggin as far back as possible and plug the nostrils with cotton balls. I groped for a handkerchief while Gineen Rosenberry grabbed my arm.

"Are you all right, Carroll?"

"My glasses. I need my glasses."

"They're somewhere around. I'll find them, but first we have to get you to a bathroom."

While she shepherded me out of the main ballroom, I could hear snatches of excited gossip:

"That was Liddell. The actor. Someone hit him."

"It was him," a falsetto voice said excitedly.

"That guy?" someone responded with great disappointment. "Looks like he got the worst of it."

Another voice. "No, Liddell is out cold."

Gineen led me out into a hallway and pressed my hand onto a marble staircase handrail.

"Carroll, darling, can you find your way upstairs? Use my bedroom, or one of the spares. I'll go back and find your glasses and see how Peter's doing."

I clutched at her arm before she took off. "Gineen. What the hell happened back there?"

"Well, I must say that Peter was out of line, slapping you like that. I was trying to step between you, then you put your hands out, and somehow Peter slipped. I think he stepped on a plate of food. His feet went out from under him and he took a terrible spill to the floor. Then one of his bullies hit you. I'll find your glasses and be back in a flash."

How many multimillionaires do you know who say things like, "back in a flash"? I groped my way slowly up the staircase, head tilted back, handkerchief blotting up the blood, while wondering just how I was going to explain what happened to my boss. Reviewers have been known to puncture the egos—and other vulnerable spots—of actors with verbal daggers, but actually scuffling with them was a bad show. One which my boss, Max Maslin, was probably not going to appreciate.

I was almost at the top of the stairs when someone came rushing past me, almost knocking me down.

"Hey, watch it," I blurted out in a voice that came out sounding like a bad Donald Duck impersonation, thanks to the handkerchief covering my nose.

Whoever it was didn't stop to apologize. I could hear the bark of footsteps on the stairs. Probably one of the hired help being summoned to clean up the mess Liddell and I had made.

I had been to Gineen Rosenberry's bedroom once before. A purely professional visit. I had interviewed her regarding last year's lineup for shows at the Orpheum Theatre. Gineen had been suffering from a cold, so the interview took place while she was cloistered in her swimming pool–size bed, propped up by a mound of pink satin pillows, working her way through an ordinary box of Kleenex. It was somehow comforting to know that even the ultrarich suffered the same agonies as the rest of us.

I was a bit surprised to find the lights on in Gineen's room. I groped my way toward the bathroom, an outstretched hand rubbing against mirror-covered walls, paintings, and the occasional bit of furniture.

I was bent over the sink, splashing cold water on my face when Gineen came in holding my glasses. She took over the first aid chores: painfully at first with Q-tips, some sort of creamy balm, and finally the old standby—cotton balls.

"There," she said, examining me with a one-side grimace. "I don't think anything is broken. Maybe you better lie down and rest a bit. Oh, and here are your glasses."

One of the lenses had been cracked. "I'll be fine, Gineen. How's that bastard Liddell?"

"He has quite a nasty bump on the back of his head. His manager called for an ambulance. Are you going to be all right?"

"Fine. I think I'll go out the back way, if you don't mind."

"Good choice. The man who hit you, Liddell's bodyguard, is acting like he's itching to make more trouble."

Gineen tugged a bloody cotton ball from my nose and replaced it with a fresh one. "He looks like a football player. Not one of the cute ones who throw the ball and run. The big ones who tackle people. If you leave through the kitchen and out the garden gate, I'm sure you can avoid him."

There is a time to fight, a time to run, and a time to duck out the garden gate. This was one of those duck out times.

"My God, Quint," Max Maslin said to me the next morning, peering at me over the glasses that had slid halfway down his rubicund nose. "Pick on someone your own size. Liddell has four inches and fifty pounds on you."

Before becoming my boss at the *San Francisco Bulletin*, Maslin had worked in the ink-stained trenches: Washington, D.C., politics, war correspondent, *LA Times* entertainment editor, the local city hall beat, and the sports page. He was a self-acknowledged expert on just about everything. He was in his midfifties, with a round face and several chins, and wore baggy tweed suits, checkered shirts, and floppy bow ties. The checks and tweeds were used to hide the small holes made from his pipe tobacco.

"He swung first," I said, passing Maslin's desk and walking into my cubicle, which was barely large enough to hold my desk, computer, and one chair. I sank into the chair and booted up the computer.

Maslin leaned against the doorjamb, and smiled down at me. "That was pretty good stuff you sent from New York."

"Pretty good stuff" was about as close to a rave review anyone ever received from Maslin.

I tilted the spare pair of glasses I'd been forced to use onto my forehead, leaned close to the computer monitor, and clicked over to my e-mail address and found some hundred and forty-two messages—the price one paid when ignoring the damn stuff for almost a week.

Max said, "I need a story on Montgomery Hines. You knew him as well as anyone, I guess."

"You guess wrong. I had a few drinks with him at parties or openings, but he wasn't a friend."

Maslin shrugged his shoulders. "So fake it. Tell a story about what a good guy and wonderful actor he was."

"Jesus, Max. I've got a stack of stuff to go through. Three off-Broadway plays from New York. The new Oliver Stone turkey, and—"

"And you're working on your book, right? Did you see your editor while you were in New York."

"I did." That had turned out to be the best part of the trip. Two years ago I'd written a book on *film noir* heroes, *Tough Guys and Private Eyes*, that had garnered some excellent reviews and pretty low sales figures. I was working on a sequel, *Before Color—Hollywood Musicals*, and the publishing house had agreed to buy it.

"Didn't Hines work in some of those old black-and-white hardboils when he was a young man?" Max asked.

"Not that I know of. Look, Max, can't you get—"

"Well he died like one—the woman in Hitchcock's *Psycho* flick. In the shower, hacked to pieces." He raised his bushy brows and smiled.

"Hey, maybe you can fit that into the story. Actor dies like Hitchcock character."

"It was Janet Leigh, a lovely blonde in the movie, Max. Have the police arrested anyone?"

"Nah. And no suspects as far as I know. Carl Dillon is handling the story. It was front page today, page ten tomorrow, then who cares by the weekend, so get me that obit by tomorrow morning, okay?"

"Okay," I grumbled, scrolling down the list of e-mails.

Max did a quick about-face and came back to my cubicle. "And I need something about your beef with Liddell. Katherine the Great was on the horn first thing this morning—she's a little pissed that you didn't come in last night and bang something out."

Katherine Parkham was the *Bulletin*'s editor, a transplanted New Englander who viewed anyone who enjoyed living on the Left Coast as slightly crazy.

Max took his pipe from his jacket pocket and rubbed the bowl between his thumb and forefinger. "She said that Liddell is likely to sue you and the paper, so she wants you to talk to Mark Selden 'as soon as Quint gets his lazy ass in the building.'"

Selden was the paper's legal advisor. "Liddell isn't going to sue anyone," I said. "He'll tell everyone he knocked me silly and make himself into a hero."

"Maybe," Max said, "but see Selden and cover your butt."

"*Camelot* opens in three days, Max. Under the circumstances, I probably won't be able to review it."

"Are you kiddin'? The Great was all hot about that. She definitely wants you to do the review." He rubbed his thumb and forefinger together. "Controversy, Quint. That's what sells newspapers, and that's the business we're in. Roast Liddell and maybe he'll take another shot at you. Now that would be a hell of a story."

I deleted the spam mail that was hoping to entice me to use their products to enlarge my penis, increase my breast size, or view other people's e-mail.

The rest of the mail was from people who either agreed or disagreed with my reviews, or wanted to meet for lunch because they had a screenplay that couldn't miss.

One e-mail sent three days ago jumped out at me—from thanatos@freemailer.com.

PYSCHO—what would you think of a remake of Psycho with a male victim in the shower scene?

Creepy. Sent to me just days before Montgomery Hines was killed. My fingers dangled over the keyboard. I try to respond to all of my e-mail—if someone takes the time to read my stuff and write me about it, they deserve an answer.

"Are you psychic?" was the response I settled on.

There was a rap on the fiberboard wall of my cubicle. I dropped my glasses back to my nose and looked up to see the smiling face of Brody Carew. Carew didn't smile often, and for good reason—his teeth were oversized and grimy, the ivory of ancient piano keys. He was a tall, skinny man in his thirties, with rounded shoulders and a curved back. He had a sullen, pinched-in face, and had abandoned his hippie-style ponytail for an *Eraserhead* cut, skinned on the sides and long and fluffy on top. He was dressed in jeans and a white sweatshirt with GOT POT? printed in bright red letters. Brody's wardrobe always told you just what he wanted out of life: to save the whales, to stop global warming, to get our troops out of everywhere, including America. What he really wanted was my job.

"Man, that was something last night. I thought that Liddell's bodyguard was going to beat the snot out of you," he said.

"You saw what happened?"

"Just the good part. You bleeding all over yourself." He exposed his ugly teeth again, said, "Peace out, baby," then strolled away humming a rap song.

Brody was low man on the totem pole in the paper's entertainment section. In addition to being the TV critic, he usually reviewed what

Max Maslin described as "that crap that no one in their right mind could sit through."

The rest of the day was dedicated to work—the obit on Hines and fleshing out the reviews of the New York shows, two of which were wonderful, and the third wasn't bad. In between that I sandwiched in a meeting with Mark Selden, the paper's legal beagle. I was cleaning up my desk and getting ready to go out and scrounge a meal somewhere when the phone rang.

"Carroll. It's Gineen. How are you feeling today?"

"Fine," I assured her. "All the pain was to my ego, not my body."

"Darling, when you were up in my room, you didn't happen to see a ruby necklace of mine, did you? Sweet William gave it to me on our wedding day. I'm sure it was on my makeup table when I went down to the party, and now it's missing."

Sweet William had been her last husband, a Southern California shopping mall developer. "I couldn't see anything without my glasses, Gineen. Wait. When I was at the top of the stairs, someone came out of nowhere and swept past me. I figured it was household help, but I couldn't tell you if it was a man or a woman."

"I know it's a bore, Carroll, but I had to call my insurance people, who contacted the police. I'm afraid they'll want to talk to you."

"That's not a problem," I told her.

"Good. The detective's name is Wyatt, and he's kind of cute in a dark, oily way. Are you coming to the *repas léger* party at the Hilton before the *Camelot* opening?"

Repas léger, French for a light meal, which meant hors d'oeuvres and lots of free booze. "I wouldn't miss it. Mind if I bring a friend?"

She emitted a light giggle, then said, "Bring a couple, and a spare pair of glasses just in case, darling."

As I hung up the phone, the lovely head of Terry Greco peeked in on me.

"Hi, Rocky," she said with a smirk. "When's your next fight?"

Terry is the proverbial ten pounds of candy in an eight-pound bag.

She's short and tightly packed. Her hair is four shades of carefully blended blond. She favors tight skirts and sweaters, claiming that her mother advised her, "If you've got it, flaunt it, 'cause you ain't going to have it long, kid."

She had been with the paper for a couple of years and juggled art, books, and restaurant reviews into her schedule. All of us at the *Bulletin* were multitaskers, and lived in real fear that each edition of the paper might be its last. Just looking at her brought out all my primal urges: sex and food.

"Any restaurants you need a hand with, Terry? I'm starving and available."

"Don't I know," she said, pulling a thick hardcover novel from behind her back. "Want to trade? You review this baby, and tomorrow night we go to Dutil's." She kissed the tips of the fingers on her free hand and made smacking sounds. "I hear the veal is fantastic."

She plopped the book on my desk. The cover featured a tall, full-figured woman with long dark hair, her hands holding up what remained of her dress while a bearded half-naked Adonis brandishing a sword leered at her.

"God," I groaned. "Not another Joan Kenyon bodice ripper."

"Don't knock it," Terry said. "The lady makes a fortune on these things. So, get me four hundred words, and we dine at Dutil's. Deal?"

I picked up the book and bounced it in the palm of my hand. "Anything this heavy deserves two dinners. Deal?"

Terry scraped her fingers down the arm of my sweater. "Okay. Pick me up tomorrow night at seven and wear a shirt and tie, Quint. This is a classy place."

"Your apartment is pretty classy too, as I remember."

She inhaled deeply for my benefit, then said, "You've got a long memory. You should have called me from New York."

THREE

I'd stayed up late working on my new book, so when the phone rang a little after seven in the morning, I was in a grumpier mood than usual.

"Carroll. I need to see you right away. It's urgent. Now." Click. Just like that. Not a hello, and definitely not a good-bye.

"Okay, Mother," I mumbled to no one but myself as I rolled out of bed.

My mother lives in the lower unit of an Edwardian pair of flats on Liberty Street, in the Dolores Heights section of the city. Dad has the upper unit. He'd inherited the property from his parents well before I came into the picture. The entire block is filled with similar buildings, all meticulously cared for, each with a blooming bottlebrush tree positioned in the front. On a foggy day, of which we have quite a few, you can imagine that you're strolling down a posh residential London back street. The Quint residence featured a fresh coat of olive green paint with glossy black accents. The curved bay windows were hand-cast and cost a fortune to replace, something I'd learned after breaking one with an errant baseball when I was about nine. The rose-tinted terrazzo steps leading to the front landing were damp and smelled of Pine-Sol. My mother goes through Pine-Sol like McDonald's goes through ketchup.

The hardware on the door leading to her unit was gleaming brass, with specks of white polish in the cracks and keyhole. Dad's brass doorknob had a dull, smeared look.

Before I had a chance to ring the bell, the door swung open and my mother rushed out to meet me, pulling me to her chest, kissing me on the cheek. She stood back and smiled at me. "Carroll, it's so good to see you," she said, making it sound as if it had been months, rather than less than a week since our last meeting.

"What happened to your face? That ruffian Peter Liddell? He hit you, didn't he? I heard it on the news. Bully. He's twice your size. I've got some vitamin E that will take care of that bruise in no time."

My mother is a shade over five feet. Her once natural blond hair has dissolved into a gleaming silvery gray. She has delicate features, bright blue eyes (bluer than Sinatra's ever were, she has assured me many a time), a tipped-up nose, and fair, clear skin that could have belonged to a woman twenty years younger. She had on a pair of red wool slacks and a white shirt, the French cuffs held together by strands of silk cord that were a perfect match to her slacks. For some reason she was wearing just one earring, a Tiffany starburst of diamonds on platinum that I knew to be one of her favorites. "What's up, Mom? Is something wrong? How's Dad?"

"Oh, don't worry about *him*," she said, cupping a hand under my elbow and leading me inside. "He's on one of his Caribbean ocean liner cruises. He plays music for a few hours every day and they pay him a fortune, plus he's surrounded by a mob of those menopausal nymphomaniacs who take those trips to revive their sex lives."

"What was so urgent?" I asked, following her over the highly polished hardwood flooring. The hallway walls were lined with framed movie posters, ones in which she, under her maiden name, Karen Kaas, had appeared—if only briefly: *Showdown*, an unfunny comedy western with Dean Martin and Rock Hudson; *Live and Let Die*, a Roger Moore James Bond flick (how many guys can say his mom was a Bond Girl?); *The Klansman*, a thankfully forgotten film costarring Richard Burton and Lee Marvin, neither of whom—according to my mother—drew a single sober breath during the shooting; and a Steve McQueen–Paul Newman flick filmed in San Francisco, *The Towering Inferno*.

There were familiar smells of Lemon Wax and Windex in the air, muted by vases overflowing with flowers from her garden. She headed straight for the kitchen—her favorite room: marble countertops, cherrywood cabinets, a huge woodblock chopping island. Ironic, since she is one of the worst cooks on the planet.

A small table was covered with a nearly completed jigsaw, a scene from *I Love Lucy*, showing Lucille Ball dancing around in a vat of grapes. Next to the puzzle box was a pair of scissors. Mom always had the scissors ready "for the pieces the silly manufacturer always makes the wrong way."

A TV situated over the refrigerator was tuned to the Turner Classic Movies channel. An outrageously young Marilyn Monroe was sprawled out on a couch and a wonderful old actor by the name of Louis Calhern was blowing cigarette smoke into her hair. The sound was muted. Both Mom and I could have probably spoken the dialogue word for word.

"Your father left some clothes for you, dear. On the chair over there."

Dad, partially because of his job as an entertainer, and partly because he was a clothes horse, or fashion plate as my mother would say, was always updating his wardrobe, and, since we were about the same size, I was the happy recipient of his castoffs. Today's batch of goodies included a navy blue blazer with a Burberry label and a rust-colored cashmere shawl-collar sweater.

"Do you want something to eat, Carroll? I have some homemade waffles that I can put in the micro."

"No," I said quickly. Mother's baked goods usually included ingredients such as brewer's yeast, wheat germ, and black strap molasses.

"Tea then." She pulled a silver plate teapot, one that she'd "rescued" from the Plaza Hotel in New York City years ago, off the four-burner stove and poured while saying, "It's about the police. I don't want to talk to them. I *really* don't."

Parking tickets, I figured. Or maybe she'd dented someone's fender. I was wrong.

"It's about Monty," she said, placing a cup of foul-smelling green tea in front of me. "There's nothing I can tell them of course, but—"

"Monty? Montgomery Hines?"

"Who else?" She stooped over and stared into my eyes. "Have you been getting enough vitamin A? I have some I'll give you, and bilberry, put a few drops in—"

"Mom. I'm fine. Why would the police question you about Hines?"

Her hand went to her earring, the fingers caressing the diamonds. "Well, I was there. Not when Monty was killed of course, it was the day before."

I took a sip of the tea and instantly regretted it. "You and Monty were . . . friends?"

"Of course." She smiled sadly. "He was a very nice man, and I never held it against him."

I tried picturing Hines and my mother together. It wasn't a pretty picture. "Held what against him?"

"Your father of course," she said, looking at me as if I had asked a particularly stupid question. "If it wasn't for Monty, I never would have met John." She patted me lightly on the head. "And then you wouldn't be here now, would you? Monty and I were in production, *Under the Grave*, a terrible movie, but I did have two lines. Monty had taken me to a club on Sunset Boulevard, and there was your father, playing piano. He caught my eye and sang 'You'd Be So Nice To Come Home To,' in that Jiffy Lube voice of his, just to me."

"Jiffy Lube?" Dad had a soft, whispery voice that had been described in many ways, but this was a new one to me.

"Yes, one of his many paramours, hoping to be the next Mrs. John Quint, hung that on him years ago." She blushed lightly, then added, "When he sings the girls get all wet, if you know what I mean, dear." She shook her head, a lock of hair falling in front of her eyes. "God, he was so handsome. Two weeks later we were in Las Vegas getting married."

This was all news to me.

"I still don't know why the police would want to talk to you, Mom."

"Because of my fingerprints, silly. When I read about Monty's death, stabbed right through the shower curtain—the bathroom was so forties, with that horrid bright purple tile they used to use. The curtain was awful. Ducks, or geese, or some goddamn birds in flight. What a shame he had to die in that room."

"Were you and Monty . . . ?" I stumbled around trying to think of a discreet way of asking my mother if she and Hines were lovers.

"Doing it? Of course not," she said indignantly. "It was not that kind of relationship. He was a friend, that's all. An old friend. I was going to redecorate his condo. It certainly needed it."

After leaving Hollywood and settling in San Francisco, my mother had gone through a number of "artistic endeavors": painting, operating a health food store, a boutique on Union Street, and her latest, home decorating.

She waggled a finger at me. "Monty was furious with you; that last review devastated him. Couldn't you have been more kind? Stay here, I've got something I want to show you."

As soon as she left I took the opportunity to pour the tea down the drain.

She came back clutching a thick photo album. She plopped it on the table and flicked through the pages. "Here we are dear. Monty and I."

It was a black-and-white studio still shot from *Under the Grave*: my young, gorgeous mother in a strapless white dress, her hair done up in an exotic bouffant. Hines stood alongside her in a tuxedo, a gun in one hand pointing off-camera.

"So, what I want you to do, my darling son, is get my earring from his apartment before the police trace it back to me. I don't think my fingerprints are on file anywhere."

"Earring?"

She flicked the Tiffany with her finger. "The mate to this. I left it somewhere in Monty's place. Probably in the damn bathroom when I was freshening up, or in the kitchen. You'll find it if you look hard enough."

"Mom, the police aren't going to let me prowl through Monty's apartment looking for your earring. I can't just break the door down, or climb through the window."

"I wouldn't expect you to John Robie it, dear. There's no need for that."

John Robie. My mother and I spoke in a sort of old-movie code— Robie being the jewel thief character Cary Grant had played in *To Catch a Thief*. She slipped her hand into her slacks' pocket and came out with a bright metal object. "Here's the latchkey. The address is the Maisonette, on Leavenworth Street. The lobby door is never locked, and Monty didn't have an alarm system."

"Did anyone see you going into his condo, Mom? Did you talk with anyone there? Leave a business card with Monty? Would your fingerprints be on any of his knives?"

"No, no, no, and no. The building is filled with dreary old people from what Monty said. And please try to get the earring quickly. I have to have it back. I wouldn't want your father to know I'd misplaced the damn thing. He gave them to me right after you were born."

FOUR

After leaving my mother's place, I stopped at the nearest Starbucks for a strong coffee to rinse away that green tea taste, then headed to work.

If you grow up in a household that is infatuated with show business, especially movies—mom is the queen of movie trivia—and you become hooked on them too, and somehow are lucky enough to fall into a job like mine, reviewing movies and plays, you develop a habit of casting people into roles, and imagining the actors who might play them.

Max Maslin had told me that Carl Dillon was the *Bulletin* reporter handling the Montgomery Hines story. I'd never met Dillon, but I had a picture in my mind of how a crime reporter should look: Humphrey Bogart, ideally, with a cigarette dangling out of the corner of his mouth, or maybe Cagney bouncing around and swinging his arms wildly for the copy boy. I'd settle for Bruce Willis, wearing one of his better hairpieces, a three-day stubble, cigarette pack pouched in his button-down shirt pocket, cocky scowl on his kisser as he pecked away at his keyboard. What I got was none of the above. Dillon was a skinny guy with close-cropped brown hair and thick glasses that gave his face a stunned look. He wore unpressed khakis, scuffed loafers, no socks, and an orange polo shirt with that famous alligator on its breast.

I introduced myself. He wasn't impressed.

"Entertainment section, man, that must be a lark. No deadlines, get to see all the latest flicks for free. It must be like stealing money."

"Not quite," I said. "Has there been anything new on the Montgomery Hines story?"

Dillon's pale forehead rose toward his hairline. "Why? You hear something that I should know?"

"I'm working on his obit, and thought I'd keep up to date."

"*Nada*, so far. Kind of funny one though, huh? Cut up pretty bad from what I hear. In his own shower. Must have been someone he was *real* close to. Some old broad who wasn't getting enough action, I guess."

"What makes you think it was a woman?" I asked.

Dillon raised his hand and made chopping motions. "The weapon. A big chef's knife from Hines's kitchen. A broad's weapon. And she was smart. Stabbed him right through the shower curtain so she wouldn't get any blood on herself. Guys like Hines, actors, even the old farts, they're up to their armpits in broads. He probably had a Viagra omelet every morning to keep him going."

"Who's the homicide detective handling the case?"

"Inspector," Dillon said. "Here in San Francisco the plainclothes dicks are inspectors." He swiveled around on his chair and pawed through a pile of papers. "Inspector Granger. Dave Granger."

"What kind of guy is he?" I asked casually.

"Big, mean, ugly. The joke is he should have been named Grave Danger." He touched the sidepiece of his glasses. "Get it? Dave Granger, Grave Danger."

"I get it. Have you been to Hines's place?"

Dillon folded his bony arms across his chest. "Why would I do that? The body's gone, the crime lab's done its thing. Nothing there now but memories, and they're not mine."

"I thought I might find something there I could put into his obituary. Old photos, some background stuff."

Dillon's cheeks bulged like a trumpet player's. He blew a stream of air at the ceiling, then said, "You're sure going through a lot of trouble for a lousy obit, Quint."

"Boss's orders. Katherine the Great wants it done right. I'm just trying to keep her happy."

"Ain't we all, pal. Ain't we all."

I headed back to my desk. Darlene, the entertainment section receptionist, waved me to a stop. She was a slender woman in her fifties, with a sharp, triangular face, and a cheerful, unbending faith in the goodness of the world. One of those persons who actually meant it when she wished you a happy day. "There's a police inspector in your office waiting to see you, Carroll."

Police? Inspector Granger? Had they identified my mom's fingerprints at Hines's condo, or somehow connected her to the Tiffany earring?

The man sitting in my chair wasn't big or ugly—he was lean, and had thick brown hair with a crooked center line. His face was so narrow it seemed crowded by large zinc colored eyes, and a slightly hooked nose. He was wearing a blue blazer, starched white shirt, and pin-dot blue tie.

"You're looking for me?" I said.

He leaned back in my chair, gave me a quick once over, then shook his head. "I'm waiting for Carroll Quint."

"I'm Quint."

He fingered the knot in his tie. "Are you really? I thought—"

"Almost everyone thinks that. How can I help you?"

He took a leather wallet from his jacket and flashed a gold badge at me. "Inspector Jack Wyatt."

The lightbulb finally went on in my head. "Oh, yes. Gineen Rosenberry told me you might want to talk to me. Any luck in finding her ruby necklace?"

"If I'd found it, I wouldn't be bugging you, would I? Tell me about it."

"If by 'it' you mean the necklace, I've never seen it, as far as I know."

He drew a piece of paper from his jacket and handed it to me. It was a color printout of a necklace—a large, carmine-red single stone dangling on a chain of small diamonds. The stone was described as a perfect 5.2 carat ruby, once owned by Marie Antoinette—insured value, $600,000.00.

"Gineen always had great taste," I said, handing the document back to Wyatt.

"So did the thief," he answered dryly. "Tell me how you happened to be in her bedroom at the time it was stolen."

I gave Wyatt a brief but concise version of what took place that night at Gineen's house. He took no notes. His eyes wandered around the cubicle. He shuffled his feet on the carpet.

"I guess you found my prints there, Inspector. I'm pretty well lost without my glasses, so I was grabbing hold of things just to stay on my feet."

"We found a *lot* of prints. The lady must have a *lot* of visitors."

"Well, I wish you luck in finding it."

"Oh, I'll find it, one way or the other." He got to his feet by grasping the arms of my chair and kicking it back from him. "If the thief is a pro, he'll do the smart thing, contact the insurance company and sell it back to them. But if he's an amateur, say someone like you, Quint, then I'll have to work a little harder."

"I didn't take it," I protested.

Wyatt inhaled deeply, then exhaled loudly. "I'm talking hypothetical here. Let's *suppose* it was you. What would you do with the stone? Try and sell it at a pawnshop?" His hands came together in a loud clap. "Bang. You're mine. Try and peddle it to some punk thief?" His hand clapped again. "He'd turn you over after he had the stone, and those insurance investigators aren't dummies—you try dealing with them, they'd know right away you were bush league and when you tried to pick up your dough, guess what?" Again with the hand clapping. "You'd be mine. And if I even had a hint that you were the thief, I'd get a warrant, search your office, your home, your car. And I'd make sure people saw me going through your stuff, Quint. People would notice, put two and two together. Bad for your reputation—you know what I mean?"

"Yes. You mean you don't have a clue as to what happened to Gineen's necklace, and you're trying to scare up some answers. Now, just theoretically, Inspector, let's *suppose* that you tried some of that search warrant bullshit." I brought my hands together in a soft clap. "You wouldn't find anything, and I'd slap a harassment suit on you, and the *Bulletin* would run the story on the front page. I know you guys like publicity, but not that kind—you know what I mean?"

Wyatt coughed out a laugh. "You talk pretty tough for a guy named Carroll. Hey, sometimes it works, sometimes it doesn't."

He went to his badge holder again, slipped out a business card, and dropped it on my desk blotter. "Suppose you do hear something, give me a call, okay?"

He bumped into me as he maneuvered his way out of the cubicle, mumbled a "sorry," and sauntered off toward the elevators.

I slipped into my chair and got to work, again starting out with checking e-mails. There was a reply to my reply to thanatos@freemailer.com, about his being a psychic.

I'M A VISIONARY. QUOTH THE RAVEN, NEVERMORE. (WHAT IS THE DIFFERENCE BETWEEN THEM AND CROWS?) MAYBE THEY WERE ALL FULL AND COULDN'T EAT ANY MORE. MEAT DOES SPOIL QUICKLY, DOESN'T IT? HAVE A SAFE JOURNEY.

"Whacko," I said under my breath as I deleted the e-mail and vowed never to open another one of his messages again.

Terry Greco swiveled by and reminded me about our dinner date that night. I finished Hines's obituary and decided it was time to take an early lunch. Darlene, the receptionist, yelled out to me, as I was halfway out the door.

"Carroll. I forgot to tell you. There was a call for you around nine."

She pulled a piece of pink scratch paper from a spike near her phone. "Charlie Reeder. He said it was urgent. He wants you to go to his place. He sounded real strange. Like he was in a lot of pain. He hung up before I could get his number."

I examined the note. Charlie was a Hollywood screenwriter who had his hay day in the eighties: a Dudley Moore comedy, a Harrison Ford thriller, and some early Sean Penn things. He hadn't had a hit in some time. He was one of those guys who could be your best friend—until he had four or five drinks under his belt; then he wanted to fight you and everyone else in the bar. But he had a repertoire of wonderful old Hollywood stories that I could never resist.

I hadn't spoken to Reeder in months. He lived in a cliffside house in Montara, some twenty miles down the coast from the city. Charlie was always changing his phone number, or having it cut off for lack of payment. That made two urgent calls in a day. At least Charlie wouldn't pour me any green tea—he was strictly a bourbon man, from breakfast throughout the entire day.

If you live in San Francisco, you have to have transportation—cabs are expensive and hard to find. The buses are never on time and often filled with pimps and drug dealers. Those little cable cars may climb halfway to the stars, but they never really stop at any place you want to go, unless you're a tourist. Parking is a major problem—the lots charge you a fortune and the city has installed meters everywhere; they even tried putting meters in Golden Gate Park, but the public finally had enough and rebelled. So, you have to be resourceful. My solution was to buy the shortest car on the market, a silver-colored MINI Cooper, which I could wedge into some very tight spots. The added benefit was that most women were wild for the car. One leggy blonde, after folding herself tightly in the front seat, told me, "It looks like a puppy wagging its tail."

Though the car was almost a year old, I'd never gotten around to attaching the license plates—it still had the dealer's paper plates, and I always slipped a map or half of a sandwich over the VIN number printed on the top of the dash—so if a meter maid was about to write out a ticket, she was out of luck. Not legal, of course, but creative. One of these days I was going to find it had been towed away, but so far, so good.

I pointed the MINI's blunt nose south on the freeway and angled over to Highway 1, which hugged the coast. The sky was cloudless, chamber of commerce blue; the sun had gone soft like a big dab of butter. I drove by small beaches strewn with driftwood and others crowded with picnickers and dozens of wetsuit-clad surfers braving the angry, dishwater-colored waves of the Pacific Ocean.

I stopped at a Burger King in Linda Mar and dashboard-dined my way to Montara. When I spotted the red-roofed Point Montara Light Station, I knew I was getting close. The 1875 lighthouse had been restored and turned into a hostel. A string of gaudily outfitted bicyclists hogged the one lane road, seemingly asking to be hit.

The turnoff to Charlie's place was an unmarked dirt road. The MINI bumped over clumps of flowering orange ice plant. A dilapidated fence with rotting posts guarded the entrance. There were two rusting metal signs splattered with bullet holes big enough to shove a Popsicle through nailed to the fence gate: One simply said BEWARE OF DOGS. The one below it was more specific. FORGET ABOUT THE FUCKING DOGS. BEWARE OF THE OWNER! The signs were a bit misleading—Charlie never owned a dog.

"Hey, Charlie," I yelled as I unlocked the gate and swung it open. Despite the blue sky and full sun, it was cool—even in summer, the average daytime temperature on this part of the coast is in the mid-fifties.

No response. I hopped back in the car and negotiated the sharp right turn that led to the house. Charlie had the place built when he was in the chips—a modernist mass of limestone, redwood siding, and glass, with a steel cantilever supporting a half-moon shaped deck hanging out over the ocean.

I parked between a pair of twisted cypress trees, their long branches spread out like great linking hands. Signs of neglect were everywhere: weed-choked flowerbeds, the cement pathway buckled by tree roots, the windows caked with dirt. The oak chevron front door was warped and the brass hardware green and crusted from the salt air.

A number of birds began to croak and argue. I used the Oscar-shaped doorknocker (Reeder had been nominated for an Academy Award, but never won). "Charlie. It's me, Quint," I yelled.

Still no response. The door was unlocked. I stuck my head inside and yelled again. Charlie's living room would have warmed my mother's heart: large modern Scandinavian furniture, Chinese art on the walls, African hand-carved masks and statues, and Greek flokati rugs scattered over the polished red Cuban mahogany flooring. Mom wouldn't have liked it in its current condition: newspapers and magazines strewn everywhere. Glasses, some with lipstick smears, littered the tables. Ashtrays overflowed with cigarette butts. There was an awful odor in the air, a smell that even the closeness of the ocean couldn't obscure.

I made my way through the kitchen and out to Charlie's sundeck. I flinched at first, not sure what I was seeing. A hump sprawled on the deck, covered by a cluster of large, shiny black birds. I picked up the nearest object, a white plastic deck chair, and threw it at the birds. Several ravens gave me fierce don't-mess-with-us looks, then reluctantly backed away from the bloated body dressed in faded jeans. I jumped up and screamed and the birds began flying away, croaking at me in anger. I edged closer to the body. I couldn't be sure it was Charlie. The eye sockets were empty, bloody holes, the flesh on the face ripped away to bare bone. Then I spotted the faded anchor tattoo on a bloody forearm. Charlie's tattoo from his years in the Navy. I lurched over to the railing and emptied my stomach of a Burger King Whopper and fries onto the rocks below.

I used my cell phone to call 911, then sat in the kitchen, where I could run out and shoo away the miserable birds, and waited for the police to arrive. It took nearly forty minutes. I whiled away the time by sampling some of Charlie's Wild Turkey bourbon, straight from the bottle, and wandering around his place—careful not to touch anything else. There was a long-barrel revolver with pearl handles sitting on the stovetop. Charlie had always kept guns in his place: pistols, revolvers, and shotguns. "If I dial the cops, then immediately call Domino's Pizza, guess who would get here first?" he once asked. All those guns hadn't done him much good.

I wiped my prints from the bourbon bottle when I heard the siren. The first patrol car to arrive was driven by a uniformed officer with a rugged, outdoorsy look. I went out to meet him. He kept one meaty hand on the butt of his service revolver while I led him to Charlie's body. The birds had come back and the officer pulled out his gun and fired it into the air to get rid of them.

"Don't tell anyone I did that," he said, "or I'll have to fill out a half dozen 'discharging your weapon' reports." He had me stand with my feet together and arms out in a crucifixion pose while he gave me a pat-down. After looking at my driver's license, he told me to wait in my car. "Detective McCall's on the way. I'll stay here and keep those miserable crows away."

I used the time to call the paper and fill them in on what I knew of Reeder's death, including the mysterious e-mail.

"Suicide? His liver give out? Or was he murdered?" Max Maslin wanted to know.

"I haven't a clue, Max. I'll keep you posted."

It was another forty-five minutes before a tobacco-colored sedan arrived.

A man with arched eyebrows and a long-chinned face climbed out of the car. He wore a western-style corduroy jacket, no tie, dark brown slacks, and dusty cowboy boots.

"Who the hell are you?" he said as a way of greeting.

I gave him my name and told him how I'd found Charlie's body. In return he handed me a business card. Detective Bruce McCall.

"Is that your car?" he asked.

"Yep."

His right hand made an opening and closing gesture. "Give me the keys, and stay right here."

After viewing the body, McCall parked his butt on the hood of his unmarked car and, unlike Inspector Wyatt, he asked me a lot of questions and took a lot of notes.

"Let me get this straight, Quint. You're telling me that the deceased, who looks like he's been that way for a few days, called you to come and see him?"

"Someone called me. I was out. He spoke to our receptionist, said he was Charlie Reeder, and that he wanted to see me, that it was urgent."

"Have you been here before?" he asked.

"A few times. Charlie liked to throw parties from time to time. Did you notice the guns in his house?"

"I noticed. Was he a collector or just paranoid?"

"A little of both, I guess. There were times when he'd have a few drinks, and sit out on his deck and plink at the birds."

"Really? That's against the law. You should have reported it to us." McCall scratched at his chin with the eraser end of his pencil. "And this e-mail that said something about ravens—what was it?"

" 'Quoth the Raven, Nevermore.' It's from Edgar Allan Poe. Then it said something about them being all full, having too much to eat, meat spoiling. And to have a safe journey."

"I want a copy of that e-mail."

"I deleted it," I told him. "Along with his previous message."

McCall stuck the end of his pencil in his ear and gave me a hard look. "That's the one you think is related to this actor who was murdered in his shower in your town?"

"Montgomery Hines, yes."

"Were Hines and Reeder friends?"

"Not to my knowledge."

"Well, then he's 'Frisco's trouble," McCall said, "I've got enough problems of my own. How often have you been communicating with this—what's his handle? Thanatos?"

"Just those two messages, as far as I know."

The pencil moved to the area between his shirt collar and neck. " 'Far as you know'? Wouldn't you remember any prior communications with a fruitcake like this?"

"I get a ton of e-mail; my mailing address is always at the bottom of my columns. But I don't remember any earlier messages."

McCall had me go through it all again. The coroner's wagon arrived as he was finishing up. He snapped his folder shut and squinted at me. "It'll take a day or two to determine exactly what was the cause of Mr. Reeder's death. He could have passed out or died of natural causes, and the birds got to him when he was already gone. If it's a homicide, you and I are going to have some long talks together."

He started off toward the coroner's wagon. "Hey, Detective. My car keys."

He turned around and gave me that squint again, and strode over to the MINI. "No license plates. That's a vehicle violation. If I had my ticket book, I'd slap a tag on you, son. Make sure you've got those plates on when we talk again." He handed me the keys. "And I don't want to read anything in your paper about this before you clear it with me."

FIVE

It had been a long, tough day, starting with the call from my mother and her revelations about her friendship with Monty Hines, then finding Charlie Reeder's body. Still, what I would remember most about that day was Peter Liddell saving my life.

Terry Greco was already seated and being fawned over by a tall, distinguished-looking man in a charcoal gray suit by the time I arrived for our dinner date at Dutil's.

I'd gone straight to the *Bulletin* after leaving Reeder's place and tried—without success—to retrieve the e-mails I had deleted from my computer. Then I had called Terry and told her I'd be a little late, but hadn't filled her in on Charlie's death. Josh Hickey, the paper's electronic whiz, informed me that due to the enormous amount of e-mails that came into the paper, they went in the trash can in a matter of hours rather than days.

"Once it's erased from the server, it's pretty much gone," Hickey had said.

"Is there any way to trace the sender through his e-mail server? It's important, Josh."

"Not if this guy is smart. He'd just use a phony name and address on his register—and if he's real smart, he'd be sending from a laptop he'd picked up at a flea market, and using a wireless Wi-Fi connection at Starbucks or a public library. If he wanted to stay hidden, he'd use an anonymous e-mail provider, change his mailing name every once in awhile, and pay for it with porn money."

"Porn money?"

"Yeah. You can buy cards for any amount at those check-cashing places. You then open an account and the money is deducted from the card—that way you never leave a credit card or a bank account number. Guys use it all the time to log onto porn Web sites, so their wives don't notice an entry on a credit card bill. Maybe the FBI or CIA could trace him, but not me, pal."

What good are electronic wizards when they can't whiz?

Darlene, our receptionist, told me she had never spoken to Reeder before, and said the man on the phone had a deep, quavering voice, and yes, it certainly could have been someone trying to disguise his voice. I told her that the police would probably be contacting her and that made her day.

I cobbled together a story on Reeder's death, listing his literary achievements, and filled it with the usual cliches: Police will not confirm whether foul play is involved until the autopsy is completed. Detective McCall probably wasn't going to like it, but he had his job and I had mine. McCall's cavalier attitude toward the e-mails puzzled me. He seemed to be more concerned about Charlie shooting at birds, and my car not having license plates, than the obvious connection between Reeder and Monty Hines's death.

Terry arched an eyebrow as the distinguished-looking man in the charcoal suit whipped out a chair for me with the finesse of a lord's butler.

"Here's your young man," he said, beaming at Terry. "*Bon appétit.*"

She was definitely worth beaming at: a black, low cut dress of liquid silk that flowed over her body like a sheet of water. Her hair fell in orchestrated layers to her bare shoulders.

Her trips to review restaurants are supposed to be very hush-hush, the owner and chefs supposedly having no idea just who she is—but the city's upscale restaurants are a small, gossipy community; everyone in the business knows when a place is doing well, when it's about to go belly up, when a top-notch chef is fed up and wants to change ranges.

And especially just who the reviewers are for every newspaper in the Bay Area.

So when a critic who looks like Terry comes to your place, you roll out the red carpet and file the check away in the trash can.

"Who's the Richard Gere–looking cat in the charcoal suit?"

"Emile Dutil, our host." She held up her hand dramatically and looked at her wristwatch. "Well?"

"I have a hell of an excuse for being late, teacher, but first I need a drink. A big drink."

Terry glanced at a waiter across the room, pointed her finger at the martini in front of her, and signaled for another.

"Here's what happened," I said. It took two martinis and the first glass of Chardonnay before I'd brought her up to date. While we were talking and drinking, Emile himself shuttled over small plates of delicious appetizers: oysters on the half shell, crabcakes, escargot in puff pastry.

"God, that's really awful about Charlie Reeder. Tell me, Carroll. Your gut feeling—was he murdered?"

"Hell, yes. The e-mails make that pretty certain, but this Detective McCall is playing it slow and easy, waiting for the autopsy."

Terry's shoulders gave a light shudder, setting off a tsunami of jiggling flesh that almost caused Dutil to spill the wine he was pouring into her glass. "Finding him like that, I don't know how you can eat."

"Lunch didn't stay with me for long." I looked up into Dutil's handsome face and asked what his recommendations were for the entrée.

We finished off dinner with a Calvados and when I gallantly offered to drive Terry home, she would have none of it. "You've had too much to drink. We're taking a cab. You can pick up your car in the morning."

Mr. Dutil provided Terry with a doggy bag that would have taken up most of the backseat in my MINI.

The cab driver dropped her off first. His eyes caught mine in his rearview mirror. Reading his scrunched up facial expression wasn't hard: *how could you let someone like that get away?*

My apartment is on the Embarcadero, roughly between the Ferry Building and the Giants' ballpark. It was a beautiful night, the Bay Bridge a string of pearl lights stretching across the bay. Ferryboats and huge tankers crisscrossed the dark bay waters. I had the driver drop me off a few blocks from my place, so I could walk off the effects of all of that free booze and food.

I was fumbling for my apartment key when I got the first hit— right in the small of the back. The keys went flying, and before I could fall to the sidewalk something struck me solidly in the stomach. I hit the ground like a sack of cement—landing on my chest. When I tried to get up, a hard-toed shoe caught me in the shoulder, barely missing my neck. Two pairs of strong hands grabbed at my arms and held me out spread eagle.

"Don't scream, asshole, or I'll really hurt you," a deep nasally voice said. He yanked off my glasses. I twisted my head and saw a knee, pant cuff, then a shoe slowly lowered over one of my outstretched hands. "Hard to write any shitty reviews with broken mitts, ain't it?" the same voice asked. The foot raised up and I screamed as it crashed into the sidewalk, inches from my hand, right onto my glasses. My spare pair of glasses. Nasally voice's partner hammered a shoe into my kidney and I curled up in a fetal ball.

Another pair of shoes came into view. Highly polished black tasseled loafers. Then a familiar, deep, sonorous voice said, "Okay boys, he's had enough. Let him go."

And that's how Peter Liddell saved my life.

I could hear them walk away, a car door open, the engine growl to life, and the car surge away.

All those hard-boiled actors I'd put in my book, the ones who portrayed Philip Marlowe, Sam Spade, even Peter Gunn, would have bit the bullet, struggled to their feet, tossed down a few shots of bourbon, gone after Liddell and his henchmen, and made them pay dearly for beating them up. I crawled around, searching unsuccessfully for my keys and glasses, then just lay there and moaned until I had enough strength to wiggle my cell phone from my pocket and make one call: "Mom," I said when she came on line. "Can you come over? I need a little help."

The next morning I slept late, waking up with a large headache and an odd smell, my mother having rubbed my scrapes and bruises with a pepper-red-hot ointment that she picked up from a herb shop in Chinatown. I smelled like three-day-old roadkill, and even after scrubbing myself near raw in the shower, the awful scent lingered. I doused myself with cologne, then cabbed it to my car and limped into work. I tried contacting the San Francisco homicide cop, Inspector Granger, but he wasn't in the office. I left my name, but no message.

Detective McCall phoned to let me know that the preliminary autopsy revealed that Charlie Reeder had a .241 blood alcohol count—four times the legal limit on a drunk driving charge. "He was flat-out drunk. There are signs of an injury at the back of his head, but that could have come from his falling on the deck. The doc says that with his liver, he wouldn't have clocked another year on this planet no matter what he did."

"So I'll print it was an accidental death," I responded.

"You will not. It's accidental when *I* say it is. There's more work to do on that head injury. I gave you one of my cards, didn't I, Quint?"

"You did."

"Great, then you'll know how to spell my name when I give the final package."

"McCall, this doesn't fit. It doesn't explain the phone call, or the e-mail. It doesn't—"

"Maybe someone saw Reeder's body, but didn't want to become involved—so rather than call the police, he called the paper. It's happened before."

"Not to me," I said, breaking the connection.

I figured there was no sense in phoning the cops to report the beating Peter Liddell's flunkies had inflicted on me: I had no witnesses, and

Liddell was clever enough to have an alibi all prepared—his word against mine. Still, as my father had preached to me as a young lad: "You're going to lose some fights, kid, but somehow, some way, make the bastards pay."

I stared at the blank computer monitor for several minutes, then began inflicting my revenge—one of my "best and worst" columns. They were fun, easy to write, and generated the most mail for the paper of any of my stuff: the best dancer, the worst dancer—Astaire in anything, Peter Lawford in those old MGM musicals; the best hairpiece—Sean Connery in *The Hunt for Red October*, absolute worst—William Shatner anytime.

This one I titled the best and worst movie fights:

BEST FIGHT IN THE RING

Hilary Swank, in Clint Eastwood's *Million Dollar Baby*. She coulda been a contender.

WORST

Stallone in any of the *Rocky* movies; watching them in slow motion makes you yearn for *The Three Stooges*.

BEST HOLLYWOOD WARRIOR IN AND OUT OF THE RING

Russell Crowe; the Gladiator picks fights with his own security guards, and usually wins.

WORST HOLLYWOOD WARRIOR OF ALL TIMES

Peter Liddell; when he isn't using a stunt man (which isn't very often) Liddell looks as if he has inhaled too much hairspray and throws his punches as if he's afraid of damaging his manicure. No wonder he surrounds himself with goons when he ventures out on the streets.

I sat back and stared at the finished product through my prescription sunglasses, my last available pair—the two pairs of regular glasses that

Liddell and his goons had ruined were in for repairs. The article was juvenile, catty, malicious—just what I wanted.

Max Maslin tapped me on the shoulder, causing me to nearly jump out of the chair.

"What the hell is that smell, Quint? And what's with the sunglasses?"

"I lost my spare pair, Max." I pointed at the monitor. "Take a look. What do you think?"

He leaned over my shoulder, pinching his nostrils between thumb and forefinger.

"Oh, Liddell is going to love this one, my friend—just love it." He straightened up, thrust his hands into his pockets, and cleared his throat before saying, "Katherine the Great wants to see you in her office. Now."

At the *Bulletin*, a summons to The Great's office was tantamount to a professional football coach calling in a low round draft pick days before the season opener—you were going to get the boot.

"Good luck," Max said, the tone of his voice conveying the message that I was going to need it. "Quint, those e-mails. Thanatos. Didn't that ring a bell with you?"

The puzzled look on my face caused him to spell it out for me. "Thanatos was the Greek god of death."

Ah, the benefits of a college education, which I didn't have. At Mission High School the only Greek word that mattered was *baklava*, and, in my own feeble defense, I can't ever remember old Thanatos popping up in a movie.

Max thrust his hands in his pockets and rolled back on his heels. "I told The Great that you figured out the e-mailer's name. Maybe that will help."

SIX

Katherine Parkham was sitting behind her desk, phone in hand, speaking in French. Her feet, clad in black suede Manolo pumps, rested casually on the desk's edge. Her eyebrows contorted in a frown at the sight of me, and she waved her free hand toward the cracked maroon leather club chair directly in front of her desk. She was a big woman, with angular features and wide shoulders. Her eyes were chocolate-brown, wide-set, and always seemed to be half-shut. Her wedge-cut brown hair was streaked with gray. She was wearing a well-cut ivory-colored pants suit and a beige silk blouse. She wasn't beautiful—more like what old-fashioned novelists used to call a "handsome woman."

Her office had all the trappings of a big newspaper executive: a coffin-shaped desk littered with manila folders, two computer screens, coffee mugs jammed with pencils and pens, three telephones, a humidor, and crystal glass ashtray. Oak paneled walls featured dark, murky oils showing four-masted schooners battling monstrous storms.

With one exception—a snowy-white unframed canvas showing a smear of black paint that appeared to be nothing more than a skid mark—the room looked exactly like it had when Boyd Wilson, her predecessor, ran the *Bulletin*. Ran it into the ground, his critics would be quick to point out. Parkham hadn't bothered with any remodeling—which gave fuel to the rumors that she wasn't planning to stay long, just long enough to find a new buyer or give the paper a proper burial, then take her skid mark painting and gallop off to another ailing newspaper in need of her special skills.

There were rumors about her sexuality—the fact that she liked to smoke an occasional cigar led certain crowds to immediately wrap her in a mantle of gayness. "She's got to be a lezbo," Brody Carew had said. Since he figured that any woman who wouldn't jump into the sack with him was gay, his opinion wasn't taken seriously.

The rumor was put to rest when the Great hooked up with Harry Crane, a raging heterosexual who owned a string of fashionable jewelry shops.

"*Au revoir*," Parkham said, dropping the phone on its cradle with a little clattering noise. "Do you understand French, Quint?"

"Just *au revoir*."

She did that thing with her eyebrows again. "Is it too bright in here for you?"

My hand touched my sunglasses. "Sorry, my regular glasses are in for repair."

"Ah," she said, swinging her pumps off the desk. "The beef with Peter Liddell."

"Two beefs with Liddell," I said. "Two beefs, two broken glasses."

"Tell me about it," Parkham said, slouching into a comfortable position in her high-back executive chair.

I did. Her first question was, "Did you call the cops about the second fight?"

"No."

"Good. You got that part right." She rummaged through the folders on her desk, finally pulling out a yellow foolscap tablet. "Max Maslin's told me about these e-mails you received, the one regarding *Psycho* and the one about the ravens. Tell me about it—from the beginning. Starting with the first fight with Liddell."

I did just that, leaving out nothing other than my visit with my mother, her missing earring, her steering me into my apartment last night, and the restaurant dinner date with Terry Greco at Dutil's.

Parkham scribbled furiously on her note tablet, interrupting only when I told her the contents of Thanatos's e-mails. She wanted those down word for word.

When I was finished she tilted her chin up and said, "What's your impression of the San Mateo cop, McCall?"

"Impatient, overly sure of himself. A stickler for the little things, which might lead him to miss the big things."

She opened the humidor, selected a long, fat cigar, slid the band off, and fitted it on her little finger. "Carl Dillon tells me that Granger, the San Francisco cop handling Hines's murder, is a hot shot, and doesn't treat the press with the dignity and respect that we deserve. In other words, Dillon can't get shit from him."

"I've got a call in to Granger," I said, "but no response yet."

That didn't sit well with Parkham. "Don't contact him until I tell you to. This could be big, Quint. This could be a *signature story*—a *Bulletin* signature piece, the kind I've been looking for since I came to this goddamn place. We've got some sort of whack job sending e-mails to *you*—he's either the killer, or knows who it is, right?"

"It's certainly possible, I was thinking—"

"Let me do the thinking on this, Quint. This cuckoo is going to contact you again; he'll probably end up killing someone else. Someone connected with show biz. He's taken out an actor and a writer. Who knows what he'll do next, or how many victims he has on his list? Why is he using you? Have you thought about that? Because you knew both Hines and Reeder? What were they? Drinking buddies? Lovers? Did they like each other? Hate each other? Did they ever work together?"

"I . . . I don't think they worked together," I said. "Lovers—no way. After four ex-wives, Charlie was past sex, from what he told me, and Hines always had some actress dangling on his arm. They both liked the booze, that's for sure. Reeder wasn't a friend, just a guy I liked to spend time with once in a while. Hines I knew only from his work, we were never buddies."

Parkham passed the cigar under her nose, inhaling as if it were a rose. "There's an Alfred Hitchcock angle here. Hines is murdered in the

43

shower, à la *Psycho*, and Reeder is attacked by crows, just like in *The Birds.* That tells us something about him, because ninety percent of the great unwashed who go to the movies today are young people who don't have a clue as to who Hitchcock was. That's why your book didn't sell—these people don't read books, and if they did they sure as hell aren't going to be interested in ones about dead actors, and they're not interested in movies where holding hands and a goodnight kiss on the first date was a big deal. Ten years from now they won't remember Tom Hanks, Brad Pitt, or Jennifer Lopez. They want special effects, huge screens, blood, guts, and raw sex. But not Thanatos. He's a movie buff, like you, and he's telling you how smart he is. Christ—you, Max, and I are probably the only ones on the paper who ever heard of Thanatos, the Greek god of death. I want you to find him, Quint."

I shifted uneasily in the chair, causing the leather to squeak. "Ah, I'm not really a crime guy. Maybe Carl Dillon could—"

"Dillon is useless," she said flatly. "He's typical of the reporters that I haven't yet been able to weed out of here. He sits on his duff and waits for something to come over the wire, to drop into his lap. He writes most of his stuff without leaving the building. He's like the goddamn CIA—they think they can fake everything by using Google and talking to people on the phone. Those CIA turkeys squeal that the reason we're in so much trouble in the Mid-East is that they can't penetrate these Moslem terror cells. Yet high school kids from Marin County and New Hampshire fly over there, drop on their knees, say 'I hate my country and I'll do anything you want,' and boom, they're wearing rags and assembling car bombs in no time." She pointed the cigar at me as if it were a pistol. "I've read your stuff, Quint. It's good. Very good. You're wasted on this show biz junk. From now on you're working on these murders exclusively. Let that punk with the goofy haircut handle your stuff for the time being."

Brody Carew. God, if he got his butt into my chair, I'd have to kill him to get him out. "We don't know that Charlie Reeder was murdered," I protested lamely.

"Bullshit," she barked. "You know it, I know it, and that cop McCall knows it. I know you can do this, Quint. Hell, pretend that you're one of those private eyes in that book of yours. Can you get back into Charlie Reeder's house?"

"I doubt it," I said. "McCall is bound to have someone watching it."

"How about Hines's place? Talk to his neighbors, see what you can find out, and stay away from both McCall and Granger."

I pushed myself to my feet and surrendered—almost. "Okay, I'll try, but I do want to review the *Camelot* opening."

I got another stern look, then her face melted into a smile. "Ah. Peter Liddell. You want to shove a few knives in his back, eh? *Et tu, Quint?* Okay, I don't blame you, but concentrate on the murders. If Thanatos doesn't e-mail you by tomorrow morning, you open a conversation with him. He has an ego a mile wide—let's use it."

"Why *he?* We don't know that Thanatos is a man. Dillon thinks Hines was stabbed by a woman, and as for Reeder, all someone would have to do was get him drunk—which wasn't much of a chore—lead him out to the deck, bop him on the head, and let nature take its course."

She slipped the cigar band from her finger, rolled it into a ball, and thumbnailed it into the trash can. "What's Dillon's reason for suspecting a woman?"

"The weapon—a knife. Monty was in the shower. Unless the killer broke in, it was someone he knew, trusted."

"Possibly some woman he gave his key to?" Parkham said. "Check to see if Hines had any keys made lately, or who he was in the habit of passing them off to. I spoke to Darlene, your ding-a-ling receptionist. What the hell is it with her? She's always so goddamn happy."

"There are worse traits," I said.

Parkham gave me a vulturelike smile. "Really? Well, Darlene thought the phone call was from a man, but I take the point. You and Sherlock Dillon *could* be right, but my fair sex doesn't usually dabble in serial killings."

"He or she calls, and gives Darlene the message. What if I was in the office when the call came in? She would have transferred it right to me, so the caller knew I wasn't there. How?"

"Don't get paranoid on me, Quint. If you were there, he hangs up, calls again around lunchtime when you're out, then gives Miss Happy-face the message." She waved a hand toward the door in dismissal.

I was halfway there when she said, "How's your father?"

I did an about-face. I had no idea that she knew who my father was. "Fine. He's working on board a Caribbean cruise right now—"

"Island hopping. Fun trip. That's where I first met him." She opened the humidor again, palmed a cigar, and tossed it at me. "Give this to John and tell him I said hello."

Max Maslin spotted the cigar in my shirt pocket and heaved a sigh of relief. "She didn't can you?"

"No, but I've been given a temporary assignment, trying to find a link between Monty Hines and Charlie Reeder. Can you think of any?"

Max scratched at his beard and puckered his lips. "Bourbon? Scotch? Vodka? Gin? Both of them were pretty good dippers."

"The Great wants Brody Carew to handle my reviews for a few days," I said, the sorrow obvious in my tone. "Except for *Camelot*."

"Carew," Max groaned. "I have nothing but confidence in him, and very little of that. Be careful, Carroll—first Hines, then Reeder. Two deaths, we don't want any more."

"The Great does. She figures we've got a serial killer on the loose and that he'll contact me again."

"Like I said, be careful, and don't come running to me if you break your legs."

It was my turn to groan. Max loved corny old jokes. "Groucho Marx?"

"It wasn't Harpo," Max said, while wiggling his eyebrows.

I sat down at my computer and immediately went to one of my favorite Web sites: allmovies.com. I entered Hines's name and was rewarded with a list of some forty-six films in which he had appeared, usually well down the credit list. I checked each film—Charles Reeder was not listed as a writer on any of them; still, in La-La Land guys like Charlie did a lot of ghost writing for so-called big name screenwriters.

I then went to the phone for the definitive source on Hollywood— my mother. She cackled on about my scrapes and bruises for several minutes, suggested an array of tonics, and when I told her about Charlie Reeder she started crying. "Charlie was such a wonderful man," she said between sobs.

"I didn't know you knew Charlie, Mom."

"Everyone knew Charlie. How did he die?"

I filled her in, leaving out the gory details.

"My God, right on that beautiful deck of his."

"You've been to his house Mom?"

"Certainly. I redecorated his living room. I had some wonderful ideas for the rest of the place, but Charlie kept putting me off."

"Have you been there lately?" I asked, because if she had, maybe the cops would match up her fingerprints from Monty Hines's condo.

"Not for more than a year."

"Did Monty and Charlie ever work together, Mom?"

"Oh, I imagine they did, somewhere along the way. Charlie was in demand as a 'chalkman,' a screenwriter called in to help out on a script—sometimes there are a dozen writers. Believe me, putting together a film is much messier than making sausages."

"I'm trying to find out if there's something that could link the two of them to the killer."

"Well, dear, why don't you toddle over to Monty's place, use the latchkey I gave you, and look around—after you've found my earring."

SEVEN

It weighed what? A half-ounce? Less? Yet, as I pulled it from my pocket it felt more like a pound—a hot, burning pound of . . . steel? Chrome? Nickel? Montgomery Hines's key—or latchkey, as my mother described it, putting a nice, old-fashioned English spin on the thing. One word on the key: Utica, the manufacturer—nothing to link it to Hines or his condo.

Hines's place was tucked into a ten-story concrete building topped with a gently sloping mansard roof and anchored by a brick veneer base. It had that solid look of buildings put up after the 1906 earthquake: a strong, broad-shouldered, powerfully graceful appearance that seemed to say "ain't no earthquake gonna knock me down, baby."

The name, Maisonette, was carved in Roman script over the arched front entrance.

I had been walking slowly up and down Leavenworth Street, wearing the repaired glasses that Liddell had knocked off at the party—the spare pair was a total loss. A typical icy San Francisco afternoon summer wind rattled windows and tossed around discarded newspapers like wounded birds. In the past twenty minutes not a soul had left the building.

Now or never, I told myself, flipping a mental coin, praying for never, which I knew had no chance of coming up. I climbed the three U-shaped steps leading to the lobby door and calmly pushed the door.

It didn't budge. I tried pulling. Same results. Dear old Mom had told me that the lobby door was never locked.

I backed away and scanned the street. No one was looking, pointing, or calling the cops on their cell phones. Why was the door locked? Hines's murder? Did that warrant a new lock? It would if I were a tenant.

The building's tenant-listing doorbell-intercom system was a neat affair, each tenant's name inscribed on a brass plate next to the bell button. Simple, Carroll, I told myself. Push one of the buttons, tell whoever answered you were Western Union. Did they still deliver telegrams? No way. UPS? FedEx? A pizza delivery? What the hell would get someone to open the door?

I tried the top unit, number twenty, listed to someone named Damas. After a long moment there was a grumbled response through the grilled microphone. "Whoisit?" All one word. He had to say it again before I figured it out.

"Me," I grumbled back, and just like magic there was a buzzing sound, and when I pushed the lobby door it swung open.

Hines's unit was on the third floor according to my mother—3B. I skipped the elevator and took the stairs in a hurry, wondering what Mr. Damas was going to do when "me" didn't show up at his door.

There was no POLICE CRIME SCENE tape on Hines's door. No warnings of any kind. I knocked on the door. If the cops happened to be there, all I had to say was that I was a reporter, etc., etc. No response. I wrapped a handkerchief around my right hand, quickly slipped the key into Hines's lock, and it worked like a charm. I went inside and closed the door. My heart was ricocheting around my ribcage. I'd never make it as a burglar.

I wrapped another handkerchief around my left hand and took a tentative step. The place was bigger than I had imagined, with period furniture and striped wallpaper. Mom would have had a ball redecorating it. The flooring was hardwood covered by an occasional Persian rug. One wall was a shrine to its owner, slathered with pictures of Hines on various film locations: Hines in western gear with Gene Hackman; sharing a cup of coffee with Al Pacino; in a doctor's smock alongside a smiling Walter Matthau; and one with a youthful, bare-chested Peter Liddell, both of them done up in pirate costumes. There was one I almost passed over: Hines sitting on a barstool, hoisting a beer with Clint Eastwood. I didn't recognize the smiling man with his arm draped over Hines's shoulder at first—a much younger, beardless Max Maslin. When Maslin had asked me to do Monty's obit, I got the feeling that he hadn't known the actor.

Most of the photos showed Hines escorting starlets to gala Holly-wood affairs. The girls always seemed to be very young, while Hines's hairline retreated gradually in each photo. There were some very rec-ognizable actresses in the photos: Lauren Hutton, Lee Remick, Elke Sommer—but they were in the background, while Hines's dates, though just as beautiful, had never lit up the silver screen. Luckily, my mother's picture hadn't made it to Hines's trophy wall.

The opposite wall was of mirrors, from ceiling to floor—mirrors of every size and shape: round, square, hexagonal, framed, unframed, gilded, frosted. It somehow reminded me of those fun house mirrors they used to have back in the days when they still had fun houses.

I found the kitchen, a 1950s throwback: chrome and yellow vinyl chairs, Formica-topped table and countertops, a turquoise range and re-frigerator, and a water cooler, the kind with the big upside-down bottle that gurgled when you filled your glass. A hardwood knife block held a selection of five black-handled knives. There was one empty slot in the block—no doubt where the knife that killed Hines had come from. There was no sign of my mother's earring on the counters or in any of the drawers. I popped open the refrigerator and saw the trappings of a fellow bachelor: cartons of Chinese takeouts, wrinkled lemons, and rows of wine and champagne bottles. The champagne labels were Cristal and Dom Pérignon, whereas mine were Chateau Supermarket.

Hines's bedroom was off a long, narrow hallway. The platform bed was made of dark, polished burlwood. The matching nightstands had twin frosted-glass tulip-shaped lamps. There was a cottage cheese acoustical ceiling, and musty purple drapes cloaking the windows.

A carved dresser with a brown marble top caught my attention.

Sitting on all that marble was a strange windmill-like device about a foot tall. It held two wristwatches and moved ever so slowly in a clockwise direction, then stopped and went the other way. I stooped over and examined the watches: both Rolexes, one stainless steel with a black face, the other solid gold. The windmill thing was a watch-winder. You shell out ten to twenty thousand dollars for a Rolex and it doesn't come with anything as modern as a battery, of course. You have to buy something to wind the beauty for you. I glanced at the Timex on my wrist and it informed me that I'd been in the condo for over fifteen minutes.

I started going through the bureau drawers and almost immediately hit paydirt. A leather jewelry box held a variety of cufflinks—some looked valuable: silver, pearls, one gold mushroom-shaped pair. There were dozens of tie clips, silver collar studs, and one diamond earring.

I was about to pocket Mom's earring when I heard the front door click open and slam shut. I dropped the earring back into the box, closed the drawer, and looked around frantically for a hiding spot. Under the bed? Or the closet? The sliding-shutter-door closet won out.

I huddled in between Hines's collection of suits and coats, the closet door opened just enough so I could monitor the outside world.

Footsteps, over carpet. Then they became louder. Linoleum? The kitchen. The sound of another door opening, then kissing shut. The refrigerator. Silence, then, all of a sudden, a blast—a popping sound that had me nearly jumping out of my shoes. What the hell was that? A gunshot?

More footsteps. A man strode into the bedroom—a big man, barrel-chested, a deep-lined muscular face, and thinning gray hair that had been carefully arranged to make the most of it. He was wearing a wide-chalk-striped dark blue suit and carried a bottle of Hines's Dom Pérignon in one hand, a glass in the other. That explained the popping sound—the champagne cork.

He took a long sip from the glass, then settled it and the bottle on the marble-topped dresser. He edged his suit jacket open, and I could see a gun holstered at his hip and a cell phone clipped to his belt. I started sweating. My cell phone. If someone called there was no way the big guy wouldn't hear the ring. It was too dark in the closet to see the right keys to silence the phone. The way my luck was going I'd set off the damn thing.

His hand came out of his pants pocket with a watch. He plucked one of the Rolexes from Hines's watch-winder with his other hand, held the two of them up to his face, and smiled. He dropped Hines's black-faced Rolex in his pocket, and, after rubbing down the other watch with a handkerchief, set it gingerly back on the winder.

He poured himself more champagne and took a leisurely look around the room, ending up by staring at the closet doors. I opened my mouth wide and tried to keep the sound of my nervous breathing from reaching him. If he came to the closet, what the hell was I going to say? The gun on his hip—a cop? The theft of the Rolex—a crooked cop?

He took a leisurely step toward the closet, then turned back to the dresser and began going through the drawers. The jewelry box caught his attention right away. He held up several of Hines's cufflinks, examining them with a quizzical look on his face, probably figuring if they were worth pocketing. One pair was—it joined the Rolex in his pants pocket. Then he held up mom's earring. He tossed it in his hand for a moment, as if it were one of a pair of dice, then dropped it back into the box.

He was pawing through the rest of the drawers when a familiar tune chimed out of his cell phone—the theme from *Mission: Impossible.*

He freed the phone from his belt and said, "Granger. What's up?"

After a half-minute or so, he said, "I'm at Montgomery Hines's place taking a last look. Hines's sister is coming out tomorrow from Iowa. I'll be over there in a few minutes."

Trying to keep my sigh of relief from blowing the closet doors open took a considerable effort.

Inspector Dave Granger topped up his glass with champagne, drained it in a single gulp, then carried the glass and bottle back to the kitchen. I could hear the sink water running, then the refrigerator door opening and closing, and finally the solid thunk of the front door slamming shut.

I waited a good five minutes before slipping out of the closet. I picked up the watch Granger had set on the winder. It looked just like a real Rolex to me—said so on the dial: SUBMARINER—superlative chronometer. Then why the switch? This one had to be a knockoff.

I put the watch back, then dug out the jewelry box. The mushroom-shaped cufflinks were gone. I retrieved my mother's earring. Hines's sister would have no use for one earring. Just before leaving I checked the refrigerator again. The opened Dom Pérignon bottle was down below half-label. Maybe the sister would have a use for that.

EIGHT

They say that timing is everything—of course they also say that falling in love is wonderful, so I've never really trusted *they*. My timing couldn't have been worse—my mother was cooking dinner when I arrived at her flat.

"Oh, darling," she gushed, tugging at my sleeve as she helped me through the door and pulled me toward the kitchen. "You're just in time. I'm making tofu cutlets with tapenade sauce, and there's more than enough for both of us."

Maybe it was that early Hollywood training—my mother dressed for cooking as if she were replacing Emeril on the Food Network: she had on an eight-button chef's jacket and a white bandana around her hair.

"Sorry, Mom, I've got a dinner date."

The stereo was playing one of my father's CDs, his fingers tinkling around with "Fools Rush In."

Mom picked up a chopping knife and began attacking a pile of parsley. "You always say that. Why don't you bring your girlfriends here for dinner?" She dropped the knife on the cutting board. "What do you have in the shopping bag, dear?"

"A book." I opened the bag and laid on the table the copy of the book Terry had given me to review. "Do you think you could skim through this and give me a review by tomorrow?"

She rapped the side of the knife blade against the counter. "Carroll, I have a business to run. I just can't drop everything and do a book review for you and . . . what are you doing?"

I was opening the drawer where she kept her towels and potholders. "Treasure hunting, and look what I found." I opened my palm and flashed the Tiffany earring I'd taken from Montgomery Hines's place. "It must have dropped off when you were doing the dishes."

She plucked the earring from my hand and beamed up at me. "How clever you are, my wonderful son." She leaned forward and brushed my lips with hers. "Thank you."

There was an opened bottle of zinfandel on the counter. I poured both of us a glass. "That's my story, and I'm sticking to it, Mom. And by the way, I've got a ticket for the *Camelot* opening for you. There's a preshow party at the Hilton."

The CD slipped over to a new track, "Let's Fall in Love," this one a vocal, my father's whispery voice making the most out of the mischievous lyrics.

Mom sipped at her wine, then said, "Damn that man, he still sends shivers up and down my spine." She shook away the nostalgia and looked me straight in the eye. "Did you find anything else of interest in my towel drawer, dear?"

"Not a thing. And I lost that key you gave me. Do you happen to know if Hines had any other keys out floating around?"

She clasped her hand to her chest in mock surprise. "How would I know that? It wouldn't surprise me, though. Monty was a scoundrel in his own little way."

Later I would wish I'd asked her what she meant by "little way."

I woke up in the middle of the night in the middle of a nightmare. Peter Liddell's goons were chasing me down a dark tunnel. I kept running for the light at the end of the tunnel and when I got close I could see a man in a dark suit heading right for me, a gun in hand, aimed directly at me.

"Shit," I said out loud, throwing the covers off and stepping on something sharp as I banged into a cabinet that should not have been there.

Terry Greco snapped on her bedside lamp and blinked her eyes rapidly. "Where the hell are you going?"

I looked down at the sharp object that had nearly punctured my instep—one of her black, high-heeled slippers. I flopped back on the bed, massaging my foot. Terry had invited me over to her apartment to finish off the doggy bag from our dinner at Dutil's restaurant: rack of lamb, tortellini, and crème caramel. Monsieur Dutil had added a bottle of champagne in order to help Terry relax while she wrote her restaurant review. Smart man. Over the next bottle of wine we'd discussed Thanatos's e-mails. Terry's opinion as to why he'd picked me to receive the messages was not comforting. "He knows you, and he was obviously aware that you knew Hines and Reeder."

When I argued that point, she chimed in, "Otherwise he'd have sent the e-mails over to someone at the *Herald*."

In a way, that made sense—the other daily newspaper had twice the circulation of the *Bulletin*. Then she added this grabber: "You're probably one of his targets, Carroll."

"They never kill the messenger, Terry."

"They do, after all the messages are delivered," she said bluntly.

I slipped back under the sheets. "I forgot where I was," I told her.

"That isn't very flattering," Terry said, leaning over to turn off the lights. She snuggled against me, rubbing her foot down my leg, pressing her breasts into my arm.

What was it? My looks? Charm? Sparkling repartee? Or maybe it had been my meeting with Katherine the Great. News of it had spread around the paper, and I became something of a hero for surviving the encounter.

Terry leaned over and licked my ear. "You're not too tired, are you?"

Or maybe it was my inviting her to the opening of *Camelot*.

Her hand skimmed along the outside of the sheet, across my chest, then stomach.

"Ah," she said huskily when she reached the area that had made a tent of the sheets. "You're not tired at all."

I rolled over and locked my lips on hers. Charm, I said to myself. That famous Quint charm.

Carl Dillon sat up straight and held his hand out to me when I stopped by to see him in the morning. It wasn't charm this time, it was fear. I had the Great's blessing, which made me the chosen one—for the moment.

"Carl, did you ever hear of Inspector Granger being on the take, or bending the rules?"

"You mean like taking bribes? Hell, they all do, I guess, but nothing I've heard for sure. These guys don't really have to. You know what a regular patrolman pulls in? Up to ninety thousand dollars a year, not counting overtime, and they all get a hell of a lot of that. Then there's four weeks vacation, sick leave, medical pay, court pay, standby pay, on call pay, and a hell of a pension. As an inspector, Granger has a base pay of more than a hundred thou, plus all of those goodies, so he's got to be pulling more than a hundred and a quarter a year. You sweep in all of those benefit cookies and it's worth another ten or fifteen grand. No one around here comes close to that, except maybe the Great."

I was impressed. "How do you know all of this?

He leaned back and laced his hands behind his head. "I'm on the hiring list. Took the test nine months ago. They call me for work, and I'm out of here, pal."

I settled in behind my computer, checked the two small pink-colored notes from Darlene—two phone calls, both from movie publicists passing on dates for previewing their latest flicks.

I took a long breath, booted up the computer, and moused over to the e-mails. Close to a hundred, most responding to my "best-worst" Hollywood fighters article; every one of them had what the reader considered were better selections. One from my mother: *Sunday brunch! Soy sausage & egg whites Benedict and chocolate soybean brownies! Bring a friend.* And

one I almost passed over: the sender was Hermes at freemailer.com—
Thanatos's mailbox provider—subject: 39 steps. Message:

OOPS! 39 STEPS. MORE THAN ENOUGH TO DO THE JOB, DON'T
YOU AGREE?

I exited my mailing site and went to good old Google, entered Hermes, and
saw listings for the upscale Paris apparel stores and, at GreekMythology
.com, an entry that showed Hermes was one of those Greek gods—the
cleverest of them all, and among his other outstanding virtues, he was the
guide for the dead to go to the underworld.

Thanatos to Hermes—why the name change? *The 39 Steps*, another
old Hitchcock flick.

I brought up the Movie Guide—*The 39 Steps*, made in 1935, five
stars, one of Hitch's first mega-hits and the first with his hallmark: innocent man, caught up in intrigue, must clear himself.

I called Carl Dillon and asked him if any suspicious deaths had
taken place in the last couple of days, where the victim had fallen down
a flight of stairs.

"Stairs? Not that I know of. What's up?"

"I'm not sure," I said, then broke the connection and punched in
Katherine Parkham's extension. Her secretary put me right through.

"Don't tell me," the Great said. "Another message from Thanatos."

"Not exactly, but I think I'd better come up and see you right
away."

NINE

You know that corny old joke about attorneys? How do you know when they're lying? They move their lips. Well, Mark Selden, the *Bulletin*'s house counsel, had solved that problem—his lips barely move at all. He keeps his mouth slightly open at all times, and his voice seems to come from the back of his throat. He could have been a ventriloquist, and at times I expected him to swallow a glass of water while he preached about the dangers of "journalistic litigation."

Selden was a small terrierlike man with dry, mud-colored hair and a face that tapered to a narrow chin. He favored dark suits and bright, flowery ties. Today's featured little yellow daises against a red background.

As soon as Katherine "the Great" Parkham had seen the Hermes e-mail, she summoned Selden to her office. They tossed around several possibilities. Parkham got on the phone and called Carl Dillon, ordering him to find out if there were any deaths involving falls down stairs in the entire Bay Area in the last few days.

She turned her attention to me. "What do you know about this movie, *The 39 Steps*?"

"It's been years since I've seen it," I said. "Maybe we should take a look."

The Great summoned her secretary and within thirty minutes her office was outfitted with a TV and DVD player, and a copy of *The 39 Steps* from a nearby Blockbuster store.

Selden looked as if he was in danger of dozing off throughout the movie, but the Great and I sat back and enjoyed. All that was missing was a box of popcorn.

It had been too long since I'd seen the flick. Shame on me. It was pure Hitchcock: handsome young hero accused of a murder he didn't commit, who finds himself handcuffed to a beautiful, icy blonde he meets on a train, and they're chased all over Scotland by the bad guys. There was what would have been considered a racy scene back then, when our hero and the blonde are handcuffed at a hotel, arguing about who was going to sleep on the floor.

The times being the times, Hitchcock skirted around the problems caused by Mother Nature for the two of them. If Hollywood filmed it today, there would be three or four scenes filmed in a bathroom along with some X-rated jokes. What is it with movies today? Producers seem to have a urinal fetish.

The 39 Steps was actually the name of a band of bad guy agents, and our hero exposes them, and saves himself, by running down a vaudevillian named Mr. Memory, a sort of human Google, who the Steps were using to bring secret documents out of the country. Ah, the good old days, before computers, cell phones, faxes, and e-mails.

When the movie was over, the Great asked Selden for his opinion.

"Old, lousy special effects, nobody falling down a flight of stairs," he said in that clipped, lips-apart manner of his. "A waste of time."

"I don't think so," I said. "The fact that there were no steps might indicate that our Greek God really isn't a movie buff, that he's just using the titles."

Selden flapped a hand in front of his face. "So?"

Funny how one short little word like that can take the wind out of your sail.

The Great said, "Maybe he's not a *total* movie junky, but he's a Hitchcock fan and is someone who knew Monty Hines and Charlie Reeder. Hines was killed in his own shower, Reeder on his sundeck."

"Both of them were drunk at the times of their deaths from what I've heard," Selden said.

"Making it easier for the killer," Parkham said. "Quint found Reeder's body covered with those damn ravens. He's using Quint to get his story out, so there's definitely a show biz connection."

Selden picked up the DVD container and said, "Maybe there's a simpler solution. The main actress, the British spy, is named Madeleine Carroll. C-A-R-R-O-L-L. The exact spelling of your first name, Quint." He paused for dramatic effect before adding, "Is this Hermes's way of telling us that *you* will be the next victim?"

That possibility had invaded my little gray cells, and I'd rejected it. But a little chill ran through my vitals—first Terry Greco, and now Selden saying that I was on the hit list. "It's just a coincidence," I said, with more confidence that I felt.

"Maybe, maybe not," the Great said. "It's something we have to consider."

Selden surveyed his fingertips. "I think it's logical to conclude that Thanatos is priming us for his next victim. Someone—probably intoxicated, because it makes it easier for him—is about to take a tumble down a flight of steps."

Parkham's phone rang. She mumbled a "Yes," then said, "Put her on."

Her face creased in anger as she nodded a few "umm hmms" and jotted down something on a notepad. She ended the call by saying, "What if I don't want to?" before slamming the receiver down.

"That was your little Miss Happy-Face, imploring me to have a good day and saying that you received two phone calls from the gendarmes, Quint. One from McCall in Redwood City, the other from the SF Inspector, Granger."

Selden turned his cold eyes toward me. "Do we have a theory as to why this person changed his name from Thanatos to Hermes?"

The Great raised her eyebrows as an invitation for me to respond.

"He could have been worried, afraid that we could somehow trace him through his e-mail name."

"Can we?" Selden asked.

"No. At least not according to Josh Hickey, our resident computer expert," I said. "If Detective McCall wants to talk to me, it's for one reason—Reeder's death was definitely a homicide."

"Let's see just what he wants." Parkham picked up her phone and squinted at her scribbled notes. "I'll put the call on the speaker, but I want McCall to think he's talking to me, and me alone."

McCall must have been at his desk waiting for me to ring in. He picked up the call on the first ring.

"Detective McCall here."

"And this is Katherine Parkham, the editor of the *San Francisco Bulletin*. I understand you want to speak to one of my writers."

"You understand correctly, lady. Where's Carroll Quint?"

"He's on a special assignment for me at the moment. Perhaps I can answer your questions."

"Since you didn't find Mr. Reeder's body, then I doubt you can. Quit stalling. Where's Quint, lady?"

The Great's eyes narrowed and she spoke softly and distinctly, as if there were a child on the other end of the line. "In England's rule of peerage, a *lady* is the title given to the wife of a duke, baronet, or knight, and since I am single, and intend to stay that way, it's a title I will never have to bear; so, *Detective*, you may call me Ms. Parkham. If we get to know each other and decide to cooperate on this matter, you may eventually call me Katherine, understood?"

"Don't get touchy on me," McCall countered. "I'm just doing my job."

The Great groaned out loud and made a gesture with her hand, as if she were tipping back a glass of beer to Selden.

"We both want to do our jobs, don't we? Since you want to reinterview Mr. Quint, I assume that Charles Reeder's death is being classified as a homicide."

"You can assume all you want, la—Ms. Parkham. Where's Quint?"

"We're not getting anywhere, Detective. I'm trying to cooperate. Since you say that Reeder was murdered, why don't you—"

"I didn't say that!"

While the Great and McCall were arguing, Selden opened a cabinet, revealing a neat little built-in bar. He selected a bottle of Johnnie Walker Blue Label Scotch, which goes for about two hundred dollars a bottle, poured two glasses, and brought one over to Parkham. He settled back into his chair and took a nip of his whisky.

"None for me," I mouthed silently at him.

"Detective," Parkham said, "here's what I suggest. You fax me a copy of the autopsy sitting on your desk right now, and whatever additional information you think might be useful, and I'll do my best to find Mr. Quint and have him in your office as soon as possible. Deal?"

"I'm not making any deals. I want to know if Quint claims to have received more e-mail from this Thanatos guy."

"I can assure you that he has not. I've been monitoring his e-mail."

"For all I know they never existed, or he sent the mail to himself. Quint is a possible suspect in two murders, and in the theft of a valuable ruby necklace."

Both Parkham and Selden gave me a wide-eyed look.

"Detective, you say *two* murders. Are you referring to the death of Montgomery Hines?"

"You bet. I talked to one of your Frisco cops." We could hear the rustling of papers. "Inspector Granger—he's handling the homicide, and he wants to talk to Quint almost as much as I do."

Parkham took a sip of her drink and rolled it around in her mouth before swallowing. "It is my impression that Quint was in New York City at the time of these deaths."

More paper rustling. "Not from what he told me. The coroner puts Reeder's death down at between the morning and evening of August the fifth. During my interview Quint said that he took the red-eye for New York just before midnight on the fifth. Frisco has Hines assuming room-temperature at six in the morning on August nine. Quint got into the airport at two a.m. that morning. He had more than enough time to stop at Hines's place. And that stolen ruby necklace—your boy's the *prime* suspect there, his prints are all over the victim's bedroom.

Now are you going to send him over to me right now, or do I have to do this the hard way?"

"Are you going to fax me that autopsy? It's public record now. I can have someone down to the coroner's office within the hour."

"Well, send your someone, because I am not going to release anything to you."

The Great let out a theatrical sigh, then said, "All right Detective McCall. This is Katherine Parkham, in the company of attorney Mark Selden, terminating this call. And I did have your permission to record our conversation, didn't I?"

"Hey, wait a—" was all McCall had time to say before Parkham hung up.

Selden's lips actually moved when he broke the silence by saying, "What is this about a ruby necklace?"

The Great stood up and began pacing the room. "This had better be good," she threatened.

"Gineen Rosenberry's necklace was stolen during the party she threw at her house the night I had the fight with Peter Liddell. She knows I didn't take the damn thing. Hell, without my glasses I could barely see her, much less a necklace. There were at least a hundred people at the party who could have snatched the necklace. And McCall is out of his mind. I had no possible reason for killing either Hines or Reeder."

"The fact that you're considered a suspect puts the paper in an uncomfortable posture," Selden said, back in his ventriloquist mode. He looked up at Parkham. "It might be a good idea if he took a vacation for a couple of weeks."

She settled back into her chair and stared at me while running her tongue around her mouth, literally chewing the idea over.

"I'm not going to lose this story," she finally said. "You're right in the middle of this, Quint, and I want you to stay there. Now, the solid truth—is there any possible reason that the police could legitimately consider you a suspect in the homicides?"

"None," I answered firmly.

"And you've just spoken to McCall once, and never to Granger, right?"

"Right." Never spoken to Granger. I certainly had seen him up close and personal in Monty's condo, but, since it involved my breaking and entering, or actually keying and entering, I didn't want to tell her about that, especially with Selden in the room. "I did speak to the cop handling the theft of Gineen's ruby, Inspector Wyatt. Just once, here in my office."

"Did he indicate that you were a suspect at that time?" Selden asked.

"He tried to bluff me, using me as a hypothetical—what if it were you? What if you did take it? That kind of stuff. I was in no shape to pinch a fork after Liddell's bodyguard whacked me."

Parkham leaned back in her chair and tapped the tips of her fingers together. "All right, here's the plan. I want to see that autopsy before Quint talks to McCall. Mark, you go down to Redwood City and pick it up right now."

Selden took a catlike sip of his Scotch, then said, "I'll send someone down and—"

"No. I want you to go. McCall is probably trying to block access, so let's show him some power." She pointed a long finger at me. "Have you come up with anything regarding visitors to Hines's flat?"

"No, I haven't gotten around to that yet."

"Just as well. Stay away from there. If someone spotted you around his building, it would only make things worse. Avoid McCall and Granger and be here in my office the first thing in the morning."

"I've got the *Camelot* opening tonight," I told her.

She scrunched her eyes and was about to say something when I jumped in with, "There are bound to be a lot of Monty's friends at the party before the curtains go up. I may be able to learn something."

She did that thing with her tongue running around her mouth again, then said, "Okay, do it." She stood up and headed for the bar. "I thought that you people out here hated it when people called the town Frisco, like McCall does."

"McCall is in Redwood City—that's a different world than San

67

Francisco. What about the e-mail from Hermes? Should we print something about that? He's flat out telling us he's going to kill someone."

"What should we do?" Selden said sarcastically. "Warn everyone with a remote connection to the screen or stage to be careful crossing streets and walking down stairs? I say we hold on to that for a bit, Katherine."

She agreed with him, then reminded me to be back by nine in the morning. I left, closing the door quietly behind me, and truth be told, if the Great's secretary wasn't right there looking at me, I would have knelt down and peeked through the keyhole. Selden's suggestion of a "vacation" didn't sit well—all I could think of was Brody Carew writing *my* columns for weeks on end.

TEN

That's your *mother*?" Terry Greco said when I pointed out the beautiful woman shimmering her way over to us. We were on the forty-sixth floor of the Hilton Hotel, which provided us with a 360-degree view of the Bay Area. The sunset had turned the evening clouds an orange sherbet color and the city was putting on its neon makeup.

None of these natural wonders compared to my mother—she was wearing a light blue, one-shoulder-bared sequined dress, and her hair looked more platinum than gray and swished around her neck with each step. Her years of dance training and modeling had given her a "walking down the runway" stride. The heels on her shoes were as thin as chopsticks.

"Christ," Terry said. "She's beautiful."

I wouldn't argue with that. A pretty picture indeed, I thought, until she got closer. She was wearing those damn Tiffany earrings.

"Hi Mom. This is Terry Greco. Terry, my mother, Karen."

The ladies shook hands and made nice comments about each other. Bracketed by two beauties, I was getting envious looks from the crowd. Terry was decked out in a bright red lingerie slip dress that displayed a generous décolletage.

"Who do you have to sleep with to get a drink here?" mom asked. "I need a martini, dear."

"Let me get you one," Terry volunteered, and made off in search of the bar.

The room was filled with the "A list": socialites and wealthy first-nighters who didn't mind paying the two-hundred-per-person tab in order to mingle with the city's movers and shakers, along with the usual politicians and media types who, naturally, like me, were free-loading.

Mom leaned forward and whispered in my ear. "My God, Carroll. What a pair of knockers. It's amazing that Terry doesn't tip over. Don't let your father get a look at her."

Terry came back with a drink for my mother and while they started feeling each other out, I mingled. I spotted Brody Carew bending the ear of Don Hampton, the entertainment editor of our rival paper, the *Herald*. Don was a great writer and a good guy. We often sat together during private previews of upcoming movies and compared notes.

Carew was wearing a white tuxedo jacket, ruffled pink shirt, and khakis stained with blotches of white paint. The young lady clinging to his side had maroon-colored hair and gold rings rimming each ear.

Hampton looked over at me and rolled his eyes. I shrugged my shoulders in a "better you than me" gesture.

Jules Moneta, dressed elegantly as usual, tugged at my elbow. He was using his straight—there were uptight businessmen in the room—voice. "Carroll, how am I ever going to get you to come out of the closet when you keep dating these extraordinarily lovely ladies. The woman in blue is new to me."

"My mother," I told him.

"Oh, sure." When he saw that I wasn't kidding he bounced his eyes back and forth from mom to me several times. "Yes. I can see it. The cheekbones, the neck. You have your father's hair and coloring. My, my, how lucky you are."

"How are things going over at Treasure Island?" I asked, snatching a glass of champagne from a passing waiter.

Moneta pulled a dreary smile. "With every two steps forward, there's a step backward. They're redoing a lovely old mansion for me that used to house Admiral Nimitz during the war. I won't be able to move in for six months or so, but I've leased a lovely boat in the sea cove harbor that I'm using as an office.

"The Island administrator is a hundred percent behind me—though I'm not sure I'm comfortable with that position—but the board of supervisors is split down the middle. Some are eager to see a movie studio blossom in the middle of the bay, while the others want to turn the Island into another damn park."

I could see where there would be some opposition—George Lucas, of *Star Wars* fame, had moved his operation from nearby Novato into the twenty-three acres of hallowed ground and prime San Francisco real property of the Presidio, the old military post that was now part of the National Park Service. The local Greens and environmentalists hadn't liked it at all, and they have as much political clout as anyone in the Bay Area.

"What about the Hollywood studios, Jules? Anybody willing to make a move up here?"

"Oh, yes, yes, yes," he said, rubbing his hands together like a man anticipating a gourmet meal. "I've got several deals working with *major* producers. George Clooney is thinking of remaking *The Maltese Falcon*, and shooting all of it right here."

That news hit me harder than anything Liddell's goons had thrown at me.

"Clooney? *The Maltese Falcon*? Tell me you're pulling my leg, Jules."

"Not at all. I'm keeping everything that's still flexible crossed for luck. Wait until you see my plans—the studios, editing rooms; and I'm going to set up two blocks of upscale housing for the actors and crews. It will be fantastic. Drop over to the Island—you'll see for yourself. And mark your calendar for August the twenty-fourth. I'm throwing an old-fashioned black-tie bash. Everyone will be there. Bring your mother and your girlfriend."

I assured him I would, then wandered the room, snapping up

toothpicks speared into bacon and oysters, and melon wrapped with prosciutto, from waiter's trays, and refilling my champagne glass at every opportunity.

An arm bumped into mine, causing me to spill champagne on my shoes.

"Oh, so sorry about that, old boy," said Rawley Croften.

I hadn't seen Croften in four or five years. It was Croften I'd replaced as the *Bulletin*'s entertainment critic. He'd been let go because he would take off for days on end, then show up as if he hadn't missed a deadline. Pills were his problem—prescription medicine. The paper had stuck with him for a long time, had paid for his stays at a couple of expensive treatment centers. Once I went to Rawley's house out in the avenues to fetch some clothes for him during a rehabilitation treatment. I peeked in his medicine cabinet, which was jammed with pain medications: Vicodin, Demerol, stimulants such as Ritalin and Dexedrine, and antidepressants like Valium and Xanax along with dozens I'd never heard of. The front office finally got fed up and let him go.

We'd been friends at one time, and he'd taught me a lot. I ended up feeling very sorry for him, and he ended up hating me—blaming Max Maslin for his being fired, and me for taking over his job.

"Still sniveling around at these affairs, are we, Carroll?" Rawley said.

He was in his early sixties, with hair dyed inky black and parted in the middle, leaving a stark white line across his scalp. He had a high forehead, his face dominated by a large, hawkish nose. He was wearing a black velvet tuxedo that, like him, had seen better days. "Dress British—think Yiddish," had been one of his favorite sayings.

"Good to see you, Rawley. How are you doing?"

"Don't bullshit me, you little twit. I still despise you." He took a swig from his champagne glass before saying, "Your work stinks. Did I teach you nothing?" He looked over my shoulder at the crowd. "Dear mummy still looks good. I might have another crack at that."

He almost got a crack in his nose. I squeezed his arm hard enough to make him wince, then said, "Be nice, Rawley."

He pulled his arm free, glared at me, said, "Your book was pathetic!" then moved off into the crowd.

There were very few actors or directors in attendance, so I wasn't able to pick up anything interesting regarding Monty Hines or Charlie Reeder. By the time I got back to my mother and Terry, they were fast friends.

"I invited Terry over for breakfast Sunday," my mother informed me with a beaming smile.

"That's nice," I said, and it would have been, except I knew I was included in the invitation. "Speaking of invitations, Jules Moneta invited me to a black-tie party on Treasure Island on the twenty-fourth, and both of you are coming as my guests."

Mom said, "Oh, goody," and Terry smiled and got into a whispered conversation with a waiter carrying a tray of drinks.

"Can you imagine George Clooney doing the remake of *The Maltese Falcon*, Mom?"

She wrinkled her nose. "It is one of those events I hoped would happen long after I was gone." She pointed a finger toward the bar. "There's that slut Gineen Rosenberry."

Gineen was deep in conversation with Jules Moneta. She was wearing a stylish evening gown, her hair curled and piled on top of her head. "Why would you say that? She's a very nice lady."

"Hmmmph," Mom snorted. "She looks like Medusa on a bad snake day. She's one of your father's *paramours*. I've seen her chauffeur pick her up from his flat in a Rolls at five in the morning."

"You're up at five checking on Dad's visitors?"

She plucked the champagne glass from my hand and took a deep sip. "How could I sleep? The woman trundled down the stairs like a drunken sailor in hobnailed boots."

Brody Carew and his maroon-haired girlfriend hurried over to us. "That's him, that's Carroll," Carew said to the big man in the wide pin-striped suit—Inspector Dave Granger.

"We have to talk, Mr. Quint," Granger said. He identified himself without flashing his badge. His voice was low and harsh. I hadn't gotten

73

a real good look at his face in Hines's apartment. He had wide-spaced gray eyes and his face was deeply creased. Carl Dillon had called him ugly, but I wouldn't go that far. He had the rugged, hit-in-the-nose-a-few-times-too-many look that some women would find quite attractive. His suit was obviously tailored for his large frame. He wore a black shirt and gray tie.

"Is there somewhere we can go?" Granger pressed. "It's regarding Montgomery Hines."

"Oh, poor, dear Monty," my mother said.

Granger turned his head toward her. He stopped for a moment to feast his eyes on Terry, then smiled lightly at mom. The smile slid away when he spotted her earrings. "Who are you, ma'am?"

"My mother," I jumped in. "You caught us at a bad time, Inspector. We have to get to the theater right now. I'll call you first thing tomorrow."

Granger's eyes kept flicking back from me to my mother's earrings. "I won't keep you long."

He wasn't going to keep me at all if I could help it. "Do you have the time?" I asked him.

Granger shot his cuff, revealing a cuff link in the shape of a handcuff and a black-faced Rolex. I'd been hoping to see one of the gold mushroom-shaped links he'd taken from Monty Hines's place.

"Ten after seven," he said. "Let's go over to the—"

"I really can't, Inspector."

He rubbed a finger along his thick nose. "I'm going to have to insist."

"And I'm going to have to resist. The paper's attorney, Mark Selden, is over by the bar. Maybe we should ask him his opinion as to whether I have to talk to you right now, or get on with my job, which is reviewing a play that is opening up in a matter of minutes."

Granger arched his back as if in sudden pain. "We'll let this one go, Quint. But I want you down at my office in the Hall of Justice first thing in the morning." He took a business card from his breast pocket and flicked it several times with his thumb before handing it to me. "Understood?" He smiled at my mother, said, "Nice earrings," then turned on his heel and walked away.

74

"What an interesting-looking man," Mom said. "If *Guys and Dolls* was opening tonight, he could have played Sky Masterson. Or better yet, Big Julie."

"Show time," I said. "We don't want to miss the first act."

The Orpheum Theatre is a short four-block walk from the Hilton. Four blocks in the highest crime area of the city: hookers of both sexes, dressed in leather, chains; transsexuals; tri-sexuals; shemales; bisexuals; buy-sexuals; muscled-up hemales; pimps; drug dealers; "straw men," people who literally spend their entire day on their knees, a magnifying glass in one hand, a straw in the other, sucking up the tiny specks of speed, meth, and heroin that fall to the sidewalk during a drug buy; and groups of hard-faced young men carrying aluminum baseball bats that would never make contact with a ball of any kind—just heads, arms, and knees.

Mom had cabbed it to the hotel and my MINI was parked a block away, so the solution was a taxi. Brody Carew and his friend, who he introduced as Soria, had latched onto us and, since we couldn't all squeeze into a cab, I negotiated a thirty-dollar ride with a limousine driver.

Soria seemed fascinated by my mother, and kept asking her questions about how she'd kept her looks. "You must be my grandmother's age and she looks like a hag," Soria informed us all. She asked my mother about a face-lift, and I could see there was going to be trouble.

"Do you have any tips for us young people, Karen?" was Soria's final mistake.

"Yes, dear," mom responded sweetly. "Never put ground glass up your ass."

The next three blocks were driven in total silence.

As for the show itself, it was a disaster—for me. I had come to bury Peter Liddell, but ended up giving him a standing ovation with the rest of the audience. The old ham had molded himself perfectly into King Arthur's robes and battle armor. His leathery voice reached the back of the theater and there were few dry eyes in the house when he gave that final "here in Camelot" line.

My mother was all wound up by the performance, and wanted to go somewhere for a drink, but I had to get over to the paper and get the review in for the morning edition.

Gineen Rosenberry saved the day by offering to take Terry and Mom over to Tosca's for a nightcap, then have them driven home.

Mom gave me a peck on the cheek and got in her final quip of the night. "At least her goddamn driver knows the way to my place."

I gave her a hug and said, "Your earrings. Did Tiffany make a lot of them?"

"God, no. They're very special." She patted my cheek. "And so are you, dear."

I went off into the night hoping that the MINI would still be where I'd parked it, all the while wondering if Inspector Granger was going to go back to Monty Hines's condo to see if a single diamond earring was still sitting in Hines's jewelry box.

ELEVEN

Katherine "the Great" Parkham and Mark Selden were waiting in her office for me the next morning.

Selden gave me a sort of sneering look and said, "I see from your review of *Camelot* that you've decided to avoid another confrontation with Peter Liddell by kissing his ass."

"I call them like I see them," I said, working to keep the heat out of my voice. "Liddell was terrific, that's all there is to it."

"I agree," the Great said. "He had *me* swooning there at the end, and I can't stand the man." She was dressed in a vanilla white pantsuit with a three-strand ring of black pearls at the neck. She picked up a sheaf of papers and waved them in my direction. "This is the autopsy report on Charles Reeder. Do you want to read it, or will you settle for my synopsis?"

"I've never read an autopsy report, and there's no reason to start now, is there?"

She dropped the papers back onto her desk. "Reeder was murdered. The back of his head was smashed in with the old reliable blunt object. The cops don't have a clue; it could have been a rock, or piece of pipe, or whatever."

The Great topped off her china coffee cup with steaming coffee from a bullet-shaped Thermos. Right about then I would have sold my grandmother's tombstone for a cup of good coffee, but none was offered.

"I think," the Great said, after a long, slurping sip, "that we're going to have to let the police have access to you, Carroll."

I nodded my agreement. "Inspector Granger was at the pre-show cocktail party last night. He made it pretty plain that if I didn't show up at his office this morning, he'd hunt me down and make life unpleasant."

"Typical overbearing cop mentality," Selden scoffed.

"Then you go see him in my place," I suggested.

Selden leaned back in his chair and folded his hands across his chest as if protecting his heart. "Granger has no interest in talking to me." He turned his eyes to the Great. "Quint should tell him as little as possible, of course. I definitely don't want him saying anything about the latest e-mail from Hermes."

"Yes," she replied, "that would be best, and I—"

"No way," I said. The Great gave me a look that would have frosted a beer mug.

Before she could read me the riot act, I said, "Look. I know this is a big story, and I'm right in the middle of it. I want it as much as you do, but I'm not going to spend the rest of my life blaming myself if this creep shoves someone down a flight of thirty-nine steps and there's one slim chance in hell that I could have prevented it by telling the cops about the latest e-mail."

The Great's eyes tightened. "You *do* enjoy working here at the *Bulletin*, don't you, Mr. Quint?"

"Fire him, Katherine," Selden said. "Let him find out just how the police will treat him without our protection."

I looked Parkham straight in the eye. "I love my job, but I like living with myself even more. Here's my suggestion. We tell the cops about the e-mail, but we leave Hermes name out of it. They already have the Thanatos information, and if we don't break the story, somehow Thanatos's name will leak out, and the other newspapers, the local TV stations, they'll all want a piece of the action."

"It'll go national," Parkham said excitedly. "The networks will jump on it."

"Right, and I'll be getting a couple of hundred e-mails a day from crazy Thanatos wannabes, confessing to every murder that took place in the last five years. So, I make contact with the guy at the Hermes address, and tell him we're going public with Thanatos, but want to keep the Hermes name out of the story, so I'll know it's really him when he mails me."

We locked eyes for several seconds and the Great surprised me by blinking first.

"You're right," she said. "This bastard may change names again, another Greek god—who would be your guess? Hades? Or one of the others?"

I had a vague idea that Hades had something to do with hell, but before I could respond Selden bolted to his feet and said, "You're making a mistake, Katherine."

It was Selden's turn to get a frosty look. She turned her finger toward him and said, "I have my faults, but being wrong isn't one of them. Can we—what's the right terminology? 'Put a wire on Quint'? Record the conversations with the cops?"

Selden's head snapped back as if he'd been slapped. "Not in a police environment, and certainly not with my knowledge of such activity."

The Great smiled at me. "He means no. So it's up to you, Quint. I want a word-for-word account of what you tell these guys: Granger, and Detective McCall from the San Mateo Sheriff's Office." She ruffled the papers on the desk. "See McCall last, let the schmuck sweat awhile."

McCall wasn't going to be the only one sweating.

She got up from behind her desk and patted the chair's arm. "Sit down, use my computer, log on to your account, and send Hermes the mail. Keep it short—no condemnations, no questions—just tell him we want to keep in contact."

I did just that, and even though it was my idea, I didn't like it. It somehow gave me the feeling of playing god—and not the mythical Greek types. I didn't like being used as a conduit for a murderer, and I didn't like having to deal with one cop who steals watches and cufflinks from a dead man's bedroom, and another cop who had me penciled in as his prime suspect in two murders. I didn't like the thought of losing my job. There were a lot of things I didn't like, including Selden and Katherine the Great leaning over my shoulder as I pecked away at the keyboard and sent the message to Hermes.

The San Francisco Hall of Justice is located at Seventh and Bryant, a five-block hike from the *Bulletin*. You won't find it listed on any tourist guides, because it's a seven-story Stalinesque concrete monstrosity the color of bad weather. The Hall houses a police station, all of the detective details, the DA's office, municipal and superior court houses, and a jail. Someone could be arrested, confined, tried, convicted, and then housed in the crossbar hotel, all without leaving the building.

I didn't want that someone to be me. I had to be very careful with Inspector Granger. I wondered how far he'd push me about Mom's earring. I couldn't let him interview my mother—while she was bright, fun, and loving, she had a hard time keeping any secrets to herself. She'd try and get cute with Granger and end up telling him everything. Was there a way for Granger to tie Mom directly to Montgomery Hines? Had Hines given her a check for the scheduled redecorating work on his condo? Granger was sure to check Hines's bank accounts.

I mentally kicked myself for not thinking of this before. And that brought up Charlie Reeder's place in Montara. Mom had worked there, on Charlie's living room.

I used my cell phone and called my mother, but she was out, no doubt shopping, involving herself in what she liked to call "retail therapy."

I stood in a slow-moving line with a lot of nervous, desperate-looking people—like myself—waiting to pass through the Hall of Justice's metal detector. A stream of men in dark suits lugging bulging briefcases streamed by, waving a nonchalant hand at the uniformed cop seated alongside the metal detector; attorneys who were too important to stand in line with the great unwashed.

It made me think of Mark Selden. Why was he so eager to throw me overboard? I barely knew the man. He'd hit me up for tickets to shows a few times, and I had taken care of him. So why was he so hostile now? "Fire him, Katherine."

I shuffled ahead slowly and when I finally came to the metal detector I saw the reason for the delay. The uniformed cop was a handsome Latin guy in his thirties with a neat mustache. He chatted with the petite elderly woman in front of me as she emptied the contents of her purse into a plastic tray. "How are you today?" "Nice weather, isn't it?" More idle chatter before he waved her through the doorframe-style detector and then a farewell "Have a nice day."

He went through the same routine with me, then cheerfully gave me directions to the Homicide detail. I had a mental image of him and Darlene meeting, marrying, mating, and filling the world with cute little kids who wished everybody a happy day. The Great probably would have strangled the guy.

There was an espresso bar near the elevator and I bought a large French Roast and sticky sweet roll, gulping down the roll before the elevator had hit the fourth floor.

The Homicide detail receptionist was no Darlene. A short woman, heavy in the chest and hips, with pencil-line eyebrows and blotchy skin, she looked bored and grouchy at the same time when I told her I was there to see Inspector Granger. Her office wasn't much bigger than my cubicle.

She grunted something unintelligible then pushed herself to her feet and ambled through a door, slamming it shut after her.

There was a green-colored chalkboard on the wall in back of her desk listing the names of the Homicide inspectors. There were spaces to show if they were in or out of the office. The names were all in pairs: Cullen-Parodi; Flynn-Riordan; Kreutzer-Moody. Granger's was the only single listing.

The woman came back and flopped in her chair without looking at me. It was another ten minutes before the door opened again and Granger stuck his head out.

"You're late," he said. "Come back here."

I followed his broad back through an aisle created by gray tweed cloth-covered wall partitions to a small room—about the size of Montgomery Hines's clothes closet.

"Have a seat," Granger said. "I'll be right back."

There were two seats bracketing a laminated oak table that was crisscrossed with graffiti. The walls and ceiling were of acoustical tile. More graffiti on the walls, but so far no one had attacked the ceiling.

I should have brought a book, or at least a newspaper. The graffiti were the usual collection of slang, curses, and profanity. Many of the authors seemed to have trouble with the "F" word—they left out the letter c.

The door suddenly opened with a bang and Inspector Granger looked down at me with an amused smile. He had a book under one arm, a coffee mug in one hand, and a folded-up newspaper in the other. He slammed the paper down on the table and said, "De Niro, for Christ's sake. How the hell could you leave out Robert De Niro in *Raging Bull*? Best damn fight flick bar none."

The paper was opened to my column on best and worst fight pictures. "You have a point," I conceded.

Granger dropped the book on the table and settled into the chair directly across from me. For a moment my whole impression of Granger changed. Suddenly he was a man of intelligence and great taste. The book was mine! *Tough Guys and Private Eyes*, a sleepy-eyed Robert Mitchum in a battered fedora and baggy trenchcoat on the jacket. There isn't an author in the world whose heart doesn't skip a beat when he or she spots someone with *their* book. Then I noticed the San Francisco Library mark stamped on the bindings. Still, it was my book.

"Did you get that coffee downstairs?" Granger wanted to know.

"Yeah."

He reached for my cup and dumped about half of what was left into his. "Our coffee stinks."

"You're welcome," I said, moving my cup out of his reach. There was only about three feet of table separating us. Granger was a menacing-looking creature up close and personal. He had large pores and a rash on his neck. The shirt he was wearing was unbuttoned at the collar, revealing tufts of furry gray hair. The shirtsleeves were rolled up to his elbows and his arms were thick with hair. The black-faced Rolex was on his left wrist.

Granger took a swig of coffee, let out a soft burp, and said, "You're a lot of trouble Quint."

"You asked me to be here, I'm here, Inspector." I reached in my pocket and drew out a copy of the Hermes e-mail—minus his name. "I received another e-mail."

Granger leaned across the table and snatched the paper from my hand. He brushed his lower lip with a fingernail as he read the e-mail printout. "Thirty-nine steps. Ain't that cute."

"That's a Hitchcock movie—"

Granger cut me off with a waved hand. "Yeah, yeah. I watch TV. There's really no way to prove that you're not sending yourself these e-mails, is there, Quint?"

"Why would I do that, Inspector?"

He turned his chair around and sat astraddle it, leaning his elbows on the chair back. "Your mother is a beautiful woman."

"She'll be pleased when I tell her that, Inspector."

"She was a good friend of Montgomery Hines, wasn't she?"

"Yes, in fact it was Hines who introduced her to my father."

"Is that a fact? And she knew Charles Reeder too, didn't she?"

"If you think my mother has something to do with their deaths, you're just wasting your time. She worked in movies years ago with Hines, and Reeder was part of a clique of actors, directors, show biz people here in the city. Everyone in the business knew Charlie."

"I think that I'm going to have to talk to your mother. Good looking lady, good dresser, too. Those earrings she was wearing last night. They looked expensive. I think I saw an earring very similar to hers. I just can't remember where. Do you know a man by the name of Stanley Damas?"

"I don't think so."

And I didn't, until Granger said, "He lives on the top floor of Hines's building. Yesterday afternoon he said that someone rang his bell. He let him in the building but the guy never showed up at his door. I wonder why?"

"Were any of the units burglarized, Inspector?"

"No one reported anything like that. But maybe someone got in to take a look at Hines's place."

"The killer returning to the scene of the crime?" I said skeptically.

"Stranger things have happened, Quint. Where were you yesterday afternoon? Mr. Damas said he got a little worried about the guy not coming to his door. Right after a murder in the building, you can't blame him for being shook up. He said he looked out his window and saw a guy on the street a little while later. Young guy, not too big, wearing glasses. What do you think of that?"

"That's a pretty vague description, isn't it? Do you have the time? I'm supposed to meet with Detective McCall before lunch."

Granger glanced at his watch and shook his head. "I don't think you're going to make that meeting Quint. I want a sample of your fingerprints."

"For what purpose?"

"Purpose? You're a suspect in the theft of a valuable necklace. Inspector Wyatt says that you admit being in the room where the necklace was kept."

"Then why didn't Wyatt ask for the prints?"

Granger tilted his chair and leaned forward so that his head was less than a foot from mine. "Maybe he forgot, but *I'm* asking you now. Is there some reason why you don't want to give us your prints?"

"Is there some reason I should?" I countered.

"Yes. To help the police clear you as a suspect, smart ass."

"It would be just a waste of the taxpayers' money," I told him. "I had nothing to do with the disappearance of Gineen Rosenberry's ruby and nothing to do with Montgomery Hines's murder."

For a moment I thought he was going to reach across the table and grab me by the neck. He was breathing hard, through his nostrils and open mouth.

"It must be hard for you, Inspector. No partner. You have to play both roles: good cop, bad cop."

"You haven't seen me play bad cop yet, Quint."

"That's a nice watch, Inspector. Rolex Submariner, right?"

Granger fingered the watch and smiled. "It's a knockoff. Cost me fifty bucks."

"Monty Hines used to have one just like that, but I'm sure it was real. I read something once, a reporter for one of the papers—not ours. It must have been a slow news day. He picked up a phony Rolex, just like yours, and went around to several jewelers in the Union Square area, telling them it needed service. Unless they opened up the watch, they couldn't tell the difference—same weight, same markings. Makes you wonder why anyone would go to the trouble of buying, or even stealing, a real one."

Granger edged his butt off the chair, then sank back down again. "You know what I think, Quint? I think you're a wise guy." He picked up the book and weighed it in his hand, looking like he was debating on whether or not to throw it at me. "You figure you're one of those tough private eyes in this dumb book of yours. That you're smarter than the cops." He stood up and dropped the book to the floor. "Let me tell you something, pal. You ain't so tough and you ain't so smart. You watch out or you may find yourself at the bottom of a staircase."

I was tired of him standing over me, glaring at me. I rose from my chair. Damned if he wasn't still standing over me. "Inspector, I'll cooperate with you in any way I can." I held out my hand. "But I don't think you need to bother my mother, do you?"

Granger enveloped my hand with his. He tried to short-finger me so that he could squeeze the life out of my hand, but I was too quick, and made sure my finger webbing made contact with his. It still felt like my hand was put through a winepress, but nothing got broken.

"Your mother's not important now. But things could change, Quint. You know what I mean?"

He turned and left without giving me time to answer his question.

I bent down and picked up the book. Inside the front cover was the library's due date return card. A page of stamped dates, the last being nine days away. San Francisco library books were normally checked out for three weeks—twenty-one days—which meant that Granger had checked the book out well before Montgomery Hines had been murdered and before I'd received any Greek god e-mails.

I laid the book gently on the table, wondering what all that meant.

TWELVE

The woman who came to the door had a green face. Her hair was covered with goop the color of grape jelly and she reeked of vinegar. Her hands were encased in plastic bags.

"Mom?" I said.

"Inside quickly, Carroll. I don't want anyone to see me like this."

I wasn't too happy seeing her like that myself. "Are you all right?"

"I'm fine, darling. Come back to the veranda."

Most people would call it a sun room, or porch, but with Mother, it was a veranda—a small redwood deck located at the back of the flat, overlooking her "enchanted garden," which was filled with dozens of rose bushes and clay pots overflowing with everything from mums to parsley. The fences were hidden behind towering walls of flowering oleander. Water spurted from the mouth of a bronze frog into a small pond filled with water lilies and fantailed goldfish.

My mother flopped onto a cushioned chaise lounge and motioned for me to sit in an adjoining chair. She picked up two thin slices of cucumber from a dish on the lounge's arm, leaned back, placed them over her eyes, and said, "How are you, dear?"

On the lounge's other arm was an item that caught my attention. A gun.

"Mom, what are you doing with a gun?"

"Air pistol is the correct terminology," she informed me. "A BB gun. It's for Herman."

That certainly cleared things up. "And who would Herman be?"

"The Nelsons' new cat. He's developed an appetite for my goldfish, and I simply have to discourage him."

"You're shooting at the cat?"

"Carroll, I'd never hit him. He just hears the noise and runs like hell."

I picked up the pistol. It had the heft, and the feel, of the real thing. I looked deeply into her cucumber-covered eyes and asked, "What's the green goop on your face?"

"Avocado. Don't you dare laugh. Sophia Loren uses it all the time and she's not exactly chopped liver. And to save you further questions the solution on my hair is honey, vinegar, and grape extract. Cleopatra used to have two cucumbers cooled in the Nile then sliced and put over her eyes while she slept, though from what I've read she seldom slept alone. The greatest fellatrix in history, dear Cleo was. Those little Hilton girls will have to work long and hard to catch up with her."

While she was in the mood for a history lesson, I asked her what she knew about the Greek god Hades, who Katherine the Great had mentioned as being a possible next e-mail name for the killer.

"A greedy boy. The king of the dead and the god of wealth. Isn't that an enviable combination? He wears a helmet that makes him invisible."

Was I the only guy who knew nothing about Greek gods? "How do you know all this stuff, Mom?"

"Disney did an animated *Hercules* about ten years ago. James Woods did the voice for Hades. I love that man. He's what we would have called a character actor in my day." She lifted up the cucumber slice from her right eye, winked at me, and said, "Did you know that Woods is fabled as having the biggest schwantz in Hollywood now?"

"Thanks for sharing that with me, Mom."

"Milton Berle, the old comedian—couldn't stand the man—but he was well known for the . . . size of his penis. Some friends found a young man endowed with similar proportions and they started a round of bets to see who was the biggest. Legend has it that there ended up being quite a bit of money wagered, and when it came time to show and tell, Berle told his opponent to go first and he'd reel out just enough to cover the bet."

I laughed out loud and Mom smiled slightly, but still launched cracks in her avocado face mask.

"I ran into Rawley Croften at the party before *Camelot*. Did you see him, Mom?"

"No. Poor Rawley. What a waste. He was a very good writer at one time. Your father has no use for him though. Rawley had become rather insistent that I go out on a date with him. I wanted no part of that, but he continued to pester me."

"What happened?"

"Your father, my dear ex-husband, can be a persuasive person. I don't know what he said or did to Rawley, but it got the job done. He never bothered me again."

I patted one of her plastic-wrapped hands. The plastic was squishy and I could smell coconut. "A serious question. When you did the re-modeling work for Charlie Reeder and Monty Hines, did they pay you by check?"

"No, dear. I hadn't really done anything for Monty, and Charlie was old-school. Cash, God bless him."

"Did you give either of them an invoice? Anything with your name on it?"

She peeled back both cucumbers and blinked. "This is just between you and me, and not *him*."

Him being my father. Each of them had a habit of telling me things that they didn't want the other to know. I crossed my heart with my index finger. "Scout's honor."

"If my dottering memory isn't deceiving me, the only scout you had any contact with was little Dorothy Bilcey. She'd come over in her Girl Scout's uniform and help you with your homework. I'd have to buy all of those awful cookies just so you could learn the art of kissing. Anyway, your father and I have a financial arrangement. For all of his faults, he is rather generous. If he had an occasion to see my invoices and incoming checks, he'd no doubt want to change things. So when I consult with someone, especially friends, I make sure it's strictly cash. Speaking of which, I finished reading that dreadful Joan Kenyon book for you." She waved a hand over her head. "It's on the potting table behind me, along with a two-page review. Unlike you, I tried to be kind to the poor woman."

I picked up the review and left a twenty-dollar bill on the table. The "poor woman" took in over a million dollars a year, but there was no reason to tell Mom, or she'd want more for her reading fee.

"Why the interest in Hades, darling?"

"The name came up in a conversation with Katherine Parkham." I told her about my meeting with Inspector Dave Granger. "He spotted your earrings last night, Mom. He knows there was one just like them in Hines's jewel box. If he tries to question you, stall him—act flustered, confused, whatever you want, just don't talk to the guy."

"Have the police found out about poor Charlie Reeder? How he actually died?"

"A blow to the back of his head. Heavy weapon. Could have been anything, Mom. A club, piece of a tree, an axe handle."

She peeled off the cucumber circles and sat up in the lounge. "I remember Charlie had an enormous refrigerator-freezer. Restaurant-size. I wonder . . ."

"Wonder what? Charlie was beaten to death, his body found outside on the deck, not in the freezer, Mom."

"I'm not senile yet," she said huffily. "All of these movie clues: Monty being stabbed in the shower, poor Charlie's body being desecrated by those birds. But Charlie was already dead before the ravens started their awful pecking. So, if we believe the killer is a perverted Hitchcock aficionado, why wouldn't he get rid of Charlie in a Hitchcockian manner?"

"He did, Mom. There must have been dozens of people killed in Hitchcock movies by having their heads smashed in."

She started peeling the plastic gloves from her hand. "You've got a point, dear—but not the main point. The killer is a show-off; he'd use something more exotic than a rock or a stick."

"Then what?"

"A leg of lamb. Charlie had all kinds of roasts and steaks in his freezer. I'm sure there was a leg of lamb in the damn thing somewhere. Hitch used it in one of his TV shows. You're much too young to remember the show. A sweet little old lady decides to bump off her husband. She whacks him in the back of the head with a frozen leg of lamb, defrosts it, then pops it in the oven. The police arrive, conduct an investigation, but can't find the weapon. Our dear old girl invites them to stay for dinner." She smiled broadly, her teeth looking brighter than ever against the avocado skin. "Leg of lamb." She started toweling off the thick white cream on her hands. "I'm going to fix a pot of tea. Care for a cup?"

I called Detective McCall's office in Redwood City, and was told that he was out of the office. I left my name and cell number and within two minutes McCall phoned.

"Where the hell were you this morning, Quint?"

"With your comrade-in-arms, Inspector Granger."

That didn't seem to sit well with McCall. He shouted, "Look out for that thing, damn it," to someone, then turned his attention to me. "Where are you?"

"In the city. I was just about to drive down and—"

"Charlie Reeder's place. Be here within an hour or I'll have a warrant put out for your arrest, and that officious, beady-eyed attorney of yours won't be able to stop me."

McCall was right. Mark Selden did have beady eyes. I was so conscious of looking at his never-moving lips that I'd never taken notice of his eyes.

I stopped at a deli, got a ready-made sandwich and an iced tea, and headed down to Montara.

TV and radio weathermen don't even have to show up for work at that time of the year in the Bay Area. They keep running the same forecast over and over. It's sort of a *Groundhog Day*, every day is the same as the day before: "Fog and overcast on the coast, extending inland in the morning hours, clearing in the afternoon."

It was a little cooler, a little windier than my last trip. There were four official-looking cars and one large bus with San Mateo Sheriff's Office signs all over it. I spotted a dozen or so unhappy-looking campers wearing orange prisoner overalls tromping around the ice plant, long spike-end sticks in hand, the kind they usually used to clear rubbage from the freeways.

A tall, rangy uniformed cop with yellow-tinted glasses held up his hand when I approached the house, as if he was stopping traffic.

"What's your business here, sir?"

"Detective McCall requested my presence. The name is Carroll Quint."

"Carroll?"

You have no idea how many times I told my mother that Joe or Pete would have been such a wonderful name. "That's right. He's expecting me."

The officer ducked his chin to his chest and said something into a microphone protruding from his shirt's breast pocket.

After a moment he advised me that I was "free to enter the premises."

Charlie Reeder's house was a mess the last time I saw it, but nothing compared to this. The paintings had been dragged from the walls, the couches and chairs were upturned, drawers pulled from bureaus and scattered around the floor.

Detective Bruce McCall came into the living room. He was in a shirt and tie. His suspenders had been pulled from his shoulders and dangled in twin loops to his knees. There were saddlebags of sweat under his arms. He pointed a gloved hand at me. "Don't touch anything."

I jammed my hands into my pockets. "There's been another e-mail, Detective. I've made a copy for you."

McCall led me into Charlie's kitchen. The refrigerator-freezer Mom had spoken about—a stainless steel behemoth—was positioned against the far wall. I hadn't taken notice of it on my last visit. Why should I? I didn't have my mother's murderous-mystery background.

"The kitchen's been checked and cleared," McCall advised me. "Have a seat."

Charlie had a little breakfast nook with a restaurant-style rolled-red-leather booth that looked out over the deck to the ocean. I handed McCall the e-mail, and slid into the booth. He stood his ground, read the e-mail, then started the questions.

"Did you give this to Granger?"

"I did. On the advice of the paper's beady-eyed attorney, and our editor Ms. Parkham."

McCall flopped down beside me and let out a whoosh of breath. "I'm not a big movie fan, Quint. When I watch TV, it's the Discovery or History Channel, or the news, so fill me in on this *39 Steps* crap."

The officer with the yellow-tinted glasses approached us.

McCall said, "Anything?" and the officer responded by raising his hand and jabbing his thumb downward, like a Roman emperor telling a gladiator to give that slave the coup de grâce.

McCall grunted and told me, "We're looking for the weapon. The killer probably dumped it in the ocean. I've got two scuba teams down there, but no luck so far."

"Can I make a suggestion?"

He flexed his arm and consulted his watch. "Make it quick. I've got a lot of work to do."

I leaned out and pointed at the freezer. "Is there a frozen leg of lamb in there?"

Before McCall could respond, I told him about my mother's theory, leaving her name out of it, of course. His eyes narrowed, his forehead wrinkled, and his tongue snuck out and licked a circle around his lips as he listened.

When I was through he pushed himself to his feet and approached the refrigerator-freezer as if he was expecting to find a bomb. The freezer door popped open, he reached in and pulled out a butcher-paper bundle the size of a small axe. *Lamb* was written in black marking pen on the paper. McCall studied it for a long time, then turned to me and said, "Son of a bitch."

THIRTEEN

There aren't any "newspaper bars" in the city anymore, those wonderful old smoke-filled gin joints where reporters and cops and judges and bookies met in dark booths and swapped lies and confidential information over fishbowl-size martinis, and the papers' printers, in their black coveralls and little paper hats made out of yesterday's edition, would sneak a beer or two during their lunch break.

After a three-hour round-robin with Katherine the Great, Mark Selden, and Max Maslin, I needed a drink. I was sitting at the bar at Momo's, an upscale grill directly across from the baseball stadium, and within stumbling distance to my apartment. The Giants were on the road, so the place was fairly quiet. I was on my third glass of wine and my second basket of crispy calamari rings when something soft and round bumped into my back.

"I figured I'd find you here," Terry Greco said. She smiled sweetly at the Hawaiian-shirted tourist on the stool to my left. How can you tell when someone is a tourist in this town? If they're wearing shorts, a light shirt, and their bodies are covered in goosebumps—they're tourists. "Do you think you could move down one for me?" she asked politely.

The guy would have moved the stadium for her if he thought it would do him any good. He and his wife had been knocking back screwdrivers and we'd been having a pleasant conversation about where to go for dinner. When they'd found out I was a local—"born and raised" in the city—they pumped me for information on spots the tourists didn't clutter up. I did what any decent San Franciscan would do—advised them not to order fish anywhere near Fisherman's Wharf.

He raised his glass in a "you lucky bastard" gesture, and moved over to the opposite side of his nice, pleasant, two-hundred-plus-pound wife.

The bartender was polishing the plank in front of Terry before her sweet little bottom hit the stool. She was wearing a butter yellow scoop-necked sweater and short black skirt. I wasn't sure about her shoes. Most men's eyes never travel that far down when they're ogling Terry, and I'm like most men.

"I'm in the mood for a *mojito*," she said.

The bartender, a good-looking dude with a wraparound mustache that made him look like a mournful bandit, jumped in with, "You're in luck, Miss. I'm Joe Mojito."

I decided then and there to drop the show biz books and write one on the corniest pickup lines ever muttered. Hanging around with Terry brought them all out.

She picked up my near-empty basket of calamari and shook it at the bartender. "And another of these." She turned her attention on me. "What's going on, Carroll? The paper's all abuzz. You were in the Great's office for hours."

"That's the price you pay when you're a front page crime reporter, kid."

"Front page?"

"Yep." My wine had cooled down to room temperature. I gulped the remains and waved the empty glass at the romancing bartender. "Tomorrow's edition, yours truly's byline on page one."

"Wow. You must be excited."

Her rum, lime juice, and crushed mint drink came and the bartender took his eyes off her long enough to pluck the empty glass from my hand. "God's truth, I'd rather be back at the old stand reviewing movies, Ter."

She sampled her drink, smacked her lips, then said, "That would be nice for both of us, I guess. Brody Carew is being a real jerk. When Max isn't around, he acts like he's in charge. I saw him going through your desk this afternoon."

"My desk?" I said loudly enough for my Hawaiian-shirt buddy to give me a concerned look.

"Yes. I asked him what he thought he was doing and he mumbled something about how he'd be moving into your spot permanently in a few days."

"Shit!" I said so loud that Mrs. Hawaiian shirt gave me a threatening look, and she was big enough to back it up.

The fresh calamari came and Terry dug in. In between bites she said, "So what's going on with the case? Any more e-mails from Thanatos? What are you and the Great up to?"

"Well, there is a new angle, but—"

"But you can't tell me? Is that it?" she pouted.

"You're better off not knowing," I advised her. "The Great is ready to fire anybody who leaks a word on this thing."

Her voice turned soft and husky, saturated with sympathy. "Carroll. You have to trust *someone*, for God's sake. You know I'd never leak a word."

"I can't do it, Terry." When she stiffened and picked up her purse, I said, "Of course there is my medical condition to consider."

She arched one eyebrow. "Medical condition?"

I shrugged my shoulders in defeat. "I do talk in my sleep."

Terry let out a lusty laugh, bringing back a smile to Hawaiian shirt and another scowl from his wife.

A hand pounded my back and I turned to see the bushy face and drooping bow tie of Max Maslin. "Sorry I'm late, boys and girls, but I had to get the story ready for the morning." He circled his hand over his head like a cowboy roping a steer. "Innkeeper. A Cherry Heering over for me, and drinks for my friends."

I'd always liked Max, but how can you have any real respect for a man who drinks a sweet, cherry-based liqueur? He pressed a "hot off the press" sneak edition of the morning *Bulletin* into my hands.

Terry clapped in delight. "They used a good picture, Carroll."

"I couldn't find one with you not smiling," Max said, helping himself to some calamari.

It probably would have looked better if I had a somber, professional look in the photo, but it's a bad habit—someone points a camera and I automatically smile. I blame it on my mother—she took enough pictures of me as a kid to raise Kodak's stock a few points. If Granger ever gets around to booking me for something, my mug shot would no doubt have a smiling face.

The twenty-four-point headline read: BULLETIN REPORTER ON TRAIL OF MOVIE FAN WHO MAY BE INVOLVED IN TWO LOCAL MURDERS.

Terry snatched the paper from my hand as the bartender brought Max his foul drink.

A family—mother, father, and three kids, all decked out in SF Giants jerseys—trooped by en route to their table.

Max said, "A friend of mine works for the *Chicago Tribune*. He came out for a few days and of all the restaurants in town, he wanted to come here. He thought it was named for Sam "Momo" Giancana, the nasty old Chicago Mafia boss. Boy, was he disappointed. The place was named after the owner's grandmother."

I'd had enough wine by then to ask a question I probably shouldn't have. "Max, why did you have me write Monty Hines's obituary? You knew him fairly well, didn't you?"

His neck snapped back a bit. "Barely spoke to the man. What gave you the idea that I knew him?"

I couldn't very well tell Max about the photo in Hines's apartment, with Max's arm draped over Monty's shoulder. I shook my head wearily and just said, "Just an impression I had."

Hawaiian-shirt's wife had been chatting with Terry. She leaned way over, balancing precariously on her stool, and said, "Are you famous or something?"

"He's something," Terry said. "I can vouch for that."

Max gave a "follow me" gesture with his head and we walked out to the front patio, where a group of young people in jogging outfits were in the process of getting hammered.

He took out his pipe and sniffed the empty bowl. "You didn't mention the Hermes development to Terry, did you, Quint?"

"No, but I'm sure she could keep the secret. She told me that Brody Carew has been hanging around my cubicle, going through my desk. I don't trust him. If he somehow got into my computer data—"

"He doesn't know your e-mail password, does he? Have you got it written down somewhere in your desk?"

"No one knows it but me, Max. But they say there are hackers that can break into anything."

Two attractive young girls wearing Stanford sweatshirts were having a beer chug-a-lug contest at a nearby table. "I'll take care of Brody," Max promised. "You take care of yourself, Quint. If we believe this guy's e-mails—and I certainly do—then he's killed two individuals, and maybe a third. He could be after you."

Everyone seemed to think I was on the hit list. "I don't think so, Max. But I'll be careful."

The girl who won the drinking contest was holding her empty beer bottle up to the sky as if it were a trophy.

Max finished his drink and handed the empty to a passing waiter. "Even if you're not on his kill list, he could be following you to see what you're up to. He picked you for a reason. He could be watching us now, so don't take any chances."

I felt a chill run down my back, just like in all of those paperback private eye novels. I scanned the crowd. Suddenly everyone looked suspicious—even the cute Stanford chug-a-lug winner.

When I got back to my stool the bartender was bent over, elbows on the counter, talking fast, making a determined pitch to Terry.

I spilled my wine in the direction of his elbows and he jumped back with the grace of a matador.

"Sorry about that," I said insincerely.

After he'd mopped up the mess and brought me a full glass of wine,

Terry leaned over and whispered in my ear. "He told me he's not really a bartender. He's an actor."

"Is that the first time you've heard that one?"

"Yep. This week." She handed me part of the paper. "Take a look at the obituaries. There's a service for Montgomery Hines tomorrow night."

The notice was short and brief: Monty's age, the date he passed. Survived by his sister, Flora Hines. Friends were invited to the service in his memory at Dumphy's Mortuary from 6 to 8 P.M. His remains were to be cremated and taken back to his place of birth, Luxemburg, Iowa. Monty had never seemed like an Iowa kind of guy to me. I would have guessed he was a Southern California boy.

I was mildly surprised that the police had released the body so soon.

"I'll bet that your Thanatos will be at the wake," Terry said, munching on the last piece of crispy calamari rings.

"You could be right. Max seems to think he's following me around. Let's get out of here."

Hawaiian-shirt and his wife decided to leave at the same time. "Would you two care to join us for dinner?" the husband asked, after clearing his throat.

"I'm sure they have better things to do," the missus said sternly.

She was right.

I kept looking over my shoulder as we walked back to my apartment. There were up to fifty pedestrians and as many cars that could have been following us. None of the people looked particularly threatening or dangerous, but I had a real fear that one of them had stabbed Hines to death and beaten Charlie Reeder to a pulp with a leg of lamb.

FOURTEEN

The guy wasn't anything special to look at: forty or forty-five, medium height, medium build, brown hair in a longish crewcut. He was wearing a baggy dark brown suit and sunglasses with lenses the size of quarters.

He had been sitting on a pier bench, chewing on a toothpick and reading a newspaper, while Terry and I had al fresco coffee and doughnuts at Red's Java House on the Embarcadero, a clapboard shack perched on Pier 3, just across the street from my apartment. It dates back to the nineteen-twenties and has a million-dollar view and a limited menu: hamburgers, hot dogs, and fries. A cheeseburger and Coke will set you back about four dollars. One unkind critic—not Terry—suggested that the best use for the burgers would be as Frisbees.

Mr. Medium ignored the ferryboats, yachts, the seagulls and penguins diving for breakfast—he was interested in us.

Terry wanted to go home before showing up at the *Bulletin*. When we took off in the MINI Cooper, Mr. Medium slid behind the wheel of a battered old tan Japanese compact.

He stayed a few car lengths behind us as I drove over to Terry's place in the Marina District. A cop? Driving a compact? Not likely. Thanatos-Hermes? Would *he* be that obvious? I did a quick through-a-red-light left turn on Bay Street and figured I'd lost him.

None of this caught Terry's attention. Even two cups of strong coffee and a jelly doughnut didn't keep her from taking an in-car morning nap. The girl could fall asleep on a roller coaster.

I poked her gently in the ear when we got to her place. She gave me a quick kiss and said, "See you in an hour or so."

I headed for the *Bulletin*, the MINI taking the ski-slope-steep Russian Hill grades in stride.

When I stopped for an arterial at Taylor and Union, who should appear in my rearview mirror but Mr. Medium behind the wheel of his compact.

Parts of the greatest of all movie car chase scenes—the classic from *Bullitt*—had been filmed within shouting distance of where I was right then.

I had a brief vision of myself as Steve McQueen, stabbing the accelerator, making a sharp U-turn, and then pulling up right behind Mr. Medium's bumper. A very brief vision. There was a steady stream of traffic moving across Union Street. A school bus lumbered slowly through the crosswalk to my left. I goosed the MINI, made a hard right turn, and tried to get a look at the tan compact's license plate in the rearview mirror. I picked up the first number and three letters as the school bus screeched to a halt within inches of my left fender. Horns started beeping and, if I was reading lips correctly, the bus driver was saying very naughty words that his young passengers were no doubt enjoying.

By the time I'd finished the right turn, the school bus was nosing my tailpipe and Mr. Medium was gone.

I drove as slowly as traffic allowed the rest of the way to the *Bulletin*, hoping to catch sight of the tan compact, but Mr. Medium was nowhere to be seen.

Whoever he was, he knew where I lived. Hopefully I'd shaken him earlier so that he hadn't picked up Terry Greco's address.

For the first time since I'd known her, Darlene, the receptionist, wasn't in a good mood when she greeted me.

"Mr. Quint, there have been all kinds of phone calls for you," she said in a highly exasperated tone. "And Mrs. Parkham insists that you call her as soon as you arrive." She brushed an errant lock of hair from her forehead. "I hope it won't be like this all day."

She handed me a sheet of notes—her usual clear, distinctive handwriting had deteriorated into childish scribble.

"All these people," she continued after a long sigh. "They claim to be this Thanatos person. One even threatened me. He said I was going to be his next victim."

"Relax, Darlene, and don't worry. These are just crackpots."

She placed her hands on her hips and thrust her chin out at me. "Isn't that just what the real killer is? A crackpot?"

It was hard to argue that point with her. "I'll talk to Katherine the Great and see if we can get someone to help handle the calls." I should have thought of that earlier. We should have been recording all of the incoming calls.

Once I was at my desk, I sifted through her notes. Most were short and to the point, the caller saying he was Thanatos. One was enterprising enough to ask for money. "For a million dollars I'll give you an exclusive interview and tell you where I buried the others." That idiot even left his phone number.

I called it. The phone was answered by a squeaky male voice. "Tower Records."

"Is Thanatos there?"

After a long pause squeaky voice said, "For the right price he might be."

"I'll get back to you," I promised him.

I took out my wallet and looked through my collection of policeman's business cards. There was McCall's, Inspector Granger's, and the one belonging to the burglary inspector, Jack Wyatt. I called Granger. He was on another line. I left my number and booted up the computer. My e-mail box was bulging—seventy-six messages, none from Thanatos or Hermes at the freemailer.com address, but plenty from the army of crackpots. A few more demands for money, but the majority were just pure Looney-Tunes stuff: "Catch me if you can." "God is making me do this." "You'll never catch me." And one from a Schwarzenegger fan: "I'll be back." My favorites were the two with attachments—photographs—one of a pasty-faced guy with a shaved head wearing a Grateful Dead T-shirt, the other a sixtyish man with a scraggly goatee wearing a San Francisco Muni bus driver's uniform.

The phone rang. It was Inspector Granger. He wasn't happy.

"You sandbagged me on that article, Quint."

"Hey, I'm just an employee. My editor wanted a story—I delivered. Speaking of which, I have a batch of e-mails from people claiming to be Thanatos, but none from the right mailbox. Do you want me to send them over to you?"

He didn't sound very enthusiastic. "I'll have somebody pick them up later."

"Why don't I just e-mail them to you, Inspector. That'll save time."

"Because I don't have an e-mail address. We're a little behind the times here. No computer, other than the one that checks criminal and DMV data."

I found that hard to believe. "No computer?"

"We're lucky we've got telephones. You know all those bullshit TV shows? *CSI: Miami*, *CSI: New York*, with six or seven cops working on one case, using all those magic electronic devices? A dream world, except for maybe the FBI and CIA."

I checked Detective McCall's business card. He had an e-mail address. I told Granger so.

"Good for him. He's probably got a digital camera, a secret decoder ring, and a secretary with big knockers. I've got none of that, so I'll send someone over for the e-mails."

"Umm, Inspector. You don't happen to have someone following me, do you?"

"I've got better ways to waste my time."

Brody Carew strolled by, gave me a wicked smile and the finger at the same time.

"Someone was tailing me this morning, Inspector. Middle-aged, driving a tan compact. I just got part of the license plate—4YPS."

"Fascinating, Quint. He's probably another half-assed reporter, trying to find out what you're up to. *If* you got the right first four digits, that means there are three numbers remaining, each running from zero to nine, so ten numbers. Ten times ten times ten gives us a thousand possibilities. Get the full plate and maybe we can do business."

He might have been right about Mr. Medium being a reporter. "I see that Monty Hines's wake is tonight. I didn't think you'd release the body this soon."

"The coroner got all he needed from the autopsy."

"Are you going to be at the wake?" I asked.

"If my social schedule allows it. Who knows? Maybe the killer will be there. I met with Hines's sister. She's anxious to get her brother's remains back home. It'll be a short affair—a few words by a preacher, then off they go. No memorial, no food or drink. Too bad. I heard Hines liked a drink or two."

It was one of those times when you open your mouth before you check with your brain. It seems to happen to me a lot. "I was hoping she'd serve champagne."

There was a long, cold silence, then Granger said, "Champagne, huh. Fancy that." Then the sound of a phone being crashed into its receiver, then the hum of a disconnected line.

I got up and followed the smell of burnt coffee to the office coffee station. There was about half an inch of thick, gooey black stuff at the bottom of the glass pot. I started up a fresh one. My cell phone rang. It was Mom.

"What time are you picking me up?" she asked.

"I didn't know we had a date."

"Dear, I'm sure you want to escort me to Monty's wake. You wouldn't want me to arrive at a function like that alone, would you?"

"Seven o'clock, Mom. And whatever you do, don't wear those diamond earrings."

She tried to get me to come early for dinner. "Sweet and sour tofu soup."

Max Maslin came by just after I'd poured myself a cup of the fresh coffee.

"Better forget the coffee. The Great knows you're in the building and she's not happy. We're both wanted in her office. Now."

In the elevator I told Max about Mr. Medium. "Inspector Granger suggested he might be another reporter."

Max fiddled nervously with his bow tie. "I doubt it, unless he's some freelance jerk with nothing better to do. I've been checking everywhere, and I can't find anything that fits with the Hermes e-mail regarding thirty-nine steps."

"Maybe some poor soul is lying at the bottom of a stairwell, and no one's seen the body."

"That's possible," Max conceded. "Have you got a story mapped out for tomorrow's edition?"

"Sort of. I was thinking of waiting until after Monty Hines's wake before working on it."

"That'll be too late. I don't want to come back to the paper to edit tonight, besides, the Great wants to stretch this thing out as long as possible. Save the wake for the next day."

"Are you going to be there tonight, Max?"

The elevator doors pinged open and Max motioned me off. "Nope. I didn't know the guy, and it's your story, Quint. You get to have all the fun. All I do is look over your copy and shuffle it to the Great."

Someone impersonating Katherine Parkham greeted us with a warm smile, an opened Thermos, china cups, and a platter of assorted pastries. "Gentlemen, let's get to work. Anyone want coffee or something to eat?"

It's amazing what a hot story can do to a cold-hearted newspaper editor. I intended to enjoy it while it lasted. "I'll take the lemon scone, thanks."

It was close to two in the afternoon when Max and I finally were out of Parkham's office. He went right to work, but I needed a little fresh air. I exited the building and took a slow stroll toward Market Street. I tried those things we've all seen in spy movies: stopping in front of store windows, stooping to tie my shoe, making an abrupt turn—and damned if it didn't work. I spotted Mr. Medium directly across the street, a newspaper held up concealing the bottom half of his face, but not those tiny sunglasses.

I bought a hot garlic pretzel from a street vendor, then crossed Market to Powell Street, one of the most congested areas of the city. Tourists waited by the dozens for a chance to hop on a cable car as pickpockets culled the crowd for an easy target. A man with hair that looked liked greased snakes was pounding away with a wooden spatula on a battered aluminum cooking pan while singing "God Bless America" in a fairly good soprano voice.

I melted in with the tourists. It wasn't long before Mr. Medium arrived on the scene, a toothpick twirling between his teeth. He seemed bewildered as he threaded through the crowd. Several panhandlers approached him, only to be rebuffed with his rolled up newspaper.

He finally gave up and started hiking back the way we'd come— toward the *Bulletin*. His tan compact was parked just across the street from the paper, in a disabled-only parking spot. There was a blue disabled-person-parking placard on its dashboard.

He unlocked the car, spit a toothpick onto the street, slipped off his coat, and draped it over the driver's seat. No holster, so he wasn't a cop. He slid easily behind the wheel, with no sign of a physical disability. Maybe he had a mental disability.

I wrote the license number down on the back of Granger's business card, then decided, what the hell, Mr. Medium looked harmless enough. I walked over to the car. There were a couple of faded and scratched stickers on the rear bumper: HONK IF YOU WANT TO SEE MY FINGER, and KEEP HONKING, I'M RELOADING. The passenger door was unlocked.

"How's business?" I asked as I opened the door wide.

He dropped the paper on his lap and said, "What the hell do you think you're doing, buddy?"

The passenger seat was littered with balled up napkins, cookie crumbs, and mangled toothpicks. I swept the junk to the floor with the back of my hand and settled into the seat. "You've been following me all day, now either you tell me who you are, or I call the police." I reached across slowly with my left hand and rapped the disabled-parking plaque with my knuckles. "The fine for misuse of this is twenty-five hundred dollars and the loss of your license, so start talking."

He turned away and looked out the window. "Go screw yourself, buddy."

I shifted my weight so I could get to my cell phone. I punched in 911 and said, "I'm at the corner of Fourth and Howard Streets. There's a man who has been using a phony disabled parking—"

His head snapped around. "Okay, okay. The name's Powers. Tom Powers. I'm a private investigator. I've been hired to investigate the theft of a ruby necklace belonging to the insured, Gineen Rosenberry."

"Prove it." I told him, disconnecting from the 911 call.

He twisted around and pulled a wallet from his suit coat. He extracted a business card, which showed him to be Tom Powers of Pacific All Risk Insurance Company.

"Anyone can have a card printed, Mr. Powers."

He flapped open the wallet and waved it under my face. There, below his driver's license, was a pale green card listing Powers as a private investigator with the State of California Department of Consumer Affairs.

"I'm an independent PI," Powers explained. "I work for a dozen or so different insurance companies."

After all those years of reading mystery books and reviewing movies, I finally meet a real life private eye and it has to be this jerk.

"Powers, first, you're wasting your time following me. I had nothing to do with stealing Gineen's ruby necklace. Second, I do everything possible to beat the cops and the city out of paying for a parking ticket, but I draw the line at misusing a disabled plaque. You're taking a spot away from someone who may really need it."

"My wife is seriously ill," he said stiffly.

"My condolences, but she's not here now, you are."

He took off his glasses, revealing a pair of small, dark, shifty eyes. The eyes of a bargainer.

"Don't make a federal offense out of it, Quint. You're in enough trouble as it is. The cops figure you took the necklace, and so do I."

He slipped the glasses back on and gave me a friendly grin. "Tell you what we're going to do. I'll make a deal with Pacific All Risk. Tell them that I've got a confidential source who is willing to return the jewels. Your name will never be mentioned, of course. They're willing to shell out thirty thousand in cash for the necklace. I give you half of the cash, everybody wins. What do you say?"

"I say the biggest risk Pacific All Risk made was in hiring you, Powers. The standard payoff in a situation like this is ten percent—that's sixty thousand. So you were planning to pocket three-quarters of the money."

"I've had my expenses." He peeled the cellophane wrapper from a fresh toothpick and stuck it in his mouth. "Following you around, last night at Momo's. Who's that gorgeous broad you picked up at the bar?"

I'd had enough of Powers. I climbed out of the car and leaned through the open window. "Keep wasting your time, it's fine with me. There's something that your friends at the police department didn't tell you. They think that someone else is following me around. A murderer. If you decide to read that paper rather than hide behind it, you'll see that his name is Thanatos. And I'm still going to call the authorities about you misusing the disabled plaque."

Powers opened and closed his mouth a few times as if deciding what to say. He finally settled on, "You know what your problem is buddy? You ain't got no fuckin' finesse," then cranked over the engine and roared off, a broken muffler making the car sound more like a ten ton truck than a ten-year-old Toyota.

FIFTEEN

I was glad we'd arrived a little early for Montgomery Hines's wake. The funeral parlor was jammed.

My mother was in her full wake regalia: she wore a hat the size of a birdbath—black naturally—as was her dress, coat, and shoes.

Montgomery's sister, Flora, was the only one there to greet the attendees. She was a tall, slim woman with short dark hair salted with silver and skin so pale and soft looking you'd think a touch would leave a bruise.

She gave a sorrowful smile when I introduced myself.

My mother engaged her in a whispered conversation for a few minutes.

We found two vacant seats in the middle of the chapel. Within a short time there was standing-room only. Hines would have loved that. The altar area was jammed with flowers and many of the floral arrangements were in the shape of a star—an ambition that Monty had never reached in life. Mom made little waves to some of the people streaming up the middle aisle to say their final farewells to the closed coffin that held Monty's remains.

"He's going to be cremated," she informed me. "Don't you dare do that to me."

I spotted several members of the local acting community and we communicated with those solemn nods people use at funerals.

The gaunt figure of Rawley Croften made a brief appearance, pushing his way to the front of the line. He slapped a hand on the coffin, then turned on his heel and marched out of the chapel.

"There's the slut," Mom said when Gineen Rosenberry made an appearance alongside Jules Moneta. She was wearing a fawn-colored suit and Cossack-style fur hat. "For her next wedding, she should wear black and be carrying a gin and tonic," sweet old Mom opined.

Moneta was his usual out-of-the-pages-of-*G.Q.*-magazine self: beautiful pearl gray suit and matching tie. He gave me a wink and rolled his eyes at the crowd. It was an eclectic mix: a goodly number of old timers of both sexes from local theatrical circles, in tuxedoes and formal gowns, and an array of tough-looking women who looked as if they'd stepped off of the stage during the intermission of *Chicago*. Directly in front of us a drunk was nursing from a long-necked brown paper bag.

I spotted Inspector Dave Granger and Detective McCall standing at the back. McCall was gesturing with both hands while Granger kept his eyes focused on the floor.

The prying eyes of private eye Tom Powers were not in view. Maybe he was hiding under the coffin.

A stocky gentleman with a neatly trimmed beard introduced himself as Reverend Foster. He was wearing a dark brown suit with a clergy collar. He gave a brief eulogy, and from the number of times he glanced at his notes, I guessed that he'd never met or heard of Monty before that evening.

Prayers were said, then the good reverend made the mistake of asking if anyone cared to say a few words about the deceased.

We sat through eleven long-winded remembrances—the speakers praising Monty's acting ability while not leaving out their own talents and portfolios. "I remember being with Monty and Richard Burton one night, and—"

"If it wasn't for my good friend Montgomery, I never would have had the role of a lifetime in *Shane*."

On and on and on it went. It made you long for those days of yore when a vaudeville audience would scream out, "Give 'em the hook," and the manager would actually use a long hook to drag the offending entertainer from the stage.

During one particularly self-aggrandizing spiel from a frizzy-haired bit player, my mother nudged my knee with hers and said, "Who's that lovely hunk of a man over there giving you dirty looks?"

I twisted my neck and locked eyes with Peter Dkany for a moment. Dkany was a muscular, jut-jawed former fireman who'd had a few small roles in a cop TV series filmed in the city. He became infatuated with acting and quit the fire department and moved to Hollywood. After a year of almost no work, he came back home, only to find that the fire department didn't want him back, and neither did his ex-wife, Sara Vasin, a beautiful East Indian who was a top-rated makeup artist. She lived in a hillside cottage with a bunch of wild parrots, and spent a lot of her time working on-location stage productions and film shootings. Sara and I had a brief "thing" shortly after her breakup with Dkany. He'd taken out his Hollywood frustration on her, giving her a black eye. He took one look at me and figured I'd be an easy victory.

Dkany had size and muscles but he didn't know how to use either. While he was flexing his biceps and telling me just how many of my bones he was going to break, I acted on an old lesson from my father: "When in doubt, cop a Sunday on the guy." Meaning, hit him first, because whoever lands the first real punch in a street fight always wins. I'd slammed the tip of my elbow into his rippling abs, which took all the wind out of his sails, in front of Sara. I knew it was something he'd never forgive me for.

I hadn't seen Sara in quite awhile. The last I heard she was in Vancouver, working on a Meg Ryan comedy.

I gave my mother a short outline of why I wasn't on Dkany's Christmas list.

"Someone should tell him that if he keeps scowling and frowning like that, he'll end up with a face full of wrinkles. That's why Al Pacino looks older than his father. Always keep your face stretched, Carroll. My God, this is dreadful. I hope that someone does right by Charlie

Reeder. Something at a saloon or restaurant would be nice. No speeches and lots of liquor. I'm sure that's what Charlie would have wanted."

Jules Moneta ended the service with a brief, classy eulogy, presenting a pleasant picture of Montgomery Hines's career that was just right—not too flowery and not a bit patronizing. It was much better than the obituary I'd written for the *Bulletin*.

The Dumphy family, which ran the mortuary, also operated the nearest cocktail lounge, a slipper of a room, long and narrow—the bar extending the entire length of the building. Wooden tables butted up against a brick wall with concrete oozing between the bricks. Three thick-wristed bartenders were pouring drinks at a fast-and-furious pace to keep up with the thirsty customers.

My mother was talking with Jonathan Ashley, an actor I'd seen at Gineen Rosenberry's party. I got in line at the bar and picked up two glasses of red wine. Someone poked me in the back. I turned and saw Rawley Croften.

"I see that you're a *reporter* now, Carroll. Chasing murderers. Well, either dance well, or quit the ballroom."

I was trying to come up with an appropriate reply to that when Croften turned on his heel and walked away.

"What took you so long?" Mom complained when I handed her a glass. "That person with the funny name who hates you is over there, looking upset."

Peter Dkany turned his back on me as soon as I looked his way. Jules Moneta strolled over and made a big deal out of meeting my mother for the first time.

"Where has Carroll been hiding you, Mrs. Quint? You look absolutely stunning. I hope you're coming to my party at Treasure Island."

Gineen was sitting alone at a table for four. I made my way over to her. Her makeup wasn't quite right—too much or too little rouge, the eyeliner not perfect, as it usually was. She looked quite sad. I wondered if she knew Montgomery Hines better than I thought she had. "Can I get you something, Gineen?"

"Jules has ordered champagne." She glanced over at Moneta. "I have a feeling that your mother does not think nice things about me, Carroll."

"If Mother Teresa had once dated my father, Mom would have prayed for her to go to hell."

Gineen laughed. She had a sort of tinkling laugh that suited her looks and personality. "Is John back from his trip?"

"Not yet."

Moneta came over, one arm linked into my mother's. "Where's that champagne, damn it."

"It's nice to see you again, Karen," Gineen said to my mother.

Dear Mother was sweet—in her own way, loving and caring, devoted to me when I was a kid—but, truth be told, she was never much of an actress, so when she said, "Nice to see you, too," she couldn't bring it off. At least the "slut" word hadn't slipped out.

A waiter came with an iced bucket of champagne and Moneta insisted on pouring all of us a glass.

I complimented him on his speech at the end of the funeral service. "Nice job, Jules."

He ran a hand over his perfectly knotted gray silk tie. "Unfortunately, when you get to be my age, young man, you have to have a eulogy at the ready."

I sat next to Gineen and told her about my meeting with the private investigator, Tom Powers.

"Powers has been following me around. Both he and the police seem to think I'm the one who took your necklace."

Gineen placed her hand on top of mine and gave it several pats. "Mr. Powers came to the house and interviewed me. I hate to pass judgment, but he seemed to be an awfully dense young man. I know you weren't involved, Carroll. Don't let Powers or the police upset you. They can be such bastards."

Speaking of bastards, the broad shoulders of Inspector Granger were bulling a path toward the bar. He was dressed in that casual half-mast tie mode that cops wear when they want everybody to know they're cops. Rings of gray chest hair spilled over his shirt's open collar. I waited until he had a drink in his hand, then walked over and said, "I found out who's following me. He's a private investigator—Tom Powers. He's working for the insurance company that carries the policy on Gineen Rosenberry's necklace."

Granger took a swig of his drink, then said, "Never heard of him."

"Where's McCall?"

"Halfway home by now, I hope. The man doesn't drink. He's spoiling our image."

"See anyone you think might be Thanatos?" I asked.

Granger drained his drink and rattled the ice cubes as if they were dice. "McCall has a new theory. He still thinks that you could be good for the murders—that leg of lamb in the freezer bit is too cute by half; where did you learn about that one?"

"At my mother's knee, and other low joints."

"Always the clown, huh, Quint. McCall figures that even if you didn't kill these two saps, you're sending the e-mails. That you just made up Thanatos out of thin air so you can get a good story." He tilted the glass and sucked in the ice cubes. They made crunching noises as he bit into them. "Not a bad theory. He also thinks that you're a fag. Imagine that, a homophobic cop who doesn't drink." He tilted his head and looked around my shoulder. "Your mother looks nice. You take her everywhere, Carroll? Or do you go out with girls, too? Or boys? The guy in the slick gray suit is cute for his age, and looks like he might float out of his loafers at any moment."

If Granger was trying to get under my skin, he was succeeding. "The lady in the fur hat is Gineen Rosenberry."

"Oh, I know the Satin Widow well. I handled the investigation on her last husband."

He'd caught me off balance. "Investigation? Bill Rosenberry died of a heart attack."

"That's what they say. He'd been mixing medical prescriptions—different kinds of pecker-picker-uppers, to keep up with his beautiful wife. Nice way to bump an old geezer off—literally screw him to death."

When I started to protest, Granger jumped in with, "I couldn't prove it, and with her connections at city hall there was no way the department would let me do a proper investigation. Her first old man died pretty much the same way. Both husbands were loaded. No wonder she isn't shedding any tears over that necklace you heisted."

At times like this it is almost always better to walk away and fight another day. But, never being one to take my own advice, I said, "What is it Granger? Are you having a bad chest hair day? You know you *really* do need a partner. Someone to balance your big bad cop side. I spoke to Hines's sister. Nice lady. Apparently she gave Monty some valuable jewelry over the years: watches, rings, cufflinks. The murderer didn't steal anything, did he? I imagine there's an inventory."

Granger pushed me out of the way and headed back to the bar without saying a word.

Jules Moneta had been gabbing with a statuesque brunette in a skin-tight red leather dress with a slit up the side that went to the waist. She turned around abruptly and bumped into me. She had long thick eyelashes and pendulous, pink-glossed lips. The thick pancake makeup didn't quite conceal an emerging twelve o'clock shadow.

"Hi honey, I'm Ramona. Are you with anyone?" Her voice was made for phone sex.

"Yes. My mother."

Ramona had a laugh like an airhorn. She dragged a long red fingernail down my sleeve and said, "Well then, be a good little boy and do *everything* that Mommy tells you to."

What Mommy told me to do next was drink up and drive her home. She handed me her empty glass. "I do like good champagne. It tastes like my foot's asleep."

She was always sprinkling her conversations with bons mots she picked up in old movies. "Who said that?" I asked. "Noël Coward? Marilyn Monroe?"

"Not when they were with me," she said with a twinkle in her eye.

On the way to the MINI Cooper, I spotted Brody Carew in a curbside conversation with Peter Liddell, fresh from the theater, and still decked out in his King Arthur makeup. A dark limo pulled up. Liddell opened the door, waved Carew into the car, then climbed in after him.

I watched the limo's taillights disappear into the darkness. Carew and Liddell. What the hell were they up to? Nothing that was going to do me any good.

Mother broke up my morbid thoughts. "If we're going to just stand here, Carroll, we might as well go back and have another drink."

SIXTEEN

If a brilliant physician developed a cure for all cancers, if a genius of a scientist discovered an additive for gasoline that completely eliminated pollution and allowed even those hunky SUVs to clock in at two hundred miles a gallon, or if the French Minister of Health suddenly reported that all Parisians were now taking a bath every day, none of those worthy stories would have received a bigger above-the-fold headline on the morning edition of the *Bulletin* than MOVIE MURDERER THREATENS LIFE OF FAMOUS ACTOR. That famous actor being Peter Liddell.

Under the headline was a somber picture of Peter Liddell in a paisley dressing gown holding a piece of paper out to a wrinkle-browed Brody Carew.

Adding insult to injury, I spilled coffee on my lap when I saw it was Carew's byline. The story moved from page one to page six—more photos of Liddell in various movie roles, and one of Carew that must have come from his senior prom. No wonder Liddell and Carew were huddling together like thieves last night. Liddell claimed that he had found a note in his dressing room—from Thanatos. I had to turn to page seven to see a picture of the alleged note:

YOU ARE NEXT. YOUR FAME AND TALENT CANNOT SAVE YOU.
THANATOS.

The lettering had been clipped from a newspaper or magazine and pasted onto an ordinary piece of paper.

I skimmed Carew's story—half of it was a suck-up to Liddell, praising his career from all possible angles, the rest a capsule summary of my earlier story.

I took a quick shower and shave and then picked up Terry Greco at her apartment for our brunch at my mother's place.

Terry was all atwitter about the Liddell story. She slid into the passenger seat and said, "Did you see the paper? Peter Liddell is your Greek god's next target."

"It's a crock," I told her. "Liddell is just using it for publicity. He wrote the damn note himself."

"Do you really think so?" she asked innocently. Too innocently for someone in the newspaper business.

I noted a small tan Toyota a few cars behind as we crossed Lombard Street, but I couldn't be sure it was Tom Powers's car. I squeezed into a tight yellow zone in front of the Starbucks on Union Street, and asked Terry if she wanted anything to eat.

"But we're going to your mother's for brunch, Carroll."

"All the more reason to load up on Danish or coffee cake."

She shook her head resolutely. "I wouldn't insult her that way."

I had downed a cheese Danish and a large cup of coffee by the time I parked in Mom's driveway.

"The least you could do is brush the crumbs from your pants and shirt," Terry told me as we climbed the stairs.

Mom greeted us cheerfully. She was outfitted in a white sleeveless blouse and black slacks with a razor sharp crease. Rows of gold bracelets jangled at her wrists. She clinked her gypsy jewelry at me and smiled pertly at Terry, telling her how charming she looked.

Charming wasn't the word I would have used—Terry was wearing cutoff jeans, a cotton, second-skin Day-Glo orange tank top that made it obvious there was nothing but her lovely self underneath, and black leather t-strap sandals. Hot. That was the word. Zipper-melting hot.

"Come in, come in," Mom said.

I turned to close the door and saw the tan Toyota again. I ran down the steps, but the car took off in a cloud of exhaust and I wasn't able to make out the plates.

"Stop playing and come inside," Mom scolded from the doorway. While she gave Terry a tour of the flat, I headed to the kitchen. A strong Bloody Mary was always the best way to start off one of Mom's brunches. While I made the pitcher of drinks I studied the jigsaw table. She'd finished the Lucille Ball in a wine vat puzzle and had just started a new one. There were just a few of the edge pieces in place. I looked at the puzzle box, which showed a colorized scene from *Casablanca*, in Rick's Café Americain: Humphrey Bogart pointing a gun at Claude Rains, while Paul Henreid and Ingrid Bergman looked on nervously.

I had the drinks fixed by the time the ladies returned. While Mom fluttered about the kitchen, regaling Terry with stories from her Hollywood days, I went to the den, booted up her computer, and checked my e-mails. Another banner day from Thanatos wannabes. Forty-three Looney-Tunes messages—the usual things: "Save me before I kill again." Two from guys who threatened that if I didn't publish their messages, "You'll be next," and one who misquoted Shakespeare: "The first thing we do is kill all the actors." The immortal bard was smarter than that. He wanted to kill all the attorneys. I scanned through the rest, then delighted in forwarding them to Detective McCall in Redwood City.

Terry brought in the pitcher, topped off my glass, and told me the food was ready.

By the time I'd sampled the drink, two new e-mails had popped up on the computer: one from Hermes:

LIDDELL IS SUCH A BIG FAT TARGET I THINK I WILL DO HIM. WOULDN'T THAT CREATE A FRENZY.

Frenzy—another Hitchcock thriller. From what I remembered, it was about a rapist-murderer terrorizing London.

The second was from Katherine the Great:

WORKING DINNER ON BOARD THE JEWEL BOX—GOLDEN GATE
YACHT CLUB—FIVE O'CLOCK TONIGHT—BE THERE.

"Carroll," Mother yelled. "Hurry back here or your eggs Benedict will get cold."

Her version of this classic egg, ham, muffin, and thick Hollandaise sauce dish consisted of tofu—scrambled with egg whites—over rice cakes and topped off with a blob of yogurt cheese. Could it possibly be any worse cold than hot?

The Golden Gate Yacht Club is tucked away in a jetty just north of the Marina Green. There were boats of all shapes and sizes in their moorings: some with their sails neatly rolled and tied, some sleek powerboats with deep V-shaped hulls.

At the entrance to the club itself was a poster with a smiling young man and woman hanging onto the mast of a ship that was slicing through heavy waves. It read, I kid you not: LEARN YOUR PORT FROM YOUR BOW WITH INSTRUCTORS WHO AREN'T SO STERN. It sounded like something Brody Carew might have written.

A middle-aged man with a melon gut and a neck the size of a fire hydrant was varnishing the deck of a small sailboat. I asked him where I could find the *Jewel Box*.

He pointed his paintbrush to the right. "Ya can't miss the damn thing. Keep walking until you see the biggest damn boat in the harbor."

He was right. The *Jewel Box* was a huge, gleaming vanilla white broad-beam triple-decked cruiser. It had a stylish, almost art deco look, with its sharply pointed bow and sleek fiberglass sides. A young man in white shorts and a blue-and-white striped shirt was waiting at the gangplank leading to the boat. He had a clipboard in hand and dutifully checked my name before allowing me onboard.

Waiting on the main deck was a familiar face—that of Harry Crane, the Great's significant other of the moment. His handsome kisser was always popping up in the society columns and he did an occasional TV ad for his nationwide string of jewelry shops. I should have put two and two together earlier—it was fitting that he'd call his boat the *Jewel Box*.

Harry was in his mid-fifties, but didn't look it with his erect posture and muscles bulging under a polo shirt.

I introduced myself and he told me that Katherine was waiting for me in the salon.

"Great looking boat."

"Ship," he corrected me. "One hundred and six feet, twin diesel engines. Sleeps twenty." He nursed a long pause, then added, "Screws forty."

No narrow vertical ladders on this baby. I walked down a wide, carpeted stairway to the guts of the ship. Inside it was more like you were in an upscale apartment rather than a yacht. The ceiling was house-size, at least eight feet high and covered in ivory-colored leather. No portholes—wide, rectangular blue-tinted windows looked out to the bay waters and neighboring boats. The walls were a soft lemon yellow, the floor travertine marble. There was a curved bar with a black granite top. A young man who could have been the twin brother of the one guarding the gangplank was behind the bar mixing drinks.

Among his customers were Peter Liddell, Brody Carew, Inspector Dave Granger, and six or seven people I'd never seen before—friends of Harry's or the Great. Carew spotted me and then leaned over and whispered something into Liddell's ear. Whatever it was caused Liddell to peer around the room with arrogant, bloodshot eyes. When he saw me he let out a sarcastic laugh.

Mark Selden was huddling with someone in a business suit on the far side of the room.

Max Maslin was sitting in an overstuffed yellow leather chair, pipe in hand, watching a wide screen TV. A golf match was on. Tiger Woods was scowling at the flight of a ball that ended up in a greenside bunker.

A stringbean of a man in a striped T-shirt carrying a tray loaded with drinks approached and asked if I was interested in a glass of wine. I was indeed. He reeled off a list of varieties and vintages. I was used to places that served "red or white." I picked up what he assured me was a "marvelous merlot with a front-forward of blackberries and lots of toast and chocolate in the middle flavors."

He watched me closely as I took a sip. I didn't have the heart to tell him that all I tasted were red grapes. Really good red grapes.

Max raised his Cherry Heering to me as I sat down across from him. A loud cheer came from the TV. Woods had holed out his bunker shot.

"I would have appreciated a little notice on Carew's front page story," I said.

Max blew a mushroom of smoke toward the ceiling. "Me too. I learned about it when I picked up the paper at the front door this morning."

That surprised me. Max copyedited all of the entertainment section articles.

"Who edited Carew's stuff, then?"

"The Great. From what Brody told me, Liddell came to him with the story. Brody claims he tried to get hold of me, but that's baloney. He went straight to Parkham. She edited the thing. Caused a hell of an uproar with the printers. They had the entire front section of the paper all slugged up and ready to go. Then the Great changed everything." He sighed and replaced his glasses. "If you thought Carew was hard to live with before, think what he's going to be like now."

I turned back to the bar. Carew's girlfriend with the maroon hair, Soria, had belly-upped alongside Peter Liddell. He held out a limp hand to her and bowed in agreement with whatever it was she was saying. Terry Greco wouldn't like Soria being there. She had argued—with both me and herself—about tagging along for the cruise, but she came to the conclusion that coming to the dinner without an invitation wouldn't go over too well with the Great.

Max said, "Doesn't Liddell have a show to do tonight?"

"No. His contract is for five performances a week, which gives him ample time for partying and beating up newspaper critics." I twisted my neck around. There was no sign of Liddell's bodyguards.

Inspector Granger was staring at me. I was trying to figure out why he and Liddell had been invited to the party when Katherine Parkham came into the room on the arm of Harry Crane.

"Drink up," she said. "We're about to get underway."

Everyone went on deck to watch as the big ship's engines came to life, churning up chocolate-colored mud from the bottom of the bay. I borrowed a pair of binoculars from a passing deckhand and scoured the marina's parking lot. Tom Powers was leaning against the side of his car, holding onto a pair of binoculars—no doubt focused in on me. There was a loud tooting of horns and we were off, the *Jewel Box*'s bow cutting through the water with a loud hiss and leaving a wake of creamy foam.

It was a beautiful summer evening, the kind that reminds you that you're lucky to live in San Francisco. For once there was no wind, the blue-green bay waters were hazed with the soft gold of the sun. The rafts anchored off Pier 39 were blubbery carpets of barking sea lions. The captain steered out toward Alcatraz. Sailboats, like neatly folded pocket handkerchiefs, slipped past us. The lion-colored hills of Marin County retreated into the haze.

Inspector Granger sidled up alongside me, close enough so that his elbow nudged mine sharply.

"Nice little boat," he said. "I was surprised to get an invitation from your boss, Parkham. She left a message on my machine asking me to be on board by four. She's been pouring booze down my throat since I got here."

"Was Peter Liddell here when you arrived?"

"Yeah. He'd gotten a head start on me. The man may be a phony, but he sure as hell can drink."

I wondered why Liddell and Granger received early invites and I was instructed to show up at five o'clock. "What do you think of the threatening letter that Liddell found in his dressing room?"

"Nice of him to go to your reporter buddy before coming to me, wasn't it? This Thanatos guy had to be damn clever to sneak that letter into Liddell's room. I checked it out. The theater has guards outside the building and all around the dressing rooms. Then there are Liddell's personal bodyguards. Tough looking hombres."

"You're right about that. How are you and Liddell getting along?"

"He wants to do a cop movie here in the city. The hero's a big, tough, take-no-prisoners kind of a homicide inspector who doesn't go by the rules, and isn't averse to taking a small bribe now and then. He thinks he may have a place for me as a consultant."

We were traveling toward the Bay Bridge. I could see the outlines of the two old airplane hangars on Treasure Island that Jules Moneta planned to turn into movie studios.

"Why would a cop have to take a bribe? You make over a hundred thousand dollars a year, don't you?"

Granger shrugged his thick shoulders. "Maybe the hero is divorced, paying out alimony. If you ever start dating girls, you'll learn that after you marry them, they tend to get tired of you, and they also tend to get the house, the car, and most of your salary."

"So Liddell's hero is going to be a sort of whore with a heart of gold."

"Something like that. Small world, huh? Our host, Harry Crane, sold that ruby necklace to Gineen Rosenberry's last husband. The one everybody thinks you swiped."

Granger pulled back the sleeve of his tweed sport coat and glanced at his watch. His plastic digital watch. "When do we get something to eat on this floating mansion?"

The answer to his question came by way of my merlot sommelier. He was ringing a triangle dinner bell, and shouting, "Dinner is served in the main salon."

I had no appetite and don't remember much of what was served. Everyone was chatting about stuff that had nothing to do with the reason we were supposedly summoned on board—to catch the goddamn jerk that had killed Monty Hines and Charlie Reeder.

Inspector Granger turned out to be an entertaining dinner guest;

some of his humorous stories about busting homicide suspects had everyone at the table—except me—laughing. Liddell was not about to be outdone by the likes of a cop, so he began telling tall tales of the fascinating life of a fascinating movie star.

After dessert—a gooey soufflé-like thing, everyone got up from their seats and headed back to the bar.

Katherine Parkham caught my eye and mouthed, "Come with me," silently.

I followed her up a circular stairway leading to the top deck, which she informed me was known as the flying bridge in yacht-talk. Harry Crane was sitting in the outdoor captain's chair in front of a control panel with enough gauges and levers to make Captain Nemo drool with envy.

There was an oval shaped Jacuzzi, a brushed-stainless-steel grill, an icemaker, and molded fiberglass seating with blue-and-white-striped cushions butted up against the railings.

The Great motioned for me to sit down, then walked over to Harry Crane. She came back moments later, puffing on a long, narrow black cigar.

During dinner the ship seemed to be moving in long, lazy circles. The sky pulsed with stars—but not for long. A finger of fog was rolling through the Golden Gate Bridge.

"You look ticked off," the Great said after she'd settled down next to me.

"The story on Peter Liddell is all—"

"Bullshit," she said sharply. "I know that, but I can't prove it, and neither can you. It's news, and it will sell a lot of papers." She flicked cigar ash onto the deck and scattered it with a deft sideways movement of her shoe. "Liddell went to Brody Carew with the story just so he could rub a little salt in those wounds his goons inflicted on you."

"Thanatos seemed to like it. He sent me a new e-mail, using the Hermes address, saying that he thought Liddell was a big fat target and he might as well do him, and that it would cause a *Frenzy*—which is the title of yet another Hitchcock flick."

She puffed repeatedly until the cigar tip glowed red. "Did you tell Inspector Granger about it?"

"Not yet, I wanted to run it by you first," I said, aiming for some brownie points.

"Quint. Do you remember anything about a San Francisco serial killer who called himself the Zodiac? Before your time, really. In the late sixties and early seventies. I had Carl Dillon pull up the old stories on local serial killers. The Zodiac really stood out. He killed five people—at least the police found five victims. He claimed he'd killed seventeen, and vowed to kill lots more. He said: 'School kids make nice victims,' and threatened to take out a school bus. Thankfully, he never did.

"He taunted the police by sending in strange cipher messages made up of shapes and symbols to represent the twenty-six letters of the alphabet. The cops broke the code. The maniac sent them all kinds of clues: maps, pieces of the victim's blood-soaked clothing. He was never caught—never identified. The police went through a total of twenty-five hundred suspects. The killings stopped. Some people think he simply died of natural causes or in an accident."

"What's the moral of the story?" I asked. "You think that Thanatos is a Zodiac copycat?"

The breeze had kicked up and the fog was all around us. Parkham shivered. She was wearing pleated slacks and a V-neck blouse. The gentlemanly thing to do would be to take off my blazer and slip it over her shoulders. But then I'd be the one shivering in my short-sleeve shirt.

She blew a big smoke ring that disappeared quickly into the fog. "I asked Inspector Granger to come about an hour before you got here, so I could liquor him up and feel him out. It wasn't worth the effort—either he's good at playing dumb, or he doesn't know what's going on. Thanatos *could* be a copycat. There are similarities: the taunting, the sending of messages, and the threats not acted on. Thirty-nine steps. Nothing has come of that."

"That we know of," I said.

She stood up and tossed the cigar over the side. "I want Thanatos caught, Quint. And I want the *Bulletin* to be involved. I don't want it to drag on for years, either. Like it or not, you're his connection. He picked you for some reason—either he knows you, or knows someone close to you. I'm giving you full rein. Anything you need from the paper, you ask and I'll deliver. Concentrate on him—nothing else. Become one of those private detectives in your book. Dig into it. Do whatever it takes. If you get into trouble, I'll stand behind you."

She started walking over toward Harry Crane, then stopped in midstride and turned to face me. "Oh, one more thing about this Zodiac creep. One of the Homicide cops started sending in phony messages to himself, allegedly from Zodiac. And you know why? So he could keep the investigation going, run up his overtime—to make a few more bucks. Keep an eye on Inspector Granger. I don't trust him."

"Who do?" I asked, repeating the answer the great Willie Mays once gave when a dumb reporter asked him why he didn't like a high inside fastball.

SEVENTEEN

Katherine Parkham's faith in me to somehow catch up with Thanatos was inspiring—it was also unrealistic, impractical, and wishful thinking stretched to the max. "I'll stand behind you." Sure, but how far behind? Her orders for me to concentrate only on Thanatos meant that I wouldn't be doing my job as a critic. The investigation could go on for months. By the time I got back to my reviews and columns, no one would remember who I was.

"Act like one of the private eyes in your book," she said. What was it with these people? Parkham wanted me to be a PI, and so did my mother. Granger claimed I *thought* I was a PI. Everyone seemed to want me to be a PI, except Tom Powers, who *was* a private investigator, and also a public nuisance as far as I was concerned.

Peter Liddell's bodyguards were waiting for him at the dock. After the *Jewel Box* was safely tied down, I strolled off the boat alongside Inspector Dave Granger. Somewhere in my devious mind I imagined a confrontation between Granger and the goons, but it never came to pass.

Max Maslin had stayed behind to chat with Parkham. Brody Carew and his girlfriend, Soria, tried to talk me into stopping for a cup of coffee.

"We barely got to speak onboard," Carew whined.

"The Great wants me to interview someone right away," I said to throw him off balance. "We can talk at the paper tomorrow."

"Say hi to your mother," Soria called after me. "She's a funny old lady."

I shuddered at the thought of passing that line along to Mom. Soria had better be careful crossing streets, etc., etc.

There was no sign of Tom Powers or his old Toyota, so I drove directly over to Terry Greco's place and filled her in on what had taken place on board Harry Crane's yacht.

"Soria," Terry hissed. "What nerve that maroon-haired bimbo had, crashing the dinner party like that. I knew I should have come along with you. So, what's our next move, Carroll?"

Since we were both naked, in her waterbed, and munching on a large bag of potato chips, the next move would have to be carefully planned or we were going to get some salty crumbs in uncomfortable places.

"Maybe we should move to the couch," I suggested.

Terry elbowed herself into a sitting position and said, "No, Mr. Horny. I mean about Thanatos. We should work together on this. A detective team. Me Nora, you Nick."

"Ah, I see. Me The Thin Man, you The Zaftig Woman."

She scrunched the empty chip bag into a ball and threw it at me. Before she decided to kick me out of bed, I said, "Do you remember Peter Dkany? He did some small parts in a TV series filmed here."

She smacked her lips together and said, "Ummmm, yummy yummy."

I took that for a yes. "Well, Dkany was at Monty Hines's funeral, and he was looking at me as if I was going to be roadkill soon."

"What's his beef with you, Carroll?"

"Sara Vasin. His ex-wife. We dated a few times."

She swung her shapely legs over mine, slipped out of bed, and made for the kitchen. "I don't see how your previous love life could have anything to do with Thanatos."

"Katherine the Great thinks that Thanatos is someone who knows me, or someone who is close to me."

She paddled back to bed lugging a new bag of chips and a can of Coke. How the hell did she keep her figure with that diet? She handed me the chip bag. "Use those big muscles of yours to open this up."

While she popped the soda top, I pulled, stretched, and tugged at the bag, finally settling for the old standby, ripping it open with my teeth.

"I think we can drop Dkany from the list of our suspects," Terry said, wiggling her butt into the mattress. "There's no reason for him to have a grudge against Hines or Charlie Reeder. And besides, he's just not bright enough to pull this off; I mean, he's a dummy, never went to college. He'd have no idea who Thanatos was. He's a hunk—but a killer? No way."

"How do you know all this about Dkany?"

"Word of mouth, darling. Are we going to munch on chips all night?"

We didn't, but somewhere in the middle of the night I woke up thinking of Sara Vasin's house on Saturn Street. There was a public stairway dating back to the 1920s very near her house. We'd walked it several times. A lot of steps. Thirty-nine at least.

Terry had Mondays off from the *Bulletin*, so she decided to sleep in. I picked up some coffee and drove home. A tobacco-colored sedan with a whip antennae was parked on the sidewalk in front of my place. Detective Bruce McCall's car.

I parked in the underground garage and took the elevator up to the sixth floor. If McCall was waiting in the lobby, I'd just let him wait.

The door to my apartment was wide open. I crept up on tiptoes and peeked inside. There were papers, dishes, and clothes all over the floor.

I slammed the door as hard as I could and yelled, "McCall. What the hell do you think you're doing? Just because you're a cop doesn't give you the right to break into my apartment!"

McCall came out of the door leading to my bedroom holding a small lacy black garment in his hands.

"Your door was open when I arrived, Quint," he said. "Either you're a very sloppy individual, or you've been burglarized."

I marched by him, entered the bedroom, and almost cried. A bigger mess than the living area: closet stripped of clothes, dresser drawers pulled out and upended, the mattress turned over.

My main concern was my collection of movie posters. They were all originals in mint condition protected by seal-tight frames: *The Sting*, autographed by Paul Newman and Robert Redford; *The Godfather,* autographed by Al Pacino and Robert Duvall; *Jaws,* with the signatures of Spielberg and Robert Shaw; and *Chinatown*, autographed by Jack Nicholson. One of the perks of being a critic is that you get to pester actors and directors up close and personal. They were my biggest investment—don't laugh. A poster from the 1932 production *The Mummy,* with Boris Karloff, sold for $535,000 at Sotheby's in 1997. If Karloff had autographed it, the price would have gone up near the million-dollar mark.

The posters had been removed from the wall, but were unharmed.

"Does this belong to you?" McCall asked. He looked over the lingerie in his hand carefully, and did everything but bite it. "Are you into cross-dressing, Quint?"

"That's a bra. Size thirty-six C. It belongs to a lady friend of mine, and I don't think she'd appreciate you sniffing it."

He dropped the bra to the floor. "There are some other things on the floor: slips, and lady's shoes by the closet."

"How do I know you didn't break in here? I just have your word that the door was open when you got here."

McCall straightened up to his fullest height, stretching his neck so that his Adam's apple protruded. He was dressed in western style again, a two-tone brown jacket and snakeskin cowboy boots. His jacket was undone, revealing a silver belt buckle in the shape of a bucking horse. Everything but a pair of holstered pearl-handled six-shooters and a horse.

"I don't appreciate that kind of talk," he said. "Do you have any idea who did this?"

An idea all right. Tom Powers. But I didn't think that now was the time to share that information with McCall.

"I don't have a clue," I told him.

His eyes were in constant motion, flicking around the room. "Could be drug addicts, looking for a score. A professional burglar never leaves this kind of a mess." He waved his arm languidly around the room. "You start tossing things around like this punk did, and it just might cover up what you're looking for."

"I don't do drugs, McCall. Never have."

He walked to the door as if he'd hadn't heard me.

"His mode of entry was professional, though. The perp used a gun to open the lock."

"A gun?"

McCall opened the door and took a pen flashlight from his jacket pocket. "Lock pick gun. Those phonies you see in the movies—guy sticking a curved piece of metal in a lock and springing it—just doesn't happen, son. The pros hook the picks up to drills, or battery operated screwdrivers, or a computer hard drive disk, and pop it in a matter of seconds."

He cupped the flashlight in his hands and shined the light into the outside lock of my apartment door. "Take a lookie."

I bent over and examined the lock. There were multiple small scratches all around the key entrance.

"If I opened the lock up," McCall said, "you'd see scratches on all the pins and tumblers. The pick guns won't always work on a really good lock, but this useless piece of junk you've got here, no problem."

I began picking up plates and cups and bringing them to the kitchen. The cabinets were half-empty, and the sink was filled with the bare necessities I kept in my refrigerator, including the ice trays. "What are you doing here, McCall? What brought you to my apartment this morning?"

"The coroner has confirmed that the blow to the back of Charles Reeder's head was indeed from that frozen leg of lamb in his refrigerator. Tell me again just how you happened to figure all that out."

"The Alfred Hitchcock connection, Detective. The birds attacking Charlie, and Monty Hines being killed in the shower. Then I remembered the TV show with the leg of lamb."

McCall wandered over to the couch and kicked at one of the cushions lying on the floor. "Remembered it, did you? Interesting. If it wasn't drugs, what do you think the perp was after, Quint?"

"Beats me."

"Is anything missing?"

That beat me too. I went over to the computer desk. The screen was twisted around and a box of floppy disks had been upended and thrown on the carpet. I booted the machine up. The screen looked normal. There was nothing of value to anyone but me on the hard disk.

"I don't see that anything's been stolen. Are you going to take a report?"

McCall shook his head slowly, then pointed his finger at the telephone next to the computer. "This isn't my territory. Call your local police, though I don't think you're going to get much satisfaction. Those e-mails you've been sending me. A waste of my time. Nothing but crackpots. What do you make of that letter delivered to the actor, Peter Liddell?"

"A phony. The real Thanatos sent me an e-mail. Said that maybe he would take Liddell out. Said it would start a *Frenzy*—which happens to be the name of another Hitchcock movie."

"You didn't send me that one," McCall accused.

"It came in late yesterday. I'll get it to you this morning."

McCall interlocked his fingers and stretched his arms out in front of him until the joints cracked. "Maybe the perp was after that ruby necklace, Quint. Or maybe it was this Thanatos fella, just paying a friendly visit."

"Maybe. Then you should get your crime lab out here and look for fingerprints."

He raised a hand in a lazy salute. "Like I said, it's not my territory. Just in case it was this Thanatos, I'd suggest you get a better lock on that door."

EIGHTEEN

The police department's dispatcher I spoke to was polite and well spoken, but useless. When I reported the break-in, she asked a series of questions:

"Is someone in the apartment now?"

"Just me."

"Is there any sign of the person or persons who broke in, sir?"

"No. I think the break-in took place last night."

"Was anything stolen?"

"No, not that I can tell."

"Do you feel that you are in any danger at the present time?"

"No."

"Have you been having any difficulty with your neighbors?"

"No, not really."

"Then I suggest you contact your insurance carrier, sir, and advise us if you discover something has been stolen."

"Aren't you going to send a policeman out to look it over?"

"Sir, there were no injuries, nothing stolen, there's not a whole lot we can do under those circumstances."

I broke the connection, fumbled through my wallet for Jack Wyatt's card. The SFPD Burglary cop was at his desk and seemed to be delighted that I had become a crime statistic.

"I guess I'm not the only one who figures you heisted the Rosenberry necklace, Quint."

"Inspector, I've been burglarized. Aren't you going to come over and check things out? Take fingerprints? Look for clues?"

"Our crime lab is up to its test tubes in *important* investigations. We can't just send them out on every small-time breaking-and-entering case. We have to prioritize. Of course, if you want to tell me where the necklace is, I'll be there in a few minutes."

"Do you know of a private investigator by the name of Tom Powers? He's been following me. Claims he works for the Pacific All Risk Insurance Company, which insures the ruby necklace."

"Powers? No, never heard of him. But if I were the thief, I'd do business with him. Just hand over the necklace, and both he and I would go away."

"Detective Bruce McCall of the San Mateo Sheriff's Office was in my apartment when I got home this morning and found the place ripped apart. He checked the front door lock, and said it looked as if the burglar had used a lock pick gun."

"What was McCall doing there?" Wyatt asked.

"He came to ask me some questions regarding the death of a man in Montara. Charlie Reeder."

"Oh, yeah. That Thanatos thing. I spoke to Dave Granger. He's interested in you, too. Keep in touch, Quint."

"McCall said the front door lock was *picked*," I said trying to control my temper. "Don't you think that warrants your coming here and doing an investigation?"

"What's McCall's bag? Homicide isn't it? Listen, most of the locks in the city look like they've been picked. You stick the wrong key in the lock, or twist it the wrong way, over time the tumblers get scratched and bent. Doesn't prove a thing. Nice talking to you."

I slammed down the phone hard enough to ring the bell, then began cleaning up the apartment. One of the advantages of having a one-bedroom unit was that there wasn't much to put away: service for four in the plate and silverware department, a hundred or so CDs, and my wardrobe. While picking through the CDs, I found a thin tube of cellophane on top of one of my father's albums. The kind of tubes they wrap toothpicks in. Tom Powers hadn't been careless enough to leave a chewed-up toothpick, but he'd left the wrapper.

I started to reach for the phone to call the cops, then remembered that it wouldn't do any good. A toothpick wrapper wouldn't be considered a priority in Inspector Wyatt's world.

I informed the building manager about the break-in and for once found someone who was interested.

"No kiddin', Mr. Quint. That's terrible. I'll call the locksmith, you better talk to the cops."

Carl Dillon was sprawled in his chair, looking bored, until he saw me approaching. He snapped into a sitting position and said, "Hi, Carroll. Anything I can do for you?"

"As a matter of fact, there is." I leaned close and talked softly. "I want to find out everything I can about a private investigator. His name is Tom Powers, but he's not listed in the telephone book."

"That's not unusual," Dillon said. "A lot of those guys are unlisted. They work for insurance companies and attorneys. Real life private eyes don't make a living off of people who call them up looking for dear old Aunt Gladys."

"You sound like you know a lot about them."

Dillon affirmed the conclusion with a nod. "That's how I supported myself through college. I worked for a big PI outfit, mostly nights and weekends. Surveillance stuff. Worker's compensation. A truck driver or fireman goes off work with a bad back, the insurance carrier thinks he's faking it and hires a PI firm, who hires a dumb kid like me to sit around in a panel truck parked in front of the guy's house hoping to film him dragging out the garbage, or mowing the lawn."

He lifted his pinkie and bit at a piece of skin near the nail. "I can't complain. I got to do a lot of studying while I was sitting there. Let's see if this Powers is licensed."

He turned to his computer, and clicked his way to the State of California Department of Consumer Affairs, then scrolled through the license section, which had a list from A to V, everything from accountants to vocational nurses. He selected "security and investigators" and clicked in Powers's name.

"Here he is. Thomas J. Powers. Licensed since nineteen ninety-nine. No record of disciplinary action. License issued in San Mateo County."

I was impressed. "All of this is available on-line?"

"Oh, sure. You can find anything on-line. That's why PIs spend most of their time behind a computer, like me."

"What about a gun? Would Powers be carrying a gun?"

"There's no mention of a concealed weapons permit on his license. And most PIs don't carry—it's too much of a financial responsibility. Their insurance premiums go way up, and they'd open themselves to civil litigation if they ever had to use the damn thing. Think of all the trouble the cops get into when they fire their weapons. It's a lot worse for a private citizen. Let's run him through ZabaSearch."

"What the hell is that?"

"A freebie search engine that does a pretty good job of locating people."

Dillon entered the database, typed in Powers's full name. "Powers is a pretty common name, the middle initial, J, should narrow it down."

Darned if he wasn't right. There were eight Thomas J. Powerses in California; none in San Francisco, but one in Colma, in San Mateo County.

"Now," Dillon said, enjoying showing off his expertise, "if you want to get real fancy, we can run a database check and really dig into the guy." He looked up at me and frowned. "Trouble is they cost twenty bucks a pop and have to be approved by the editor."

"Katherine the Great has given me all the authority you'll need. Run it, Carl."

He did just that, and within minutes his printer came to life and started spewing pages—a total of twenty-three pages, most of them in tight-lined, abbreviated legalese that was confusing to me.

Dillon came to the rescue. "Let's see what we got," he said, high-lighting information with a yellow marking pen. "It shows he's licensed as a PI. Here's his date of birth, his Social Security number. He filed for bankruptcy sixteen months ago." He shuffled some more pages. "Once owned a house in South San Francisco: Thomas J. and Marie S. Powers. Now it's just in Marie's name. Probably because of a divorce. A few small claims filings. Previous address on Forty-third Avenue in the city. Latest address is on Ferrando Way, in Colma."

He switched over to Yahoo! and ran a map of the address, then scooped the pages into a pile, tapped them together neatly, and handed them to me.

"There's a lot of repeated information, but I highlighted what I thought you'd like to see."

I skimmed through the documents. "And all of this for twenty dollars?"

"You'd be surprised what you can find just by sitting on your ass in front of a computer, if you know where to look."

I thanked Dillon and headed for my cubicle, feeling like a kid who just found out where Mom hid the Christmas presents. The feeling of mirth soon disappeared. Brody Carew was sitting in my chair, bent over the computer keyboard like a mad scientist.

I rolled the data check papers into a tight sphere and jammed them into Brody's ear.

"Get the hell away from my desk."

"Hey, man," Carew squealed, his hand going to his ear. "That hurt. I was just using the word processor, leaving you some ideas." He struggled to his feet, massaging his ear. "I figured we could work together on this." He leaned out into the corridor, then sat on the edge of my desk. "I'm not just talking about the *story*," he hastened to explain. "I'm talking book. Big book. You and I—coauthors. I figure with my connections with Lid-dell, and your publishing connections, this could be big. Really big. After the book, a movie. Liddell is all hot for it. I sketch it out, you fill up the pages." He cocked his head like a dog waiting for a biscuit. "What do you think?"

"I think if you don't get out of here, I'm going to play proctologist with this rolled up paper."

It took him a moment to pick up on that, and when he did he stood up, his face suddenly red and sweaty as if he'd just finished a run or jog. "Don't act tough with me, Quint. I know all about how Liddell beat the crap out of you. I try to do you a favor, and you push me around." He tapped his chest with his thumb, right in the middle of his Homer Simpson sweatshirt. "I'm doing the major reviews here from now on, pal. Remember that. You're toast."

Max Maslin came by and kept me from breaking one of my father's rules: never fight with anyone you know you can beat easily; it doesn't prove anything—to you, or him.

"We're wanted upstairs, Carroll. Right now."

The rest of the day was spent in conference with Katherine the Great and Mark Selden. Selden suggested that we publish some of the most obviously phony and objectionable e-mails from people claiming to be Thanatos.

"We don't put in the full address, just the mail."

I disagreed, but was overruled by Parkham.

"I think it's okay. I'll pick the ones we use." Then she dropped a little bombshell. "We're going to print the latest e-mail from Hermes, where he claims he'll go after Liddell and start a *Frenzy*, and we'll play up the Hitchcock connection."

I started to protest, but she held up a hand like a traffic cop. "Mark, Max, and I have talked this over, Quint. We all think that the letter to Liddell was a phony, but we can't be sure. We won't use the Hermes name, of course."

I looked over to Max, but his eyes were riveted on the carpet.

Selden tucked his thumbs into the pockets of his vest and said, "We would be in a vulnerable position if we don't publish this and something serious happens to Liddell. Quint, have you passed this message along to the police?"

"I told Detective McCall this morning. I found him in my apartment, which had been burglarized."

That got everyone talking at the same time. I filled them in on the details, including my suspicions regarding Tom Powers.

Selden, ever the attorney, asked, "Why did this detective drive all the way to San Francisco to see you, Quint?"

"He wanted to thank me for finding the murder weapon used on Charlie Reeder. A frozen leg of lamb."

"You better tell us about that," the Great said, the annoyance clear in her voice.

"The cops couldn't find the blunt instrument that bashed in the back of Charlie's skull. I suggested they look in the freezer for a frozen leg of lamb. It's a murder weapon from an old Hitchcock TV show, a wife kills her husband with a frozen leg of lamb, then pops it in the defroster and then into the oven—then serves it to the cops for dinner."

Selden actually got a little excited—his lips quivered. "That confirms one thing, that the killer is a true Hitchcock old movie–TV expert. Who else would know such a thing?"

"Quint did," Parkham said dryly. "And I damn well want that in tomorrow's paper. *Bulletin* reporter IDs murder weapon. Now is not the time to be modest."

I said, "If you enter Hitchcock's name in Amazon.com under books, you get hundreds of hits, so anyone could have gone to a bookstore or the local library and picked up on the leg of lamb thing."

Max pulled at the knot of his bow tie and unbuttoned his shirt collar. "This is getting out of hand. We're reporters, not cops."

"Calm down," Selden advised. "We are giving the police our full cooperation. As Quint says, the burglary has to do with the stolen necklace, not Thanatos." He arched his eyebrows at me. "I hope we're not going to have to watch another movie. Katherine tells me that *Frenzy* is another old Hitchcock thing."

"I've ordered a copy," Parkham said. "We can view it later. Quint. I want you to call Inspector Granger and tell him about the Liddell/*Frenzy* e-mail, I don't want him finding out by reading the paper. Has there been anything else from Thanatos or Hermes?"

"Not since I checked this morning. There were more wannabes. I e-mailed them to McCall, and I'll send copies to Granger."

Parkham steepled her fingers and looked over the tips at me. "If nothing happens, and if we don't hear from Hermes by tomorrow morning, you're going to contact him again, keep the dialogue going."

When I didn't give her an argument, she sent out for sandwiches and coffee. A lot of coffee. It was after four in the afternoon when Max and I finally got out of there.

We went right to work on the story for the morning edition. When we finished I gave Granger a call and told him about the *Frenzy* e-mail.

He was his usual charming self.

"Detective McCall filled me in. Hours ago. He said someone had broken into your place and messed up your lingerie. I know the movie, *Frenzy*, it was on Showtime a few weeks ago. Not bad, except that as usual, the police looked awfully stupid."

"Imagine that. I've got a batch of e-mails from crazies that you're welcome to, Granger."

"Do me a favor. Unless they look promising, just send the stuff to McCall."

"Why would I want to do you a favor?" I said.

Granger laughed loudly; the laugh transformed itself into a hacking cough. When he could finally speak he said, "We're partners in crime, aren't we, Quint? We should stick together."

I was cleaning up my desk when I remembered my middle-of-the-night thoughts on Sara Vasin. It had been some time since I'd spoken to her, and I'd forgotten her phone number. I found it on the Rolodex. Her voice on the answering machine picked up the call on the first ring. "Hi. I'm out. You know what to do."

I left my cell number and gathered up the papers on my desk, the ones with Tom Powers's address.

NINETEEN

The town of Colma, just a couple of miles south of San Francisco, has been called the "City of the Dead" and the "Necropolis of San Francisco." It has a population of just over two thousand above the ground, and more than a million below ground. There are more than a dozen cemeteries, serving every race, creed, and religion, as well as a pet cemetery. There's a card club, a few small farms, the usual shopping center, and one great old saloon, Molloy's, whose history dates back to the early nineteen-hundreds when it hosted boxing matches, including the likes of the great Jack Johnson, Stanley Ketchel, and James Jeffries.

Wyatt Earp, of cowboy fame, is buried nearby. He once refereed a match at Molloy's between Bob Fitzsimmons and Tom Sharkey, Earp giving the match to Sharkey on a technical foul—which didn't go over too well with the crowd, who thought Fitzsimmons was the winner. Earp packed up in a hurry, with what some thought were his gambling winnings from betting on Sharkey, and moved to Alaska for a time.

I was glad that Carl Dillon had printed a detailed map for Tom Powers's address. I drove past streets lined with small ranch-style homes with tar-and-gravel roofs and weed-choked runt lawns. The neighborhood changed abruptly into a cluster of light industrial buildings: junkyards, storage shacks, abandoned gas stations, and one tempting-looking burrito place.

I took a left on Ferrando, and drove up a dusty road that narrowed into one lane. The hillside was upholstered in yellow oxalis and purple lupine, the colorful weeds engulfing most of what must have been a potter's field cemetery, with crumbling tombstones sticking out from the ground like rotting teeth. A hand-painted sign nailed to a redwood gate informed me that I was approaching The Ocean View Trailer Court.

The hill leveled off, giving me a bird's eye view of the trailer park, which was engulfed by a ring of towering eucalyptus trees. You could climb to the tops of those trees and still have no chance of seeing the Pacific Ocean. I counted forty-one trailers parked in an awkward, H-shaped hunk of land. The majority seemed to be narrow, thirty- to thirty-five feet in length, probably one bedroom, pint-size kitchen, and bathroom. There were a couple of vintage, once shiny-skinned Airstreams, their sleek aluminum shells oxidized and marred by dents.

I drove cautiously over the pothole-filled road into the park. A dog howled from somewhere nearby.

I parked, switched off the engine, and listened to its ping. Howling dogs always made me nervous. The air was so thick with the smell of eucalyptus, it made me think of cough drops.

I heard the creak of a door opening. A man lurched awkwardly down the metal steps of what was by far the best-looking trailer in sight. He appeared to be in his mid-seventies, with a florid face and bulging stomach. He was bald except for a few untidy strands of wispy gray hair settling about his ears. He had on faded black pants and a baggy white shirt—the label of a pack of Lucky Strike cigarettes visible through the front pocket.

I climbed out of the MINI as he limped his way over to me. He had a longneck bottle of beer in one hand, a cigarette in the other. A small transistor radio playing big band music from the forties hung from a leather cord around his neck.

"Howdy," the man called, "what can I do for ya?" He waved the hand with the cigarette across his chest. "We're full booked up."

"I'm meeting Tom Powers," I told him.

He stopped within a foot of me. His face was a mesh of tiny inter-twined wrinkles. His voice had a juicy southern accent.

"Fella, that's about the smallest damn car I ever did see. Duke's the name. What's yours?"

I didn't feel like going through the Carroll routine with the old-timer, so I just said, "Joe. Which trailer belongs to Tom?"

Duke took a pull on his Lucky, then a sip of beer. "Whattcha want with Powers?"

"Business."

Another puff on his smoke, followed immediately by another sip of beer. The man didn't even take the time to exhale. He belched loudly. "Powers ain't here now. Maybe I can take a message."

"No. He told me to wait in his trailer if he wasn't home."

Duke frowned, and while mulling that over slipped the beer bottle under his arm, dug the pack of Luckys from his shirt, and chain-lit an-other smoke.

"You another one of those private eyes, Joe?"

"Something like that."

The radio switched to a sultry voiced singer doing "Love for Sale." Duke adjusted the volume loud enough to raise some of the dead in the nearby cemetery. "Know who that is?" he said.

I listened a few moments, then guessed, "Diana Krall?"

"Who? No, that's Julie London, boy. Once married to the guy who did *Dragnet*, the old cop show on TV. She's my life support. I gave strict orders to the wife. When I'm in the ground, and just before they start piling dirt on the coffin, she's gonna play a Julie song. If that don't get a rise out of me, nothing will. I'm dead."

Duke cackled over that one for about a minute, then it was back to puffing and sipping.

"Powers's trailer," I reminded him. "Where is it?"

Duke pointed the beer bottle down the road. "The green one at the end of the block. You're welcome to wait in my place with me. We could play cards. You like gin rummy?"

"Thanks, but Tom told me where he keeps the spare key."

I hopped back in the MINI and drove at loitering speed until I reached Powers's trailer. I parked around the back. The red-and-white-checkered curtains in the trailer across the road parted and I got a quick glance at a pale elderly face before they were jerked shut.

The windows to Powers's trailer were covered with wrinkled aluminum foil. The screen door was open, the weather-blistered wooden one right behind it locked.

There was a chance that Powers had the place alarmed, but I figured him to be the lazy type, like the painter whose house is the worst on the block, or the electrician who never gets around to fixing his own lights and switches.

I used the spare key I found in the MINI's tool chest—an eighteen-inch-long tire iron. I jammed the sharpened end into the spot just below the door lock and gave a quick pull. There was a loud cracking noise, the door swung open—no bells or alarms.

I checked the unit across the road. The checkered curtains didn't move. Duke was probably tapping an arthritic foot to a Glenn Miller song. I slipped the tire iron into my waistband, then went inside and closed the door behind me.

I guess breaking and entering is easier the second time around, because there was no pounding heartbeat or sweaty palms as there had been when I keyed my way into Monty Hines's condo.

I found the switch and snapped it on. A fluorescent ceiling light pinged to life. The place had a locker room smell about it—unwashed clothes, moldy walls. A small ceiling fan, black with grime, turned in endless circles. A television screen fluttered like a flag nobody saluted.

There was a closet-size kitchen, checkerboard linoleum floor, a lumpy, root-beer-colored couch, its arms repaired with duct tape. No paintings on the wall, just a calendar with a picture of Salma Hayek in a tiny white bikini.

Alongside Salma's photo was a floor-to-ceiling bookshelf, the books landsliding in toward a series of old shoeboxes. I checked the boxes. The tops were off, the insides filled with mysterious black plastic devices with wires dangling from them, ranging from thumb to cigarette pack size; telephones in various degrees of disassembly, camera lenses by the dozens.

I scanned the book titles: *How to Make Silencers for Handguns, Surreptitious Infrared Audio Monitoring, Fast Eddie's Guide to Lockpicking, Updated Telephone Techniques, Spy Bug Techniques.*

The opposite wall was filled up with a gray metal four-drawer filing cabinet and another cheapo bookcase stuffed with three video recorders, two monitors, racks of video and audio recording tape, and an ancient typewriter that looked as if it should have been in a museum.

I opened up the top drawer of the cabinet and found a semiautomatic pistol with a cracked checkered grip. There were filing marks on the end of the gun's extended barrel. I picked it up, found the button for the clip release, and pushed. The clip was filled with bright brass bullets. I fingered them free of the clip. They fell to the linoleum floor like lozenges. I dropped the gun and kicked it in the direction of the sofa. In addition to the gun, there were dozens of manila file folders, the typed label names ranging from Abadale to Cullen. Drawer two started with Davis and finished with Lamont.

I switched to drawer number four and found the file for Quint. It wasn't very thick, but there was a packet of four-by-four photographs, twenty-six in all, showing me walking near the *Bulletin*, behind the wheel of the MINI, and strolling back to my apartment with Terry Greco.

There was a file card listing my address, and a sheaf of data sheet information similar to the one Carl Dillon had run on Powers.

After I replaced the file I fingered my way through the Rs, and came across the file for Rosenberry, Gineen.

More pictures: Gineen in her bedroom, casually dressed, looking annoyed, in front of her makeup table, alongside her bed, and one with her back turned, apparently heading for the door.

I could tell that Gineen hadn't known she was being photographed from her posture, and the way her head was turned—showing the shade of a double chin and some wrinkles on her neck. She never got in front of a camera unless her makeup was perfect and the cameraman was professional enough to catch her in the right light.

So Powers had some type of hidden camera with him when he'd visited Gineen. Why? What the hell was the bastard's game? I slipped the photos of Gineen into my coat pocket and turned my attention to the football-shaped table covered in green felt, like a gaming board, in the middle of the room.

On the table was an abalone shell ashtray filled with chewed up toothpicks and jumbled up plastic sheaths like the one I'd found in my apartment. Alongside was a red coffee mug with the initials NRA and a picture of crossed rifles. It was filled with fresh toothpicks. There were three computer screens, and a maze of electronic gadgets. Two of them caught my eye. The first was an odd shaped instrument: an opened hard drive, with a computer mouse duct taped to it. The hard drive had been stripped. Two AAA batteries were glued to the housing. An angular, sharp-tipped screwdriver had been soldered to the drive casing. I picked it up, activated the mouse, and Shazam—the hard drive began humming and the screwdriver started vibrating like crazy. A homemade lock pick.

The second goody was a piece of black plastic the size of a deck of cards, with four sharp prongs on one end and a lanyard on the other. Stamped on one side were the words BANTAM STUN GUN 775,000 VOLTS. I picked it up carefully, found the on/off switch, and flicked it on. The nasty little thing started to throb in my hand. I switched it off and dropped it in my pocket alongside the photographs.

There was the sound of an out-of-tune motor pulling up in front of the trailer, the engine dying in an anguished groan. A car door opening, then closing. Footsteps hurrying up the front steps, then slowing to a halt. Powers had spotted the damage I'd done to the door.

"Who's in there?" he called out in a deep-chested voice.

"The boogie man, Powers. Come on in. The door was broken when I got here."

Powers kicked the door open and strode into the room, one arm cocked, the fist closed ready to throw a punch, the other holding a white plastic bag.

"What the hell do you think you're doing here?" he demanded.

"You know, that's the same thing I asked Detective Bruce McCall of the San Mateo Sheriff's Department when I found him in my apartment this morning. Of course, my front door wasn't broken in, you used the computer generated pick gun to get in."

"You're crazy," Powers said, marching over to the green felt table. He grabbed the pick gun and dropped it into one of the shoeboxes on the bookcase.

"I can have you arrested for breaking and entering, Quint. I'm calling the cops, right now."

"Be my guest. I'm sure they'd be interested in that gun, the one with the scratches on the barrel for the silencer you made. That's a no-no, Tom."

Powers hammered the edge of his hand against the edge of the table like a karate expert warming up. It suddenly dawned on me that he might just be a karate expert, which turned it into a hit and run situation; I'd either have to hit him pretty damn quick, or run the hell out of there.

"I'm a licensed private investigator and I have the right to—"

"You don't have a gun permit, and if the Department of Consumer Affairs finds out what kind of a racket you're running, you won't have a license for long."

He started rocking back and forth on his feet, planning his next move. I beat him to it, moving in quickly and slamming an elbow into the middle of his chest. He screamed, and the white bag fell from his hand.

While he was cursing me, I picked up the bag. Inside was a video rental. The movie was *Frenzy*.

I grabbed Powers by the arm, spun him around, and slammed the tip of my elbow square into his chest again. His face turned a cement gray color, and he collapsed to his knees.

"You son of a bitch, Powers. It's you. You're Thanatos."

"No, no," he said, trying to catch his breath.

I picked up the videocassette and slapped him on top of his head. "Then how do you explain this?"

"Not me," he gasped. "I bugged your place. I listened to you and Mc-Call. You told him about the movie." He placed both hands on the ground and pushed himself up, almost falling down again in the process.

I threw the cassette against the wall and took the stun gun from my pocket and shoved it into Powers's neck. His body twitched as if he'd been electrocuted, which was what was going to happen soon if he didn't come clean.

"It's true, Quint," he rasped. He nodded his head toward the bookcase holding the cassettes. "It's there. The recording. Marked with your name."

He was telling the truth. About the tape anyway. I slotted it into a machine on the table and soon heard the sound of footprints, someone whistling a tune I couldn't recognize, then my own voice shouting, "McCall, what the hell do you think you're doing. Just because you're a cop, it doesn't give you the right to break into my apartment." I ejected the tape and shoved it in my now bulging pocket.

Powers had been busy while I was doing all this—he was on the floor by the couch, stooping over to pick up the semiautomatic pistol. He gripped it in both hands and pointed it directly at me.

"Who took the written test for your private eye license for you, you moron?" I said. "Look on the floor. Those round little brass things are bullets."

Powers swallowed hard and said, "Get out of here. Leave me alone."

"Not until you tell me where the bug is in my apartment. How many are there?"

"Just the one. In the phone in the front room."

"I'm going to have the place swept, Powers. And if I find more than one bug, I'm going to take them all to the cops."

"There's just the one." He waved the gun barrel toward the door. "Get out, damn it."

"In a minute. First, tell me why you went to all this trouble? Why are you so certain that I'm the one who took Gineen Rosenberry's necklace?"

Powers wobbled for a moment, then flopped down onto the sofa like a runner whose legs have gone out. "I got a call. A man said it was you. That he saw you leaving the party that night with the necklace."

"What man? Who?"

Powers set the gun onto his lap and began massaging his chest. "Why'd you hit me so hard?"

Actually, I'd pulled the punch. The tip of an elbow is the most lethal weapon in the human anatomy's arsenal. That was the blow that killed the great magician Houdini, puncturing his stomach muscles and rupturing his appendix. "Tell me who the man is, or I'll hit you harder. Who?"

He paused for a moment, as if marshalling his thoughts. "I don't know. Really. But he had you pegged; what you were wearing that night, the bloody nose. Everything. He had to have seen you."

I looked at the racks of recording cassettes. "Did you tape his call?"

Powers shook his head as if it weighed a ton. "No. You can't tape everything, Quint."

"How many calls?"

"Just the one. I swear it."

His face was getting its color back, his breathing returning to normal. In a minute or two he'd have his strength back and want to go after me. I had two choices: hit him again right then, or leave. I headed for the door.

I patted my jacket pocket. "I have those surreptitious photos you took of Gineen Rosenberry. If I show them to her, she'll go after you with a battery of attorneys. You'll end up out of work and in jail. If this man calls you again, you tape him, and you call me right away. Get it?"

"Got it."

"Good." I opened the door and he called out one last question.

"Quint. How did you find me? Find my address here at the trailer court?"

"I used a private eye, Powers. A competent one."

TWENTY

Thanatos/Hermes was right about one thing—his latest e-mail had started a frenzy. I was treated like a celebrity when I arrived at the paper the next morning.

Carl Dillon was in a chipper mood, telling me that he'd been receiving calls from mainstream press types trying to get an angle on the story.

"I believe someone has planted bugs in my place," I said. "What's the best way to find them?"

"Easy. Give the place a complete security sweep. I can recommend someone."

Dillon gave me the name of a firm called Argonaut Investigations. I called them from his desk and made an appointment to meet with them at my place at nine the following morning.

Darlene was back to her usual cheerful self, thanks in part to the two assistants who were handling the incoming crank calls.

I made for my desk. Max Maslin was sporting one of his rare smiles.

"The Great just called me, Carroll. Returns were the lowest anyone can remember, and ad revenue is picking up."

Returns were the unsold papers that sat in street-side vending machines and a real indicator of how popular the paper was. Low returns meant high sales.

I'd just settled down behind my desk when Brody Carew stopped by to say, "Hi, partner. Nice trick with that leg of lamb. Don't forget our book."

Carew calling me partner brought me out of my morning high. There were pages of new e-mails from Thanatos impersonators. Nothing from the real McCoy. I called Katherine Parkham and told her the news.

"Well, then, you get in touch with him. Make it short. Pitch him for a meeting, mention the thirty-nine steps, and tell him that you have to cooperate with the police, but that you are keeping his e-mail address to yourself. Hell, send him some of the stuff from the crazies. Anything that will get him involved, involved enough to make a mistake."

"I don't want to push Thanatos into another killing."

"Nobody's going to push this guy, Quint. It's the other way around. He's pulling our chain. We've got to get to him somehow. And oh, by the way. Be here in my office at six. You're going on TV tonight."

"TV?"

"Yes. Live, from my office. Channel seven. Better get here a half hour early so we can go over the script and they can make you up."

"Into what?" I said to a dead receiver.

I worried over the message to Hermes/Thanatos for close to an hour, and finally sent him:

THE POLICE DO NOT KNOW ABOUT THIS ADDRESS FOR YOU. THEY'RE BUSY LOOKING FOR A VICTIM AT THE BOTTOM OF A FLIGHT OF STAIRS. WHY DID YOU PICK ME?

Max and I batted around a story for tomorrow's paper, then I gave him a toned-down version of my encounter with Tom Powers at his trailer.

"Did you check to see if there's a bug in your telephone?"

"No. I haven't been home yet. Someone Carl Dillon recommended is coming over to check it out in the morning."

"Do you think someone actually called Powers and said they saw you with Rosenberry's necklace?"

"Yes, I do. Someone really wants to put the screws to me, and I can't figure out why."

Max closed his eyes and massaged his temples. "It's too much of a coincidence, the stolen necklace and Thanatos popping up at damn near the same time."

"I know," I agreed, "but what the hell is the connection? Both Hines and Charlie Reeder were dead at the time the necklace was stolen."

"Talk to Gineen Rosenberry," Max suggested. "Get a list of everyone who was at the party that night."

I took his advice and dialed her number. Gineen was at home, she said she'd have her secretary fax the information to me. "I hope you're being careful, Carroll. All of this has me very upset."

I assured her I was being careful. "When am I going to see you again?"

"I'm glad you called, Carroll. Your mother was actually quite nice to me the other night. She had a suggestion, that we have some sort of a memorial for Charlie Reeder."

"I didn't know you and Reeder were friends," I said.

"Not friends, but associates. Jules recommended him. He came in at the last minute and did some rewriting on *The Caring Ones* last fall. It didn't save the play, but it did help it stay in the theater for a few months. He was very professional, and I guess I owe him something."

I remembered the play, a tearjerker about a man dying of AIDS. I hadn't known that Reeder was involved.

"I'm sure Charlie would have loved a going-away party, Gineen."

"It won't be anything fancy, just his close friends. Jules is going to set it up at the officers' club on Treasure Island. Perhaps you can get me a list of who should come. Include some of the people at Sara Vasin's parrot parties. That's where I first met Charlie."

Sara's parrot parties. Damn, I'd forgotten that Charlie had attended. Sara loved to throw weekend lunches during the times that a group of wild parrots came and picked her cherry tree clean. She'd invite people from the local theater groups, who would oooh and aww over the parrots' antics. Sara had the birds literally eating out of her hand.

"I'll get right on it," I told Gineen.

As soon as I hung up, I dialed Sara's number, only to get her machine. When I tried to leave another message, I was cut off. I tried again—same thing, which meant her machine's recorder was full.

Sara's place was on Saturn Street, in the Corona Heights section of the city, just above the Castro District. Visitors are surprised to learn that the Castro wasn't always a gay enclave. Before it became the "center for alternative living," as our rival newspaper likes to call it, the Castro was a rough-and-tumble neighborhood dominated by Irish longshoremen, teamsters, cops, and firemen.

I drove by narrow, curving streets with names like Temple, Mars, and Uranus, before finding a parking place on Seventeenth Street, two blocks from the entrance to the Saturn Steps. A two-block walk from a parking spot to your house in this area is considered pretty damn good. Sara rented a single slot in a nearby neighbor's garage for several hundred dollars a month.

The Saturn Street Steps are actually two parallel sets of steps that climb a steep block-long hill. The city put in the set of concrete steps some twenty years ago. On the opposite side of a divider, which is planted with shrubs and small trees whose upkeep depends on the generosity of the nearby homeowners, is a set of the original lumber and packed earth steps. Every fifteen steps or so there's a landing with a dilapidated bench set into a concrete bulkhead.

There is an eclectic mixture of housing bordering the steps: Victorians, modern bungalows, and quaint cottages. The owners of the properties all have one thing in common—strong legs and backs, because everything, from furniture to groceries, has to be lugged up the steps. Sara had used me as a pack mule on more than one occasion.

It really was a lovely spot, but like many lovely spots in the city, it had been taken advantage of by drug dealers and hardcore homeless individuals, what my father would call "godamn bums," who slept in the shrubs, sold their drugs, urinated on the steps, then moved on. Burglaries, rapes, and overdosed teenagers were all part of the mix now.

Sara's house was near the top of the third landing, some forty-five steps above street level. I negotiated the crumbling wooden steps leading to her property. The seven-foot-high redwood fencing had faded to a gray ash color. There was a doorbell alongside the gate. I rang several times before stooping down and unearthing a cobblestone, underneath which Sara had kept a gate key. I hoped it was still there, because I hadn't climbed a seven-foot fence since puberty.

I was in luck. I opened the gate and walked into what could have been a Tuscan garden.

The house was bungalow style, with broom-stroke apricot ocher plaster walls and a red tile roof. There were full-size fruit trees: cherry, nectarine, plum, and pear; and miniature lemon, lime, and orange trees. Terra-cotta urns and jugs sprouting geraniums, impatiens, and purple flowering rosemary dazzled the eye. Wrought iron baskets of fuchsia hung from tree branches. Hidden behind a bamboo hedge were Sara's marijuana plants. The deck looked out onto a panorama of the city stretching from the downtown area over to Potrero Hill.

There was a sudden screeching and several feral parrots flew from the pear tree. Sara had given me a lesson on the birds, which are the size of a robin, a brassy olive green in color with a red head, and officially known as the red-masked conure. Their place of origin is Peru, and no one knows for certain how the flock, estimated from sixty to a hundred, ended up in San Francisco. They are noisy critters that can't be taught to speak and who have a habit of biting their owners' fingers, so they either escaped their cages or were set free. They don't seem to have a problem breeding, because the flock size stays pretty consistent, despite the attacks of cats, owls, hawks, and a falcon or two who think they look delicious.

They're also territorial as hell and consider Sara's garden as their personal property. One bright redheaded parrot soared past my face and let out a threatening shriek to let me know I was going to be treated like an invader.

Like many parrots, they have a long lifespan, but it would be hard to beat my favorite bird of all time, Winston Churchill's parrot, Charlie, who is reported to be alive and well today, and kept out of the public eye because he still spouts a few phrases the great man taught him, such as "Fuck Hitler."

A lavender trellised archway led to a Dutch door with heavy wrought-iron hinges.

I pounded on the door and called out Sara's name. There was no hidden key that I knew of, and the lock looked sturdy—probably too tough for Powers's computer-generated pick. The window curtains were drawn, one torn, a detail that didn't register with me until later.

I tried the obvious—turning the doorknob slowly, one part of my brain hoping it was locked. It wasn't. I opened the door slowly and stuck my head inside, fearful of inhaling that terrible scent of death. All I smelled was rosemary, lemons, and lavender.

"Sara, it's Carroll," I called out to an empty house. The furniture was rustic; some of it she'd purchased directly from a farmhouse in Tuscany. The kitchen table was set for lunch or dinner: plates, glasses, silverware.

I strolled around, winding up in the bedroom. Everything neat as a pin, a pair of freshly ironed jeans and a yellow blouse laid out on the bed. Her "Louie," a Louis Vuitton monogrammed feed-bag-style purse that she took with her everywhere, was on the dresser. I peeked inside: wallet, passport, compact, keys, a couple of Power Bars, an assortment of lipstick and makeup tubes. All the things she wouldn't leave home without.

Sara's answering machine was in the kitchen, on a counter next to a massive oak chopping block. The message indicator number showed that she had thirty-two calls waiting for her. I wound the machine back and listened to the calls: Four from her ex- Peter Dkany: the first soft and gentle, the second sweet love words, the third—"Where are you?" The fourth—"Where the hell are you?"

There were calls offering jobs—two of those from Vancouver; a number of quick "call me back" messages, the caller assuming that Sara would recognize their voices—I certainly didn't. Calls from girlfriends, boyfriends? One cheerful call from a woman wishing Sara: "Good luck. No more traveling! I hope you get it." There was no explanation as to just what "it" was. Toward the end of the tape was my phone call to Sara, sounding anything but cheerful.

I strolled back to the kitchen and checked the refrigerator, which was filled with enough food to throw a party. The sink was spotless, the dishwasher empty. Everything was spotless—too spotless for Sara. She always had a few books and newspapers spread around the place; bowls of berries and nuts out ready for the parrots; bags of peanuts for the squirrels; a couple of opened wine bottles, plates of cookies. Someone had carefully cleaned the place.

I hurried back to the bedroom and went through her purse again. Her PalmPilot pocket computer wasn't there. I went through the house—it was nowhere to be found. It had a cell phone, digital camera, access to the Web. She used it as a calendar and as her address book; it held her client list, recipes, just about everything. She'd thought she'd lost it one time and came close to having a breakdown. She wouldn't let it out of her sight after that.

I took another tour around the place, and before exiting noticed the torn window curtain again. Sara had the mustard-colored curtains made of heavy-duty, fire resistant theatrical fabric. The jagged tear was some three feet long. It would require someone quite strong to make a tear like that in the thick cloth. Thanatos, you miserable bastard, I said to myself.

TWENTY-ONE

"You're in the wrong place," Inspector Dave Granger told me. "Missing Persons is down the hall."

"I'm afraid, really afraid that Sara Vasin is more than just missing."

Granger hauled his feet from his desk and swiveled his chair so that he could look out the window facing the bumper-to-bumper traffic edging its way toward the Bay Bridge.

"You're a lot of trouble, Quint. Do you have any idea just how much grief your articles are giving me? I'm getting calls from all over the state—idiots telling me that they're Thanatos. Cops who are sure they've found the next victim. Some klutz sheriff from Bakersfield phoned me this morning saying that aliens had cut figures in a cornfield. He's sure that they're Greek letters and symbols and have something to do with the murders. He wants me to fly down there and check it out."

Granger swiveled back to face me. "And now the FBI wants to horn in. They can't stand seeing us get all of that newspaper coverage without their name being in the mix."

"Sara Vasin, Inspector. I think she may be the thirty-nine steps victim."

Granger was in his shirtsleeves, the sleeves rolled up, and he was wearing the cheap digital watch, not the Rolex. He had a gold ring on the ring finger of his right hand. I knew a lot of divorced men who made the transfer from left hand to right. He twisted the ring as if it were uncomfortable.

" 'You think,' " he said sarcastically. "The only problem is that there's no body."

"Her house is empty, and as clean as a marine barracks. Her purse is there, with all of her identification and makeup. One very important item is missing—her pocket computer. It's her business lifeline, her calendar. Maybe she entered the name of the person who came to the house. Maybe that's why it's gone. The killer took it. And then there's the torn curtain on the window by her front door."

Granger let out a loud groan. "You know, Quint, talking to you is like straddling a tightrope and watching the strands slowly unravel at the other end. *Torn Curtain*, another damn Hitchcock movie, right? Thanatos snatches the damsel in distress and leaves a clue that only you—our hero—can figure out. Give me a break. Somehow I missed that one. Just what's the significance of the torn curtain?"

"It was a spy flick, Paul Newman and Julie Andrews. The curtain was the iron curtain of communism."

"So now Thanatos is a commie?" Granger stretched his arm over his head and yawned, not bothering to cover his mouth. "This Vasin woman. What's she to you?"

"We used to date. She's a theatrical makeup artist. One of the best."

Granger arched his eyebrows. "A girlfriend? Does Mommy know?"

His taunting act was wearing thin. I leaned my elbows on his desk and said, "Jesus probably loves you, Inspector, but everyone else thinks you're an asshole. This woman is missing. Are you going to do anything? Or should I just put an article in the paper, saying that I dropped all of the information onto your fat lap and you did nothing about it?"

"My, my. We're a little touchy, aren't we?"

"Roll down your shirtsleeves, Inspector. I'm curious to see if you're wearing cufflinks today."

Granger clenched and relaxed his fists, as if he was squeezing a ball. "Detective McCall buzzed me yesterday. Told me all about the alleged break-in at your apartment. He thinks it was a drug deal. He told me you show-biz folk are big with coke."

"I tried sniffing Coke once, but the ice cubes got stuck in my nose. Sara Vasin's house is on Saturn Street, the area with the steep stairs. More than thirty-nine of them, and she's missing."

"So where's the body? We're not that dumb, Quint. I've checked all of the John and Jane Does who have come in the last week. Nothing that would indicate that any of them fell down a flight of steps. And I—" He began trawling through a stack of papers on his desk. "Saturn Street, up by Seventeenth and Market, right?"

"Yes, it's right off of—"

"Ord Street." He brushed his lower lip with a thumbnail as he studied a report. "Unidentified WFA, approximately thirty-five. A hit and run victim. Place of incident, two-hundred block of Ord Street." He got to his feet and reached for his jacket. "Come on, let's go see the medical examiner."

The medical examiner's office was located on the main floor of the Hall of Justice, but you had to go outside the building to enter it. Granger stopped at the espresso bar in the lobby and bought two cups of coffee. Handing me one, he said, "You'll probably wish this was something stronger. The report indicated that the body was severely damaged. Whatever ran over her was big and heavy."

We started walking, Granger muttering a "Hello," or "What's doin', pal," to passersby who called out his name.

"Did Vasin have any identifying marks, Quint? Scars? Tattoos? That kind of thing."

"Yes. A tattoo. Links around her left ankle. Her husband, ex now, had an identical one—they were supposed to link them together for all time."

Granger pushed open the glass door leading to the medical examiner's office. There was a long counter extending the length of the room. On the other side were walls of file cabinets and ten or so desks, but no one to man them.

"Wait here," Granger told me, as he walked through a door marked EMPLOYEES ONLY at the end of the counter.

A slender man with a long pointed nose suddenly appeared from the back of the room. He was smiling and humming a song. He wore a starched white doctor's jacket freckled with tiny blood spots.

"Are you being helped?" he asked cheerfully.

"I'm waiting for Inspector Granger," I told him.

His smile deepened. "Grave Danger, we call him down here. Sends us some of our most interesting cases."

"You're the medical examiner?" I asked.

"Yes, but I prefer coroner. Sounds a lot better, doesn't it? Medical examiner is so politically correct. When I tell people my title now, they think I check records for people studying to be a doctor." Another broad smile. "Oh, well. Back to the job."

He hummed his way through the same door Granger had disappeared through. I had no problem with a man being happy with his work, but a coroner? That happy?

Ten minutes later Granger opened the door and motioned for me to join him.

"Quint, I'm afraid the victim is your friend Vasin. The tattoo is there, around her ankle, just as you described it. I could ask you to view the body for a positive identification, but I don't think it's necessary, and, unless you've got a real strong stomach, not advisable. Do you know if she had a passport?"

"Yes. She did."

"Then I can verify her identity with a fingerprint comparison. You mentioned an ex-husband. Is he still in the picture?"

"Yes. Peter Dkany. I saw him the other night at Montgomery Hines's wake."

In a surprisingly tender gesture, Granger patted me softly on the shoulder and said, "I'm very sorry for your loss."

Even more surprisingly, he sounded like he meant it.

We walked outside and I deeply inhaled the exhaust-filled air.

"I have to ask you this, Quint. Was Ms. Vasin a doper?"

"She had a couple of small marijuana plants in her garden, and I guess she was what would be called a recreational user of other stuff.

But she was never hooked on anything. She couldn't be, and keep her job. I never joined in, it was one of the reasons we drifted apart."

"Her blood test showed traces of THC, tetrahydrocannabinol, the stuff that gives marijuana its kick, as well as alcohol, point seven. Point eight is considered legally over the limit."

"I've seen her smoke some grass, along with a glass or two of wine," I told him.

Granger took a pack of cigarettes from his coat pocket, shook one free, and lit up with a disposable lighter, coughing at the first inhale. "It's a good thing the ME did a complete autopsy, because he found something else in her blood. Flunitrazepam. Rohypnol."

It took me a second or two for that to register. "Roofies? The date rape drug?"

"Exactly. Not only is it colorless, tasteless, and odorless, all traces of the stuff leave the body after seventy-two hours."

"Was . . . was Sara sexually assaulted?"

"No, she was not." He dropped the cigarette on the floor, squashing it with the sole of his shoe. "I give these damn things up at least once a day."

"So what does it all mean?" I asked. "The killer has a drink with Sara, maybe they share some dope, then slips the Rohypnol in her drink, rolls her down the stairs, and then runs her over with his car?"

"That's one scenario. I called the crime lab from the ME's office. They're on their way over to Ms. Vasin's house. So am I. You're welcome to come along."

"Thanks, but no thanks."

Granger unbuttoned his jacket and hooked his thumbs into his trousers. "We'd better exchange cell phone numbers, and I'm going to ask you for your fingerprints, Quint, and this time I don't want an argument."

I raised my hands in mock surrender. "This time you won't get one, Inspector."

.   .   .

Katherine Parkham waved me over to her desk. There was a squad of television technicians in the office, two cameras, and a battery of lamps. Her face had been made up, giving her skin an odd orange tint. "You're late. We start in twelve minutes. You'll have to go on with no makeup, I want—"

"I'm not going on television, boss. This afternoon I found Thanatos's thirty-nine steps victim. A woman I knew by the name of Sara Vasin."

"Oh, God. I'm sorry. Where and how was she killed?"

I gave her the details, including my trip to the city morgue.

She pinched the bridge of her nose, as if she had a headache. "Carroll, can we be certain that this woman's death is linked to Thanatos?"

"I'm certain."

A makeup technician hurried over to Parkham. "You've ruined your nose. I'll have to touch you up."

"Screw off," the Great growled, sending the technician backpedaling.

Parkham grabbed a notepad and pencil and rifled off some questions to me. When she was finished, she said, "I'll go on alone. We'll announce there's been another victim. I'd like you to get together with Max and get something ready for the morning edition. I know it's personal, I know it's tough, but we have to run the story. Agreed?"

"Agreed," I said and went down and met with Max Maslin. There's a paper policy that there is to be absolutely no consumption of alcohol within the premises. Max figured if the Great could violate that policy, we could too. He pulled a pint from his desk drawer.

"If that's Cherry Heering, I'll pass," I told him.

"Vodka. I keep it for medicinal purposes." He went into a very bad W. C. Fields impersonation: "I keep a bottle of it handy in case I see a snake, which I also keep handy."

He poured us shots in paper cups. Warm vodka in paper cups, not exactly a James Bond martini.

We went to work piecing together a story.

I checked my e-mail. No response from Thanatos/Hermes to my earlier message. I wondered if he was watching Parkham on TV at that moment. How would he feel about the discovery of Sara's body? A faked hit and run. Why? There was a chance that he'd left some clues: tire prints, skid marks, paint transfers. There could have been a witness. Had Sara screamed? Or was she too drugged up to do anything? She was probably unconscious. But the sound of a car impacting a body could draw attention by itself. I thought of sending the bastard e-mail, telling him exactly what I thought of him, but Max talked me out of it.

"He'd just gloat, Carroll. Don't give him the satisfaction," Max said.

Darlene came in and handed me some papers.

"This was faxed to you by Mrs. Rosenberry," she said, making a clicking sound with her tongue when she saw the vodka bottle.

It was the list of the guests who had attended Gineen's party the night her necklace was stolen. I gave it a cursory glance. Two names jumped out at me: Max Maslin and Rawley Croften.

"I didn't see you at Gineen's party, Max."

"I made a brief appearance—had a drink and got out of there as quick as I could. Those parties aren't my cup of tea, old friend."

"Did you see Rawley Croften there?"

Max closed his eyes and massaged his temples. "I did see Croften. Briefly. As soon as he spotted me, he took off. He still thinks I was responsible for him getting the boot."

"Interesting, Croften being at the party. He certainly knew Charlie Reeder and Montgomery Hines, and he was at Hines's wake."

"Are you telling me that Croften could be Thanatos?"

"Why not? He's as big a movie buff as anyone, he'd know all of those Hitchcock flicks better than the two of us. And he's got a grudge against the *Bulletin*."

Max took out his pipe and clamped it between his teeth. "I don't know. I just can't see old Rawley as a killer."

"He was a prescription pill addict—maybe he still is."

"What about Sara? Did he know Sara?"

I frisked my memory, but couldn't come up with anything regarding Croften and Sara.

I found out why Max usually nursed a Cherry Heering. Two shots of vodka and he was half in the bag.

"I really liked Sara," he said mournfully.

I didn't remember seeing Max at her parrot parties. "How well did you know her, Max?"

"Fairly well. That was before you dated her. She used to let me fill up my pipe from Cheech and Chong."

He saw the puzzled look on my face.

"Those were the names she had for her marijuana plants."

A shadow loomed over my shoulder and Max looked up at Katherine Parkham with wide eyes. He reached for the pint bottle, but she beat him to it.

She held it up to the ceiling light fixture and squinted her eyes. "Jesus, this is cheap crap. Let's go up to my office and get a real drink."

I ran Rawley Croften's name past the Great. She had never heard of him, but thought he was worth checking out.

"Did you tell Granger about Croften?"

"No."

"Let me handle it," she said. "Was Carl Dillon working at the *Bulletin* when Croften was here?"

"No," Max said. "Rawley was long gone by then."

"Good. I'll put Dillon on Rawley, we'll see what he can dig up."

She'd better hurry. The way things were going, Dillon would be wearing a badge, a blue uniform, drinking free coffee before we caught up with Thanatos.

It had been another long, hard, tough day. I needed a soft shoulder to cry on. My mother called on the cell phone, upset about the fact that she hadn't been given credit in the paper's story for figuring out that the weapon used on Charlie Reeder was a frozen leg of lamb.

"Mom, I just didn't want the police pestering you."

She didn't buy it, and told me that from now on, "You'll have to solve your own murder cases."

I told her about Sara. I had taken her to Mom's flat once.

"Oh my God. That's awful, Carroll. She was such a sweetie. You must be feeling terrible. Come over and I'll fix you something special."

I said the first thing that came to my mind. "Can't do it, Mom. I'm having dinner with Katherine Parkham."

"I saw her on TV. Her makeup made her look like Tom Hanks in drag."

"I don't think I'll pass that on to her, Mom. Love you. Call you tomorrow."

There are times when you feel like the bottom of that proverbial barrel, and nothing—not food, drink, sleep, or clever conversation—will help you climb out of the damn thing. Times that literally try men's souls. I was thinking of going somewhere where I could be alone and feel sorry for myself when two warm hands cupped my ears.

"Hi," Terry Greco whispered. "Guess what? I'm working on something that may take Thanatos off the front page."

I grasped her hands and pulled them to my chest. "What is it?"

"Suicidal twin kills sister by mistake."

I sat there in confused awe for a moment, then started laughing, and then crying.

"Come on big boy," Terry said, pulling at my arm. "My place, or my place?"

TWENTY-TWO

There were no left-over gourmet meals that night at Terry's. We called out for a pizza and when it came, washed it down with Diet Pepsi—Terry's only apparent concession to weight control—and had cookies scatter-shot with chocolate chips for dessert.

I gave her a highly sanitized version of my trip to Tom Powers's trailer.

We tossed around the names of invitees to Gineen Rosenberry's party.

Terry picked up a cookie, and between bites said that if Powers was telling the truth, then someone on the party list had called him.

"It would have to be someone who knew me, and that Powers was handling the case for the insurance company."

Terry tossed a piece of cookie to me. "Carroll, you're going to have to start reading the *Bulletin*. There was a story on the theft, just three paragraphs on page seventeen, and it mentioned the insurance company and Powers. Gave his phone number, too."

There was only one way the paper would publish an article like that; someone had to call it in. Powers himself no doubt, looking for a little ink.

"I'm surprised Max Maslin didn't tell me about it," I said, padding to the refrigerator and retrieving a beer—Bud Light. God, Terry was on a crash diet.

"Maybe he missed it," she said.

"Max doesn't miss much. Tonight he told me he was friends with Sara, before I was seeing her."

"*Seeing*. Was it more than that? A love affair?"

"More of a *like* affair. We liked each other, but we didn't have much in common; she smoked dope, dabbled with other stuff, I'm strictly a wino; she was into rock and heavy metal, I'm still stuck in jazz and swing. It was, as Mr. Porter said, 'Just One of Those Things.'"

She plucked the beer bottle from my hand, and said, "Mr. Porter who?"

"Cole Porter, for Christ's sake. Who else?"

She ballooned her cheeks, sloshed beer around her mouth, swallowed, and said, "I know, I'm kidding you. Cole Porter, short guy, wrote all those things Sinatra sang, fell off his horse, injured himself, couldn't walk right, and went gay. That Cole Porter."

"Let's hope Katherine the Great never has you doing obituaries, Terry. Did you ever meet Rawley Croften?"

"No. Who is he?"

I gave her Croften's background, including his grudge against Max, me, and the paper, and the fact that he knew at least two of Thanatos's victims.

"Do you think he could be the guy?" she asked.

"I don't know—I can't see him with any real motive, unless he wanted to kill Max or me, but why has he waited this long? He had the hots for my mother—maybe he still does. Mom says my dad scared him off, but that was a long time ago. He looks pretty feeble. The Great is having Carl Dillon check him out."

She picked up the party list and waved it in my face. "How many people on this list knew Montgomery Hines, Charlie Reeder, and Sara?"

"Good question," I said. I only recognized some forty of the ninety-two names—those all being people "in the business": actors, directors, writers. The rest were probably friends or business associates of Gineen's and Jules Moneta. It was impossible to draw any real conclusions from the list. And besides, there are always a handful of crashers at these affairs.

Terry had another idea. "All of this started at the time that Peter Liddell came to town. He probably knew Hines, and—"

"I'm certain he did," I said, remembering the photo of the two of them on Monty's trophy wall.

"And he must have known Charlie Reeder."

"I'm not sure about that," I said. "I don't know that they ever worked together."

"Carroll, all of those Hollywood people know each other—it's an incestuous town, they go to the same restaurants, clubs, whorehouses."

"True; so let's say that Liddell and Charlie were acquaintances, if not friends."

She poured some beer into her empty Pepsi glass and dipped a cookie into it. "I wonder if Sara had ever worked on one of Liddell's projects?"

"It's possible, but there's no way that Liddell could be Thanatos. He just doesn't fit the role of a serial killer."

"I agree. But what about one of his toadies?" She took a bite of her beer-soaked cookie.

"How can you eat that thing?"

"It's pretty good," she said, in between munches. "Your mother would probably like it."

I was saved a response when my cell phone rang. It was Inspector Granger.

"Quint. I've got a guy who wants to talk to you. He claims to be Thanatos."

"Put him on the line," I said, wondering what the gag was.

"No can do. He's out of my reach. By about fifteen feet. He's hanging over the side of the Golden Gate Bridge and says he'll jump if you don't get over here right now."

"Who is it?"

"He won't tell me, Quint. Hear a siren yet? Because I sent a radio car to pick you up."

"If you sent him to my place, it's the wrong place." I gave him Terry's address.

I hadn't ridden in a patrol car since I was a junior in high school. The cops had picked up me and a buddy for fighting with some local roughnecks. The two officers, both sour-faced veterans, had stopped en route to the station house to get some coffee and doughnuts.

My buddy and I sat alone, uncuffed, in the back of the car for some ten minutes before we decided to make a break for it. As we raced up Dolores Street we laughed and talked about how stupid the cops were. The next day another friend wised me up to the fact that it was a standard police procedure—letting young dummies escape so that the cops wouldn't have to haul them in, contact their parents, and then write out reports for an hour or more, which kept them off the streets where they belonged.

"They were drinking coffee and wondering if you were too stupid to run away, Quint," my streetwise friend had informed me.

Terry Greco seemed to be enjoying the ride. She was leaning forward, talking to the young uniformed driver, as we sped past the Marina Green toward the bridge.

I called the *Bulletin*, and spoke to the night editor, Ed Hutcheson, who told me he'd send someone out to the bridge as soon as possible, and in the meantime to wait for a call from Katherine Parkham.

I had done some research on the bridge for a Hollywood producer who wanted to film a scene there. You've seen the Golden Gate in hundreds of commercials, TV shows, and movies. First-time viewers are sometimes disappointed because the bridge isn't really golden, more of an orange vermilion color. One of the more famous film scenes was from Hitchcock's classic *Vertigo*, though the part where Jimmy Stewart dives into the bay to save Kim Novak was pure Hollywood set stuff. A rubber-suited Navy SEAL wouldn't survive the rocks and currents near Old Fort Point under the bridge.

The Golden Gate is the Mecca for the suicide-prone—on average there's a jumper every two weeks, and only a couple of dozen of the three thousand plus jumpers have survived the two hundred twenty–foot plunge to the icy waters.

The driver rode the siren all the way to the visitors' parking lot on the south side of the bridge.

Inspector Granger was there to meet us. He was wearing a dark blue windbreaker with SFPD in white block letters across the chest and a baseball cap. The wind was howling and he had one hand on the top of the cap as we climbed out of the radio car.

I introduced Terry, and Granger said, "You were at the party at the Hilton. Little red dress, right?"

Terry dimpled her cheeks. "Yes, but—"

"Isn't there someone about to jump off the bridge?" I interrupted. "Have you identified him, Granger?"

"No. He's a WMA, late thirties, balding, thick glasses, wearing cords and a UC Berkeley sweatshirt."

"What's a WMA?" Terry asked, as we started following Granger onto the bridge's pedestrian walkway.

"White male adult," Granger said, as we walked around a police barricade. There was a group of a hundred or more spectators craning their necks to get a look at us. Traffic had slowed to a crawl in both directions.

"Ghouls," Granger said. "One jerk was yelling at the guy, 'Jump you chickenshit.'" He grabbed my hand and held my elbow too, so that I couldn't shake free.

"Quint, the man climbed over the four-foot guardrail. He's standing about fifteen feet below, on a thirty-two-inch girder that the bridge people tell me is called the chord. I haven't been able to get a rope on him. He's just sitting there. I'm surprised the wind hasn't pushed him off the damn thing."

"And he told you he was Thanatos?"

"That he did. He's been spouting off about Hitchcock movies, says the leg of lamb thing was brilliant, that 'you stupid cops would never have figured it out, if it wasn't for Quint.' He's a big fan of yours, and says he's sent you e-mails telling you that he's Thanatos, but you won't believe him."

"Do you, Inspector?"

"Not enough to climb over the railing and go down and talk to him about it. The firemen will put a safety harness on you." He turned his attention back to Terry. "You look chilly, little lady, take my windbreaker."

As Granger struggled out of his jacket a husky fireman came over and slipped a black webbed Velcro-strap safety harness around my thighs and stomach.

"Ever worn one of these?" he asked casually.

"No. Are they safe?"

"Oh, yeah." He snapped the clip from a piece of nylon rope onto one of the loops in the harness, and added, "Especially if you're on the end holding the rope. Good luck, sir."

My cell phone rang. It was Parkham. I explained my predicament.

"Goddamn it, we haven't got a camera out there. I want pictures of you going over the side and talking to this man. What do we know of him?"

"He's white, bald, wears glasses."

"Wonderful. Is there any way you can stall things 'til I get a crew out there?"

"I'd like to stall it forever," I said. "Climbing over the bridge railing isn't in my job description."

Terry came over and I cupped the receiver and told her, "It's Parkham. She's mad because we haven't got a camera crew with us."

Terry rooted around in her purse and pulled out her cell phone in triumph. "But we do. Two megapixels, I can take all she needs."

Granger was waving an arm at me. "Katherine, Terry Greco is with me. She has a camera on her cell phone."

"Who is she?"

"She does our restaurant reviews, and—"

"Right. I know her now. Let me talk to her."

I handed Terry my phone and hustled over to Granger. The wind had picked up. I approached the railing cautiously. The nighttime view was breathtaking: Angel Island, Alcatraz, the Bay Bridge, and the skyline of San Francisco. It must have been the reason nearly all of the jumpers took off from the east side of the bridge; the west side looked out to nothing but the vast Pacific Ocean. I could make out the running lights of ships heading out to sea.

"Are you ready?" Granger shouted over the wind.

"No. I'm never going to be ready for this."

Terry ran over and gave me a kiss, then stood back and began snapping pictures.

The fireman I'd spoken to earlier gave the rope a little tug and said, "Don't worry. There's no way we can lose you."

I saw that the rope stretched out to a winch on the front end of a fire engine.

"Maybe one of the firemen should come with me," I said to Granger.

He shook his head, then jabbed a hand downward over the railing. "He says it's you and you alone, Quint. The price of fame, I guess. Come on, get going, or the guy is either going to freeze to death or slip and fall."

I placed my hands on the railing. The metal was wet, cold, and slick. I wondered briefly if there was a patron saint for newsmen, then started to climb over the railing. Granger held onto my shoulder and the firemen called out encouragements.

I stood on the outside of the railing, nothing but air between me and what was below. I crouched down and got my first look at the man. He was sitting with his legs dangling over the edge of the beam of metal Granger had called the chord. He turned his head to the right, saw me, and smiled.

I clasped the bottom of the railing, clinging to the rope as I was slowly lowered to the chord. When my feet made contact with solid metal, I stood there for a moment. Later I described that moment as "getting my bearings." What really happened was that I was frozen with fear. What the hell was I doing there?

The rope went taut, then loosened again, and I edged my way closer to the man. He pretty much fit Granger's description: balding, glasses, harmless-looking, really.

"How's it going?" I asked in a croaking voice I didn't recognize.

"Not bad," he said. He twisted his buttocks on the cold metal, trying to get comfortable. Put a fishing pole in his hand and he could have been on the cover of *Field & Stream* magazine.

I looked up and saw Terry hanging over the railing, her phone camera clasped between both hands, Granger leaning over her shoulder.

I edged closer, until I was within a couple of feet of him. He slapped his hand on the chord, inviting me to join him.

I made the mistake of looking down just as a freighter steamed under the bridge. My legs turned to jelly and my feet slipped out from under me. I dangled in midair for what must have been a few seconds but felt as long as a Kevin Costner movie.

The rope was yanked back and I landed awkwardly on the chord, scraping a knee in the process.

"You okay?" the man asked. His voice sounded vaguely familiar.

"Oh, yeah. Just great. Tell me, Thanatos, why are you doing this?"

"Doing what? Killing people or sitting on the bridge?"

I groaned loudly into the wind. His voice was squeaky, like the wacko who had e-mailed me and left his phone number.

"Let me make a wild guess. You work for Tower Records, don't you?"

"Video manager. Twelve years in September. The Web is killing us. I wish Amazon.com was never invented."

"We all have our crosses to bear." I stretched an arm out to him. "Why don't we go somewhere warm, where we can talk, and I can take your picture and tell the American public all about you?"

He inched his butt a few inches away. "You're just saying that so I won't jump."

"I'm just saying that because I'm freezing, I think I broke my leg, and I suddenly have to go to the bathroom."

He laughed. Giggled really, then put a hand on his trousers and opened and closed his zipper.

"I had the same problem, but I let it go." He tilted his head down to the bay waters. "I wonder if I hit a boat?"

"What's your name?" I said. "When you're not being Thanatos?"

"Bill. Bill Cosby, like the old comedian, though we're not related."

"I kind of figured that out." I gave the rope a sharp yank and was pulled to my feet. "Come on, Bill. Let's get out of here. There are all kinds of TV cameras up there waiting to get a look at you." I reached out a shaking hand in his direction.

He responded by leaning back, swinging his legs over the chord, and jumping to his feet, all in one graceful movement.

"I'm not afraid of heights, Carroll," he told me. "Hang on to my arm if you're nervous."

I was. I did. And I barely resisted the urge to drop to my knees and kiss the ground once we were both safely on the other side of the railing.

We drove back to Terry's place and I dove into a bath and then a bottle of Chianti. Granger stopped by to take a brief statement and inform us that William Cosby was a certified nut. I was dozing and mumbling by the time he left.

TWENTY-THREE

Sam Mercer, of Argonaut Investigations, the security expert Carl Dillon had recommended, arrived at my apartment late the following morning. I had the place pretty well put back together: clothes in drawers and closets, posters on wall, dishes in place.

Mercer was a short, thickset black man with a shaved head and a rough, sandy voice.

He scanned my apartment and said, "I hear someone's bugging you."

"Someone told me he'd put a bug in my telephone."

Mercer tilted his head and frowned. "He told you?"

"Under duress."

"Yeah. I bet." Mercer took a palm-size electronic device from his briefcase. There were four little red bulbs and a small antenna on one end. "Let's see if your man under duress was telling the truth. This baby will pick up analog, digital phone taps, room bugs, concealed camera videos, any kind of radio frequency transmissions."

He pointed the device toward the phone and one of the red bulbs went on.

"We've got a bingo, Mr. Quint." He set the device down and took a screwdriver from the briefcase and began dismantling the phone.

"Phones are great—they have microphones, speakers, transducers, and plenty of power that can provide an eavesdropper with everything he needs to listen in on you." He upended the guts of the phone and smiled. "Here it is. A dual-capacitor you can pick up at RadioShack. All you have to do is know which wire to strip, install this sucker, and you're in business. It records both sides of a phone conversation, and anything that's said in the room within twenty or thirty feet of the phone."

"This sucker" was a piece of black plastic with green things the size of a vitamin pill welded to it.

"The man under duress," Mercer said. "Do you know how much time he had to install the bug?"

"Several hours at least. He picked my front door lock. His name is Tom Powers; he's a private investigator. Ever hear of him?"

"No. Did you call the cops?"

"Yes. They weren't interested."

Mercer let out a loud chuckle. "Well, maybe if you show them the bug, they'll change their mind." He looked around the room again, then said, "If it was me bugging you, and I had a few hours, I wouldn't stop with one."

He picked up his detecting gizmo and began waving it around the room. It was silent, until we entered the bedroom.

"He bugged the phone in here, too," Mercer said.

"The son of a bitch told me he'd just bugged the living room phone."

"Maybe you didn't put him under enough duress, Mr. Quint."

Mercer removed the telephone bug then picked up his detector and began canvassing the room. He pointed it toward the ceiling and suddenly it was Christmas—all four of the device's lights started blinking.

Mercer pointed toward the ceiling smoke detector.

"Do you have a ladder?"

"No."

"Strong chair?"

That I had. I stood by, my arms ready to steady Mercer, as he pried the smoke detector's lid free.

"My, my. Your under duress friend was busy. Hand me that bigger screwdriver."

After a minute or two of tinkering, Mercer jumped to the floor. "The man knows what he's doing, I'll give him that. The smoke detector is hardwired, no batteries, so he just installed a camera—the Web sites that sell this stuff like to call them spy cameras."

He handed me something the size of my thumb, with a wire attached to one end.

"See the screw on the end of the flat part there? That's the camera. He drilled a hole in the smoke detector's housing, put the camera on the inside, and replaced the housing in the ceiling. Even if someone was curious enough to give it a good look, all they'd see was the screw." Mercer gave another long chuckle. "Maybe that's why he put the damn thing in there, Mr. Quint. He was hoping to watch you screwing somebody."

"I should have killed the son of a bitch," I said hotly.

"I wouldn't do that," Mercer advised. "At least not 'til you pay my bill, sir. If you have a cell phone, I should check it out."

I went back to the kitchen where the phone sat on its charger. "Are cell phones any safer than regular ones?" I asked Mercer as he waved his magic machine at my cell.

"Worse. The general rule is that if it has an antenna, then it's not secure, period. If someone had the right equipment installed on your cell he could monitor your calls from a couple of miles away." He handed me back my phone. "This baby is clean, right now. Takes about a minute to put a bug in there, so don't leave it lying around out of sight."

"Life is getting to be like a science fiction movie," I said. "A bad science fiction movie."

"You see any good ones lately?" Mercer asked as he headed for the door. At least he didn't tell me to have a good day.

Right then my idea of a good day was driving down to Powers's trailer and ramming his lock pick down his throat. The camera in the ceiling had been a waste of his time. I'd slept at Terry's last night. Phone calls? I couldn't remember any calls I'd made from the apartment phone that had amounted to anything since that party on the *Jewel Box*. Powers probably drove to my place to plant the bugs right after we sailed away from the dock. He knew he'd have a minimum of a few of hours to get his dirty deeds done. The bugs I could understand, since he really believed I'd taken Gineen's necklace, but the camera? Overkill. The pervert had gotten a good look at Terry Greco when he'd followed us from Momo's the other night—that was the reason for the camera.

Terry Greco was all smiles when I arrived at the *Bulletin*. The pictures she'd taken of me and Mr. Cosby had made the front page of the paper. He was smiling and happy. For once, I wasn't smiling. I looked like Dustin Hoffman in that scene in *Marathon Man*, after Lawrence Olivier, playing a former Nazi concentration camp dentist, tortured Dustin with some down and dirty oral surgery. If someone were to put a caption on the picture, the balloon over my head would have said: "I want my mommy!"

There were other pictures, with Cosby and me standing close to each other on the bridge girder, one with Inspector Dave Granger in profile as he snapped a pair of cuffs on Cosby.

"The Great loves me," Terry said. "She thinks I may end up winning a PPA award."

"PPA?"

"Press Photographers Award." She nipped me on my ear with her teeth. "And I owe it all to you, Carroll. You were so goddamn brave, I couldn't believe it, you going over the railing like that."

I couldn't believe it either. A Hemingway quote popped into my mind: *Courage is grace under pressure.* I certainly hadn't felt courageous, graceful, or brave, and wondered what I would have done if the fireman hadn't tied a rope to me, if I had just taken a stroll across the bridge, heard a man yelling for help, looked down, and saw him clinging to that cold steel chord. If Terry or Inspector Granger hadn't been there, would I have climbed over the railing? I remembered another quote about bravery often being mingled with cowardice—men appear to be brave just so they won't look silly in front of their friends.

Brody Carew rapped on Terry's door and gave me the power fist. "Great job, partner. I'm proud of you."

Terry dug a compact from her purse and checked her makeup. "He's certainly in a good mood. Partner?"

"Yes. We're working on a book together. Brody's putting the numbers on the top of the pages, and I'm filling in the words."

"Poor Brody. He's his own worst enemy."

"Not while I'm around. Listen, there's something I have to tell you."

Terry listened with wide eyes when I described the bugs and camera found in my apartment. I had expected her to be angry, really angry, but life is full of surprises.

"Really," she said in an excited whisper. "A camera over your bed. How long has it been there?"

"Since the night of the party on the *Jewel Box*."

She pursed her lips and frowned. "We weren't in your bed after that, were we?"

"No."

She took a tube of lipstick from her purse and brushed her lips with it. "Imagine that, someone filming us, and watching any time he wanted. He'd probably play with himself while he watched. Kinky, huh? This man, the private eye—"

"Powers. Tom Powers."

"Do you think he could have slipped into my place and planted a camera?"

"I don't think so, but I'll check, just to make sure."

Someone made a deep coughing sound and we turned to see the tired face of Inspector Dave Granger.

"You have the right to remain silent, Inspector," I said. "Anything you say will be misquoted then used against you."

"Very funny, Quint. Hi, Terry. Is there somewhere we can talk? A place where three people can sit down together?"

"Sure," Terry said. She led us to the coffee annex.

Granger was looking haggard, in need of a shave and a fresh shirt.

He sat down gingerly in a chair and accepted the cup of coffee Terry handed him.

"Thanks, Terry." He measured sugar, almost to the grain, into his coffee. "I wanted to keep the two of you updated on what's going on. Mr. Cosby is in San Francisco General, the psycho ward, under fifty-one-fifty of the Welfare and Institutions code. I can keep him for seventy-two hours. He's confessing to everything, except shooting Abe Lincoln."

"Poor man," Terry said.

The *poor man* had me dangling from a rope two hundred plus feet over freezing water. I thought that should have been a hanging offense, but I didn't say so.

Granger pulled at the knot of his tie and unbuttoned his shirt collar.

"The lab report on Sara Vasin came in this morning. Traces of her blood were found on the wooden steps leading from her house down to Ord Street."

I pictured the steep steps in my mind. "Just a fall down those steps could have killed her."

Granger circled the spoon in his coffee. "It didn't, though I believe the killer thought so. The back of her head was crushed by the vehicle that hit her, but the ME thinks it's quite possible that she suffered a severe head wound prior to that."

Terry let out a soft moaning sound, then poured me a cup of coffee.

"So what's the scenario?" I asked Granger.

He shifted his weight, took a small white pill from his shirt pocket, put it on the tip of his tongue, and washed it down with coffee.

"This is just my gut feeling," he said. "Vasin knows the perp. He's in the house with her. They have some wine, smoke some dope, then he slips the Rohypnol into her vino. When she passes out he cleans up after himself, making sure he hasn't left any fingerprints, any strands of hair. Then he uses the old reliable blunt instrument."

Granger fixed his eyes on mine. "Not a leg of lamb, or anything from Vasin's freezer—I checked that out. Maybe it was something he brought along for that specific purpose. He whacks her hard, decides she's dead, and then drags her outside. I figure this would have been around midnight. He pushes her down the steps. This is a risk for him, there are neighbors, but it was a foggy night—I checked the weather report.

"He thinks she's dead, he takes off. But Miss Vasin didn't die easily. She's alive, barely. She crawls, looking for help. She makes it to the street, and someone, person unknown, runs over her."

"Couldn't it have been Thanatos?" Terry said. "He saw she was still alive, and hit her with his car."

"That's possible," Granger conceded. "But I'm betting the perp was long gone by then. The driver of the vehicle must have known what he'd done. He probably stopped, saw Vasin's condition, realized that no one had witnessed the accident—and that's what he thought it was, an accident, the woman somehow getting in front of his car."

"It sounds probable to me," I said. "Was there anything in the street? Skidmarks? Parts of the car?"

"There a lot of skidmarks all over that street, the problem is tying the right ones to the incident. There was also a lot of Miss Vasin's blood, but nothing that can lead us to the driver. Have you heard from Thanatos again?"

"No. I checked this morning. Some sixty more screwballs claiming to be Thanatos, but nothing from him."

When Granger started to get to his feet, Terry said, "Aren't you going to tell Dave about the bugs and camera, Carroll?"

I hadn't been planning to, but now the cat was out of the bag. Granger listened patiently, but he didn't take any notes.

"I'll pass the information along to Inspector Wyatt, but right now, if what you tell me is true, it would turn out to be your word against Powers's."

"The man *told* me he planted the bug," I said.

"Yeah, but he'll deny he said it now. And he'll deny the bugs are his. Anyone can be a James Bond today, you can buy the equipment all over the Web. There's even a shop near Fisherman's Wharf that sells the stuff."

Terry inhaled to get Granger's attention, then said, "Isn't there something you can do, Dave? The man could have filmed Carroll and me in bed."

"Terry, I'll do what I can, but I can't promise much."

Terry. Dave. The two of them were on a first name basis since I dangled from a rope below the Golden Gate Bridge.

Granger thanked her for the coffee, told me to keep in touch, then lumbered away to the outside world. He looked like he might drop to the floor from exhaustion before he made it to the elevator.

"Poor Dave," Terry said. "I bet he didn't get any sleep last night."

"You'd probably win that bet. Tell me, did Granger make a move on you?"

"Certainly he did," she said in a tone a teacher might use after a school kid asked a very dumb question. "And he seemed surprised when I told him that I wasn't available at the moment, that you and I had a sort of arrangement."

"Sort of?"

"For the moment," she said sweetly. "The trick is to find out how long the moment lasts."

TWENTY-FOUR

Things calmed down for a day—no e-mails from Thanatos/ Hermes, no breaks into the investigations of the deaths of Hines, Reeder, or Sara Vasin—at least none that the police were letting the public, or the press, know about.

I'd driven down to Tom Powers's trailer, vengeance in mind. His car was gone. I knocked on the door—it had been hastily repaired. No response, and I didn't want to push my luck by breaking in again.

Duke, the park manager, seemed to take a keen interest in my car, blowing smoke and spilling beer on the MINI's hood as he asked me about miles per gallon and if I'd ever "done the back scuttle" in the front seat.

I had no idea what he meant, until he started explaining that "the little darlin' would have to have at least one of her legs stuck out the window when you was doin' the nasty."

I was back in my mother's good graces, thanks to my involvement in the Golden Gate Bridge rescue. Being in her good graces unfortunately meant going to her place for dinner.

I dragged Terry along, and made a pitcher of martinis while Mom showed Terry her scrapbooks. I put three olives in my drink, because they were probably going to be the best food available all night.

The *Casablanca* jigsaw puzzle Mom had been working on with Bogart, Bergman, Rains, and Henreid was coming along nicely.

When the ladies came in to get their drinks, I asked Mom about my father.

"He should be back any day, dear—suntanned, wind blown," she batted her eyelashes innocently at Terry and added, "sexually sated for the moment. I spoke to Gineen the . . ." she almost said "slut," but out of courtesy to Terry's tender ears, simply said, "Rosenberry. She's put together a memorial for Charlie Reeder at the officers' club on Treasure Island. I helped her with the attendee list. Tomorrow night, Carroll. Six o'clock. I expect you'll be picking me up around five."

I felt guilty for not getting back to Gineen regarding Charlie's affair. Quite truthfully, it had slipped my mind.

Mom picked up a puzzle piece and squeezed it into Bogart's arm. It wasn't the right piece, and it didn't quite fit, but she got it in there.

Suddenly she said, "You know, Carroll, this murderer . . ."

"Thanatos," Terry said.

"He's just like the midgets in *Casablanca*, isn't he?"

I was used to my mother's goofy statements, but Terry was really confused.

"Midgets? *Casablanca*? The movie?" she asked.

Mom took a healthy—or, if you're anti-booze—unhealthy swig of her martini, and said, "Yes, dear. Exactly."

Terry dove into her drink and looked at me for support.

"In the scene at the end," I said. "Where Bogart tells Ingrid Bergman and Paul Henreid to get on the plane for Lisbon, you can see the airplane in the background. Special effects weren't very special back then—it was just a plywood cutout, about half the size of a real plane; so, to make it look the right size, the director, Michael Curtiz, hired a few midgets and had them walk around looking like they were working on the plane."

Terry held out her glass for a refill and said, "Fascinating. But what has that to do with Thanatos?"

Mom whisked herself into an apron before answering. "He's there, Terry. Right in plain sight, but we're not seeing him. Time for one more drink before dinner."

If Mom was right, what was I missing? A famous line from *Casablanca* came to me: "Round up the usual suspects." Who were the usual suspects in this mess? I had no clue. I was like a blind man in a dark room looking for a black cat that wasn't there.

"What are we having, Mrs. Quint?" Terry had the guts to ask.

"Tomatoes fresh from my garden, soymilk-garlic pasta, and tofu flan for dessert."

Terry and I nearly got into a knife fight for the last of the tomatoes.

We drove back to my place and used copious amounts of cheap red wine to flush the soymilk and tofu from our systems.

Inspector Dave Granger stopped by to update me on his investigation of Sara Vasin's death. "I interviewed her ex-husband, Peter Dkany. He's an excitable guy. Owns a Hummer, which is big enough to have been the vehicle that ran over Vasin. The lab went over it, but didn't come up with anything. It had been given a steam cleaning recently. Dkany claims he cleaned it up after an off-road trip around Lake Tahoe."

Granger put a dent in my bourbon supply and seemed reluctant to leave. Maybe he was hoping that I'd doze off and leave him alone with Terry. I started yawning loudly and he finally got the message and took off.

"I thought he'd never leave," I said, heading for the bedroom.

"He's kind of cute," Terry said.

I could have thought of a lot of words to describe Granger. Cute was nowhere on the list.

The buzz at work the next morning was about Peter Liddell claiming to have found another threatening letter from Thanatos, this one allegedly slipped under the door of his suite at the Fairmont Hotel. Liddell must have had a falling out with Brody Carew, because he went straight to a television station with the story.

Katherine the Great was getting edgy, calling me every few hours, asking about new e-mails. There were dozens from the usual wannabes, which I forwarded to Detective McCall. Regular old-fashioned snail-mail from the post office had been arriving daily; many of them composed with letters cut out from magazines, like the ones Liddell was sending himself. They were opened with gloved hands by Darlene, copied, then delivered to Dave Granger and McCall.

Just before quitting time, an e-mail arrived under the hermes@ freemailer.com address:

NICE JOB—WOULD YOU HAVE CLIMBED OVER THE RAILING TO SAVE ME?

I fired back a quick answer:

PLEASE GIVE ME THE CHANCE.

There are some perks that go along with that fifteen minutes of fame because your picture was plastered all over the local newspaper: friends you haven't spoken to in years call, the people you deal with every day—fellow workers, waiters, parking lot attendants—give you a smile, as if you'd just done something cool. The fifteen minutes pass very quickly, and you're back to being just some guy in the crowd.

Then there's the downside: people who didn't know your name from Adam suddenly know too much about you, which is how I landed in jail.

En route to Charlie Reeder's memorial service on Treasure Island, Terry Greco and my mother were engaged in a fascinating—to them—conversation about which movie stars had boob jobs and which were blessed by nature. Among those who had "store boughts" according to Mom were Jane Fonda—"Too little too late," opined Terry—Halle Berry (say it isn't so), Jessica Simpson, and Hilary Swank, which I didn't believe.

Terry, one of God's truly blessed creatures, was fascinated by Mom's story regarding Melanie Griffith. Supposedly Melanie had taken off two weeks during the filming of *The Bonfire of the Vanities*, a movie so bad that the star, Tom Hanks, had allegedly walked up to the author, Tom

Wolfe, in a restaurant, and apologized for the whole thing. "Griffith used her vacation time to enlarge her breast size by about two full sizes, which required reshooting all of her earlier scenes."

When the conversation switched to Hollywood face-lifts, I upped the radio volume and listened to the Giants getting blasted by the New York Mets.

I took the Treasure Island off-ramp, and spiraled down to the former site of the 1939–1940 World's Fair. Treasure Island is the world's largest man-made island—roughly a mile long and half a mile wide—and was built specifically for the fair. It butted up to the natural Yerba Buena Island, which forms a sort of midspan anchor for the Bay Bridge.

After the World's Fair, Treasure Island was converted into a naval base. It's a truly beautiful, somewhat neglected spot, and provides the best view of San Francisco's waterfront. While Yerba Buena, once known as Goat Island, is hilly, Treasure Island is perfectly flat. The Navy has moved out, and their former housing quarters are being used as rental units. The island has its own fire station, a police station, a large art deco administration building that dates back to the fair, and a sea harbor that once was the take-off spot for the famed Pan Am China Clipper ships, which, before the war, flew all the way to Pearl Harbor, a twenty-hour flight. That was back in the days when flying was an adventure—sleeping quarters, fine dining, pleasant flight attendants. The passengers wore suits and dresses for dinner. Now, of course, they squeeze hundreds of us, after traversing airport security searches, into those sardine cans with wings, toss us food that makes my mother's cooking look good, and the overworked, underpaid flight attendants frown when you order a double gin, because liquor only aggravates those passengers who are pissed because they can't use their cell phones, or their laptop battery died, or they're tired of waiting to get to the restroom.

Even first class has succumbed to the great unwashed. Thanks to the *Bulletin*'s travel editor, I'd been bumped up to first class for my last flight to New York City. Spacious seats, good food, plenty of booze, but my seat neighbor was a three-hundred-pound foul-mouth with a pirate's beard who was wearing soiled sweats and sockless flip-flops, and who was badly in need of a bath. And you wonder why United dropped the "friendly skies" commercials.

"We're going to the Charlie Reeder memorial," I told the bored security guard leaning against a fence post.

"The officers' club is straight ahead," he told me.

He was right. I parked the MINI among a cluster of BMWs, Jaguars, and SUVs.

A three-piece band was playing tunes that would have made Duke, the trailer park manager, tap his foot in glee. The dance floor was empty, but the bar was three-deep with Reeder's friends. I could picture Charlie sitting on a cloud, looking down, chuckling over the fact that his boozing buddies were ordering nothing but the best—Chivas Regal Scotch, Grey Goose vodka, Boodles gin, Wild Turkey bourbon—rather than the rotgut they normally quaffed. Not in tribute to Charlie, but because Gineen Rosenberry was picking up the tab.

Terry and Mom went off in search of the ladies' room, giving me time to find Gineen. She was sitting at a banquet table, deep in discussion with a handsome middle-aged man in a gray suit. The next husband for the Satin Widow?

I was about to say hello to her when Jules Moneta came by carrying two fluted champagne glasses. He pressed one of them into my hand and said, "Follow me."

He was wearing an immaculate cream-colored linen suit that I would have had wine-coffee-mustard-stained after the first wearing.

He led me to an oversize golf cart and said, "Hop on. You've got to see this, Carroll. It's absolutely fabulous."

He took me on a quick tour—the first stop, the yacht club. He curbed the cart and pointed to a black-and-white powerboat.

"That's mine," he said. "The *Sea Queen*, and don't try to make anything of it, the name was on the boat when I leased it. Fifty-five feet—a dinghy compared to Gineen's boyfriend's Titanic."

Jules started the cart again. "You know, Carroll, there's something about a good-size boat—it's so much better than a stuffy office. I use it for my business meetings. You take a producer or banker out under the bridge, give him a chance to catch a salmon, or a big shark, and he's much more agreeable when you hand him that contract to sign." He gave me one of his winks. "Besides, it's not like they can get up and leave anytime they want. It's good to be the captain."

We traveled just a few blocks, to one of the island's two massive old airplane hangars. Along the way I asked Jules about Rawley Croften. "I ran into him at Hines's wake. Have you seen him lately?"

"Have I ever. The man's been an absolute pest for months. He's written a screenplay—one of those slasher things where everyone gets hacked to death."

"Did you read it?"

"Skimmed through it," Jules said. "It really wasn't bad. The hero, of course, is a tough, wise-cracking veteran newsman who solves the murders."

"Jesus, Jules. Doesn't this ring a bell with you? The Thanatos murders?"

"No, no. The plot is set in Seattle, and victims are Microsoft employees. To my surprise there was some Hollywood interest. We had lunch together, Rawley, a Universal producer, and myself. There were concerns of course—Universal didn't like the demographics, the main character was much too old. Nobody goes to the movies to see old people anymore. They want the hero to be a stud in his twenties. Rawley didn't much like that at first. His bark is worse than his bite—literally. He embarrassed the hell out of me—lunch at Aquas, and he slips his upper teeth out during the meal! Thought no one would notice it. Didn't seem to stop him from munching his food, though."

"Is the deal dead?" I asked.

"No—just in Hollywood limbo, and you know how that is. Ah, here we are. Really something, isn't she?" Jules said, twisting his neck upward and screwing his eyes into slits. "Eighty feet high, three hundred thirty-five feet long. The walls are two feet thick, solid concrete."

"Very nice, Jules. But I'm happy with my apartment at the moment."

He rooted in his pocket, came out with a key ring, and opened a regular-size door situated near the building's huge sliding hangar doors. "You could have a war start outside and you wouldn't hear a thing inside this baby."

We entered the "baby." Jules flicked on the lights. There were balloons and colorful strings of Chinese lanterns hanging from the ceiling, a large red-white-and-blue banner with G. R. PRODUCTIONS in front of a bandstand, and tables set up for Jules's upcoming party.

"I can build them anything they need here," Jules said, his gleaming burgundy wingtips making clicking sounds on the concrete flooring. "They need a Chinatown set, a police station, a waterfront scene, a western storefront; anything they can build in Hollywood, I can duplicate right here." He draped an arm around my shoulder. "I've rented out the other hangar to some bible thumpers who are making religious documentaries, but they only have a three month lease."

Jules finished up the champagne in his glass, then threw it against the wall. For a moment I thought he was going to yell *mazel tov*.

"This is it, Carroll, the beginning of Hollywood North. We're going to make a fortune, a bloody fortune, and show those pompous young bastards running the studios in Southern California a thing or two."

"I wish you well, Jules," I said sincerely.

He gave me the arm around the shoulder routine again. "Carroll, a nice story in the paper wouldn't hurt, you know."

"You're right. Unfortunately, I'm temporarily assigned to this murder thing."

Jules waved me to the door. After he locked up after us, he said, "Are you keeping notes on the investigation? It could make for a hell of a movie—maybe not the big screen, but a TV movie of the week. I know some people who would be interested, and we would film it right here, Carroll."

"First we have to catch the bastard," I said, as we drove back to Charlie Reeder's memorial service.

"The police must have some idea of who this creature is," Jules said. "They can't be complete fools."

"Don't be too sure of that. So far they've come up with zip."

"Incredible," Jules said. "Why kill two old duffers like Monty and Charlie?"

"Sara Vasin was no duffer, Jules. She was young, vibrant, beautiful."

"I didn't know her that well. She was the one who gave the parrot parties, right? An actress?"

"She was a makeup artist," I told him. "One of the best."

"Well, I still say the police are bumbling fools. Complete incompetents."

When we arrived back at the officer's club, Detective McCall was there, slouched against the fender of his unmarked car. His arms were folded across his chest. When he spotted me he snapped to attention and marched over in our direction.

"There's one of the bumbling fools," I told Jules.

A wide smile broke out on McCall's face as he pulled a pair of handcuffs from his belt. "Carroll Quint, I'm placing you under arrest. You have the right to—"

Jules used his best general-talking-to-the-troops voice. "What's going on here? Is this man some kind of an actor, if so I—"

"Shut up," McCall shouted. "If you want to be arrested for interfering, I'll be happy to accommodate you."

McCall wheeled me around and snapped the cuffs on.

"Just why are you doing this?" I said.

"You're under arrest for the murder of Thomas J. Powers."

"Who the devil is Thomas Powers?" Jules asked.

The cuffs were painful as hell. "Listen McCall. This is ridiculous. Can you take these off so we can go somewhere and talk about this?"

"Oh, we're going somewhere to talk. The San Mateo County jail."

"My mother and girlfriend are inside. I drove them. Can I at least give them my car keys?"

"I'll get them," Jules volunteered, wriggling his hand into my pocket. He seemed to take a long time in finding the keys.

"Call Katherine Parkham and tell her what happened," I yelled to Jules as McCall dragged me to his car. "And have her get me a real attorney. Not Mark Selden."

I tried to find a comfortable position in the backseat of the police car while handcuffed. It's not possible. Detective McCall was playing the strong silent type. Almost every question I asked, including where, when, and how Powers was murdered, was answered with, "Wait until I have you booked and charged, then we'll talk."

"Just tell me this. Why do you think I had something to do with Powers's death?"

"I have a witness," McCall said as we pulled into the garage of the San Mateo County Hall of Justice.

"Witness? Who? He or she is crazy. What's the witness's name?"

"Oliver Moriarity."

"Who? I never heard of the man."

McCall parked the car, then turned around to look at me. "His friends call him Duke."

TWENTY-FIVE

The handcuffs were removed by a female sheriff's deputy with carrot red hair and chipmunk cheeks. She wiped my palms clean with cotton swabs, my fingerprints were taken, then I was propped up in front of a stage and they took my mug shot.

I was strip-searched—a truly humiliating experience—given a pair of orange coveralls to wear, then McCall escorted me to a cell and remained mum while I yelled about my right to a phone call and to see an attorney.

"Sleep tight," he said just before slamming the cell door shut. The clanging noise rang in my ears as I surveyed my surroundings. The room was six feet by nine feet—a fact I learned by pacing it off dozens of times. There was one bed, one toilet, and one sink.

I washed my face, then sat down on the narrow, steel bolted-to-the-wall bed. The stained and spotted mattress was a couple of inches thick. One sheet—clean, one blanket—pretty clean, no pillow. And no window—the cell door was a solid sheet of metal with a peephole, which opened up only from the other side.

I'd hoped for a cell with bars running from floor to ceiling so I could run a tin cup across the bars and scream, "Let me out of here, you cheap screws!" the way those prisoners did in the old Warner Brothers movies.

They'd taken my watch, so I had no idea of the time, but figured it had to be somewhere around ten or eleven at night.

The peephole slid open and a pudgy sunburned face stared at me for several moments before saying, "Did you have your dinner?"

I know those Warner Brothers actors would have told the guard just what he could do with dinner, but I just said, "No, sir. And I'm starving."

The guard came back after a few minutes. He was a pleasant guy in his thirties with bushy blond eyebrows that turned up at the ends.

"Might not be too warm," he said, handing me a plastic tray that held a plastic cup, plastic knife, fork, and spoon, and a plastic plate filled with some kind of red meat and brown gravy. A smaller plate featured a piece of chocolate cake.

"Meatloaf," the guard said. He gave the room a quick scan. "You probably won't be here long. I hear they're going to move you to our celebrity cell. Scott Peterson spent a lot of time there. It's nice—there are bars and you can see the TV in the hallway."

The trial of Peterson, successfully prosecuted for killing his lovely young wife, Laci, had taken up a lot of newspaper ink and TV time in the fall of 2004.

"Peterson's over on death row in San Quentin now," the guard informed me. "He'll probably die of old age right in his cell."

"When can I call my attorney?" I said, poking at the meat with the fork.

"That's not up to me. You'll have to talk to the detective handling the case."

"He won't talk to me," I complained. "He won't listen to anything I say."

The guard shrugged his shoulders, then pulled a folded up newspaper from his back pocket and dropped it on the bed. "If your attorney shows up, I'll bring him to you. Here's something to read while you're waiting."

It was an old copy of the *Bulletin*, the one with my picture on the front page.

I was asleep when the door clanged open again. The same guard stood there with a man I'd never seen before. He was in his forties, with sparse hair brushed forward in the style of a Roman emperor. He wore a dark suit, white shirt, vest, but no tie, and looked as if he'd dressed in a hurry. In his hand was a thick black leather briefcase.

"I'm Ronald Moyer. Gineen Rosenberry and Jules Moneta asked me to stop by and see you."

"You're an attorney?"

"Of course I am," he said in a low, breathy voice.

"Fifteen minutes," the guard informed us. "I'll be right outside if you need me, Mr. Moyer."

Why the hell would Moyer need the guard? He was there to save my butt.

"I'm innocent," I told him. "Get me out of here."

Moyer placed his heavy briefcase on the bunk and surveyed the cell. "Tiny, isn't it? I've never been inside one before." His shoulders shuddered. "I suffer from claustrophobia, so let's make this brief. I'm not a criminal attorney, however, I will contact someone to help you first thing in the morning."

"How about first thing right now? I'm a little claustrophobic myself."

"I'm afraid there's nothing we can do 'til the morning, Mr. Quint. If, as you say, you're innocent, there shouldn't be a problem."

"There's a major problem. I'm here in this goddamn cell! Bail me out. Do something for Christ's sake."

His vest had a chain that stretched from pocket to pocket. He pulled out a fat gold watch and gave me a sad smile. "I wish I could, but bail would have to be set by a judge. And that won't be possible until tomorrow afternoon at the earliest, from my understanding."

"Why did you bother to come down and see me, Mr. Moyer?"

He picked up his case and banged on the cell door. "As a favor to Jules and Ms. Rosenberry. I hope I was of some help. Keep the faith. I'm sure all of this will be cleared up in the morning."

"What's the name of the criminal attorney who will be handling my case?"

He seemed surprised by the question. "I'm not certain at the moment, but I'll find you someone proficient in these matters."

I grabbed him by the shoulder and he flinched. "Tell me, Moyer, just what is your area of legal expertise?"

"Civil litigation." He extracted a business card from a vest pocket and handed it to me. "Any time I can be of service, don't hesitate to call."

"I'm calling right now. Get me a criminal attorney who knows his ass from a hole in the ground!"

"There's no need to become angry," he said in a professional tone.

The guard opened the cell door just in time to prevent me from being charged with assaulting an attorney.

I spent the night tossing, turning, dozing off, and listening to my fellow prisoners flush their toilets and let out an occasional scream. I thought about Rawley Croften—his movie script; I had to get a copy of it and see if there were any ties-ins to the Thanatos murders. Mostly I tried to anticipate the questions McCall would ask. What had that old codger Duke told him? What did Duke know? If I admitted breaking into Powers's trailer, McCall would throw a burglary charge at me. Burglary didn't compare to homicide, but in my own naïve way I felt that I could never actually be charged for killing Powers—simply because I hadn't. The breaking and entering: I'd used the tire iron from the MINI on the door and on Powers's shoulder. Could the police match the marks on the door to the tire iron?

When the peephole slid open again Detective Bruce McCall's nose came into view.

I sat up and was looking at the newspaper when the door opened.

"Ready to give us a statement, Quint?"

"Sure. Can I borrow a pen or pencil first?"

He squinted at me for a moment before responding. "Why?"

I waved the paper at him. "To circle real estate ads. I'm going to buy a house or condo with the money I get from suing you for false arrest."

He just grunted and slammed the cell door shut.

Another guard opened the door almost immediately, with a breakfast tray. Scrambled eggs, cottage fries, toast, and coffee.

McCall returned when I was mopping up the last of the eggs.

"Let's go, Quint. I want to finish up with you early. Try anything stupid and I'll put the cuffs on again. Real tight."

I followed him down a row of cells, the doors all shut—the occupants unseen, unknown, and probably just as frightened as I was.

We took an elevator down to the third floor. McCall kept his right hand resting on the butt of his revolver, as if daring me to make a break for it.

He put me in a room with an oak table surrounded by six folding chairs. No windows, but a large rectangular mirror on one wall, that I assumed was a two-way mirror. I imagined hard-faced district attorneys on the other side watching my every move.

At least there was a clock. It ticked away in loud Big Ben tones. Seven-forty-six. It was more than twelve hours since McCall had first snapped those cuffs on me.

At nine minutes past eight the door opened and McCall and Inspector Dave Granger trooped into the room. They looked like two cats getting ready to play with a mouse. Granger had a steaming cup of coffee in hand.

"How are they treating you, tough guy?" Granger asked, as he pulled out a chair and sat down.

"The food is better than my mother's," I said truthfully.

McCall said, "Cut out the jokes, Quint. You're in a lot of trouble."

"So you tell me, Detective. I'd like the specifics of why I'm under arrest."

"After you've answered my questions," McCall said.

I was tired, my stomach felt like a cement mixer, and I was scared out of my wits, but I was also getting damn annoyed with McCall.

"Detective. Did you ever read much of Mark Twain?"

"What the hell has that got to do with anything?" he wanted to know.

"Twain once said 'never get in an argument with someone who buys ink by the barrel.' The people at the *Bulletin* aren't going to stand by while one of their reporters is mistreated by the police."

McCall waved my complaint away. "My captain has spoken to Parkham. And you've seen your attorney, so now all you have to do is answer a few of my questions."

Granger slid his coffee cup over to me. "Listen to the questions, Quint. You don't have to answer, but hear the man out."

"I'll handle this interrogation," McCall said hotly. "You're here only as a courtesy, Granger."

"I've got two homicides in my city, McCall. You've got two in San Mateo County, and you tell me that Quint is guilty of all four, so ask away, I'm all ears."

McCall flicked on a tape recorder and gave the date, time, and my name.

"I have reason to believe that you are responsible for the death of private detective Thomas J. Powers, Mr. Quint."

"That's ridiculous. I haven't killed anyone."

McCall took a notebook from his jacket pocket, reviewed some notes, and then said, "Do you deny that you visited Mr. Powers's trailer on the afternoon of August the nineteenth—this past Wednesday?"

"I was there."

"And you were there two days prior, on Monday?"

"Yes. I was, but—"

"And on both occasions you spoke to Mr. Oliver Moriarity, the manager?"

"I spoke to an old guy named Duke."

"And you told him your name was Joe, right? Why did you give him a phony name?"

"I didn't." My first lie. "Duke is elderly, hard of hearing, was drinking, smoking, and had a portable radio around his neck going full blast. He must have misheard me."

"You told him that you were a private investigator," McCall read from his notes, "and that Powers had told you where the spare key for his trailer was."

"Incorrect." Another lie. It was time to shut up until I spoke to a criminal attorney.

McCall sucked in his lips so they virtually disappeared. When he finally spoke, saliva flew from his lips. "Mr. Moriarity may be elderly, but there's nothing wrong with his memory. He was sharp enough to identify you from the picture in your newspaper. He'll make an excellent witness. You broke into Powers's trailer, didn't you?"

"No." Third and absolutely final lie.

"The door to his trailer was forced open."

"So was the door to my apartment, Detective."

"Why did you go to see Powers?" Granger asked, drawing a scowl from McCall.

"I believed he was the person who picked the lock to my apartment. I confronted him, he admitted he had. He also admitted putting a bug on my telephone. I hired a professional security expert to find the bug. There was also a bug in my bedroom phone, and a camera in the smoke detector in my bedroom."

McCall dropped his notebook and ground his hands together. "That must have made you mad, Quint. Mad enough to kill him?"

I took a sip of the coffee Granger had given me before responding. "Powers was alive when I left him on my first visit, and on Wednesday he wasn't there, neither was his car. I spoke to Duke that day."

"Oh yes, you certainly did, Quint. He remembers the visit, remembers your car, he even remembers it doesn't have a license plate. You admit you were inside Powers's trailer."

"Yes. Once. Like I've already said, he was alive and well when I left."

McCall leaned back and smiled. "Tell me, how did you get Mr. Powers to admit that he planted a bug in your place? Did you beat the information out of him?"

"He's bigger and looks stronger than I am, Detective. I threatened to have his license suspended, and he told me about the bug."

"What was the reason for your second visit?"

"Powers had lied to me. There was more than one bug in my apartment."

McCall pulled at his little finger until the joint popped. "We found your fingerprints all over Powers's trailer."

"I told you I was there."

He popped another joint and gave me a slippery smile. "We also found your prints in his car, Quint. How do you explain that?"

I told him the truth, how I'd spotted Powers following me, and had confronted him in his car.

McCall popped the joint on his middle finger. "You tell us you found Charlie Reeder's body, and that you'd been to his house several times before that." He nodded toward Granger. "The Inspector informs me that you also found the body of a former girlfriend, Sara Vasin, and that your prints were found on her furniture. What about the other victim of this so-called Thanatos—Montgomery Hines? Were you ever at his place?"

Granger said, "I've checked Hines's place thoroughly—there's no evidence of Quint ever being there." He reached over and dragged his coffee cup back to his side of the table. "Listen, McCall, this is all very interesting and by the book, but let's get to the nitty-gritty. How was Powers murdered, and when was he murdered?"

McCall closed his eyes, rubbed them, and took a long time in answering. "Powers was shot to death, with a pistol. One that has a silencer attached to it, and that also has Mr. Quint's fingerprints on the clip."

"I can explain that," I said quickly. Even though I was telling the truth, I could feel the sweat popping out on my forehead. "When I got to Powers's place, the door was open. I went inside. I saw the gun. It didn't have a silencer, but there were marks on the barrel that looked suspicious. One of the books on Powers's shelf was about how to make silencers, so I emptied the damn thing, just took out the clip and popped the bullets out."

McCall reached in his pocket, took out a small piece of paper, and slapped it on the table like a blackjack dealer upturning an ace. "This is a ticket for BART, Quint. It was in your wallet. Do you use BART often?"

The Bay Area Transit System ran high-speed trains all over the Bay Area. I seldom used it, and I told McCall just that. "Once in awhile, I'll take it from the Embarcadero up Market Street to one of the theaters."

He leaned forward, pausing for dramatic effect, then said, "Mr. Powers's car was found at the South San Francisco BART Station, which isn't more than a couple of miles from his trailer. It was parked in a disabled only zone, the driver's door open, as if someone left in a hurry. I have people at the station now, circulating photographs of you."

"I've never been to that station. Powers was parked in a disabled zone across from the *Bulletin* when I first spotted him. He had a hand-icap parking placard, said it belonged to his wife."

Granger joined the conversation. "Did you do a GPR test on Quint?" he asked.

McCall wasn't happy about the interruption. "Yes. It was negative, but he could have been wearing gloves."

"What's a GPR test?" I said.

"Gunshot primer residue," Granger explained. "If you had fired a weapon recently there would be trace quantities of noncombustible primer mixture ingredients, barium and antimony, on your hands and clothes."

I remembered the woman deputy swabbing my hands—in every movie I could remember the cops always gave the suspect a paraffin test, dipping his or her hands into a waxy substance.

McCall was anxious to get on with it. "I have a witness who puts you at the scene, Quint. I have your prints on the murder weapon, and on the victim's vehicle. It would make it easier for everyone concerned if you just told us the truth."

"I didn't do it, and that's God's truth. I'll take a lie detector test, anything you want, because I didn't do it!"

"Maybe Quint has an alibi," Granger said, after taking a long slurp of coffee. "When was Powers killed?"

McCall went back to his notes. "The coroner estimates the date and time of death as between ten p.m. on Wednesday, August the nine-teenth, and four a.m. the following morning. Obviously Mr. Quint re-turned to the trailer park for a third, and final time."

I was having trouble calculating the dates, but when they fell into place I heaved a large, audible sigh of relief. "In point of fact I do have an alibi, gentleman. I was home, in bed."

"In bed," McCall said between clenched teeth. "Let me guess. You were alone, and there are no witnesses."

"No. I wasn't alone, Detective. I was in the company of a young woman, Terry Greco. And Inspector Granger can verify that I was there after ten, can't you, Inspector?"

Granger peered into his coffee cup as if it was a crystal ball. "Yes. I was at Quint's place questioning him about the death of Sara Vasin from a little before nine o'clock to well after ten. Quint had been drinking pretty heavily. I wouldn't think he was able to drive by himself. He was in the company of a woman when I left him."

All of the wind had gone out of McCall's sails. "And who is she?"

"I told you. Terry Greco. She works for the *Bulletin*," I said. "You were playing with her bra when I found you in my apartment. I'm certain she will corroborate what I've told you."

McCall gave Granger and exasperated look. "Do you believe this? His alibi is someone he works with and sleeps with."

"I know the young woman," Granger said. "She assisted me in the rescue at the Golden Gate Bridge. She seemed very professional." He pulled his cell phone from his belt. "I have her number on my cell. You can call her now and maybe clear this up."

McCall bolted from his chair and walked around in small circles for a minute or so. "Inspector, if you're pulling my chain, I'm going to have your job."

Granger scratched his head without mussing his carefully combed hair. "McCall, you and I both have civil service jobs. I'd have to kick the mayor in the balls in front of witnesses to get fired. I'm a busy man. I have questions to ask Quint about the deaths of Montgomery Hines and Sara Vasin. I'm trying to help you out." He flipped open his cell phone and punched a few buttons.

"Is this Miss Greco? Inspector Granger here. Someone would like to talk to you." He handed the phone to McCall who took it carefully, like a vet might handle a fragile bird.

It took about forty minutes to go through all the paper work and procedures of getting out of my orange jumpsuit and back into my clothes. During all that time Detective McCall never offered anything close to an apology for arresting me. He warned me that I wasn't off the hook, and that even though my alibi had been confirmed, I could have hired someone to murder Tom Powers.

"You're involved in this, Quint. I know that. Powers found out that you had stolen that necklace, and you had him killed. You haven't seen the last of me."

Dave Granger was waiting for me in the lobby of the Hall of Justice.

"Need a ride back to town?" he said.

"Why are you being so good to me, Granger?"

"I misjudged you, Quint. That rescue on the bridge. You showed some guts."

There was more to it than that, and we both knew it.

TWENTY-SIX

When we were in his car and on the Bayshore Freeway heading for San Francisco, Granger said, "You were in Montgomery Hines's closet that day, weren't you, Quint?"

"You expect me to admit to a crime?"

"There's no crime if you were given a key by *someone*, and asked to retrieve an item that belonged to that someone—say a diamond earring."

"You've spoken to my mother?"

There was an accident up ahead. Granger pulled a flashing red light from under the dashboard, rolled down the window, attached the light to the roof, and sirened his way along the shoulder of the road. A California Highway Patrol officer waved him to a stop.

"SFPD, Homicide," Granger told the officer "This gentleman's wife was shot and is near death at SF General Hospital."

The cop gave me an appraising glance. The look on his face showed that he wasn't too happy with the final outcome, but he backed off and waved us through.

"Goddamn young cops," Granger said. "A few years ago they wouldn't have thought about stopping a car with a flashing light. A badge could get you out of a speeding rap, parking tickets, you name it. I remember getting off work at midnight and driving straight to Las Vegas. Close to six hundred miles. I made it in record time. I was stopped by the highway patrol four times, flashed the badge, and was sent on my way. Not anymore. Professional courtesy is a thing of the past."

I almost asked if the badge could get you out of the theft of a watch or cufflinks.

"What did my mother tell you?" I said, once Granger had the car back up to freeway speed.

"Terry Greco called me from your mom's house after McCall arrested you. I went over and spoke to both of them. They were pretty upset. What's with that green tea Mom makes?"

"She told you about the earring, didn't she?"

Granger swerved to avoid pebbles falling off the back of a construction truck. "Of course she told me. I'm a professional, and damn good at what I do. Not like McCall. He has such an itch to charge you with this private eye's murder, that he didn't scratch the right people." He twisted his head and smiled at me. "He should have made sure you didn't have an alibi before booking you. Take some friendly advice. If there's a next time with McCall, have an attorney with you. And never volunteer for a lie detector test. They're about as reliable as flipping a coin. That line you fed McCall about getting Powers to admit he planted a bug by threatening to have his PI license taken away. That would have lasted about as long as a doughnut in front of my ex-wife, if I had been handling the interrogation. You roughed him up a little, right?"

"You keep expecting me to cop out to crimes, Granger."

"And I would have pressed you as to just what made you so sure Powers was the one who bugged your place. What was it? He left something behind? One of your neighbors saw him?"

"A toothpick wrapper. Powers's car was loaded with toothpicks and discarded wrappers."

Granger took a pack of smokes from his shirt pocket and used the car's lighter to get the cigarette going. "Your mother told me what a tough cookie you are, Carroll. She also told me who your father is. John Quint."

"It's not a secret."

"It was to me. I'm a fan of his. I'm not going to bother your mother about the Montgomery Hines investigation. The crime lab tells me that the stab wounds indicate that the killer was at least five foot nine, and he had to have a good deal of strength to inflict the type of wounds Hines's suffered. The fact that she did some interior designing stuff for Charles Reeder doesn't seem relevant to me."

"I keep asking—why are you so good to me, Inspector?"

Granger took a drag on the cigarette, and blew the smoke at the windshield. "You know damn well why. You were in the closet, weren't you?"

"I was."

"And you saw me temporarily borrow one of Mr. Hines's watches and a pair of cufflinks, neither of which proved to be relative to the investigation, so they were returned."

"They were?"

"Yes. So I don't see a problem between us, do you?"

Let's face it. I owed Granger. If he hadn't come down to Redwood City and backed up my alibi, I'd still be there, batting questions and answers back and forth with McCall. Granger wasn't doing this out of friendship—he was worried that I'd spill the beans about Hines's jewelry—but somehow I preferred the sharp, slightly bent cop to the straight and stupid McCall.

"No problem, Inspector. Has anything new turned up on Sara Vasin's murder?"

Granger ground out the cigarette in the ashtray. "The crime lab says that Peter Dkany's Hummer tires don't match any of the skid marks on the street," Granger said. "I canvassed the neighborhood. Two guys who live on Ord Street, just down from the spot where Ms. Vasin's body was found, had their vehicles parked on the street, and both had some damage to their cars—scrape marks on the fenders and doors. The paint transfers were dark blue. Dkany's Hummer is black."

"I don't think Dkany is Thanatos."

"Well, he has you pinned as the person who killed Vasin, so watch out for him. I haven't dug into Powers yet, but can you think of a link between him and the other victims?"

"No. Unless he came across something that connected someone to the murders."

"He wasn't investigating the murders, just Rosenberry's necklace. It could be that his death has nothing to do with these murders."

"Except for one thing," I said. "Me. I seem to be at the center of all of this and I can't figure out why someone fingered me as the thief."

"There has to be a reason, Quint. Work on it. Figure it out before we have another victim."

That probably would have been a good time to tell Granger about Rawley Croften, but I held off—the Great had sent Carl Dillon to see what he could find out about Rawley, and she wouldn't appreciate me bringing the cops in before Dillon reported back to her.

I wasn't paying much attention to Granger's driving. He had taken the South City freeway exit and was heading toward Colma.

"You're taking me to Powers's trailer?"

"McCall gave me the okay to look the place over. Of course, that was before you wiggled out of jail."

For once, Duke was nowhere in sight. Granger parked in front of Powers's trailer. There was a maze of CRIME SCENE ribbon across the trailer porch, and notices proclaiming that anyone entering the premises would be arrested and prosecuted.

Granger ducked under the ribbons. There was a padlock on the front door, but that didn't stop Granger. He used a Swiss Army knife screwdriver blade to unscrew the lock's hasp.

"Welcome to the scene of the crime," he said when the door swung open.

There were dried bloodstains on the floor, but everything else seemed about the same as when I'd been there.

Granger put on a pair of rubber gloves, interlaced the fingers of his hand, and tamped the gloves tight, then gave me a pair. "Put these on, Quint. How do you think the killer got ahold of the gun with the silencer?"

"Powers kept it in those metal cabinets. I was telling McCall the truth—I unloaded it before Powers came home that day."

"That was nice of you," Granger said. He opened the cabinet draw-ers, then slammed them shut. "You'd think that Powers would be a little more careful with an illegal gun after that—hide it in a better place. I talked to someone I know in the sheriff's office while you were turning in your bright orange pajamas. The weapon was found alongside Pow-ers's body, in his bedroom. There was no apparent sign of a struggle. So how did the killer get *his* hands on the gun?"

I had no answer to that the question. Granger turned his attention to the boxes containing videos and audiocassettes. "Powers was a busy boy." He thumbed through a pack of CDs with names and dates hand-written on them.

"What are you expecting to find, Granger?"

"Damned if I know, but I don't think Powers's murder is just a coin-cidence. Coincidence is like a rubberband. Stretch it too far, and it snaps. Let's see if we can find something on these tapes that snaps things in place for us. Powers put a camera and bugs in your apartment—maybe he did the same with someone else involved in the murders."

He slotted one of the cassettes into a video recorder and the two of us watched a man with a neck brace come out of the front door of a ranch style house and go to the curb to retrieve his garbage can. The can had been knocked over; garbage was all over the street. He returned to the house and came out with a broom and dustpan and began pick-ing up the garbage.

"Exciting work being a private eye," Granger said. "The guy with the brace must have been faking an injury, so Powers kicks over his garbage can and films him bending over cleaning up the mess."

We sat through an hour and a half of Powers's video and cassette recordings, learning nothing other than that he was good at his slimy job. Granger fast-forwarded through a group of videos showing men working on construction sites, playing softball, golf, swimming, throwing their kids up in the air, and my favorite, a guy being driven around town by a woman in a bad blond wig. He exited the car with dark glasses and a white cane, then carefully made his way over to a public phone booth in a gas station lot, took off the glasses, and, after paging through the phone book, made a call. He then did the white cane and glasses bit back to the car.

The audiocassettes featured voices of men and women talking about work, their spouses, the stocks they were buying and selling. The pick of that litter was one featuring a deep breather who, if a female answered the phone, asked, "What are you wearing?" The surprising thing was that about half of the women told him.

Granger had finally had enough. "I'm going to let McCall go through the rest of this crap. Let's look at the bedroom."

I hadn't been to the back portion of Powers's trailer. There was a narrow hallway, off of which was a small bathroom. The bedroom light was on. There was a strong smell of cordite. It looked as if Powers's cleaning lady had taken the last six months off. The room was a shambles: unmade double bed with jumbled sheets and blankets, clothing tossed everywhere, used tissue paper on the floor. Dusty venetian blinds shielded the windows. A clouded mirror hung lopsided over a raw pine bureau. A bedside lamp with a shirred paper shade sat over a lone telephone. The chalked outline of Powers's body was next to the bed. A line of bullet holes ran like a wavy snake across a row of old telephone books propped up against one wall.

Granger picked up one of the books and thumbed through the pages until he found the lead end of a bullet. He waved the book in my face. "Powers was playing with his silenced gun in here. Target-practicing or showing off to someone. The San Mateo Sheriff's Department listed the weapon as a twenty-two caliber long barrel Ruger MKII semiautomatic. Perfect gun for a silencer." He took out his knife and pried the bullet free. "The cartridge is lead, a subsonic load which helps keep the noise down; you can't really silence a bullet. Subs have less penetrating power. Only eight percent of pistol wounds are fatal, but Powers's killer wasn't taking any chances. According to the report, he was shot five times."

"I never came back here," I told him.

"You didn't miss much. Let's go."

He stopped at the cluttered table in the front of the trailer and picked up a handful of toothpicks. "Too bad the killer wasn't dumb enough to leave something like this behind, huh?"

We drove back to San Francisco exchanging small talk: baseball, my father's career. Granger pulled the car to the curb in front of a familiar house.

My MINI was parked in Mom's driveway.

Granger offered his hand and I shook it.

"I drove Terry home from here last night. Nice lady."

"She is indeed," I agreed, climbing out of the car.

"Nice apartment," he said, revving the motor.

I slammed the door shut, bent down, and leaned in through the open window. "I liked you better when I didn't like you, Inspector."

"Easy, tough guy. I never went inside, just made sure she got through the door safely. Let me know when you get arrested again."

TWENTY-SEVEN

Mom was full of hugs and kisses. She raved about what a wonderful policeman Granger was: "I knew he'd get you out of jail, darling."

Getting away from her without having to eat or drink anything wasn't easy, but I held firm.

I stopped at a nearby Peet's for a cup of coffee. The jail grub wasn't bad, but the coffee had been on par with my mother's green tea. I then called Terry at the *Bulletin*. She spoke in hushed tones, explaining that she had tried to get in touch with Katherine Parkham after I'd been busted by McCall, but the Great had been out on her boyfriend's yacht. She then called Max Maslin, who contacted attorney Mark Selden, who told Max, "I'll take care of it."

"The Great sent an attorney down to Redwood City this morning, Carroll, but you had already gone. You better let her know what's going on."

"I will. Then I'm going home for a shave, shower, and some real food."

"I'll bring the food," she said. "Half an hour."

Katherine the Great didn't sound to be in a very good mood. I told her the gist of what had taken place.

"Are you certain that the police are satisfied that you had no involvement in the private investigator's death?"

"Dead certain," which wasn't the correct response.

"Don't get witty with me."

"I have a alibi—I was with Terry Greco at the time Mr. Powers was murdered."

That seemed to appease her a bit. "I have an appointment I can't put off, but I want you here, in my office, at five o'clock, Quint. Understood? And have a story ready for tomorrow's edition regarding your arrest."

Terry Greco came into the bathroom while I was in the shower and said those magical words, "I think you dropped the soap," before climbing in with me.

She snuggled close and whispered in my ear as she soaped my back, "Is it true what they say about men in prison? Did the guards molest you? Do gangs go after the new boy—fresh meat, isn't that what they call you jail cell virgins?"

I turned and planted a kiss on her lips.

When we broke for air, she said, "I brought burgers and fries. I was sure you'd be starving."

"I am, I am," I said, nibbling on her shoulder. "It's a good thing we spent the night together when Powers assumed room temperature, or I'd still be in that cell."

She began soaping my chest in small tight circles. "Dave Granger was really helpful. He called someone in Redwood City and found out just when Powers was killed, and I knew right away you couldn't have done it. We were together that night—all night—at your place. And Dave was there for a while, too."

So Granger knew of my alibi before he came to Redwood City, but he'd let McCall go through the interrogation—why? To make McCall look like a fool? To let me sweat a little? Probably a bit of both.

"That Detective McCall wasn't at all happy when he spoke to me on the phone this morning," Terry said. "He threatened me with prison if I was lying."

The soap circles were getting larger. "McCall's a jerk. Granger seems very fond of you. He told me he likes your apartment."

"He saw me to the door, like a gentleman, but that's as far as he got, though he made it clear he wanted to come in. He said he's divorced, but they all say that."

I leaned back against the cool tile and let the water pound on my skull.

"Carroll, darling," she purred. "I have some bad news."

"What?"

There was a clattering sound and she said, "I dropped the soap."

It wasn't until after munching down the reheated burgers and fries that I remembered I should call Gineen Rosenberry and thank her for sending Ronald Moyer down to my prison cell—not that he was much to be thankful for. She was full of concern.

"I'm glad you're all right, Carroll. I thought Jules was going to have a heart attack when he told me about your arrest. Do you think that Mr. Powers's death has anything to do with my stolen necklace? Maybe it's cursed. It belonged to Caroline Astor and before that to Marie Antoinette."

"I don't think it's cursed, Gineen—just stolen. Powers was in a job where he'd made a lot of enemies."

"Well, I won't shed a tear if I never see the necklace again. All of this death and violence—I can't handle it. I think I'll go to Switzerland."

"You mean move there?"

"No, no. Just for a vacation, and to visit my money. Everything is just so depressing now. Is your father back yet?"

Ah, my father. A man who was an expert at cheering up depressed widows. "No, but he'll be home in a day or two."

"Tell John I want to talk to him as soon as he arrives."

I promised to do that.

"Be very careful, Carroll. Something very wicked is going on, and whoever is behind it is truly evil."

I broke the connection and turned to see Terry devouring the last of the french fries.

"What's cursed?" she asked.

"Gineen thinks her ruby necklace is cursed."

"It is. I saw it once and said, 'Oh damn, I wish it was mine.' Powers must have found out who stole it, and that's why he was killed."

"It's possible," I conceded. "I've got to get back to the paper. The Great wants me in her office at five o'clock."

"Be careful, Carroll. All these murders. I worry about you."

"So do I," I said truthfully.

I pecked out a story on the events leading to my being jailed and released. I've written thousands of articles about hundreds of people, but writing about myself was the hardest thing I'd ever done.

Max Maslin checked the copy and agreed—he edited it and used his byline on the finished product.

With everything that had been going on, I had forgotten to check my e-mails. There, in amongst the many, was one from Thanatos/Hermes.

I'VE LEFT YOU A CLUE. HH ALMOST FOUND THE BAD GUYS THERE. COME ALONE, TONIGHT, AT TEN O'CLOCK. I'LL BE THERE. DON'T WORRY, YOU WON'T SEE ME, AND I'LL NEVER HARM YOU. YOU'RE MY GOOD LUCK CHARM. BRING THE POLICE, AND I'LL DO WHAT THE NEXT VICTIM DOES.

Both Max and I bolted down a slug of his cheap vodka before riding the elevator up to the Great's office.

Mark Selden was there, looking grumpier than usual. Maybe his billable hours ended at five o'clock. Parkham didn't offer drinks or coffee and she gave Max a withering look when he stuck his empty pipe in his mouth.

She zipped through Max's story, simply saying, "Print it." Then she turned her steely eyes on me. "I'm sorry I wasn't able to act faster after your arrest. I don't like my people being pushed around by the police."

"Thank you." I handed her the latest e-mail and she studied it for nearly a minute.

"This jerk is playing us for saps," she said. "Why can't the police trace these damn e-mails?"

"I haven't told them about this one yet," I said. "The last time I did talk to Inspector Granger, he told me the e-mails were a dead end. The good guys' technology hasn't caught up with the bad guys' technology yet."

Selden joined the conversation. "Who the devil is HH?"

Parkham popped open her humidor and took out a cigar. "Any ideas on that, Quint? Thanatos obviously thinks you'll figure out who he's talking about."

"He's overestimated me. I haven't a clue at the moment. Did Carl Dillon find out anything interesting on Rawley Croften? I'd bet he'd know who HH is."

She began shuffling through the papers on her desk. "You think Croften's a possibility for Thanatos? Dillon didn't learn much, except that Croften's been writing mystery novels for the past few years, under an aka, Roy Dent. Four books, none of which have done very well. He lives in a home in the Sunset District on Thirty-eighth Avenue."

"That's close to Golden Gate Park," I said. "Croften has written a screenplay, and Universal Studios had bought an option on it. Apparently it's about a serial killer in Seattle. I think we should let the police know about him."

"We look at him first," Parkham said. She picked up a phone, punched in some numbers, and said, "Dillon. I want you to go out and sit on Rawley Croften's house. Right now. If he leaves, follow him—but don't be seen. And be careful. Do you have my cell number?"

Apparently Dillon didn't, because she recited it to him, hung up, and said, "We still have to figure out this HH crap."

"Would someone be kind enough to explain to me exactly who Mr. Croften is?" Selden asked.

Parkham said, "He's the man Carroll Quint replaced on the paper, and apparently he wasn't very happy about it. A drug addict, and he's no kid, Mark. In his sixties."

Max had his pipe out again, and was tapping the stem against his teeth. "HH. It has to be a character in a Hitchock movie or TV show. He almost found the bad guy *there*. Where? It must be somewhere in San Francisco. How many movies did Hitchcock shoot here?"

All eyes turned on me. "Three. I think. Let me consult with an expert."

I stood up, went to the window, and used my cell phone to call my mother. She was either out, or too wrapped up in avocado and coconut oil to answer the phone. I left her a message to call me back as soon as possible.

The Great had her cigar going by the time I got back to my seat. "She's out," I said, not identifying my source. "The movies I know that were filmed in the city are *Vertigo, The Birds,* and *Family Plot.*"

"He's already used *The Birds* with Mr. Reeder," Parkham said, picking a piece of tobacco from her tongue and depositing it in an ashtray. "*Vertigo*, I'm familiar with. What was *Family Plot* about?"

"Hitchcock's final movie, and not one of his best. Bruce Dern played a cab driver and Barbara Harris a phony psychic. She was nominated for a Golden Globe award."

Parkham said, "*Vertigo* had a scene under the Golden Gate Bridge, and at Mission Dolores Church. Didn't Kim Novak end up falling off a church roof? Maybe Thanatos is talking about a church."

"It's possible," I said. "But I don't remember an HH in the movie."

"I like it," Selden said, glancing at his watch and getting to his feet. "Quint should go to the church, and find out about this clue Thanatos is leaving there. Maybe we'll get lucky and Dillon follows this Rawley character out there, though he doesn't sound very promising to me. Quint is in no danger—the other three victims were either drunk, or drugged, and were helpless when they were murdered. Thanatos won't attack someone young, sober, and who he thinks might possibly be armed or accompanied by the police."

"Are you coming with me?" I asked.

He shot his cuff again and showed me his watch. "Can't do it. Katherine, I have an appointment with Mr. Bagley of the CBA Corporation in just a few minutes."

CBA was one of the firms rumored to take over the paper.

The Great poked her cigar in Selden's direction and waved him to the door.

Max said, "If Carroll goes to the church, he has to have some kind of protection. We should call the police."

Parkham blew a perfect smoke ring toward the ceiling. "I agree. Is there any one of them we can really trust?"

"I don't know if I trust Dave Granger, but I wouldn't mind having him as a backup," I said.

Parkham rolled the cigar from one side of her mouth to the other. "Thanatos would know what Granger looks like. He was on the front page with you and that idiot who threatened to jump off the bridge. The bastard says no cops, or he'll do what the next victim does. He's telling us he's got another murder in the works."

"Maybe it's Quint," Max said.

I didn't think so, but I wasn't absolutely sure. "If he wanted to do away with me, he wouldn't give me a warning like this—he'd just shoot me or run me off the road."

"We could use some of the building security guards," Parkham suggested.

From what I'd seen of the guards, I'd be better off on my own.

"Thanatos is preening, waving a red flag at me—he's going to leave me a clue. I have to go."

"I'll be your backup," Max volunteered. "He doesn't know what I look like."

"Don't be too sure," I told him. "He could be someone who works for the *Bulletin*, for all we know; a reporter, pressman, delivery guy."

That didn't sit well with Parkham. "I don't think we have anyone around here who is as clever as Thanatos. So, what's the verdict, Quint? You go to Mission Dolores?"

"We're not sure that's the right place," I said. "I don't remember Jimmy Stewart finding any bad guys there. What we have to do is run through Hitchcock's list of films and see if there is an actor or character with the initials HH in the mix."

Parkham tapped an inch of ash off her cigar, and said, "We don't have time to go to the movies. The e-mail says ten o'clock tonight, damn it. We have to get our shit together. I don't want to miss a chance at nailing this maniac."

"We'll have to rely on Google and movie Web sites to figure out just what he's talking about," Max said.

Parkham groaned and pushed herself to her feet. "Okay, let's get to it. Quint, you print out everything you can find and the three of us will go through it." She picked up the phone. "Chinese or pizza?"

Chinese won out. Parkham called in the order and headed across the room. "The bar's open, and Maslin, if you feel you have to, you can light up that pipe of yours."

TWENTY-EIGHT

It seemed like a hopeless task. Hitchcock had been involved in sixty-two films, dating back to something called *The Passionate Adventure* in 1924, and then there were the eight seasons that *Alfred Hitchcock Presents* was on television.

I found a Web site that detailed the sites used in *Vertigo*, and Mission Dolores topped the list. Jimmy Stewart followed Kim Novak to the church's graveyard, but there wasn't an actor or character with the initials HH in the flick.

The cloying sweetness of Max Maslin's pipe combined with the stink of the Great's cigar was making me dizzy. Or maybe it was the aroma from the cartons of moo goo gy pan, spicy shrimp with almonds, Szechwan beef, and Mandarin duck.

Max suddenly jumped to his feet, waving a printout from the Movie Guide Web site. "I've got it. HH is H. H. Hughson, in *To Catch a Thief.*"

I snatched the paper from his hand—the list of characters had the great English actor John Williams playing Hughson. I'd seen the movie dozens of times—it was one of my favorites. Williams played the stuffy insurance man who helps retired cat burglar Cary Grant catch the jewel thief who's been copying his distinctive style.

"It fits," Parkham said, peering over my shoulder. "It ties right in with the theft of Gineen Rosenberry's necklace."

"There's only one problem," I told them. "The movie was shot on the French Riviera. There's nothing to connect it to any place in San Francisco."

"There has to be," the Great said, helping herself to more of the duck.

Max puffed hard on his tubby pipe to revive the fading embers. I was glad the *Bulletin* was housed in an old concrete monster built in the 1930s when buildings still had windows. I cracked one open as far as I could and inhaled fresh air.

"Think," Parkham coaxed. "Where did HH find the bad guys in this movie?"

"On the tiled roof of a Riviera villa, which was actually a set on a Paramount Studios back lot in Hollywood."

We batted the possibilities around for awhile. Max came up with an idea—Gineen Rosenberry's house was a mansion.

"Yes, but it's not villa-style, and it doesn't have a tile roof."

We worked over the rest of the films and came up with absolutely nothing.

I was finishing up the last of the moo goo gy pan when my cell phone rang.

"Carroll dear," my mother said. "I'm sorry I didn't call earlier. I've been up in your father's flat all day cleaning, and then I went to dinner with the girls."

"Mom, can you think of anyone, an actor or a character, who appeared in an Alfred Hitchcock movie with the initials HH? And it's not John Williams in *To Catch a Thief.*"

"Why in the world would you want to know that, dear?"

"Another e-mail from Thanatos. He said he was leaving a clue, and that HH almost caught the bad guys there. It would have to be a place here in San Francisco, or close by."

"Someplace distinctive?"

"Probably," I said. Parkham was pointing at the wall clock. It was close to 9 P.M.

"Like a windmill, dear?"

"Windmill?"

"Yes. We still have one in Golden Gate Park, don't we? Joel McCrae, in *Foreign Correspondent,* was in Holland and chased some nasty Germans to a windmill, but they got away—it was one of the highlights of the film."

I had gone through the cast and characters of that film. Joel McCrae was a ruggedly handsome, underrated actor who did most of his work in westerns. Gary Cooper had been Hitchcock's first choice for the starring role, but Cooper hadn't been interested in doing a "thriller." I rummaged through the printouts on the Great's desk and found the one for *Foreign Correspondent.* "There's nobody with the HH initials in it, Mom. McCrae played a guy called Johnny Jones."

"Indeed. But when his editor sent him to Europe, he had him use a more continental name: Hadley Haverstock. HH."

"Jesus Christ," I said.

"Now you're getting into Mel Gibson territory, dear. I hope I was helpful."

When I broke the news to Parkham, she said, "Who the hell is Joel McCrae?"

Katherine the Great sent three of the paper's security guards—in plainclothes—out to Golden Gate Park. They were instructed to park on the Great Highway, within a quarter of a mile from the windmill, and wait for her instructions. She insisted on driving with me out to Golden Gate Park. Another of the paper's guards was trailing us in her Mercedes. Max Maslin was in the backseat of the MINI, sucking on an empty pipe.

"Keep your cell phone on," Parkham instructed. "All the time. In your shirt pocket. If I don't hear you breathing or your heart beating, I'm calling 911 and the guards. I think the son of a bitch has finally made a mistake. *Foreign Correspondent* is sixty years old, and outside of Quint's mother, nobody's heard of it. Quint, is it out on video or DVD?"

"Yes. I'm sure it is. Nearly all of Hitchcock's films are."

"Good. Max, I want you to check with the big movie rental outfits. If they have a copy of the damn thing, find out who they rented it to."

Max said, "Maybe the police should check on that, we don't have—"

"I thought I could count on *you*, Maslin," the Great said angrily. "Use your brain. Tell them we're running an article on old films, and that whoever you talk to will have his name splashed all over the *Bulletin*. This creep may work for a video place like that idiot on the bridge—he has to have something to do with old movies."

"The public libraries will have it on video," I pointed out.

"Then we play the same game with them," she said. "Tell them we're doing a Hitchcock article and want to know how well his old movies are doing."

"It pops up regularly on Turner Movie Classics, boss," I told her.

She grunted a little as she climbed out of the MINI. "Find out when it was last broadcast." She brushed the wrinkles from her skirt with the palms of her hand. "I haven't been in a car this small since college. And then it was in the backseat. Have you got a flashlight?"

I fumbled through the glove compartment and found one the size of her cigars. I could never remember using it. I flicked it on and played the beam across the dashboard. The MINI's dashboard clock showed 9:42. We were cutting it close. I went back to the glove compartment and retrieved the little stun gun I'd taken from Tom Powers's place and slipped it into my jacket pocket.

Max Maslin gave an audible groan as he maneuvered his way out of the car.

Parkham took a cell phone from her purse, asked for my cell number, and dialed it.

I answered. She spoke loudly into her phone and ordered me to do the same.

"Go ahead, Thanatos, make my day," I said in what I thought was a pretty fair Clint Eastwood impersonation.

Max brought things back to a somber reality by saying, "Carroll, there's a man who's killed several people waiting for you in the park. Watch yourself."

It had all seemed like a sort of game until then: a mental jigsaw puzzle with me trying to fit real people, not small pieces of cardboard, into place.

The night air was cold and clear. Parkham had on a beige belted polo-type coat. She slipped out of it and handed it to me. "You're going to freeze your buns off in just that blazer. Wear this, and keep us posted via your cell phone. My bet is that Thanatos planted whatever it is he wants us to find hours ago. He had to assume that you'd figure out his HH clue in a short time, and send out the gendarmes. He's a madman, so don't take any chances. We'll be close by."

She opened her purse and took out a small revolver with stag horn grips. "This is registered to me, Quint. Don't use it unless you have to, and I want it back as soon as this is over. It's loaded, all you have to do is pull the trigger, so be damn careful where you point it."

I slipped her coat over my shoulders and put the gun in the pocket.

Golden Gate Park is one of the city's crown jewels, over a thousand acres in the shape of a long rectangle, built back in the late 1870s on what used to be nothing but rolling sand dunes. Amongst the more than two millions trees from around the world planted in the park are small lakes, horse trails, a polo field, casting pools, a nine-hole golf course, and children's playgrounds. I drove slowly down John F. Kennedy Drive, one of the park's main arteries, past the newly refurbished Conservatory of Flowers. The bulk of the copper-clad de Young Museum seemed out of place amidst the towering silhouettes of trees and shadowed groves of shrubs and bushes.

By the time I reached the buffalo paddocks the fog had started moving in.

Two windmills had been built at the far west end of the park—one had been dismantled, the other, the Dutch Windmill, dated back to the early 1900s, when it was actually used to pump water all over the park.

The best time to view the windmill is in the spring when it's surrounded by thousands of blooming tulips.

The worst time to see it is on a cold summer night. The fog had penetrated the trees and there was a heavy scent of the Pacific Ocean a few hundred yards away.

The closest streetlight was nothing more than a yellow halo in the fog.

I parked the MINI, killed the lights, and switched off the engine.

I waited a few moments, then got out and slammed the door with more force than was necessary.

"I'm here," I whispered into the cell phone in my shirt pocket.

The Great whispered a "good" back to me.

I could see the outline of the windmill—it looked sinister, like a place that could be full of spiders, rats—maybe it was haunted. I must have reviewed a dozen haunted house, dormitory, and mountain cabin movies in the last year. There was one common thread in all of them—when lovely, curvaceous young women went to investigate those howlings sounds or banging noises, they were always dressed in their most revealing underwear.

I didn't think I'd see any Victoria's Secret babes at this windmill—and I didn't think I'd see Thanatos either. Mark Selden was right. He wouldn't risk exposing himself. He would have to think that a coward such as myself would never come alone, that there were police hiding behind trees and shrubs.

The mayor had ordered the park swept of the homeless camps that were frightening the tourists—but it was common knowledge that there were a hundred or more squatters, modern-day hippies, druggies, and just plain all around no goodnicks curled up in sleeping bags or under newspapers throughout the park every night.

I was glad the Great had provided me with her coat—it kept the chill away. Still, if Thanatos had lured me there to do me harm, my father would never forgive me for being found dead in women's clothing.

There was a carpet of rust-colored pine needles on the trail leading to the windmill.

A noise. Footsteps. Heavy footsteps. More than one person. I melted into a dark patch of cypress trees.

"Someone's coming," I said in something louder than a whisper, while digging Parkham's gun from the coat's pocket.

Suddenly two figures in orange and chartreuse flashed by. I saw the outline of a man's face, then a woman's, a blonde with her ponytail hurling from shoulder to shoulder. The woman had a good-size Airedale on a leash keeping pace with her. The dog's head tilted in my direction, gave a loud bark, then vanished into the fog with its owners.

Dedicated joggers braving the cold, fog, and park animals to get in their daily four or five miles.

"Screwball joggers," I said into the cell. "Man, woman, and dog."

The Great answered back in a voice full of tension: "It's two minutes to ten, Quint."

Ten o'clock. Why ten? Midnight seemed like a much better fit. I flicked the flashlight back on and made my way cautiously toward the windmill. Bats? Would there be bats inside the damn thing? There was a scurrying noise in the woods. I swung the light around and caught a brief glimpse of a raccoon in prison-striped fur.

I was within a dozen yards of the windmill when I heard a ringing sound. I froze. The MINI's car alarm? I played the light around and saw something nestled in a thicket of ferns. A brown paper bag. I picked up an arm-length tree limb from the ground.

"What's going on?" Parkham demanded.

"An alarm. There's something in a paper bag."

"We're on our way. I'll notify the police."

I hugged the trunk of a thick cypress tree, stuck my arm out, and poked at the bag with the branch. I counted to ten, then ten again, before peering out from behind the tree. The flashlight beam showed that two items had spilled from the bag. One was a small alarm clock—the red digital numbers showing it was three minutes after ten. The other item was a toy train—a red engine hooked up to three passenger cars.

TWENTY-NINE

The Dutch Windmill looked much less sinister in the light of day. Some sixty feet in height, its concrete base supported a large circular balcony and the windmill mechanism. The fabric covering was missing from the four blades, giving it an Erector Set effect.

Two black-and-white police cars were parked side by side, almost rubbing fenders, blocking the pedestrian walkway leading to the windmill. Inspector Dave Granger was talking to a group of men and women in work clothes—heavy shirts and jackets, knit caps, and gloves. Gardeners, I figured. They walked all over the area, stopping to bend over occasionally and pick up a stick, or a crumpled-up piece of newspaper. Granger came up with a dirty sock one time, holding it away from him as if it smelled as bad as it looked. They finally migrated to a small shack, alongside the windmill, that I hadn't noticed last night.

They'd been at it for an hour or so. I was sitting in the front seat of Granger's unmarked car, sipping on a cool cup of coffee from his Thermos. I had taken him through the whole scenario late last night—showing him exactly where I'd walked and where I had found the clock and toy train.

Granger hadn't been a happy camper when Katherine Parkham called him and told him of what she had dubbed "the windmill caper." He blew a fuse when she told him about Rawley Croften. The fact that the Great had had Carl Dillon staking out Croften's house didn't appease Granger in the least.

Dillon's stakeout effort had been a bust. There was no sign of Croften, just a light in his front room that stayed on all night. Dillon called the house after Parkham had informed him of what took place at the windmill. The phone was answered by a machine, a voice simply saying, "Leave a message."

The Great wasn't all that bright and cheery herself since she hadn't had enough time to get the "caper" in the *Bulletin*'s morning edition. Granger had lobbied her to hold off on the story until he had a chance to do some investigating.

It had been close to one in the morning before Granger released us from the scene. I'd gone directly home and to bed, only to be awoken by Granger's call at seven-fifteen and told to "get your ass back down here."

He plodded toward me. He looked tired and weary—and rather pissed off.

"This is all a lot of bullshit," he said, when he slid in behind the steering wheel.

"I agree, Inspector."

He looked at me through bloodshot eyes. "Did you drink all of my coffee?"

"There wasn't much left," I apologized.

Granger drummed his fingers on the steering wheel. "Let me ask you an important question—do you have an expense account?"

"In fact, I do."

"Good, because I'm hungry as hell."

He started the car, which threw up a fountain of dust as the tires yawed through a dirt trail before hitting asphalt.

I was trying to hook up my seat belt when Granger said, "Don't bother. We're not going far."

He was right. It was just a few hundred yards to the Beach Chalet, a terra-cotta-tiled building that was built during the depression by famed architect Willis Polk. It had been put to use as a teahouse, an army station, and a rough-and-tumble waterfront bar. After years of shuttered-up abuse, the National Parks Service reopened it and turned it into an upscale restaurant with a quiche and chardonnay atmosphere.

Granger parked in a red zone right in front of the place. I was starting to envy Carl Dillon's choice of leaving the newspaper racket to become a cop. The parking alone was worth it.

The Chalet's main floor is a sort of museum, featuring murals of how life was during the 1920s in San Francisco. The restaurant is on the second floor, with a nice view of the ocean on those days when the fog lets you see it. This was one of those days.

A group of Japanese tourists had commandeered half of the main dining hall. We found a table near the window and Granger went right after my expense account, ordering a Bloody Mary, Dungeness crab omelet, hash browns, and sourdough toast. I settled for coffee. I had no appetite at all.

"The consensus of the gardeners is that the paper bag could have been placed in those ferns anytime within the last few days," Granger said after sampling his drink. "It's not an area of priority to them."

"Which means Thanatos probably wasn't anywhere near the wind-mill last night."

"He was probably within binocular range, and laughing his ass off at all of us. Tell me, what's your take on this Croften guy."

"He hates me, hates the *Bulletin*. He knew Hines and Reeder, and he is, or was, a pill freak. And he'd be familiar with everything Hitchcock did."

"So he could be Thanatos. Damn you, Quint. I can see why your boss wanted me left me out of the loop, but you should have clued me in. I ran a quick check on Croften. No criminal record. Did he know Sara Vasin?"

"I'm not sure," I said.

"Did he know you knew her?"

"Same answer. Sara was given a roofie—Rohypnol, which is an anti-depressant—and Croften was a pill junky. If he doesn't have them in his medicine cabinet, he'd know how to get them."

Granger screwed his eyes shut. "I'll take a real good look at Croften, but he's a little old to be carrying bodies around and throwing them down stairs."

"Maybe he has an accomplice," I ventured.

"Don't make it more complicated than it is." The waitress brought Granger's order and he dug in. "You know what all this means, don't you?" he asked between mouthfuls.

"Thanatos is showing how clever he is, and sending us off on some wild goose chase."

The crab smelled awfully good. I reached over and speared a slice of toast. "The toy train was the clue he wanted us to see."

Granger nodded his head in agreement. "I came up with four Hitchcock movies where a train played a role: *North by Northwest*, where Cary Grant and Eva Marie Saint have a quick bang in her compartment; *Shadow of a Doubt*, where Joseph Cotten plays a serial killer of old women, who falls off the back of the train at the end; and *The Lady Vanishes*. In that one an old lady supposedly disappears on the train. Then there's my favorite, *Strangers on a Train*. Two guys meet on a train, one is a complete whack job and thinks he has a deal with the other guy—each of them will kill someone for the other, so that they will both have perfect alibis. Not a bad idea."

I was impressed. I lathered strawberry jam on the toast. "You've been doing your homework, Inspector."

"My sister is a librarian here in the city. She gave me a slew of books on Hitchcock."

"Did she also give you that copy of my book?"

He shoveled in a huge chunk of his omelet before responding. "*Tough Guys and Private Eyes?* Yeah. I wanted to see if I could learn anything about you from the book."

"And did you?"

"You take a nice picture and you're nuts over movies no one has ever heard of."

At least that explained the check out and due date on my book. Granger didn't check the books out, he simply helped himself to what he wanted with the assistance of his sister. Another example of his using his job to curry favors for himself.

"You're the expert, Quint. How many other train movies did Hitchcock make?"

"I'll ask my mother," I said, sneaking a second piece of toast from his plate. "Thanatos said the clue would point to his next victim, so my bet is on *The Lady Vanishes*. He's telling us he's going to kill a woman."

"A lady. On a train? Who takes trains nowadays? There's a bullet train to Los Angeles, and Amtrak will take you all the way to Chicago, as long as you're not in a hurry."

The *Mission: Impossible* theme chirped out on Granger's cell phone. He stood up and walked a few yards away as he answered the call.

I took the opportunity to spoon up some of his hash browns. I wondered what the Great would say when she saw the meal on my expense account: breakfast, bribing a cop.

Granger returned with a gloomy face and gloomier attitude. "That was my office. The alarm clock was a cheapo battery-operated job made in China that can be programmed to go off up to a week in advance. From what we've been able to learn so far, you can buy them in department stores, drug stores, damn near anywhere. Same thing with the little red train. Neither of them helps us a hell of a lot."

"So, outside of our guess on the next victim, we didn't learn much from all of this."

"Not exactly," Granger said. "We know that Thanatos is familiar with Golden Gate Park. He left the bag in a spot where some kids or homeless folk wouldn't stumble across it. I can see him checking out the windmill, even clocking the gardeners to see where and when they do their cleanup work. We also know that he's got you zeroed in, Quint. He was banking on you figuring out that HH puzzle in his e-mail." He finished up the potatoes, emitted a light burp, then said, "He knows he can count on you to unravel these goofy clues. Hadley Haverstock, Christ. Only you could have picked up on that."

"Actually, it was my mother."

Granger mopped up the remains of his omelet with the last piece of toast. "Then maybe he knows your mother. And she is a lady, so we'd better keep a good eye on her. I'll make sure a radio car from Mission Station makes passing calls by her flat every hour or so. Nothing like the sight of a black and white to discourage the bad guys."

That got my attention. I never really thought that I was a target, but Mom? Would this maniac go after her? Rawley Croften. What had he said at the preshow *Camelot* party? He'd like another crack at her? I took it as just a vulgar statement, something to get me riled up.

"Another thing we learned," Granger said as he pushed away from the table. "When you buy a guy breakfast, you steal half of it."

The barrel of the pistol moved in a slow ninety-degree arc as it followed the target, which suddenly froze as if it knew it was in danger. My mother's finger drew back on the trigger and a BB shot out and pinged into a brick not six inches from Herman, her neighbor's cat.

Herman made an abrupt U-turn and took off for the fence. Mom waited until he was almost atop the fence before firing off another round, which missed Herman's tail by the length of the whiskers on his nose.

"I'm getting pretty damn good at this," she said proudly.

"You're going to hit him one of these days," I cautioned her.

She drew the airgun's barrel up close to her lips and blew on it, like a corny gunfighter in an old western. "Then he shouldn't try rustling my goldfish, Sheriff."

We were drinking iced tea on her veranda. Rooibos iced tea, which actually tasted pretty good. Don't feel bad, I'd never heard of it either. It's made from an herb that grows only on some South African mountain, is mahogany red in color, and, according to Mom, is supposed to be helpful in preventing cancer, heart attacks, and strokes.

"Very good for the libido too, dear," she added, "though with Terry around I imagine that's not a problem for you."

"Mom, I'm worried about you. So is Inspector Granger."

"David? What have you told him about me?"

David? Granger had struck out with Terry. He was probably only fifteen years younger than Mom. Would he try hitting on her?

"Inspector Granger and I think that there is a possibility that Thanatos has you on his victim list."

She dropped the airgun into her lap and picked up her tea glass. "Really Carroll, I could expect that from you, but not from David. Why in the world would this monster be after me?"

I told her of the events at the windmill and the toy train Thanatos had left in the ferns.

She drew her legs up under yoga style and smiled with excitement. "The train is the clue, isn't it? Hitchcock loved trains—they are long, roundish, and hard. Like a gun, or a penis. He was very big on subtle phallic symbols."

"Yes. Uh, David . . . Inspector Granger and I think it may point to *The Lady Vanishes*."

"And the two of you associate *me* with the victim in that film. She was *elderly*, Carroll, and quite fat. I'm not at all flattered."

"Thanatos isn't flattering people, Mom. He's killing them. There's a chance that he's someone who knows me, and therefore knows you. When is Dad coming home?"

"I heard from him earlier this morning. The cruise is over, but he's stopping somewhere in Florida for a couple of days. The Keys area, I think."

"Did you get a phone number?"

"No. There was some young woman in the background yelling at him to hurry. 'The plane won't wait.' Something like that."

"Did you tell him about what's going on here? Thanatos? The murders?"

"I never got the chance, dear. The woman—she sounded *very* young—kept pestering him. I simply hung up. I don't have to put up with that. Why are you so anxious to talk to your father?"

"I want him home, here with you. I'm worried about you. I don't think you should be alone until this creep is caught, Mom."

She uncrossed her dancer's legs and bounced gracefully to her feet.

"Then *you* can move in, dear. Your bed is still in your old room." She arched an eyebrow. "It's a single of course. But there's plenty of room here for your friend Terry."

She saw the pained look on my face, and took a shot that went right to my heart.

"Of course, maybe David would want to stay. Did you notice all that hair around his neck and on his arms? I'll bet he looks like a gray gorilla when he's naked."

That was an image that would take years to burn out of my memory bank.

THIRTY

Sometimes life *is* like the movies. Clues pop up when you expect them. Unfortunately, I didn't pick up on them right away.

Terry Greco was not at all interested in staying with me at my mother's place.

"I just couldn't, Carroll—I mean, not while she was there."

"We could try camping—bunk out on the veranda."

"I think it's admirable of you, staying with your mom, but count me out."

We were back on the deck of Red's Java House, across from my apartment, munching from a box of chocolate doughnuts the size of silver dollars that Terry had brought along, surrounded by bug-spattered bicyclists, rugged-looking workmen in dirty coveralls, and cool and collected yuppies glued to their laptops. A squadron of seagulls was circling overhead, occasionally dive-bombing down to pick up discarded food wrappers.

"Terry," I pleaded, "don't leave me alone with her—at least stop by for dinner."

"I like your mom, Carroll, and I don't want to insult her, but she's so damn neat, and I'm such and a slob, and her dinners are—"

"I know, I know. I'll pick up some barbecued ribs and coleslaw for tonight."

A middle-aged biker dressed in a canary-yellow spandex torso out-fit that fit like a glove smiled at Terry. You had to have guts to wear something like that—the problem was this guy had too much gut. He sucked in his stomach as he climbed on his bike. The seat looked to be about the width of a quarter. My buttocks involuntarily clenched together.

"We should try that, Carroll. Rent some bikes and ride around Golden Gate Park."

I nudged the suitcase I'd loaded up at my apartment with my foot. "I've seen enough of the park for a while, Ter. Come on, you can have the bed, I'll sleep on the floor."

"How long do you think you'll be living with your mother?"

"Just until my father gets back from Florida."

"Do you really think that she could be in danger from Thanatos?"

"Granger does. And if he's worried, I'm worried."

One of the workmen, a burly guy with so much fine gray dust on his face, hair, and clothes that he looked like a walking statue, was ogling Terry. "Dave is pretty sharp."

"You girls are pretty chummy with him. Mom calls him David, and thinks that he'd look like a gray gorilla without his clothes on."

"Really? She said that?"

"It's not something I'd make up."

Terry tossed a doughnut toward a pelican perched on the pier rail-ing, spreading its wings to the sun.

"I'm worried about you too, Terry. And so is Granger. Thanatos could be after you, not my mother," I said, hoping to change her mind about staying with me that night.

"That's ridiculous," she bristled.

"No, it's not. There's safety in numbers. He'd never try anything with the three of us at my mom's flat."

She changed the subject abruptly. "Brody Carew is driving us all crazy. He's real tight with Peter Liddell, and he wanted Max to run a story on Liddell, who's upset because one of his checks bounced. Liddell told Brody that if the money matter isn't cleared up, he's leaving the show."

That didn't make any sense. Gineen Rosenberry wasn't the type to stiff actors, or anyone else for that matter.

"It had to be an accounting error," I told her.

"Max said the same thing. And Brody talks endlessly about the book the two of you are writing."

"Brody is living in a dream world." Statue-man was moving in closer. His eyes looked like raisins thumbed into cookie dough. "Come on, Ter. Let's get out of here."

She stood up, slipped her purse strap over her shoulder. "Baby back ribs? From Big Nate's?"

"You've got it." I picked up the suitcase just as statue-man made his pitch.

"Excuse me ma'am," he said respectfully, while staring at Terry's attributes. "But I think you've been taking too many pills."

Terry seemed perplexed. "Pills? What do you mean?"

"Gorgeous pills, ma'am. Give us poor boys a break and lay off them for a while, huh?" He looked over, sized me up, and added, "Can I give you a lift somewhere?"

"You just did," Terry said sweetly. "That was a new one."

"Nice try," I told him as I steered Terry toward the MINI.

Mom had mixed feelings—she loved having Terry as a houseguest, but she hated the thought of ribs and coleslaw—until she'd had a couple of martinis and some of the wine I'd brought along.

"These are delicious," she said, skinning the meat from the bones with her teeth. "Messy, but delicious."

While I did away with the paper plates and remains of dinner, Mom helped Terry move her stuff into my old bedroom.

Over coffee on the veranda, we brainstormed on the Thanatos case.

"I have a theory," Mom said. "I think Thanatos is using *you* as a McGuffin, Carroll."

"A Mc-what?" Terry asked.

"A McGuffin is a plot gimmick," Mom explained. "Alfred Hitchcock invented the word himself, and used one in nearly all of his films. It's sort of a peg to hang the real story on. In *Notorious*, it was the Nazi uranium hidden in wine bottles; in *Psycho* it was the embezzled money; in *North by Northwest* it was George Kaplan, the spy who didn't exist. Hitch wasn't the only one to use it, of course; in *Casablanca* it was that silly letter of transit. Everyone concentrates on the McGuffin—while the villains go about their nasty deeds. That's what's going on with you, son. You're in the spotlight, and he's moving around unnoticed in your shadow."

She got a little teary-eyed telling stories about Charlie Reeder. She pulled out her scrapbook and showed Terry the movie still photo of her and Monty Hines.

"Love your hair," Terry said, tapping the picture with a fingernail. "Mr. Hines must have been quite a ladies' man."

"You're half right," Mom chuckled. "Half-lady, half-man. Dear old Monty was a tranny chaser."

That perked up my ears. "Tranny chaser. You mean he liked—"

"Shemales, dear. Transvestites. 'Chicks with dicks' is what they used to call them in Hollywood."

"What about all those starlets he was dating?" I asked.

"Arm candy. After being chased all over the set by horny producers, directors, writers, and actors, it was a pleasure for us girls to go out to dinner or a show with Monty. It kept up his macho image, and gave us a much needed rest."

I thought back to those rough-looking women at Monty's wake. And the obvious transvestite who'd been talking to Jules Moneta in the bar after the service. What did she say her name was? Ramona? I couldn't remember ever seeing Jules with anyone in drag—at least in public. He favored sleek-looking young Latin men who knew how to walk, talk, and dance correctly.

There was some rustling in the garden. Mom got to her feet and switched on the outdoor lights, catching Herman sneaking up to the fish pond. She picked up her air pistol and snapped off a quick shot, causing Terry to spill coffee on her lap.

Mom apologized and went off for a wet towel.

"Carroll," Terry said, "your mother isn't going to come popping into your room with the gun tonight, is she?"

"I'll lock the door," I promised her.

Mom came back with the towel and a paper bag, which she tossed to me.

"I washed and cleaned your car while you were in jail, dear, and found those on the floorboard."

I opened the bag. It contained the pictures of Gineen Rosenberry I'd taken from Tom Powers's place.

I spread the photos out on the coffee table.

"Not at all flattering," Mom said. "Could I have a copy to pop out when your father drops by? Why did you take them?"

"I didn't. Tom Powers did—obviously without Gineen's permission. And no, you can't have a copy."

Terry picked up one of the pictures and studied it carefully. "I wonder if Powers put a camera in her bedroom like he did in yours, Carroll."

That got Mom's attention. "Camera? Bedroom? What are you talking about?"

"You explain it to Mom, Ter," I said, heading for the kitchen. Why the hell hadn't I thought about Powers's bugging Gineen's place? There was no reason for him to. She was his client—the insured, but Powers was a twisted bastard. It should be checked out.

When Gineen came to the phone she sounded drowsy, unsure of herself.

"Gineen, I'm sorry to trouble you this late, but something's come up. The private investigator, Tom Powers. I was at his trailer and found some pictures he'd taken of you, at your house."

"Of me? Why?" A gasp. "Who's seen them?"

"Just me, not the police." A small white lie, but a necessary one. Gineen wouldn't appreciate my mother having viewed the pictures. "And there's nothing revealing in them; he must have taken them when you showed him where the necklace was last seen. But Powers planted some bugs and cameras in my place, he may have done the same to you. I've

249

got an expert who can check it out in just a few minutes. Can I bring him by in the morning?"

There was a long pause. I could hear movement, rustling, the tinkling of glasses. I wondered if she was alone.

"Can I bring him?" I repeated.

"In the morning?"

"I can try and get him there before noon, Gineen."

More movement, more tinkling, a sob. "What is going on, Carroll? My God, the world is falling apart. If I'm not here, talk to Bernard, I'll tell him you're coming."

Bernard was her chief butler, an uptight Aryan who had little use for low class people such as myself.

"Thanks, Gineen."

She mumbled something I couldn't understand then hung up.

I called Argonaut Investigations, got their answering machine, and left a message for Sam Mercer that I had an important job for him in the morning.

When I got back to the veranda, Mom was shuffling a deck of cards.

"It's a little early for bed," she said. "How about a friendly game of three-handed poker?"

Terry thought that sounded like fun.

Poker isn't fun for or with my mother—she's a serious player, and she cheats, something she'd picked up from her brother, Nick "Crime" Kaas, my con man of an uncle. My father had dubbed him with the "Crime" nickname, because "Crime never pays," for anything: be it food, liquor, or lodging.

Uncle Crime had fascinated me as a kid with his sleight of hand magic tricks, but as I got older Dad hinted that I'd better make sure I always knew where my wallet was when I was around Crime.

I was down some twenty dollars before I figured out where Mom had marked the aces and kings with *white-on-white*. She'd used a nail whitening pencil to make small dots on the white borders of the cards. Even if you know the marks are there, it's difficult to see them.

When Mom caught on that I'd caught on, she suddenly got sleepy and shut down the game, with thirty-two dollars of Terry's money in her apron.

"Your mother was sure lucky tonight," Terry said as we made our way to my bedroom.

I closed the door and locked it. I saw no reason to burden Terry with the fact that my mother was a card cheat, so I just said, "Remember that old saying, never play cards with a man called Doc, and never eat at a place called Moms? You know about her food, and the next time she brings out a deck of cards, just think of her as Doc."

THIRTY-ONE

Sam Mercer had commitments early in the morning, so it wasn't until eleven o'clock that I was able to meet with him at Gineen Rosenberry's house. Her gleaming black Rolls was parked in the curving brick driveway. Jamie, her discreet, muscle-bound chauffeur, giving it a touch up wax job.

Bernard, the butler, greeted us formally, his voice firm, expression grimly set.

"Good afternoon, gentlemen. Miss Gineen is out. She instructed me to allow you entrance."

He was short, square-bodied, with ginger-colored hair and sandy eyebrows. He was wearing the casual butler's uniform: starched button-down light blue shirt, gray slacks, and suede shoes.

I once—after a few glasses of wine—asked Gineen why she put up with the stuffy jerk, and she had a good answer: "He doesn't steal, and he annoys people so much that they don't get a chance to annoy me."

Mercer was neither annoyed or impressed. "Where's the lady's bedroom, Jeeves?" he said, causing Bernard to stiffen his back and step aside.

We went through the ballroom where the party had been—the party that had ended with Peter Liddell and his goon using me for a piñata—and up the beautiful marble staircase leading to the second floor and Gineen's bedroom.

Before ringing the doorbell, Mercer had examined the photographs

Tom Powers had taken of Gineen. The majority were of her bedroom, and Mercer reckoned that that was the logical place for Powers to plant a bug, since it was the scene of the theft.

"Can you think of any valid reason for Powers to bug the house?" I'd asked him.

"Valid—maybe, in his mind—but not legal. He could have been worried that the thief would contact Ms. Rosenberry directly, and knock him out of any chance of picking up a recovery fee."

Bernard was never more than a few feet from us, his eyes taking in every move Sam Mercer made.

Mercer waved that same little magic electronic box he'd used at my place. As soon as he pointed it at the phone next to Gineen's massive bed, the lights went on.

"Be careful with that," Bernard commanded as Mercer began taking the phone apart. It was one of those French ivory-and-gold contraptions.

"Bingo," he said when he found the bug. "Same little goody he used at your apartment, Mr. Quint."

Bernard was visibly upset. His reputation as an inscrutable master of the mansion was taking some big hits: first the theft of the ruby, and now his mistress's bedroom had been electronically violated.

Mercer swept the rest of the bedroom, and then the additional dozen or so phones located throughout the house. Bernard refused to let him into his personal quarters.

"I am certain that this cretin did not gain entrance to my room!"

I wondered what Bernard was hiding in there. Pornography? A huge ruby? Gineen seemed certain of his honesty, but a pope would be tempted to stick his hand into the collection box if he thought there was a six-hundred-thousand-dollar necklace inside.

Bernard wouldn't tell me where Gineen was, but he did grudgingly allow as to how he would inform her that she was to call me as soon as possible.

He ushered us outside, and on the way to our cars Mercer handed me an envelope.

"My bill for the sweep of your apartment, Mr. Quint. I'll mail you the one for today's business."

I waited until Mercer was in his car and on the road before peeking at the bill. Four hundred dollars! He'd been at my place a total of thirty minutes tops. Maybe Carl Dillon should forget about the police department and go back into the investigation business.

I called the *Bulletin* on my cell phone and spoke to Max Maslin. There had been no new developments on the Thanatos case.

"The Great is getting edgy, Carroll. Rumors are flying that the paper may be sold by the time we go to press in the morning. Mark Selden is walking around smiling and whistling."

"Quit trying to cheer me up, Max. When will we know for sure?"

"Your guess is as good as mine," he said in a voice thick with gloom. "Your cop buddy was by, asking me a lot of questions. I guess I'm on the Thanatos suspect list."

"Granger? Why would he think you're involved."

"Beats me," he said, and then transferred me to Darlene, who told me that there had been eleven more telephone calls from people claiming to be Thanatos that morning, one from my mother about dinner that night, and one from Rawley Croften.

" 'Come if you dare,' was what he said, Mr. Quint. What does he mean by that?"

"I'll have to ask him." I called Inspector Granger's cell number. He sounded annoyed, and growled that he was "too busy to talk right now. I'll get back to you."

Too busy. Doing what? Investigating Max? I'll always remember a line my father used when I was fifteen or so. He'd taken me to a 49er football game and I was coming back to our seats with a couple of hot dogs. A guy was pestering him with questions about why he hadn't gone to a particular party. Dad didn't see me and pointedly told the guy, "Too fucking busy, and vice versa."

. . .

Some folks see miles of nothing but sand dunes and scrub and think of maybe putting in a garbage dump, or letting the city, state, or federal government come in and spend millions of taxpayers' money for a nice park, with a golf course or two.

An enterprising man by the name of Henry Doelger saw all that barren, empty land south of Golden Gate Park and thought about building houses. Which he did, starting in the 1930s, some thirty thousand of them, all remarkably alike: two story, attached, redwood-framed row houses, on a twenty-five-foot-wide lot, with common side walls, a full basement, and a stucco front in a hodge-podge of styles: a touch of French Provincial, a bit of a Spanish tile roof, a flat-faced moderne.

It was the old "build it and they will come," theory. He built the houses and the city came along with the streets and eventually, streetcars, schools, libraries, police and fire stations.

Croften's place on Thirty-eighth Avenue was a dirty-elephant-hide gray color, with a wrought iron balcony big enough to hold a few flowerpots. Given the city's crazy real estate market, it was worth more than Gineen Rosenberry's stolen necklace.

There was a small dry patch of lawn, badly in need of a mowing. The garage door was open. In the driveway was parked a gleaming racing-green Jaguar convertible.

Croften was wiping the vehicle down with a chamois cloth. He was wearing baggy cords, a white crew neck sweater, a jaunty red and white polka dot bandana tied around his neck, and one of those tweed caps the British wear when they putter around the garden. The perfect outfit for a gentleman cleaning his convertible.

He snapped the chamois when he saw me.

"Carroll. I didn't think you'd come. That policeman you sent, Granger, was an obnoxious bastard."

"I didn't send him, Rawley. It was his own idea."

He dipped the chamois into a bucket of water, wrung it out, and began wiping down the convertible's sleek hood.

"Then he lied to me. He claimed that you and that horse-faced woman running the *Bulletin* think that I may be this inept murderer."

"You have to admit you're a pretty good candidate, Rawley. All those Hitchcock clues—right up your alley."

"And yours too, as well as the real killer's."

"Beautiful car," I told him. "It must cost . . . what? Sixty thousand?"

"Seventy-four thousand eight hundred dollars. Plus tax and license, of course."

"Your books must be doing well. Or has Hollywood come through with that movie offer?"

He straightened up and massaged the small of his back with one hand. "You know about that. How sweet. Have you read the books?"

"Not yet."

"Well, do so. Out of professional courtesy, if nothing more. I wallowed through that tome of yours."

I had edged up close to him during our conversation. He didn't look that well in the light of day. His skin had an unhealthy gray pallor and his facial wrinkles were deeper than his age warranted.

"Your Inspector Granger seemed rather upset at me, Carroll. The fact that I didn't answer my phone last night. Was it you that called? Just after ten? I was in a barbiturate state of grace—dead to the world. This was about the time the killer delivered you a package in Golden Gate Park, I take it."

"Did Granger tell you what was in the package?"

"No. He didn't tell me much of anything, just asked a lot of inane questions."

He tossed the chamois toward the bucket of water. It missed by a good two feet.

"Come," Croften said, opening up the Jag's passenger door. "I'm getting tired. Let's sit for a bit."

"I'm not really in the mood for a ride," I said.

"It's only got a couple of hundred miles on it. Mostly I just roll it in and out of the garage. I like to sit behind the wheel and watch the neighbors stare."

He shambled to the other side of the car and slid behind the wheel in a series of slow, awkward movements. He patted the passenger leather bucket seat. "Come, sit, and I'll tell you who your Thanatos is."

He sounded like he was giving orders to a dog, but I got into the car. For all the money Rawley had spent, there wasn't much more wiggle room in the Jag than there was in my MINI.

Croften's hands gripped the steering wheel tightly. "I am dying, dear boy. I had to tell the policeman, so I might as well tell you."

"You're sure of that, Rawley?"

"Positive. And so are the six or seven doctors I've seen. Prostate cancer. I was diagnosed three years ago. Had an absolutely gruesome operation. They thought they got it all, but alas and alack, that's not the case."

"What about treatments? Radiation?"

"Been there, done that, and will not go back again. I never was one for pain, Carroll—that's one of the reasons I got started on those filthy pills. I've probably got a few months left, at the most."

"I'm really sorry to hear about this, Rawley."

He turned and clacked his false teeth at me. "Of course you are, because I'm telling you personally. If you'd happened to read about it in the newspaper, you'd say something like, 'Oh, too bad for Rawley,' then pour yourself more coffee and flip to the sports page."

"No. I'd remember the good times we had, and the things you taught me, and I'd feel lousy."

"Don't get morbid on me, for God's sake." He fiddled with some switches on the steering wheel and the radio came on, a classical station playing something that sounded vaguely familiar.

He patted the dashboard and said, "I hear that there's a place in Texas where they will bury you in your car. It was silly of me to buy the thing—spur of the moment, thought it might cheer me up. And what else was I going to do with my money? So, I took a loan out on the house and bought the car. There's really no one worth leaving it to—no children, no family, so I might as well take it with me."

I was beginning to feel as if he was going to give me a deathbed confession. "Is there anything I can do for you, Rawley?"

"Yes. See that Universal carries through with the movie. They've made an offer, I've accepted, but I'll be gone before it goes before a camera." He looked at me levelly and cleared his throat. "It's foolish and vain, but I'd like to feel that I'm leaving something behind. Something worthwhile. Under my own name. Does that make any sense to you?"

"Sure it does. I'll do what I can."

"Good. I've made provisions in my will, and, as much as I dislike you, I trust you."

With that ringing endorsement in my ear, I said, "You were going to tell me who Thanatos is."

"It's someone who knew all of the victims very well, someone like Max Maslin. He and Monty Hines were soul brothers when Max worked for the *LA Times*. Monty would date all of those dim-witted starlets, wine and dine them, ply them with promises of stardom, then turn them over to Max, while he chased after some fag in a wig and padded bra. Max and Charlie Reeder buried many a bottle in their time, and Charlie once told me that Max hated him because Charlie walked off with an actress Max was madly in love with."

"Even if that was true, it doesn't prove a thing," I argued.

"Then there's pretty Sara. Max was madly in love with her—before you entered the picture."

I opened the Jag's door and exited the car. "I'm not buying it. You're just still pissed at Max because you think he was responsible for the paper getting rid of you."

"Think? I know it for a fact"

"And you told all of this to Inspector Granger, didn't you?"

"Yes. He obviously needs all the help he can get."

"You're wrong about Max, Rawley."

Croften leaned forward, switched on the engine, and goosed the accelerator. The Jag's motor made that deep-throat rumble that only the most expensive sports cars can make.

"My film, Carroll. You promise to do your best?"

"I'll do what I can."

259

The sarcasm was back in his voice. "Please, do better than that, and for God's sake don't give it a bad review." He slipped the gearshift into drive. "I think I'll take her for a spin around the block today. What have I got to lose? Are you going to Jules's party at Treasure Island tonight?"

"Yes. I'll be there."

"Bringing Mommy? She looked lovely at the *Camelot* party. Sorry I spouted off like that about her—I was a little high at the time."

The Jag rocketed out of the driveway before I could say anything.

I crossed the street to the MINI thinking that I had wasted my time and put myself in an impossible position regarding Croften's movie deal. Studios don't ever listen to the writer once a deal is made—he's the last man on the artistic totem pole. They certainly weren't going listen to me seriously. It showed just how far gone Rawley was. And his ramblings about Max being the killer. Ridiculous.

I started up the car and drove off, anxious to be gone by the time Croften got back to his house.

Since I was so close, I drove past the Dutch Windmill, my mind on what Croften had said about Max Maslin. I just couldn't see him bedding down with Monty Hines's gullible movie starlets, or losing the love of his life to Charlie Reeder. Falling in love with Sara Vasin? That was certainly possible.

There were just two or three people strolling around the windmill. I parked and leaned my head against the backrest, and closed my eyes. Max's picture on Monty's wall. His denials that he knew the man. Why? I thought back and remembered a party at Charlie Reeder's place in Montara—an all-male affair for some reason—Max getting plastered, belligerent, and leaving early. And Sara. Max said she shared her marijuana with him. Was there more?

And what was I to make of Rawley Croften? Was he really dying? Or was the whole thing made up just to throw me off track? It would be interesting to see what Inspector Granger thought of Rawley's story.

The truth was that Thanatos could be anybody: some failed scriptwriter, a has-been or never-was actor. A stagehand, one of Sara's makeup gang, or a caterer, a bartender that works at some dive that Monty or

Charlie frequented. Or one of those stand-ins that hang around a movie location set for twelve hours a day and are paid in coffee, sandwiches, and the possibility of seeing their faces on the silver screen. A complete nobody, who just happens to have this one obsession—killing innocent people, and getting away with it. Why did he choose me? Who was next?

I must have dozed off, because something tapped against my window, causing me to jump up and bang my head against the car's roof.

It was a cop, on horseback. I rolled down the window and he leaned over in his saddle. He was a broad-shouldered man with leathery skin pretty close to the color of his saddle.

"You all right, sir? Just checking. You were here when I rode by an hour or so ago."

"I'm fine, officer, thanks."

I started the car and took off, thinking of Carl Dillon as a cop, riding through the park on a sunny day while I racked my brain to come up with a new column.

THIRTY-TWO

Carl Dillon seemed to be the only one at the *Bulletin* who looked to be in good spirits. He waved me over to his desk and said, "I just got my notice from the police department. I take the physical next week. If I pass, I'm out of here."

I wished Dillon luck and thanked him for setting me up with Sam Mercer of Argonaut Investigations. I also wondered what kind of a finder's fee he was getting out of the deal.

There were no smiles or happy sayings from Darlene. She handed me a short stack of notes, and said, "More calls from the sick and perverted, Carroll. Have you heard anything about the sale of the paper?"

"Not a word." It was my turn to try and cheer her up. "But no news is good news."

"No news sucks," she said, then slumped back into her chair.

Max Maslin gave me a curt nod of the head. I leaned against the door to his office. "I know why Inspector Granger has you under the magnifying glass, Max. Rawley Croften told him he thinks you could be Thanatos."

"Who told you this?" Max wanted to know. "Granger or Croften?"

"Croften. I saw him out at his house. He says he's dying. Just has a few months left to live."

Max scratched at his beard with the stem of his pipe. "What else did he tell you?"

"That you and Monty Hines were pretty friendly at one time, that you . . . dated some of the starlets Monty knew."

"It seemed a shame to let them go to waste, though I'm not very proud of myself for doing it. Did he tell you that Charlie Reeder and I once had a fight over a girl?"

"He did mention that."

Max clamped his teeth on the pipe stem and made clicking sounds. "Let me guess. He told you that I had him fired."

"Oh, yeah. And he told me that you were once in love with Sara Vasin."

Max's face reddened; whether in a blush or in anger, I didn't know.

"The man's a pill freak, Carroll, and he despises me. You can't believe anything he says." He got to his feet. "There's no sense moping around here waiting for the axe to fall. I'm going home."

"What about Jules Moneta's party? We could all use a good party right about now."

Max patted the front of his tweed coat. "It's black tie, and since it looks like I'll be unemployed in the very near future, I don't want to waste my money on renting a tuxedo. See you in the morning—I hope."

I booted up my computer and opened my mailbox. In the middle of a page and a half of Thanatos wannabes was one from Hermes.

FIGURED IT OUT YET? IT DOESN'T MATTER NOW.

Doesn't matter now? Had he already killed the next victim?

I dialed my mother's house and heaved a sigh of relief when she picked up the phone.

"Carroll, dear, Terry and I are getting ready for the party. You better get here soon. And we've decided we're not going to risk ruining our dresses or hairdos in that little car of yours, so unless you can get Gineen, the you-know-what, to share her Rolls Royce, we'll take a cab."

"I'll be there in half an hour," I promised, then immediately dialed Gineen Rosenberry's number. Bernard, the butler, answered. He sounded snootier than ever.

"Oh, yes. She returned an hour ago, I was just about to give her your message."

"Hi, Carroll," Gineen said when she got on the line. "I'm glad you caught me. Jules is picking me up any moment. We're going to meet with some producers on his boat before the party. What's up?"

"We found a bug in your bedroom phone, Gineen. Tom Powers must have installed it the day he came to see you."

"My God. He actually listened to my phone calls?"

"He could have. And he could have heard . . . any conversations you had with anyone in the room."

I would have to tell her that if Powers made any tapes, they would be in the hands of the San Mateo Sheriff's Department, and that the ever-tactful Detective McCall would have access to them. Telling her that over the phone felt a little too cold. Tonight at the party would be soon enough. I tried to phrase the next question as delicately as I could.

"Gineen, were there any phone calls or conversations that could be embarrassing to you?"

There was a very long pause before she replied, "No, I don't think so. I've been so busy with *Camelot* and sorting things out with the production company that I really haven't had much time for a social life. Carroll, I'd like to have a private, serious talk with you. Sometime tonight, at the party. Would that be all right?"

I assured Gineen it was and wondered what she meant by "serious" as I made my next call to Inspector Dave Granger.

"I received another e-mail from Thanatos." I read the message to him, and then told him that Tom Powers had bugged Gineen's bedroom phone.

"Powers was a busy boy. No camera in the bedroom this time?"

"No. The man I had check for the bugs suggested that Powers may have put it in to monitor any calls Gineen might receive from the thief—something that would have prevented him from earning his finder's fee. Powers straight out told me that if I turned the ruby over to him, he'd cut me in for part of the insurance company's finder's fee."

"That makes sense. Of course, Powers could have listened to the Satin Widow auditioning for husband number three. You're not behind one of those curtains, are you, Quint? You and Rosenberry seem awfully chummy."

"She's interested in my father, not me," I said.

"Can't blame her for that," Granger volleyed back at me. "The e-mail from Thanatos. He's bragging as if the dirty deed has already been done. Any ideas on who it could be?"

"I just spoke with my mother. She's fine. Terry Greco's with her. We're all going to the party at Treasure Island tonight."

"What party? I don't remember getting an invitation in the mail."

"Jules and Gineen are celebrating the opening of their film studio. It's black tie, Inspector, and you're wasting your time if you believe that Max Maslin is Thanatos."

"Gee, thanks for the information. Since you know my business so well, in gratitude the least I can do is write one or two of your columns for you. Call me if you have any more brilliant ideas."

I tried to get in a "touchy-touchy today," but he hung up too quickly.

I was sitting on a lounge chair on Mom's veranda, sipping a glass of her special iced tea, all decked out in one of my father's tuxedos—a midnight blue Armani single-breasted thing of beauty. The jacket, pants, and shirt all fit perfectly, but his shoes, black patent leather loafers with little bows, were a little too tight.

Herman, the neighbor's cat, crept into the yard and made his way stealthily toward the fish pond. I picked up Mom's BB gun and pointed it in his general direction.

He stared at me for a few seconds, then correctly figured that I was not the man my mother was, and slinked closer to the pond.

Herman wasn't afraid of me. It got me thinking. Monty Hines wasn't afraid of Thanatos—he'd let him into his condo, and was comfortable enough to take a shower while he was there.

Charlie Reeder must have let Thanatos in, too. All those weapons at his disposal, but Charlie hadn't felt the need to use one.

Both Hines and Reeder were easy targets—past their primes, not real physical specimens. Thanatos could take his time with them, kill them when he was ready.

Sara was a woman, but one who was in great physical shape—a dedicated runner, an exercise fanatic. She could have whipped both Monty and Charlie with one arm tied behind her back.

She'd let Thanatos into her house, too. She must have. If it was someone who had tried to break in, get the jump on her, she would have put up a hell of a fight.

So she wasn't afraid of Thanatos, but *he* was of *her*. He'd drugged her so that she couldn't put up a fight.

So why target Sara as a victim? Why not another feeble old-timer? A case could be made that Thanatos hadn't killed Sara—that he'd hit her, pushed her down the stairs, left her for dead, but she survived only to be run over by someone else.

If Granger was right about coincidences, then Thanatos killed Powers, also.

Powers was relatively young, and he had a gun, but he let Thanatos into his trailer. And allowed him access to *his* gun. Why? Powers had nothing to do with show biz, so if Thanatos was his killer, it had to be because Powers had learned something about Thanatos. How? The bug in Gineen's phone? She said she hadn't really had time for a social life.

The BB gun was suddenly yanked out of my hand. Mom snapped off a shot at Herman, who scooted for the fence.

"Your father called earlier. He'll be home tomorrow. There's no time for a drink before the cab gets here, Carroll. We'll have to take a traveler." She pirouetted slowly. "How do I look?"

"Fantastic," I said, without exaggerating. She was wearing a black backless dress with a fringe skirt and spiderweb bodice.

"Wait until you see Terry. You'd better bring the gun along just to keep the wolves at bay." She dropped the BB gun to the couch. "He'll probably be there, won't he, dear? Thanatos, I mean."

"It's a possibility, Mom."

I passed on the BB gun, but the little stun gun I'd taken from Tom Powers fit perfectly into the inside cigarette pack pocket of the tuxedo jacket.

I sat in the front seat with the cabdriver, while the ladies sat in the back. Terry was wearing a milk-chocolate-colored dress, cut low, with spaghetti straps scoring her bare shoulders.

I expounded on my theory of Thanatos making a mistake in picking Sara as a victim, while Mom and Terry sipped at their travelers: gin and tonics in disposable plastic cups.

The cabby, a thin guy with a ruddy face and a Giants cap perched on his head, had a hard time keeping his eyes on the road. They kept ping-ponging from me to the rearview mirror.

"Maybe Thanatos didn't pick Sara," Terry said. "Maybe she knew something about him, or suspected something."

"Sara apparently let him in," Mom pointed out. "She wouldn't have done that to someone she suspected was a serial killer."

We batted possibilities back and forth all the way over to Treasure Island. When we approached the sea harbor I spotted Harry Crane's yacht, the *Jewel Box,* tied up to a dock.

I pointed out the boat to the girls. "That means Katherine Parkham is here. We may learn something about the *Bulletin.*"

When we parked, the cabby jumped out and opened the back door. He removed his cap, revealing a streak of pale skin, like a bandage between his sunburned face and receding hairline.

"I probably shouldn't say dis," he said in a voice I recognized as pure San Francisco outer-Mission District, where, for unknown reasons, native-borns talk with a Damon Runyon New York accent. "But you two dolls could do a lot better than dis guy. All dis murder stuff. You sure you don't wanna go somewhere else? Without him?"

"You're right. You shouldn't have said it." The meter read twenty-eight dollars and sixty cents. I dug out my wallet and handed him twenty-nine dollars.

"What about a tip?" he protested.

"Don't play the horses," Mom said, grabbing my arm.

There had to be more than two hundred people at the party. The hangar had been gussied up since I saw it last: tented food stalls, three or four bars, waitresses in gypsy-style off the shoulder blouses carrying trays of drinks. A ten-piece band was playing dance music, the volume at a level that made you raise your voice to be heard.

I spotted the Great's distinctive profile. She was talking to Mark Selden. He wasn't smiling.

"Be right back," I told the girls.

"Bring nourishment," my mother said.

Selden was leaning forward, almost up on his toes as he spoke earnestly to the Great. He spotted me, and frowned.

"Good evening," I said.

"Maybe, maybe not," the Great said flatly. "I imagine you're curious about what's going on regarding the paper."

"Very much so."

"Well, nothing. The deal fell through, so we're back to status quo."

"It could still happen," Selden said with little enthusiasm. "Quint. Do you think there's any chance your friend Gineen Rosenberry would be interested in buying the *Bulletin*? I hear she's ready to abandon the movie business."

"What are you talking about?" I asked.

"One of the lawyers representing the bank that was going to finance our deal told me that Rosenberry is seriously thinking of pulling the plug on all of this. Too many headaches, too little return. Like throwing money into a bottomless pit. And if she does pull out, the whole deal will collapse. I think owning a newspaper would give her a better tax advantage, and think of the prestige."

269

"Your attorney friend may be pulling your leg," I told him. "Gineen hasn't mentioned anything to me about quitting the production company." Though I wondered if the serious talk Gineen had mentioned could be about that.

The Great held out an empty glass to him. "Fill it up, Mark. You'd better have one, too."

When Selden marched off toward one of the bars, I told Parkham about the latest e-mail from Thanatos.

She frowned and wrapped herself in her arms. " 'Figured it out yet? It doesn't matter now.' What do you make of it, Quint?"

"He's telling us he's murdered the next victim."

"What else is he telling us?"

"I wish I knew," I said. "My best guess is that it has something to do with the toy train he left in the park. Hitchcock's movie, *The Lady Vanishes*. He killed some woman, and has hidden her body."

"Not just a woman, a lady—that narrows it down."

The band was doing an up-tempo version of "Feelings."

"Jesus," the Great said, "can you get someone to turn that noise down? I can hardly think. Why didn't they just hire your father? Where is he?"

"He should be back tomorrow. I'll talk to Jules about the music."

Mom and Terry had one of the waitresses bracketed and were holding glasses in each of their hands.

"This is Diana," Mom said, introducing the tawny-haired waitress to me. "She says stick to the champagne. The liquor is watered down something awful."

I thanked Diana formally and took a champagne glass from her tray.

"Have you seen Gineen Rosenberry?" I asked.

"No," Diana confided, "but Brad Pitt was over there by the bandstand a few minutes ago."

Sparks nearly flew from Mom's and Terry's heels as they hurried off in pursuit of a real live movie star.

I made my way through the well-dressed crowd, stopping to say "hello, how are you," along the way. Every single member of the Bay

Area's acting guild had to be in attendance. Gineen and Jules were toasted, blessed, and adored by them all.

"Isn't it fantastic," said a tall, curly haired man whose main claim to fame so far had been carrying a spear in the local opera production of *Aida*. "Hollywood North."

I finally found Jules, in earnest conversation with a glum-faced man in a cook's outfit.

"The shrimp are not chilled properly," Jules scolded. "And the salad has much too much mayonnaise."

"And the music's too loud," I added. "My boss, Katherine Parkham, editor of the *Bulletin*, says that if it isn't toned down, she's going to write a column on just how lousy a party you throw, Jules."

"You're not serious?"

"Parkham is."

"Cooks and musicians," Jules fumed. "They never do what you tell them." He signaled to a passing waitress, pointed to the bandstand, and whispered something in her ear. He then fingered my jacket lapels and said, "Beautiful tuxedo. Is it new?"

"One of my father's," I confessed. "Where's Gineen?" I asked, scanning the crowd. "I'm worried about her. She hasn't seemed to be herself the last few days."

"I saw her a while ago. She's not feeling well. She may be leaving early. A touch of the flu, I think."

"There's a rumor floating around that Gineen may be pulling out of the production company, Jules."

"What? Ridiculous. Who told you that?"

"Mark Selden, the *Bulletin*'s legal counsel."

"Legal counsel," he scoffed. "Another fucking attorney. They stir up things just to try and bring in some business."

I didn't bring up the fact that Moneta was an attorney himself. "Gineen is fully committed to the company," he continued. "Now and for the foreseeable future, believe me."

"She told me she might be going to Switzerland for a vacation and to visit her money."

"Yes," Jules said. "And why not? She has that beautiful villa that's just a fifteen minute helicopter ride from Zermatt, which has the best summer skiing in the world." Jules's face broke into a wide grin. "It's going to happen, Carroll. Right here, in this hanger. *The Maltese Falcon*, with George Clooney as Sam Spade, Angelina Jolie, and, get this, Bill Murray as the fat man, played by Sydney Greenstreet in the original. They say they can blubber him up the way they did Eddie Murphy in *The Nutty Professor*."

I drained my glass in a gulp and went in search of a stronger drink.

Terry grabbed my elbow. "Brad Pitt took off for greener pastures. Your mother is searching for Charlie Sheen."

Mom never found Sheen, or any of the other "stars" that were supposed to be at the party: Mark Damon, Ray Liotta, and Burt Reynolds.

We danced, dined, sipped champagne, and had a good time intermingling with the local guests. I kept hoping to see Gineen, so that we could have that "serious talk" she'd mentioned on the phone, but no one I spoke to had seen her. Maybe Jules was right, and she'd left the party, though she'd have to be feeling pretty bad to do that. I spotted Rawley Croften jawing with Jules. He looked strangely out of place with his over-dyed hair and velvet tuxedo, like a villain in a silent movie.

While I was fetching my mother a glass of champagne, Ramona, the transvestite I met at the bar after Montgomery Hines's wake, approached me. She was in leather again, all black this time. It looked as if it had taken a shoehorn to get her body into the dress.

"Hi, good-looking," she said. "Do you have your mommy with you tonight?"

"In fact, I do. Enjoying the party?"

"I *always* enjoy Jules's parties. You meet the most interesting people."

"Like Montgomery Hines? Did you know Monty well?"

"Dear old Monty. The Banana Queen. I saw him from time to time. Lately he was into threesomes or moresomes."

"Banana Queen?"

"Monty was well endowed and his manhood was shaped like a banana." She made a curve in the air with her index finger. "That made him an interesting date."

The things you learn by asking questions. "Are you in show business?"

"Showing *it* is my business, honey." She dug into her purse and came out with a card. She handed it to me. It featured a flattering picture of her, a phone number, and the message: DON'T LET YOUR MEAT LOAF. CALL ME! "If I'm too exotic for you, I can always fix you up with someone a little more motherly."

The bandleader mercifully announced the last dance of the evening as I was twirling around the floor with Terry. She smiled, and looking over my shoulder said, "Here comes Inspector Granger."

Granger's version of black-tie was just that: tweed jacket, white shirt, and black tie.

He said hi to Terry, and spoke to me, while keeping his eyes on Terry.

"Quint. We have to talk."

"We are talking," I pointed out.

"I can tell when I'm not wanted," Terry pouted.

Before Granger could protest, she swiveled around and sashayed away.

"You're a damn lucky man, Quint. What the hell does she see in you?"

I sometimes wondered myself. "What's up, Inspector?"

He wandered over to a table littered with half-empty glasses and paper plates smeared with bits of leftover food.

"What can you tell me about Brody Carew, Quint?"

"Brody? Why? You can't possibly even consider him as a Thanatos candidate."

"Why not? He knew Montgomery Hines, right?"

"Probably."

"And Charlie Reeder?"

"Yeah, I guess he knew Charlie."

"And Sara Vasin?"

"It's possible," I conceded, "but Brody, as obnoxious as he is, he'd have no reason, no motive, and—"

"He has no alibi for his time during the murders of the three of them."

Granger started moving toward one of the open bars. He caught the eye of the barman who was putting his stock away. Granger flashed his badge and said, "Black Jack, over." He dropped a five dollar bill into the bartender's tip glass, saw my shocked face, and added, "Make that two of them."

"You can't be serious, Granger. Brody Carew?"

He was silent until the drinks were brought, then picked up his glass and eased his shoe onto the footrail of the bar. "Unlike your fictional cops, Quint, us real cops don't wait for PIs or amateur detectives to lead us to the bad guys. Thanks to all the press this case is getting, the chief gave me some help. I'm no longer the Lone Ranger. I've got four Tontos working with me, and one of them was running criminal checks on everyone at the *Bulletin*. And guess what? Your buddy Carew has a rap sheet. One attempted rape, and two assaults."

"Brody? That's hard to believe."

Granger sampled his drink and winced. "They watered this down." He reached into the tip glass and retrieved his five-dollar bill. "Carew also does cocaine, speed, grass, and all of those designer drugs you show people love."

"He admitted this?"

"No, he admits nothing. His girlfriend with the maroon hair spilled the drug stuff. Carew can't deny what's on his rap sheet. The rape case was eventually dropped; the victim was nineteen, claimed she met Carew at a party, and that he slipped something in her drink. When she woke up she was naked in his bed."

"When did this take place?" I asked.

"Six years ago, in Denver. The assaults are more recent—three years ago, both in San Jose. Similar situations—an argument in a club, Carew waited outside and coldcocked the victims while they were walking to their cars. He used a brick on one guy, a piece of rebar from a construction site on the other."

A chill went down my back. I'd thought of Carew as an idiot, a creep, but relatively harmless.

"This still doesn't mean that he's Thanatos," I said. "Why? What the hell would be his motive?"

Granger drained his glass, and picked up the one I hadn't touched.

"Your job, Quint. I figure you're his next victim."

"That's crazy—nobody kills four people to get someone's job."

"I've had cases where the victims were killed because their cell phone went off in a theater. One nice, quiet family man poisoned five pregnant women because he said he didn't want them to go through the pain of giving birth. His wife had died giving birth to their last son. The world is full of these nutcakes."

"Did you arrest Carew?"

"Not yet," Granger said. "I report, and the chief and the DA decide. I'd say there's a good chance they'll give me a thumbs up. It's not going to look very good for your newspaper, is it?"

My mother and Terry joined us. Mom had had more than her fair share of champagne by now.

She beamed at me and Granger. "Well gentlemen, this party's over. Where to? Carroll, did you call for a cab?"

"A cab?" Granger said. "I'll give you a ride back to town."

Mom thought that was delightful. So did I, because I wanted to talk to the Great, who was heading for the exit with Harry Crane.

"Inspector, if you could drop the ladies at Mom's house, I'd appreciate it. I have to talk to Ms. Parkham."

I kissed Mom on the cheek, hugged Terry, told them I'd be with them in an hour, and trotted off after the Great.

THIRTY-THREE

I caught up with Katherine Parkham and Harry Crane as they were approaching the *Jewel Box*.

"Boss. Can I talk to you a moment? It's important."

Harry gave her a peck on the cheek, and said, "Take your time, Kate," then hurried up the gangplank.

"I hope you've got some good news, Quint. I've had enough of the bad stuff to last me the rest of the month."

"It's pretty bad."

She groaned, then grabbed the handrail and started up the gangplank. "Then we'd better sit down."

She plopped down on a cushioned seat at the rear of the boat, gave me a wary look, and said, "Shoot."

I told her about my conversation with Granger. Her moan was louder than the *Jewel Box*'s throbbing engines.

"Brody Carew? The police are serious about this?" she said.

"Inspector Granger isn't sure if they will formally charge Brody. It's up to the chief and the district attorney."

Parkham leaned forward and ground her face into her hands.

"Do you realize what this will do to the paper? It's *our* story. We're running it page one every day. We're feeding Thanatos's messages to the public, telling them that we're on top of it, ahead of the police. And now one of my reporters is Thanatos? No, damn it, I won't accept it."

"I don't think it's Brody," I said.

She bolted to her feet. "Damn right it's not." She flopped back down again. "Christ. What if it is true? I'm finished. So is the *Bulletin*. Damn the man. Even if Carew isn't Thanatos, we're going to look like complete fools. How the hell was he hired with his criminal background?"

Harry Crane came by, a look of concern on his handsome features.

"I take it the trip to Half Moon Bay is off, Kate?"

"Way off," she said. "Let's get back to the yacht club." She turned to me. "My office, seven o'clock in the morning."

I hurried down the gangplank and stood on the dock and watched the *Jewel Box* get underway. The Great was standing on the deck, cell phone in one hand, her other arm waving frantically up and down.

Out of the corner of my eye I saw Jules Moneta's boat, which was moored at the far end of the pier. It was dark, tied up tight to the dock. Maybe Jules could save me a cab ride home. His house in the Diamond Heights section of the city was about a half mile from Mom's place.

I hurried back to the hangar. Jules's car, a yellow, shark-nosed Porsche hardtop coupe, was parked in a spot especially reserved for him. There was a queue of people waiting for taxis. A young woman wearing a fur-collared coat waved to me.

"Hi, Carroll."

I waved back. She looked familiar, but I couldn't think of her name. She came over and extended her hand.

"Doris Lowry. It's been some time since we've met."

"It sure has," I said. It came back to me now. Doris was one of Sara Vasin's best friends. She'd been at the parrot parties, and helped look after Sara's place when she was away on location.

"God, it's awful about Sara, isn't it?" Doris said. She was an attractive woman in her mid-thirties with thick chestnut-colored hair. "Have the police found out anything yet?"

"Not that I know of. But I'm sure they're working on it."

Doris hugged the collar of her coat to her neck. "And just when she was so happy, finally getting a job right here, so she could stop all of that crazy traveling."

I recognized her voice now, from Sara's phone message tapes: the cheerful woman saying something about good luck, I hope you got it.

"Sara had a job offer in San Francisco?"

"No." She tapped her foot on the sidewalk. "Here, with Mr. Moneta's production company. He offered her a steady job as head makeup artist for his company. Sara was really excited about it, the money was really great and she said she'd have her own office here on Treasure Island, and would also be involved in the selection of local actors who could—"

A horn beeped. A taxi had pulled up and a tall man in a plaid over-coat shouted at Doris. "Come on. Let's get going."

"Are you *sure* it was Jules Moneta who offered Sara the job?"

"Oh, yes, absolutely. I haven't heard her that happy in ages."

Doris said something else, but I wasn't paying attention. My mind was reeling. Jules offering Sara a cushy, well paying job? He'd told me he barely knew her, that he *thought* she was an actress.

I leaned against the fender of Jules's Porsche. Jules had told me that Gineen wasn't feeling well, might be going home early. How? A cab? Jules had given her a lift tonight. I used my cell phone to call her house.

It took several rings before Bernard, the butler, answered the phone.

"Rosenberry residence," he said in a voice full of gravel.

"This is Carroll Quint. Is Gineen there? I have to talk to her."

"She is not in residence," Bernard announced.

"Are you certain? This is important. Where is she?"

"Somewhere else, which is none of my business, and certainly none of yours."

"Bernard, I'm really worried about Gineen. Are you sure she didn't come home by cab, or that she didn't call for the Rolls?"

"Positive," he said in that snooty tone of his. "I've not seen Mrs. Rosenberry since Mr. Moneta picked her up this afternoon."

I pocketed the phone and hurried into the hangar. Everyone had left, except the cleanup crews.

"Have you seen Mr. Moneta?" I asked a stoop-shouldered man folding chairs and stacking them onto a pallet.

"Left about ten minutes ago, mister. I think he said he was going to his boat."

I started running. The *Sea Queen* was Jules's office. Gineen had told me that she and Moneta were meeting with some producers before the party on his boat. I couldn't find anyone at the party who had seen her. Could she still be on the boat? *The Lady Vanishes* popped into my mind. Moneta. Could he be Thanatos? Yes! Jules knew Monty Hines well enough to give a hell of a eulogy at his wake. That should have gotten me thinking right then. Jules was not the type to be chummy with small-time actors. He knew Charlie Reeder, and, though he denied it, he knew Sara Vasin well enough to offer her a job. But why would he want to kill them?

The answer hit me with a near physical force. To set the stage! He made up the Thanatos/Hermes character and killed three innocent people to set the stage for his real target—Gineen Rosenberry. Mark Selden's information about Gineen getting ready to pull the plug on the production company had to be true, and that may have been why she wanted to have the "serious talk" with me tonight.

And Tom Powers. His murder had to be connected with the others. He'd bugged Gineen's bedroom phone. She'd told me her calls were related to business, *Camelot*, and the production company. Some of those conversations had to have been with Moneta. What the hell had Powers learned that could have caused Jules to kill him?

I was gasping for breath by the time I got to the *Sea Queen*. The boat's running lights were on, her motor turned over, and the hull tugged against the mooring lines.

I paused for a moment, my hand going for the cell phone. Call Granger? Tell him my suspicions? What if I was wrong? What if Gineen was somewhere dancing in the arms of a new lover? What if Jules was partying on the boat with Ramona and some of her friends? Deep in my gut I knew that wasn't the case, but I had to see Jules and confront him before calling Granger.

I swung my legs over the railing and slipped aboard. There were two stout metal-framed fisherman's chairs with padded arms and molded footrests bolted to the deck at the stern of the boat. An open sliding door led to a small room with a couch, TV, and stuffed chairs.

The engines were revving up and down. I figured Jules was in the engine room, wherever that was. I ducked my head and tiptoed down the steps to what must have been the living quarters.

A door to a small bedroom was ajar. There was a woman in a red dress lying on her side on a narrow bed. The honey-colored hair. It was Gineen Rosenberry.

I went over and touched her gently on the shoulder. Then I saw the strip of tape across her mouth. She was unconscious, but breathing deeply through her nose. I dug out the cell phone to call Granger. There was movement behind me. I turned back just in time to see Jules swinging a big wrench directly at my head. There was a loud cracking sound, an immense shot of pain, another impact, then darkness.

I woke up feeling cold, very cold. I tried moving. I was sitting down on something hard. My hands were tied in front of me, the rope then fastened around my feet. My shoeless feet.

I shook my head to get my eyes into focus. What I saw wasn't at all encouraging. The west side of the Golden Gate Bridge, shrouded in fog. The *Sea Queen* was moving out to sea.

In addition to the pain, I felt nauseous. The smell of diesel oil, the rolling of the boat. My glasses were crooked, half-on and half-off, and I could only see through one lens.

I tried moving, but the end of the rope tied around my feet was fastened to a brass cleat on the boat's bulkhead.

I sat there shivering and shaking for several minutes, trying to wiggle free.

"You've got a hard head, Carroll."

I looked up to see Jules. He was standing with his legs spread apart, drinking from a bottle. He leaned down and pointed the tip of the bottle at my mouth. I could see the label—Cruzan Rum. I opened my lips and Jules dribbled in a shot.

"Feeling better?" he asked.

I held out my bound hands. "Get this rope off of me."

Jules got to his feet and shook his head sadly. "No can do, old boy. It's your own fault. You never should have snuck onto the boat."

"What should I call you? Jules? Thanatos? Or Hermes?"

He went into that sad shaking of his head mode again. "You figured it out, didn't you, Carroll? Tell me how, and I promise you a painless death. We've got about twenty minutes before we're there."

"Where, damn it?"

"The Farallon Islands. The water around there is a breeding ground for great white sharks." He leaned down and ran his hand down the arm of my tuxedo jacket. "I hate to ruin it, but there's no choice, is there?"

He removed my glasses, tucked them in the jacket's breast pocket, then moved to the side of the boat, opened a compartment, and hauled out a white plastic bucket filled with something foul smelling. He placed the rum bottle between his legs and waddled over with the bucket.

"I'd close my eyes if I were you," he said, before upending the bucket over my head.

The stink was awful, and the liquid was cold and slimy.

"Chum," Jules said. "Bits of meat, fish entrails, lots of blood."

He went back, got another bucket and dumped that one over me, then tapped me none too gently on the head with the rum bottle. "Sit tight," he said. "I have to check the wheel and Gineen. Be right back."

I watched him walk away. Jules Moneta. One of the midgets from Casablanca. He was always there, and I never paid him any attention, never considered he could be involved in the murders. I tried working on the rope knots again. They were tight, digging into my flesh. I contorted my body as best I could to get some of the shark chum onto the ropes, into the knots, hoping to loosen them, to give my hands some squirm room.

Jules came back, the bottle of rum tucked under one arm. He squatted down next to me. He opened his right hand. There were three green pills in his palm.

"Rohypnol. Roofies," he said. "I truly am sorry about this, Carroll, but the best I can do is to make it a little easier for you, but if you cry, scream, or plead for mercy, I'll throw you over. You won't last more than a minute before you drown, unless a shark gets to you first. My suggestion is that you take the pills. You'll be asleep in a matter of minutes and won't feel a thing. But before you get the pills, you have to tell me just how you figured it out."

"You made too many mistakes," I told him.

"What mistakes? What are you talking about?"

"Sara Vasin. You told me you barely remembered her, that you thought she was an actress. I listened to her telephone answering machine messages. Sara told a friend about your job offer, Jules. Her friend called and left a message congratulating her."

"Which friend? You're bluffing, Quint. It won't do you a bit of good."

"Then how did I know about your job offer to Sara?"

It shook him for a moment. "Women. You can't trust them. I told her to keep quiet about the job." He jabbed me in the forehead with the rum bottle. "Tell me which friend, or so help me I'll start cutting you up and feeding you to the sharks piece by piece, and Thanatos's next victim will be your goddamn mother!"

I believed him. His eyes were wide open, the veins on his forehead were pulsing wildly. "The woman didn't leave her name, but the police will figure it out, find her, then you'll be toast. I told the police my suspicions. They know I'm here. You're screwed."

He rocked back and forth on his heels for a few seconds, then his face softened, and so did his voice. "You're still bluffing, Carroll. I saw you talking to that police inspector at the party, less than an hour ago. He wasn't interested in you or Thanatos, he was too busy drooling over your big-titted girlfriend. And even if you're telling the truth about that phone message to Sara, so what? I offer jobs to dozens of people every day. The police will never suspect me. And you haven't told them anything, or they'd be here now."

"You're wrong, Jules. I called Inspector Granger from my cell phone just before I climbed onto this damn boat of yours."

He leaned to one side as he reached into his front pants pocket and came out with a cell phone. Mine. He flipped the shell case open, pushed a few buttons and smiled.

"Don't call me stupid, Carroll. I checked your last dialed numbers. You called dear old Gineen's house. What did Bernard tell you? That she wasn't home and he had no clue where she was, right?"

"Actually Granger called me," was the only answer I could come up with.

Jules reared his arm back and heaved the phone into the ocean. "You're so predictable, Carroll. You want to act the part of one of the brave detectives in those movies you adore, don't you? It's rather funny—I never worried about the police." He leaned against one of the fishing chairs. "They were looking for a serial killer, a monster, a lunatic. But I'm none of those. You were actually my inspiration for this whole thing—your book, those movie reviews of old thrillers, the master criminal always confounding the police, only to be tripped up by the lone wolf hero." He laughed loudly. "There's no happy ending for you this time, Carroll."

I shivered uncontrollably and felt the slimy chum running down my arms into the rope. "You've been stealing from Gineen. That's what this is all about, isn't it? To get rid of Gineen."

"Stealing? That's a harsh word. Embezzling? Even that doesn't fit the package. I've been investing her money in the production company. There have been difficulties, a great many of them, which are manageable, with enough money. She wasn't really *committed*, Carroll. She was starting to have doubts, talking to her bankers. She liked the parties, meeting the stars, all that bullshit, but she just didn't understand. I'm going to make pictures. *Great* pictures."

"Metro-Goldwyn-Moneta. Is that it?"

Jules took a pull from the rum bottle. "I decided months ago that I wasn't going to let Gineen ruin this for me."

"So you killed three innocent people."

"Innocent? I'd hardly call Monty Hines innocent. He was an old pederast whose career was over. Totally over. He'd been pestering me for work, and he'd been dying to get into my knickers for years, so I went to his place, played him along, got him drunk, told him that I'd invited a positively smashing redheaded transvestite to join us, then insisted he take a shower before we all jumped into bed. Stabbing him through the curtain was a nice touch, I thought."

"Everyone knew Monty was a tranny chaser, Jules. The police will start questioning the ones Monty favored, like your friend Ramona. She'll bring your name into it. It's another nail in your coffin."

"Ramona," Jules scoffed. "Give me some credit, dear boy. I'd never get within a mile of that creature with my clothes off. She knows nothing."

"What about Charlie Reeder?" I said. "Charlie wasn't an angel, but he certainly didn't deserved to die like that."

"He was a sick man. Very sick. He told me so himself. He knew he didn't have much longer to live. So you see, I did the man a favor. The frozen leg of lamb was a brilliant touch, wasn't it? I simply checked the Web under Hitchcock, unusual murder weapons, and there it was. I brought it with me, told Charlie it was a gift. He was already too drunk to think anything of it. I knew the police would never figure it out, Carroll. I counted on you again, and you came through."

"What about Sara? She wasn't sick. She was a beautiful, vibrant woman."

"You're running out of time, mate. I wouldn't wait much longer to take those pills. Yes. You're right about Sara. I hadn't planned on killing her. She called me, out of the blue. She'd heard about the movie studios, wanted to know if there was work for her, she was tired of traveling. While we were talking, I remembered those steps by her house. Hitch's movie, *The 39 Steps*, just popped into my brain. It would be perfect to have a woman victim before Gineen disappeared. I made a date, met her at her house. Brought the roofies with me. You know Sara. She liked her grass, her coke. It wasn't hard to drop the pills into her wine." He placed the pills in my hand, then asked, "Can you reach your mouth?"

God's truth, I was tempted. Swallow the pills and end it all—no pain, no icy ocean water, no damn sharks. I tilted my head toward my hands, made a loud coughing sound and dropped the pills into the puddle of chum on my lap. As long as I was alive, awake, I had a chance. I wasn't going to let him kill me without putting up one hell of a fight. I had to keep him talking, and hope that I could get my hands free from the ropes.

Jules took another pull from the bottle. "Last chance, Carroll. Take the pills now, or it'll be too late."

I shuddered, sobbed, then dipped my head to my hands and licked and made slurping sounds.

"Good boy," Jules said. "I've got to make sure we're on course, and bring Gineen topside." He paused on the way to the sliding doors. "Do you know who I originally had planned for victim number three?"

"Me, you prick."

"No, no. You've been my lucky charm. The night of the party at Gineen's, your brawl with Peter Liddell worked out beautifully for me. I'd seen Gineen dressing before the party—trying to decide which jewel to wear with which dress. Since I was in a bit of a cash bind, the ruby necklace was the ideal solution. While everyone was distracted, I simply went upstairs and pocketed the necklace."

Cash bind—no wonder Peter Liddell had complained about not getting his money for the *Camelot* performances. "Then it was you who brushed by me when I was going up to Gineen's room."

"Yes. You scared me a bit, then I remembered you're blind as a bat without your glasses, and you had a handkerchief over your bloody face. Victim number three was going to be Rawley Croften. Another person who wouldn't be missed. And you'll love this. The Hitchcock clue was going to be a compass, under Rawley's corpse, with the needle broken—pointing *North by Northwest*. Clever, eh?"

"Fantastic," I said, adding a slur to my voice. "I know you killed Tom Powers, I just can't figure out why."

Jules let out a low, bitter laugh. He was enjoying this—telling me how clever he was. In his mind I was the only one he could, or ever would, let in on his nasty secrets. A captive audience of one.

"I've no remorse over killing that little bastard. Gineen told me that you'd found out that Powers had bugged her phone. Well, I found out before you. Powers called me. He'd heard several conversations between Gineen and me, and it dawned on him that my voice was the same one that had called him to say that you stole the ruby from Gineen's bedroom. He tried to blackmail me. Said he'd identify me, tell you and the police that I was the snitch. That automatically would have prompted Gineen to make inquires that would have been very embarrassing to me. She was already a little too curious, mentioning more than once that I had seen the necklace in her bedroom before the theft. That's why I called Powers and pointed the finger at you."

Jules took another swig from the rum bottle. "I couldn't let Powers get away with it, Carroll. He wanted to meet with me, come to my house. No way, Jose. I took BART down to the peninsula. He picked me up in that trashy old car of his. He wanted ten thousand dollars. I wanted to hear the tapes. He drove me to that hovel of a trailer of his and played them for me."

"You could have given him the money, Jules. You didn't have to kill him."

"After Gineen vanished, he would have figured it out and asked for more. Blackmailers always do. And the fool wanted more than just money. He wanted a job, in the movies! In *my* movies. As a technical adviser. He had an idea for a television show about a private investigator. He said he could make it exciting, yet true to life." Jules shook the bottle as if to see how much rum was left. "He had one pet peeve, Carroll. He said that he hated it when he saw a show where someone shoots a revolver with a silencer attached. 'It can't work,' he said, and went into a long, boring explanation as to why you'd have to use a semiautomatic pistol. Then he took me back to his seedy bedroom and showed me his indoor firing range—all those old telephone books. He got his pistol and fired it to demonstrate how a real silencer worked. Then the idiot handed the gun to me to try. It took me all of two seconds to realize this was the perfect solution. I simply shot him. The silencer worked wonderfully well."

"The police will still investigate you after Gineen's disappearance. And I'll be missing, too. You'll never get away with it. They'll put the pieces together."

"I think not. They'll think that both of you were victims of our friend Thanatos. I'll send an e-mail to the *Bulletin* saying just that. Your dear mother will no doubt grieve, but she'd never suspect me, and Gineen has no family, no sons or daughters. Her parents are dead. I'm the executor of her will. She's left most of her monies to charities." He gave a wolfish smile. "And I'm one of the charities. You've got about ten minutes, I reckon. If you believe in God, I'd start talking to him right now."

He turned and went back into the boat. Ten minutes! The Farallon Islands, barren rocks that once housed a lighthouse and are now part of a marine sanctuary. I remembered watching a television special filmed there, where some of those idiots get into diving suits and are lowered into the water in cages so they can film the great white sharks chomping on seals, otters, and smaller sharks. I went into my contortion mode, working the knots, but they wouldn't give. I grunted, groaned—frantically rubbed the ropes against my now chum-slick lap and knees, all the while mumbling what I hoped were the right words to the Hail Mary. There was some movement. My right wrist turned a fraction of an inch. Another fraction, then real movement. I kept working it and finally the wrist slipped free of the knot. My hand slid out—it was numb—I wriggled the fingers frantically, stuck them into my mouth to warm them, which was a mistake. They were soaked with the chum.

I coughed and spit for what seemed a long time.

There was a grunting sound, some thuds. I could just make out Jules dragging Gineen by her feet through the sliding glass doors.

The fog was all around us now, low to the water, like mustard gas.

The *Sea Queen* was bobbing in the waves. My left hand was still tied in a knot. If I could get it loose, get my feet untied—

"Carroll. You still awake?" Jules called.

He dragged Gineen over by me. She was still unconscious, bound and gagged with duct tape. Jules went to the compartment, brought out another bucket of chum, and poured it over Gineen.

I slipped my cold, numb hand into the tuxedo and freed the stun gun. It slipped out, falling to the deck. Jules was busy getting another bucket of chum and hadn't noticed.

"Jules," I said in a slow drowsy drawl. "One more drink. Please."

He crouched down and peered at me. I prayed that he didn't see the stun gun, which was somewhere between me and the bulkhead.

"Still not out, eh, Carroll. All right. Time for a final-final, then, awake or not, I've got to throw you in."

He went back through the sliding doors to get the liquor. My one free hand searched frantically for the stun gun. My fingers slipped over the damn thing just as Jules returned, bottle in hand.

"Truth be told, I need a another good belt myself, Carroll."

He knelt beside me and tilted the bottle to his lips. I could see his Adam's apple moving. Then he leaned out and held the bottle out to me.

I jabbed the stun gun into his forearm. He let out a loud scream, then fell backwards, tripping over Gineen's unconscious body.

I dug my heels into the deck and scooted myself over to the cleat holding the end of the rope. I clawed at the knot with my one free hand, chewed at it with my teeth. It came free just as Jules got to his knees.

He was holding his forearm against his chest and swearing.

"You son of a bitch! You rotten son of a bitch!"

I looked around for the stun gun. Jules ran over and kicked me in the side. I wrestled for his knees and he fell to the deck. He used both hands to pummel me, his fingers going for my eyes.

I bit down on his thumb hard enough to draw blood and a loud howl from him.

My left hand was still in the knot, useless. My bound legs gave me no chance to stand up.

Jules scurried away and glared at me, his eyes narrowed, his teeth bared. He grabbed the end of the rope and started pulling me toward the rear of the boat.

"You're going over, you prick!" he screamed.

I tried grabbing onto something, but there was nothing to grab. A strong wind had kicked up, and the boat was rolling back and forth. I was being inched closer and closer to Jules. If he picked up a weapon— the bottle, an axe—I was a goner.

He wrapped the end of the rope around his chest, under his arms, leaned backwards, and dragged me several feet.

He was laughing now, laughing and spewing out undecipherable curses. I curled my knees back and lunged out at him with all the strength I could muster. My feet caught him on his knee; he lurched backward, struck the bulkhead, and tumbled awkwardly over the back of the boat. Into the ocean, holding onto the rope!

I skidded across the deck, knowing full well that Jules could still end up pulling me overboard.

I crashed into one of the fisherman's chairs, quickly wrapped myself around the base, and squeezed tight, like a rodeo cowboy holding onto a bucking bronco.

The tension from the rope seemed to have increased with the weight of Jules's body adding pressure, the knots digging deeply into my left hand and both feet. The pain was becoming unbearable. Then, suddenly, the tension was gone, the rope slack.

I crawled over to Gineen, put my ear close to her nose. She was breathing softly, steadily. My breathing was full of great gasps and sighs.

I lay on my back for a minute or two, trying to gather my strength, letting my heartbeat get back to normal.

Then it dawned on me that we were heading out to sea, and that I knew as much about sailing as I did about brain surgery.

My right hand was back to feeling normal. I undid the rope knots and made my way toward the front of the ship to the helm, or whatever they call the place with the steering wheel.

I fished my glasses from the tuxedo's breast pocket. They were smeared with the chum. I wiped them on a clean part of my shirt and took stock. Beside the wheel there were two sets of levers, a bunch of gauges that meant nothing to me, a monitor with a picture of the ocean and two small islands straight ahead, a small green screen with a line going around it, and a compass with the needle pointing in a westerly direction.

On the ceiling was something that I was familiar with—a radio. I picked up the mike and said, "Mayday, Mayday. Coast Guard, this is the *Sea Queen*. I'm in a lot of trouble. One man overboard, an injured woman, and I don't know what the hell to do."

There were some cackling sounds, then a woman's voice very calmly said, "*Sea Queen*, this is Coast Guard November Mike Charlie Niner. Read your message. What is your location?"

"The Pacific Ocean, somewhere near the Farralon Islands. I may be heading right for them."

She asked me my compass heading, told me what levers to push, which ones not to touch, then coached me through turning the boat around back toward the city.

"We have help on the way, *Sea Queen*. What is the nature of the woman's injuries?"

"She's been drugged," I said. "She's still breathing."

"Have you made attempts to rescue the man overboard?"

"Hell no," I said, then went back to help Gineen.

THIRTY-FOUR

I t's finished," my mother said proudly, putting the final piece of the *Casablanca* jigsaw in place. She stepped back to admire her work: A piece of Ingrid Bergman's hat was missing, and parts of Paul Henreid's suit belonged to Bogart's, and vice versa—minor details to Mom.

She was flitting around like a butterfly because my father had called from the airport to say that he'd be home shortly.

"Well, I'd better be going," Inspector Dave Granger told us. He'd stopped by an hour ago "for a couple of minutes" and had decided to stay once he learned that my mother was serving cocktails and wine rather than green tea.

Granger had been waiting when the Coast Guard cutter had towed the *Sea Queen* to the dock at the old Fort Point Lifeboat Station. An ambulance had hustled Gineen Rosenberry and me to the hospital. That was some sixteen hours ago.

Luckily, Gineen was fine; the effects of the drugs Jules Moneta had given her had worn off, but the shock of learning about Jules had hit her hard. Harder than the blows he'd landed on my head. I had a headache, but no concussion, and some minor scrapes and bruises.

There was still a lingering smell of that damn shark chum, despite two long showers.

Granger had interviewed me at the hospital, as had Katherine the Great. She'd come to my room with Max Maslin, Mark Selden, two more lawyers, a stenographer and photographer, ready to do battle with Granger, but the inspector was more than willing to turn me over to the *Bulletin* hierarchy.

"We'll talk soon," he'd said before leaving the room.

The Great did everything but promise me the keys to the *Jewel Box* as I laid out the details of Jules Moneta's last voyage. I didn't want the yacht, I wanted my old job back, and she assured me I'd have it.

The sedative the docs gave me finally kicked in, and the next thing I knew it was after eleven in the morning, and I'd woken with a head full of slamming doors. The beautiful smiling faces of my mother and Terry Greco were there to greet me.

The doctor came in, gave me some pain pills, and I checked out as fast as I could.

Gineen had already been released and was "recovering at home." I spoke to her on the phone for ten or twelve minutes, and she must have said, "I can't believe it," twenty times.

The Coast Guard was searching for Jules's body, but according to the seaman who'd manned the wheel of the *Sea Queen* while it was towed home, either sharks, or, if he'd gotten tangled up in something on the ocean floor, crabs were making a meal of him.

Mom had insisted on Terry and I having lunch at her place. Unfortunately, I was too weak to argue with her, and lunch turned out to be baked tofu cutlets and roasted garlic soybean scallops.

Terry promised to make it up to me with a freebie review dinner at Postrio, and later dessert, a Godiva chocolate cake, at her place.

When Granger showed up, I broke out Mom's booze. For a gruff, bent, moody cop, Granger could be an interesting guy. He estimated that it would take a week or more to definitely tie Moneta to the deaths of Monty Hines, Charlie Reeder, Sara Vasin, and Tom Powers.

"The chief wants everything wrapped up in a nice, neat package, Quint, so drop down to my office tomorrow and we'll tie up some loose ends."

After saying good-bye to Mom and Terry, he motioned for me to follow him to the front door.

"Did you call Brody Carew?" I asked him.

"Why would I do that?"

"To tell him you were wrong about him being Thanatos."

Granger shook his head and chuckled. "If I called everyone I was wrong about, I'd never get any work done. Quint. You done good. Damn good."

When I got back to the kitchen, Terry was putting dishes in the sink and fluttering her eyes at me. "Let's go," she whispered when I slid up beside her, "before she asks us to stay for dinner."

Mom came over and before I could tell her we were leaving said, "You two must want to spend some time together. Let me clean up what's left, and then you can—"

Her mouth dropped open and I followed her eyes to the doorway, where my father stood.

"Hi, everybody," he said.

Mom stood frozen in place for a moment. Terry, who was wearing jeans and a tight bubblegum pink T-top, said, "Oooh." Her nipples popped out like those timers they put in turkeys to let you know when the bird is done.

Dad has that kind of effect on women. "Instant Cary Grant," someone had called him. He'd picked up a deep coppery tan on the cruise gig, and there seemed to be a few more strands of gray around his temples.

He opened up his arms and enfolded Mom, giving her a long kiss, then hugged me tight.

I introduced Terry, and he bowed and kissed her hand. "It's a real pleasure meeting you," he said in what from now on I'll call his Jiffy Lube voice.

"I missed you guys," Dad said. "What say I take us all out to dinner?"

"No, no," Mom said quickly. "Carroll and Terry were just leaving. We can see them tomorrow."

"Okay," Dad agreed. "Anything interesting happen while I was away?"

You might wonder how my father could have missed all the news about Thanatos. Well, one of the reasons he keeps his youthful appearance is that he has no interest in what's going on in the world, if it doesn't have something to do with his small portion of the planet. If the Thanatos story had made it to *Variety*, then he'd know all about it.

"Quite a bit," Mom said, waving a good-bye to me. "Carroll had an exciting adventure. I'll tell you all about it after they're gone."

"Great having you back," I told him. "Let's have lunch tomorrow."

Terry grabbed my hand and said, "Your mother wants us out of here in the worst way." Her eyes twinkled. "I wonder why?"

I went up to my old room and got our luggage. We could hear them making small talk.

She: "How was the cruise?"

He: "Oh, same old thing."

She: "I imagine there were dozens of merry widows chasing you around the ship."

He: "Nah, it was a quiet cruise. I brought you back a present. I put it upstairs in my place. Want to take a look?"

There was a sound that could only be two people kissing. I hurried to the door. Eavesdropping on loving parents—especially divorced loving parents—was something I tried to avoid.

She: "Yes. I would."

He: "Were there any phone calls? Any interesting mail?"

More kissing sounds. I opened the front door, but Terry hung back.

She: "Your agent called."

He: "Oh, did he leave a message?"

I grabbed Terry's arm firmly and closed the door.

"Damn men," she grumbled on the way to the MINI. "Your mother is being romantic and all he's worried about is his agent's telephone call."

"That's show biz, kid. But speaking of romantic, why don't we skip going out to dinner and go straight to your place and order out for a pizza."

"You call that romantic?"

I wrapped my arm around her waist and hugged her close to me. "You, pizza, chocolate cake, what could be more romantic? We can stop at my place first and pick up the *Casablanca* DVD. I want to take a closer look at those midgets."